NIGHT SHADOWS

CHILDREN OF NOSTRADAMUS, BOOK 2

JEREMY FLAGG

NIGHT SHADOWS

Limitless Publishing, LLC
Kailua, HI 96734
www.limitlesspublishing.com

Formatting: Limitless Publishing

ISBN-13: 978-1-68058-979-5
ISBN-10: 1-68058-979-2

Dedication

This book is dedicated to the kids who related to comics more than the world around them.

And to Chris Cary, for reminding me to live in the moment and keep going, even when life's a struggle.

Prologue

"Madame President, we're under attack."

The General huffed and puffed as he climbed over the shattered wood of her broken entryway. Two members of the Secret Service sat slumped by the door, knocked down by the burly man. She didn't hide her anger as she stood behind her desk and pointed at him. "Sir, what do you think you are doing?"

"President, the Facility is under attack."

She bit her lip, aware of the severity of the situation. She stepped around her desk, letting her fingers slip along the edge of her desk to press a red panic button as she did so. She didn't like the General, but she could do little to stop him. His rank and seniority afforded him certain latitudes she wouldn't otherwise have allowed.

"General, I would appreciate—"

"Later," he said.

He motioned to the orb suspended above her

1

desk with a slight hand gesture. As the orb began projecting several screens of vibrant light, he poked at the air with his finger, moving one window to the side and opening several more. Within seconds, multiple monitors showed feeds from the Facility.

"Is this live?" she asked, stepping out from behind her desk and watching the man.

"Yes. We have five Children who breached the Facility."

"Only five?"

He ignored the comment. She eyed the fallen Secret Service men. They were some of the most trained men in the world and this brutish ancient geriatric bested them? There was something amiss with the current situation.

Her eyes narrowed as she glared at the screen. "I recognize that one." The president pointed to the screen. "She's your Paladin." She leaned in to witness the woman fling a man against a wall as if he weighed nothing. The Child only paused when soldiers landed their shots. Even then, bullets did little to stop her as they bounced off her skin.

"She was my Paladin. She went AWOL on a mission in the Danger Zone. It appears she has some extremely powerful friends."

They watched as one man hurled what appeared to be lightning from his body. The bolts surged from his palms, tearing away from his chest in loud snaps as they smacked into the generators. The chain of electricity erupted from his bare chest.

The president stared in disbelief at the magnitude of such an ability. "What is it they want?"

The General shrugged his shoulders. "I was

hoping you could explain this. The Facility has been your pet project since it opened. What *is* it they want?"

In another image, young girl severed the wires of a synthetic, tearing through them as if they offered a mere inconvenience. The president stood in awe with how swiftly each of the Children moved; the people obviously had worked together before. She hadn't imagined it possible a group of Children acting in such perfect harmony.

"There's a mentalist," she mumbled to herself. She recognized the fluid manner in which the team operated, knowing what one another did half a complex away. Their mouths moved as they spoke to ghosts. Somewhere, somebody coordinated this assault.

"More so than that, I want to know why your Warden is doing absolutely nothing in response to this threat?"

A single screen focused on the Warden. His eyes were open, but he seemed to be staring off into space, oblivious to the world around him. The president knew that expression; he was lost in his thoughts, relying on his abilities to do the dirty work for him. She had only met him a handful of times before discovering what he was. He evaded a death sentence, manipulating her at first with promises of greatness and later with threats from his newfound army.

"You don't seem particularly alarmed, Madame President."

She knew the General well enough to know he had a morsel of information he left unsaid, while he

3

poked and prodded at her until she snapped. If she was the most powerful woman in the world, he was her husband by influence. The General controlled the military forces of the United States of America, and because of the threats of mentalists, terrorists, and Children, he had been given enough resources to wage a domestic war.

"What are you attempting to get at, sir?"

"Since our rendezvous with the Facility a few days ago in an attempt to apprehend Conthan Cowan, I've been doing some research into how the Facility is run."

"You mean your spies have been at work."

"That's the funny thing," he said. "My spies had nothing to report. The place is clean, not a single person reported anything out of the ordinary. While I would like to believe that's true, let's be honest— in a compound housing some of the darkest research known to mankind, not even one crooked guard?"

"Perhaps the Warden runs a much tighter ship than you? It doesn't appear he has soldiers defecting."

The man's scowl revealed she touched a nerve. They had worked together long enough that she knew how to get under his skin. A simple threat to his effectiveness as a general would send him over the edge and she'd witness his legendary temper.

"It reminded me of something we haven't seen in decades, Madame President. I decided to use the video and audio from the synthetics located within the Facility. You'd be amazed at how well they can see. During the fire fight a few days ago, the people along the walls stopped firing, ignoring their prime directive of keeping the Facility safe. The Warden, he sat in nearly an identical state then as he is now."

The threat loomed in the air. She knew he was holding something back, something that would implicate her as the mastermind behind the Facility. She had been careful, spending decades to reach this point; every association and every tie to her was distant at best. Whatever accusation he was about to hurl, she was ready to discredit.

"The man you made Warden of the Facility..." He paused and stared down at her, his expression holding every ounce of seriousness possible. "Your Warden is a mentalist."

"You are a fool..."

She expected him to respond with criticism, mocking her, tearing down her authority as the president. She expected him to threaten her position of power, one titan of America threatening to dethrone the other. She expected many things, but the gun being drawn from his waistband wasn't one of them.

The black metal flashed before her eyes. She wasn't sure if the general was augmented with cybernetics or if he been doing this so long he was just fast. The muscles in his arm were developed to the point where his hand didn't move as he held the weapon. His face seemed void of emotion, not giving away any hint of what would happen next.

"This is treason."

"This is saving America."

Threatening her had become commonplace for him, along with claiming he served the "American way." When she won the revision of the twenty-second amendment, removing her term limit, he hadn't drawn a gun, but he made it clear that he believed she would lead America down a dark road. Now, decades later, it seemed their clandestine quarrel was about to reach its apex.

"If you kill me, you'll be hanged for treason."

"You'll be found overcome with grief, gun in your hand, and the tabloids will believe every word."

There was nobody else in the country who could manipulate the media as well as her. During the Culling, they circumvented riots as they imposed martial law and used the media to justify intrusion into the homes of innocent Americans. There might not be anybody who could rival her, but he came close. However the next fifteen seconds panned out, the survivor would control the most powerful nation in the world.

She lunged at his hand, shoving the gun upward. A shot fired into the ceiling of the Oval Office. Grabbing her wrist with his free hand, he pried her fingers off his gun hand. He leveled the weapon at her head again. She kicked at his knee, sending him toppling to the ground. As he dropped she jumped over her desk and fell off the side, the massive oak furniture between them.

"I'll have your head," she yelled.

The scanner built into the desk drawer read her fingerprints and popped open. She reached in and pulled out her own weapon. As she rested her finger on the trigger, the small power cell begun spinning, prepping the laser discharge.

Lifting her head just enough to see over the desk,

she found that the General had a sturdy grip, his gun pointed at her. He fired again, sending her to the ground for cover. She wasn't a novice in a fight, but the General had spent his entire life training for situations like this.

"Madame President," a voice yelled. "We're here to…"

More shots fired, ending the sentence before they could finish. She lay approximately fifteen feet from the entrance to a safe room. If she reached the shelter, nothing short of a missile strike could harm her. There was no way she could make it to the wall, open the door, and get inside before he shot her in the back. Even if she was lucky and made it to the door, in the half second it took for her to push her way through he'd have a bullet penetrating the back of her head.

"Give up now," she said. "It's the last warning, General."

The thumping of feet filling carpeted corridors got louder as her reinforcements flooded the building. He may control the manned military, but the synthetic army served under her control. While the military had utilized them for the last decade, she hadn't been a fool. She grabbed the edge of the desk and looked over as the General turned around to confront the three synthetics strolling into the room. Even the fastest shooting wouldn't save him now. His reflexes and manpower couldn't stop nearly a half ton of metal.

"Ready to stand down now?"

She couldn't hide her grin as the General turned toward her, holstering his gun. She figured he would try and fight his way out of the scenario. For some reason, she didn't expect the veteran soldier to be taken prisoner; he struck her more as a fight-to-the-death type of guy.

"Vazquez," he said, his voice just above a whisper.

The crash of the bay window shattering seemed quiet compared to the explosions of the synthetics' heads. Each of the manmade soldiers ruptured, sparks flying in all directions. The burst of light and sound didn't slow her as she got to her feet and ran toward the hidden panel in the office.

Her hand pressed the release latch on the door. It slid open quickly, sending her stumbling forward. She turned just in time to see the flash of gun powder from the General's gun. The pain was sharp as she toppled to the ground half inside the entrance to the safe room. The hurt moving down her side told her that his bullet pierced the muscle in her arm. She pulled her feet inside the threshold, causing a glass to slide shut. Several bullets ricocheted off the door, as the general emptied the last of his ammunition into it.

She moved back to her feet while gripping her wounded arm, trying to keep the blood from pouring out. Their eyes locked, both wearing disgusted looks. The man had tried to assassinate her. The second time it had happened in this very office. Both times she walked away victorious. The irony wasn't lost on her as she began to laugh hysterically.

He reached up to his ear and mumbled something. She knew he was asking for an extraction. Her guards were already swarming the White House. Any other man would be slaughtered before he got out the doors, but it was obvious he came here ready for this encounter. He was almost as resilient as she.

"You had your chance." She looked down to the blood seeping out of her arm. In the bunker beneath the White House there was enough technology to patch it up without much fuss. Hissing as she pressed the wound hard, she hobbled down the hallway toward the elevator.

"You wanted a war, General, you've got one."

Chapter 1

2033

Violating curfew was punishable by death.

Her roommate convinced her to go to the party at a friend of a friend's house. She hadn't wanted to go, there was a biology exam in the morning and she needed to study if she was going to pass. That test had been the focus of her life for the past two weeks. She could hear her parents scolding her if she got anything less than an A. "Your sister made it into med school with a perfect 4.0."

She hated her sister.

She jogged lightly down the street, heels clacking along the sidewalk. It was only eleven thirty and the streets of her borough were empty. Lights filled the windows of many buildings, but the blinds were pulled tight. She wished she was behind one of them, home, tucked away in the safety of her pajamas with a cup of herbal tea. But no, she had decided it was more important to mingle with a cute boy in her sociology class. She sounded like her sister.

His house had been in the next borough. It looked a lot like hers, cars lining one side of the street and the long rows of brownstone buildings stretching down the road. Every so often there would be a gap between the buildings, an alley leading to the backyard or small sheds where they stored the outside trashcans. Unlike in her borough, there was no grass between the buildings and the sidewalk. The little bit of grass in her part of the burbs gave some semblance of space. Here, it felt as if each building was packed as tightly as could be. It wasn't far from the truth. She lived in one of the nicest areas of New York City, but it had become crowded to the point of unlivable.

Her hand had the telltale signs of smudged makeup as she wiped the tears from her eyes. As her fingers touched her cheek there was a sharp sting from where a bruise was already starting to form. It had been going well before that. They were drinking. He had been brave enough to reach out and put his hand on her shoulder, tracing a line to her hand. He had been unlike the guys at school.

The booze had clouded her judgement. It was her fault for getting drunk. The conversation had been light until somebody brought up the D.C. Treaty and what it meant for Democratic States of America. His fingers were wrapped around her hand, giving it gentle squeezes as people expressed their views. She finally spoke. "This fight is about the corrupt being in power." His gentle squeeze turned to a painful grip.

His father apparently worked for the government

and he didn't like her answer. She didn't find that out until later. As they made out she let him lead her to the bedroom. She was pretty sure she'd regret the sex in the morning, but after so much studying, it was time to let loose and be a real college student. As he shut the door, his hand swung, striking her across the face. He tried to wrestle her to the bed, but she fought back. Her dad had taught her to struggle. His screams echoed when her knee connected with his groin.

Panicking, she ran down the stairs and ignored the shouts from the others in the living room. Opening the door, she ran outside. It wasn't until she reached the end of the block she figured out what they had been yelling about. Curfew. It was only a matter of time before somebody spotted her.

A light shone down the road as a vehicle turned onto the street. The terror set in as she looked for an escape, her hands shaking. She took several steps on a staircase leading down to a garden level apartment. She ducked, pressing her back to the brick, attempting to hide from the light as it passed by. There was barely a hum of the engine as the car continued down the road. She didn't dare look up to see if there were officers in the seat or if the car was driving itself. Either way, it meant the police were somewhere nearby.

She pulled at the straps on her heels and slowly removed her shoes. The lights dimmed and she took a breath, trying to steady herself as the alcohol pulsed through her veins. She crouched on the stairs, watching as the vehicle rounded the corner, going to inspect another street.

Her feet hit the ground and she was off in a sprint. She ran down the sidewalk, her bare soles aching as her feet made contact with the cement. In one window, a woman pointed at her, motioning for a hidden spouse to see. Ignoring the woman's frantic movements, she was determined to make it back to her house before being caught.

She reached the end of the street with her chest heaving from the strain. She leaned against the lamp post for a moment, trying to gasp for breath. The world started to spin. She tried to remember how many drinks she had consumed. There had been beer, then tequila, did she have that glass of wine? She ignored the spinning and took several steps further. Without warning, she threw up against a car door.

She braced her hands against the side of the car, and it started to vibrate as lights flashed on and the vehicle emitted a piercing siren. She pulled away and stumbled back. The alarm served as a reminder of how bad the crime had been a couple years prior. Crime had become negligible, nobody would dare come outside to check on it, but it meant the police would be there.

Horror seized her as a humanoid figure stepped from the shadows of a nearby house into the light of the pole she had been resting against. She didn't need to see it up close. The stiff motions gave away its inhumanity. She dropped her shoes and ran. The fear clinging to her pushed aside the alcohol. Her feet were silent as they pounded against the pavement, so that she could hear the metallic scraping coming up behind her.

She rounded the corner and made it to her street. Her father, a bank executive, had bought her the house, satisfied that his daughter would live in a safer part of the city. The row houses were set back from the street a dozen feet, each with a short metal fence in the front protecting a small patch of grass from intruders. Her chest ached, but she knew if she didn't make it to her house, the machine would use one of its lasers to bore a hole in her head.

She peeked over her shoulder and saw the machine closing the distance between them. It was only a matter of seconds before it grabbed her shoulder and threw her to the ground. It'd drag her to the local precinct, from which if she was lucky, she'd be banished to the Outlands—if not, death. She was about to pass her neighbor Karen's house. She turned right, busting through the gate, running up the stairs. She banged on the door, loud enough that if there was anybody inside, they'd hear her.

The machine was slowing, but only a short distance from her. She banged harder until the lights in the house went dark. She could see curtains quickly drawn, but nobody answered. She pulled at the handle frantically, trying to wretch the metal door open.

She slowly turned to look over her shoulder at the machine standing at the gate. It was designed to look like a human. It had limbs like a person, but its hands were oversized, making it difficult to ignore the pointy fingers. In the darkness she couldn't distinguish further details, but she felt the blank skull staring at her. A single spot on the forehead housed a camera capturing the terror on her face.

It took another step forward and fell into a hole in the ground, vanishing from sight. She let go of the metal door handle and rubbed her eyes again, trying to figure out what happened. She took a step down the stairs to see where the machine had vanished. She couldn't help but wonder if she had imagined the whole thing. Had her paranoia gotten the best of her? Had she been so scared of being discovered she invented the incident?

She gasped as a flash of metal fell out of the sky and landed in the street. The machine hit the pavement, sending a spray of asphalt in every direction. Car alarms up and down the street came to life. Flashing lights filled the small neighborhood, casting light on the crumpled pieces of the machine that had been chasing her.

She looked down the road; her doorway was only a few entrances away. She would have to cross and get dangerously close to where the machine had landed. A metallic hand rose and the machine started to stir, lifting itself out of the crater it had created. She wasn't sure how it was capable of still moving after the landing.

Ten feet away from the crater, a man appeared out of nowhere. His bulky frame was illuminated by headlights flashing on and off. He didn't budge, standing behind the machine as it pulled itself out of the hole. The hood of his sweatshirt covered his face, making him appear even more ominous. She didn't know who he was, but for the moment, it appeared she was safe until the machine killed the man.

A scream slipped out as she twisted her ankle

and stumbled the last few steps. She reached out to catch the pavement, but hands wrapped around her waist, halting her fall. The guy who wore a black hoodie underneath his leather jacket had rescued her from a collision with the ground. She didn't know if she should say thank you or cry out. Despite saving her life, he looked like the kind of man her parents warned her about.

The machine's legs pumped faster, closing the distance. It reached the sidewalk and a car fell out of the sky, landing on the humanoid body.

"You need to run," said the man holding her.

"My house is just down there," she said, trying not to slur her words.

"You can't go home."

"But..."

"They know who you are. They'll come for you. You need to run. Head north and don't look back."

A screeching filled the air as the machine pushed the car off. His hands let go of her waist. She ran down the sidewalk, passing by where the machine tried to free itself. She continued running, unsure of where she headed. She glanced back to the man who rescued her. He didn't seem fazed by the killing machine that just moved a half-ton vehicle.

The synthetic glanced at her before turning back to the man. It had made its decision about which was more important. She eyed the crushed car and wondered where it had come from. "Did it fall out of the sky?"

The synthetic reached down, its hip opening up. It pulled out a gun and pointed it at the guy trying to save her. She wanted to scream at him, tell him to

16

run away. There was no way he could survive if the machine shot him, and they were created to never miss. Ever since synthetics took to the streets in an attempt to stop rioting, they had become efficient watchdogs.

The end of the gun pulsed red, firing a single bolt at the man. The light vanished before it touched his forehead. She didn't have time to see what happened, but the synthetic fell to the ground, an unmoving heap. He destroyed it.

"Child," she whispered under her breath.

The man stepped forward and between her blinks, he vanished from sight. She ran further down the street, out of the range of car alarms and the eradicated synthetic. As she approached the gate leading to her house, she slowed. Her father would be furious to find out what she did. He would lecture her, threaten to take away his money and force her to go to school on her own.

"It's over," she mumbled. The street seemed to continue, vanishing into darkness. The life she knew was over. But thanks to a random man, a Child of Nostradamus, she had the opportunity to live.

Speeding past her house, she continued into the unknown.

***

The ruins of Boston were quiet as the ghosts of nearly a million people milled about the empty streets. A chilling breeze touched Conthan's cheek, forcing him to pull his hoodie over his head. The stars were out and the waning moon illuminated just enough of the city for him to see the bar further down the block.

The church overlooked the bar, an ominous tower acting as a gateway to his home. It was a year to the day he had arrived in the dead city, swept away from the world he knew by a series of unfortunate accidents. A year ago, he discovered he was capable of opening portals defying the laws of physics. Three hundred and sixty five days ago, he discovered he was a Child of Nostradamus.

He closed his eyes for a moment, soaking in the stillness. In between long blinks he could still see Jed's face as the dying man handed him an envelope. Inside were the ramblings of a dead psychic, a woman predicting his future. He often wondered what would have happened if he had said no and never taken the piece of paper. Unfortunately Eleanor Valentine had found a situation in which he was most vulnerable. He had stopped trying to figure out if she caused his future or if she manipulated it. The circular logic had become the bane of his existence.

The moment he thought of the dead artist, he knew he would see *her*. Sarah lay there on the ground, her face hidden by bone plating. She had been the first Child of Nostradamus he ever met. Thanks to Eleanor, he went on a mission to rescue her. Covered in an exoskeleton, she had been the one who rescued him from a violent pyrokinetic. Now, the image of her smoldering face haunted his every waking moment. He thought he'd take solace in the fact he blew out the brains of the man behind

18

her death, but even that left him filled with sadness.

"Sarah," he whispered. "I'm trying."

He woke in the middle of every night to the sound of the Warden laughing at him, mocking Conthan's attempts to be rid of him. Each night he was determined to expunge the man, one deed at a time.

The look on the girl's face tonight as he told her that life as she knew it was over was all too familiar. She was one of dozens he rescued from the government. Each time, he broke the news that their reality was about to change. Then he saved their lives. This synthetic was like every one before, determined to eradicate him just before he crushed it. He hoped he would feel better, destroying government property and rescuing an innocent victim, and each night he thought back to Sarah. It didn't get easier.

He tucked his hands into the pockets of his leather jacket, trying to ward off the cold. He leaned against the wall of the balcony overlooking the city, exhausted from another night without sleep. The moment he crawled into bed the dreams would start again. Instead, he decided he'd stay up here and watch the sun rise and when the others woke, he'd chug another pot of Dav5d's disgusting coffee.

After half an hour of staring off toward the bay, the sun started to light the world. Purples and oranges chased off the grays of the night. Below, breaking through the pavement of the street, grass struggled to reclaim the city, determined to turn it into a forest one day. Every now and then a small creature scurried through the brush, and it reminded him life, despite all odds, found a way to continue.

Heavy boots scraped the stone behind him. His muscles tensed, but he fought the urge to spin around. Dwayne leaned against the stone next to him, staring out to where the light broke through the buildings. He made no attempt to speak

"I couldn't sleep," Conthan said, trying not to make it a big deal. The man gave a slight nod

He was slightly larger than Conthan, nearly three inches taller and significantly thicker through the torso. A human lightning bolt, he could hurl electricity from his body like it was no big deal. His arms were perfectly smooth, any hair burned away by his abilities. Conthan had been unsettled at first by his lack of eyebrows and how it made his brown eyes stand out even more than normal. If he had passed the lug on the street he would have never given him another look, but after seeing what he was capable of, he was impressed.

"It's the nightmares."

It was almost comical when Dwayne raised where his eyebrow should have been. Conthan had kept the nightmares secret for months, waking in the middle of the night screaming. Vanessa couldn't help but hear his thoughts and eventually she laid it out on the table for them all. She admitted she suffered from them too, almost identical to his. He knew he couldn't hide his thoughts from her, but it was awkward having everybody know how much the Warden haunted him.

"Remember what I told you that night?" Dwayne asked.

He nodded.

20

"It doesn't get easier."

Conthan raised his eyebrow at the man. It hadn't been too long after the escape from the Facility before Dwayne and Jasmine had it out. She was willing to be part of the team as long as there was a mutual enemy, but she had issues in particular with Dwayne. He didn't understand it until she sent Dwayne to the ground in a bloody heap. She made sure each of them knew how she had been tortured by the man. She didn't want to physically wound him, she wanted to permanently tarnish his reputation. It worked.

Conthan found it ironic—the older man could provide sagely advice, but in the heat of the moment, he wasn't nearly the idol he portrayed. Only Alyssa joined Conthan in objecting to the radical abuse. They had saved Jasmine from being killed by the same military she served only for Dwayne to torture her for intel about the Facility. He was surprised Vanessa didn't comment. Her moral compass pointed toward good, but her means weren't always as righteous.

He waited for Dwayne to apologize but the man didn't speak again. The sun broke over the water and the city filled with hues of orange and red, a growing fire breathing life into the decaying buildings. For a moment, between the shift in color where Conthan believed things were like they were a year ago. There weren't super powers and there were no government conspiracies. For a moment he forgot everything but the flood of light.

The minutes passed and Dwayne turned and headed back into the church. Conthan watched the man pull the front of his jacket closed as his boots dragged on the stone.

"Why did you come up here?"

Dwayne stopped but didn't turn around. Several seconds passed before he responded. "I wanted to see a new day the way I used to." He disappeared into the doorway and Conthan was left by himself.

"Wow, now that was a line to exit on."

Conthan turned back to the light, letting the rays touch his face. The warmth battled to push away the cold of the morning. It had been a year since his life went crazy and he discovered he was a Child of Nostradamus. However, meeting a mentalist, fighting alongside a bunch of wanted Children, attacking a government facility, and killing a telepath was only the starting point of weird. It was a week later that the world went to hell.

Marshal law happened overnight, and not for the first time, but it wasn't like before. They weren't securing the borders or hunting down homegrown terrorists, they were moving toward the center of the country. Quickly, it became apparent a civil war had bubbled to a head and the American populace was the last to be informed. The Midwest became a battlefield and at first it was difficult figure out who was fighting. It wasn't until the propaganda started to appear on the internet that it became clear.

The military had staged a coup against the President of the United States of America. At first it seemed a lost cause for the leader with no army. Without the military Cecilia Joyce and her presidency were going to come to a fateful end. It had been a bum rush against Washington D.C.

while all of the world watched, waiting to see who would emerge victorious. Rumors involved everything from illegal experiments to the head of the military and Joyce being ex-lovers using government might to settle a falling out.

As the military released its soldiers into the streets of D.C., the residents waited. Those who could not flee hid in their basements, hoping the city itself wouldn't be leveled. Satellites from foreign nations projected the entire event, showing thermal scans and detailed maps of the soldiers working their way through the streets. It appeared as if by sheer might the battle had already been won.

Joyce hadn't maintained her presidency for so long without being formidable. The red dots on the thermal maps began to vanish, blips ceasing to exist. It appeared as if soldiers were being slaughtered in the streets by ghosts. They had wondered if there were Children involved, possibly more mentalists.

Dav5d almost sounded elated as he spoke. "Synthetics."

Cecilia Joyce, a devious mastermind, lured in the military forces who expected to only find opposition from the CIA, FBI, and Secret Service. However, under the cloak of secrecy, she had been amassing a synthetic army. Her army moved with a single goal, eradicate the opposition, and eradicate they did. In the history of the United States, never had so many lives been lost in a single war let alone a single fight. Now she reigned supreme over the United States of America and asserted herself as more than capable of fending off the radical Free Republic.

A year ago he lived in a sane world. Now, as he absorbed the heat bathing his skin, a new world was in the midst of being created. Each time he thought about it, he couldn't help but wonder: was *this* the event Eleanor had warned them about, or was it going to get worse?

***

Her throat closed, silencing her screams. She raked her elongated claws against the black liquid surrounding her body, threatening to consume her. Her fingers pushed through the liquid, but it refused to break away from her skin.

Vanessa gasped and gurgled as the liquid poured into her throat. Her lungs filled, and her panic turned to terror. It wasn't the thought of drowning that shook her, it was being devoured by this thing. As her breathing stopped, the whispers in the back of her head taunted her. The hissing of a man's voice grew louder with each moment, filling her head.

She fought in the center of an overgrown garden. The moon hung overhead, its light casting eerie shadows on the dozens of sculptures of people upon pedestals. Vines creeped from the ground, surrounding what once was a beautiful fountain in the middle of the garden filled with statues. Each of a person, frozen in position for eternity. Their faces had looks of horror chiseled across their rocky features. Now, Vanessa stood atop one of those

look bad, she was amazed at the transformation she had gone through in such a short time. She pulled a black tank top over her head and pushed together the Velcro on the sides just under her wings. She looked over to the closet where the robes still hung, reminding her of the personal journey she undertook. She pulled the black leggings up over her bulky legs. At some point she would have to ask for Jasmine for more age appropriate fashion, but for now, it was practical.

The whispers at the edge of her thoughts raced in, growing louder as her senses shook away the last of her sleep. There were fewer voices to listen to this far from civilization, each one distinct enough she could sort out the owners without using her gifts. There weren't many of them left; only the Nighthawks remained in the wastelands of Boston. The rest of the Children escaped, fleeing to a town in upstate New York where they could attempt some semblance of normalcy. Now, it was six voices, six sets of thoughts bombarding her mind.

With the slightest effort she focused on one of their voices and pushed away the others. She could listen to everything crossing their mind. Unlike her teammates', her gifts appeared long before the Nostradamus Effect. Born a mentalist, she was a rare human with the ability to manipulate the world with only her thoughts. She was a telepath, and until a year ago, she believed she was the last. They were few and far between, eradicated during a period of American history referred to as the Culling. Years late, fate, cruel and ironic fate, blessed her as a Child of Nostradamus. Undergoing drastic changes, she'd had her young adult life robbed from her as she became the gargoyle she was now.

Unlike other Children of Nostradamus, she had the ability to hide. Mastering her telepathy, she could blend in, hiding the green skin and growing wings from those around her. It wasn't long before she found herself in the Outlands. Escaping humanity, the Angel of the Outlands was born. Only recently her assumptions about mentalists, or even her own abilities, had come into question. Now, she was fully aware there were more, and they had learned to use their abilities in manners that never crossed her mind.

She shook her head as the Warden came to mind. That vile creature had left his mark, corrupting her thoughts like a plague and haunting her dreams at night. He claimed he had won the fight, and while he was dead, she wondered if he had been right. Would the memory of him, or the totality of his abilities, be enough to haunt her for the rest of her life? In the back of her mind, in a place she tried to lock away, the stain of his presence remained.

Chapter 2

1993

The bottle opened with a pop. The last two pills fell into the palm of his hand. He stared at the red circles and contemplated throwing them away, avoiding the chalky taste that drowned out the faux strawberry flavoring. As if in protest, bile rose in his esophagus, burning at his throat. He popped the antacids in his mouth and chewed, trying to ignore the disgusting taste coating his tongue.

He threw the bottle at the corner of his office, where it bounced off one wall and then the other until it landed in the silver waste basket. He grabbed a bottle of water stored in the mini fridge hidden underneath his desk. He popped off the cap and stopped as the plastic touched his lips. The dying plant on his desk caught his eye. Its leaves were starting to whither and fall away.

"You're the only person who understands me, Simon."

He poured some of the water into the colorful

pot. He had been told the walls of the complex were shielded from the radiation, but he had a feeling Simon suffered from radiation poisoning. He hoped that was the reason behind its slow demise and not lack of care. He wouldn't be surprised if the plant was responding to his own health; he felt as wilted as the plant looked.

"Mr. Davis, your one thirty has arrived."

He jumped at the squawking over the telephone intercom. The heartburn in his chest continued, a rumble stinging in his throat as he thought about the meeting he was about to attend. He wanted nothing more than to cancel and reschedule the day after tomorrow. While he was a far ways from Washington D.C., his bosses liked to remind him he was still their subordinate.

"Send him to the conference room, Cindy," he said into the box.

He leaned forward in his high back office chair, resting his forehead against his forearm. Staring him in the face were thousands of little notes on a giant calendar resting on his desk. He turned his head and looked at the computer. Cursing at the machine's inability to do as he told it, he ultimately gave up and went back to writing notes. He wasn't entirely sure if he could even turn it on without his secretary providing emotional support. He couldn't help but feel the calendar and computer were a metaphor for his life. Working at the Advanced Development of Sciences for the last year made him feel antiquated.

The door to his office opened and Cindy stood there holding a thermos with coffee. She gave a slight huff at her boss's condition. "Mr. Davis, you need to pull yourself together. You can't go into a meeting in this state."

It was only a matter of time before the stress ate away at his stomach or began turning his hair gray. He hadn't seen his family in a month and while they talked every night, he already missed his son's first teeth, his crawling, and now his constantly saying, "Mommeeeee." The president had assigned him this detail, told him to prove himself, and she patiently awaited his success or failure. Right now, his team was still fresh, but he had faith that there was a way he could protect the future of mankind without the mindless bloodshed that resulted from the Culling.

He pushed himself up and grabbed the folder on his desk. He had been reluctant to take this meeting, but when the President of the United States of America and the Secretary of State demand you see a specialist, you nod your head and say absolutely. He tucked the folder under his arm and stepped into his assistant's office. The look on Cindy's face gave away her lack of amusement. She took the folder from him and set it on a table along with his coffee. She was, for all intents and purpose, his work wife. He carried the stress of the entire fate of mankind; she made she he was fed, clothed, and that his desk was always stocked with antacids. She was a Godsend for him.

"Seriously, Mr. Davis? There is no way you're walking into this meeting looking like a homeless man stole a suit." She fixed the button on his shirt. It was the first time all day he realized he buttoned his shirt incorrectly. Her fingers corrected his mistake along his increasingly growing gut. He didn't resist as she took off his tie and flipped his collar. "You do not have to like this man. You do not have to like what he says. But you need to remember why you are here, Mr. Davis. You are attempting to stop a genocide. You are attempting to research and understand the future of our coexistence with mentalists. You are doing God's work."

His shoulders straightened at her compliment. He didn't want to think more of the position than what it was, but she did have a knack for boosting his confidence. Cindy straightened his tie. She always managed the perfect length. She had spent thirty years practicing on her late husband and even now, she still did it with a sense of pride. He admired her gusto and ability to stay positive. A smile started to spread across his lips as she licked her thumb and wiped a smudge from his cheek.

"Why are you here?" she asked.

It was a game they played. "I'm here to save innocent lives."

"Why are you really here?"

"Mankind needs people to protect those who cannot protect themselves."

She gave him a pat on the chest. "You're ready, Mr. Davis. Go save them."

He leaned in and gave her a kiss on the cheek. She smelled of lilacs, and for a moment, he was reminded of a woman from the past. He rest his head on the back of his chair and eyed her curiously. She might not look the same, but there was something in her demeanor at that moment that evoked a tender lady who changed the course of his future. He rested his hands on her shoulders and the smile grew wider.

"Cindy, you are an amazing woman."

She blushed.

"Did you ever..." He knew it was going to sound crazy. "Ever receive a letter from a woman you never met?"

She gave a slight giggle. "Mr. Davis, I'm sure a handsome man such as yourself receives letters from interested ladies all the time. Your wife is a lucky woman. Me, though, my suitor days are long gone."

She unknowingly answered his question. "All right, Cindy, it's time to go save the world."

"It's what we do." She handed him his thermos and file and feigned a slight salute as he walked into the waiting area of his office. He continued onward, into the hallway leading toward the more public areas of the facility. The hallways were bare, almost to the point that they became a maze if you hadn't walked through them before. Past the offices of his research team and through the sleeping quarters of his security staff, he found himself standing at the metal doors separating him from the lobby. He slid his ID badge through the slot and listened to the computer inside read the card.

Like every time before, he jumped as a spot in the wall opened and a scanner appeared. He always wondered what kind of advancements the government had made, technologies that had yet to reach the public. The idea of a machine doing his work for him didn't rest well. He barely used the computer in his office and most often found himself still using the typewriter to send memos to his staff. But there was something fascinating, alluring even, of what was possible. His research facility was one of the most advanced in the world. He had scientists working on things he barely understood. During department head meetings he would have to ask the men to dumb down their explanations so he could comprehend enough to relay it to his superiors.

His chin rested on the device and a bright blue light shone in his eye. He blinked in response and the device flashed red at him. Several more blinks passed without success. It wouldn't be the first time he had to contact his head of security to open the doors for him. He relaxed his face and took a steadying breath as he returned it to the pad. The light appeared and a moment later flashed blue as the doors opened. He was thankful the security was in place to keep his operation safe, but there were times when he wondered if the doors were there to keep the bad people out, or to keep the good people in.

The public lobby was grand. The building was meant to be flagship of its kind, housing the world's brightest scientific minds and promoting technological growth for the entire race. The president had created the center to show the other nations they were dedicated to being the best humanity had to offer. Its mission had changed with the emergence of mentalists, a rare breed of human with extrasensory mental abilities. He had only ever met two. The first had been a gentle, caring woman who, only an hour after meeting him, attempted to assassinate the President of the United States of

America. The action resulted in the Culling, a massive American initiative to eliminate all mentalists. In turn, a freedom group destroyed multiple nuclear power plants to warn the government.

He, Mark Davis, was the man in the middle trying to save these people from elimination.

As he stepped into the three-story lobby, he gave a slight nod to the secretary at the front desk. He always found it funny how she sat there, in an empty room nearly every day. The center was hours away from civilization, just inside what they started calling the Danger Zone. People living in the area had been shipped away to prevent radiation poisoning. Inside these walls, they were safe from the exposure, but even guests were required to take medicine to prevent long term effects. The loss of the center to radiation was the only reason he had been granted the ability to take it over.

The woman gestured to a gentleman sitting in one of the plush seats to the side of the desk. Mark was surprised as the man stood—he had to be nearing seven feet tall. It was rare that anybody made his six foot six stature feel small, but the man dwarfed him. However, where Mark was a large man in all aspects, this man was thin, almost wiry, his body appearing to be stretched a bit too far. He was very aware of the long spindly fingers wrapping around his hands as they clasped.

"Hello, Mr. Davis," the new arrival said with a dry voice.

"Dr. Volkov, it's a pleasure to meet you."

It wasn't entirely a pleasure. The man had been

assigned to his team. Up to this point Mark had the luxury of hand-selecting his staff. He had flown across the world, requesting the participation of some of the brightest men and women in existence. The center continued to fulfill its mission, advancing the sciences in at least a dozen fields, but there was one he was under constant bombardment to advance: the study of parapsychology.

"I fully understand I am not here upon your request, Mr. Davis. I am hoping despite being thrust upon you in this horribly bureaucratic manner, you will find my talents to be quite useful."

"Blunt and to the point," Mark said. "I can appreciate that."

"I am eager to prove myself, Mr. Davis."

"Mark," he corrected. "You can call me Mark."

The man gave a slight nod. "Ivan."

"You'll be set up with an office and a private lab. I currently have department heads discussing who will be joining your team. The government is giving us an uncanny amount of leeway and funding to make advancements with this project."

Before they reached the security doors, a gentleman in black pants and a black turtleneck stepped out from a room behind the front desk. The shirt hugged the man in a way that revealed the muscles underneath, forming to his chest and hugging his narrow waist.

"Goddard," Mark said with his best authoritative voice, "what have I said about weapons in my facility?"

"I appreciate your concern, Mr. Davis," the man said, dismissing Mark, "but this is still a military operation. All the men assigned in the research areas have been assigned non-lethal projectile weapons, but any many working the perimeter or in the main entrance will be armed."

"I will…"

"Per order of the President of the United States of America," the man said flatly.

Mark understood the argument was over. He might be in charge of the center, but for the moment, one arm would always remain tied behind his back. He didn't like it, but he learned by this point that nothing ever went entirely in his favor.

"Goddard, this is Ivan Volkov. He will be heading up our parapsychology division. If you could begin working on his credentials, it would be much appreciated."

"Yes sir," Goddard said with a slight nod. "We need to discuss some of the transient population who have been spotted in the area. It seems there are a number of people who refuse to vacate their homes. None of them appear to pose any sort of security risk. But if I were the domestic terrorists, hiding amongst the locals would be the first tactic I would use to attack one of the most secluded research facilities in the Northeast."

He hated to admit it, but Goddard wasn't an idiot. He had proved valuable in multiple situations where they had received threats from terrorists. While the interior of the building was extremely secure from the outside world, Mark knew firsthand the dangers of pissing off a mentalist.

"See to it," he said, "but as always, use non-lethal tactics."

The man nodded in response. Mark had to wonder if the nod was a subordinate agreeing or an asshole begrudgingly accepting authority. He tried to ignore what may actually happen beyond these walls. He was a pacifist, but the world being created around them wouldn't be won with good intentions. Men like Goddard still had a place, and while he didn't like the man, he did need to rely on him.

As they walked away Ivan whispered to his newly appointed boss. "Brutes will never understand enlightenment."

Mark gave a light chuckle. He was quickly becoming a fan of the new department chair. "Let me show you your facilities. After that I can take you to meet Ariel."

"That's her name?"

Mark nodded. "Wasn't this in your files?"

The man shook his head. "She is only referred to as the child of Project Nostradamus."

Chapter 3

2033

"The man has a church?"

Jasmine nodded.

Conthan stepped out from behind a trashcan in the alley. He had opened the exit portal just outside their destination. The green trashcan hid them from prying eyes as they teleported between Boston and Hell's Kitchen. The small alley opened onto a street lined cars in various states of disrepair. With the missing tires, burned out hoods, and shattered windows, it looked more like a nuclear bomb went off here than north of Boston.

"I'm for the man and everything," Conthan said, "but isn't this getting a bit ridiculous?"

Jasmine didn't reply to his rhetorical question. He turned to see her pulling the hood of her shirt over her head, hiding her face. She wrapped head until only her eyes could be seen. He pulled his own hood over his head, mimicking her movements.

"You'd think I'd be used to this."

"Yes," she said softly, "you would."

He flipped her off. "You owe a dollar to the bitch jar."

She silently held up her hand, extending her middle finger in response.

He eyed the church, shocked to see the chaos of midtown hadn't reached its doors. The fence along either side exhibited amateur graffiti, but not on the building itself. Either the keepers of the church had been vigilant about washing the walls, or the vandals stayed clear of the building. Where the cars had no windows, the church still held a beautiful rose window high above the four sets of double doors.

A dozen steps led up to them. Both Conthan and Jasmine froze as they checked the street. In both directions, there was almost nobody, only a few people walking with their eyes focused on the ground. Conthan raised his eyebrow at her. She nodded. He and Jasmine were the least friendly of the bunch. He didn't like her attitude, and she didn't acknowledge him most of the time. It had become a game at this point, seeing how far he could push her. He frequently referred to it as his second superpower.

In this duo, he was the escape artist, she was the muscle. He couldn't help but chuckle. *I'm such a pimp. My bodyguard is an impervious battle-crazy woman*, he thought to himself.

It was sad Vanessa wasn't around to smile at his twisted thoughts. He had to admit he was getting fond of having somebody hear his inner monologue.

Once he got over the shame of having dirty thoughts about his team members, everything else was a piece of cake. Now, without her on the mission, he would have to save the comment for when he saw Skits.

They walked across the street, stepping around a woman pushing a carriage filled with her belongings. He stopped to watch as she started mumbling to herself. She hobbled behind the carriage, stopping long enough to look in a trashcan. It broke his heart to think people lived this way. Though it wasn't much better living in a barren wasteland being irradiated.

Jasmine pointed to her eyes and forward to the doors. He nodded in reply. It had taken him forever to get used to her ability to carry an entire conversation on a mission without speaking. At least with Vanessa they would speak mind to mind, but Jasmine, she just expected them all to be mind readers.

They jogged up the stairs and she pressed her face to the door, listening for people on the other side. Conthan spun about, watching the street, making note of every living person. He scanned the nearby rooftops. There were six people within eyesight, each of them going about their business. He couldn't help but wonder how many cameras scanned his face, looking for defining features. Dav5d made sure they were scrubbed from every database available to the world, but Conthan believed somewhere, somebody was studying his features, waiting till they could capture him.

Jasmine pulled at the large wooden door. As she

41

did, Conthan noted the metal cuffs around her wrists. It was almost exactly a year ago he had first fought her in the courtyard of the Facility, and since then she hadn't removed the jewelry around her wrists. The few times he had gotten close to them, he noted there were no seams. He wondered if they had been grafted directly onto her body, but knew better than to ask. It dawned on him they may not be accessories for her abilities, but maybe something more akin to handcuffs. Someday she wouldn't treat him like a pariah on the team and he'd be able to ask her about them.

The entry was larger than he expected, a lobby big enough to hold a few hundred people. The area spanned the width of the church, paintings of the disciples hanging along the way, tipped and uneven as they detailed the spread of Christianity throughout the world. The building was old, so old that the plaster slipped from the walls, exposing the bricks underneath. Tables held unlit candles, available for parishioners to take with them to the service.

Conthan listened to the sound of murmuring as they reached the doors leading into the nave. He reached for the handle, stopping to see Jasmine make the sign of the cross. In over a year he had never asked if she was Catholic. Her complexion hinted at the Latin American blood in her veins, but it never crossed his mind she might be a religious person. She continued to surprise him.

He pulled the door back and she slipped inside. When she didn't call for him to wait, he followed. Jasmine's body didn't move, but her head turned back and forth, absorbing the scene. Conthan listened to her whispering a prayer to herself. He didn't have the heart to tell her God didn't look down upon this house anymore.

Light fought to enter through blacked out windows, leaving the massive room shrouded in shadows. Great pillars reached to the ceiling, the masonry covered in discarded crutches and prosthetic limbs alongside several wheelchairs.

The room was the size of a basketball court and along each side, columns rose to arches that seemed to direct the viewer toward the apex of the church. People shuffled their feet about the floor, kicking up broken tile. He could only imagine how beautiful it had been once upon a time. Now it seemed another forgotten relic in the age of technology.

A couple hundred candles looked as if they were floating in the air, casting an eerie glow about the room. As he passed the columns and walked closer to the sanctuary, he noticed the people holding candles were wearing little more than rags. The stench of body odor and urine filled the air, and even those who looked like they could be citizens of financial means wore a modest attire.

The people stood, the pews either missing or stacked against the wall in shambles. At the times in the service when they should have knelt, they remained standing, rocking back and forth and muttering something in a language Conthan couldn't make out. He pushed his way past the first row of people in a hope to get closer to the front of the church. He wished he could teleport through the crowd to avoid the scent rubbing off on him.

A woman next to him gave him the once over. He was worried she would begin screaming at the top of her lungs. She extended a hand holding a candle, the dripping wax coating her skin. As he received the candle she went back to rocking back and forth, muttering the same indecipherable phrase as before.

The crowd stopped moving and their heads lifted, waiting for something to happen at the front of the church. Conthan continued to push through them. A man with only one arm held a candle, staring hopefully to the altar. Where there should have been an arm protruding from his shoulder there was a short stub, looking as if the rest had been crushed years ago.

From somewhere among the crowd a drum sounded, one loud bang after another. The room froze at the thunderous noise. Without movement, the smell seemed to increase. Conthan wished he had something to cover his nose.

A man moved across the front of the church, holding a golden staff with a cross upon it. The man wore a tattered robe, making him look like a homeless monk. Each of the members of the audience stared intently at the man, waiting as if he'd provide sagely words. Several people stood around the man at the altar, but only he seemed to belong in this broken house of worship.

From this distance, it was hard for Conthan to make out much about the man. He was bald, with a slender, stretched-looking face, but otherwise, Conthan didn't believe he'd give the makeshift priest a second glance on the street.

"I welcome you here this twilight," the man opened. His deep voice rang out over the crowd, whose murmuring dropped suddenly. "You have gathered this day to bask in the radiance of our saviors. You have come from near and far so that you too may be able to gaze upon those mighty supreme beings. You have gathered so that your souls may take refuge in the light of our new gods."

Conthan noted the silence in the parishioners. The man's voice enthralled the masses. A man at the head of a crowd—Conthan found it difficult to not question his motives. Religion had never been part of his life. Was it even a religion? Where did the line between divine and cult lie?

"Angels have fallen from the skies." He raised his hand up, motioning to the windows high above. "Many say Nostradamus predicted the end of the world, but what he truly predicted was the end of life as we know it. Living among us are Children of Nostradamus, emissaries of the Lord himself, come to save our poor wretched souls."

The mumbling of the crowd made it obvious they were in agreement. Conthan turned around to see Jasmine studying the faces of those around them. He shot her a look, asking what they should do about the situation. She ignored him and continued scanning the participants.

"Never thought I'd be concerned about being called a god."

"As our brethren are raised above humanity, allowed to stretch their wings, we must support them. For it is the Children of Nostradamus who have been called upon by a higher power to do

God's work."

He wondered if the man giving the speech had ever met a Child in person before, or if he was just running his mouth. Perhaps it was even possible he was a Child himself and he was turning his flock into his brainwashed slaves. Conthan couldn't imagine somebody being stupid enough to congregate with this many people and brag about your affiliation with the most hated individuals on the planet.

Conthan started to search through the crowd as the man continued to boast about the higher power responsible for his ability to teleport. The faces of the people around were weathered, eyes sunken, their skin dirty, their clothes frayed and their hygiene questionable. This flock weren't Children, they were simply people attempting to get off the street before curfew took place.

As he jumped from one face to the next he froze. Close to the front of the church there was a man in a brown bomber jacket. He stared directly at Conthan. It wasn't the man himself that was awkward, it was that he continued to stare with his large smile stretched from one ear to the next. Conthan didn't need to think about it very long before he recalled the two men in the Warden's office. They hadn't moved the entire time he fought the large man, almost like empty shells.

"What the hell?" he mumbled to himself.

He pushed forward through the shoulder-to-shoulder crowd. The man in the bomber jacket had vanished, nowhere to be found. Conthan spun about, looking for where he could have gone to.

The priest continued his sermon as Conthan worked his way to the front of the church. As he got closer he could see that the man was older, at least in his sixties, and his most prominent feature, the beaklike nose on his face.

"These gods deserve our unyielding support. These gods deserve our devotion. These gods deserve nothing less."

Conthan turned back to the crowd, scanning the faces again. Twenty-Seven had told them these gatherings had become commonplace. One of the refugees she safeguarded had spoken about the church and how it had become increasingly common to see a Child of Nostradamus among the congregation. Since the Facility, it had become even harder to find Children. Either they hid underground, or the government was finding new ways to silence them.

"It is likely even now, we are amongst gods. They walk among us, testing us, making sure we are loyal to their cause."

When Conthan turned, the man made eye contact with him. It was possible the priest himself was a Child. If he was, it was disturbing to think he had created a cult to worship himself. But after the last few months, something like this didn't shock Conthan anymore. He continued to force eye contact with the priest, waiting for him to out him and Jasmine.

"These gods will save us."

The man looked back into the crowd and then to Conthan again. Conthan turned in the direction the man had been gazing. For a moment, he thought he

47

saw familiar spikes of hair. He pushed into the crowd again, shoving people aside as he worked his way to the side of the church.

"Gretchen?" he called loudly enough everybody nearby could hear.

"Let us stand strong as our faith is tested." As the monk delivered the warning, the doors to the church exploded open, splinters flying in all directions. Conthan didn't need the dust to settle to know there were synthetics about to storm the house of worship.

"Gods save us!" the man yelled.

The crowd rushed from the doors, storming the altar of the church in an attempt to protect themselves. There were no easy exits, and even if they could run, the synthetics would follow. The robots held up their hands, revealing the small armaments mounted to their forearms. Conthan recognized them as street patrol, with no major weapons, but as vicious as their heavy duty cousins.

The muscles in his body clenched and before he had time to process, his powers awakened. He could summon portals in midair without a problem. Opening them between two touching objects or opening one inside a mass, that required effort. The portal stretched open effortlessly beneath the feet of the closest synthetic, swallowing it whole as it fell through.

A team of six turned to five. The world slowed down for a fraction of a second as his powers searched for an exit. Somewhere over the Hudson River, a robot fell into the wastewater of New York City.

"They are among us!"

Dav5d referred to it as non-linear thinking. Just because a portal opened facing one direction didn't mean the exit had to do the same. He closed his hand and opened a portal underneath Jasmine. As she dropped into the blackness, she fell out of the returning portal behind the machines. He might not get along with her, but they had practiced enough that they were dangerous in a fight.

She grabbed on to the head of one synthetic and pulled hard, trying to tear the skull from the body. One fired bullets at her chest, but the slugs fell to the ground. Jasmine had probably utilized her gift before the doors exploded, making her skin as dense as the bracers she always wore. The downside to her abilities was that her muscles didn't adjust as quickly. For the first few seconds, she was slower, clunkier, and incapable of doing anything other than be a human shield.

He closed the portals as the synthetics turned to face their adversaries. He secretly hoped somebody in the crowd had a weapon and would join in the fray, but the threat of death had sent them fleeing. If he was capable of opening larger portals, he could drag all the synthetics into the river. However, there were unfortunate limitations to his abilities.

Conthan stood ten feet from the closest synthetic. "Hey, tin bucket, how about you pick on somebody your own size?" He had to wonder if the increase in synthetics meant an increase in human operators or if the machines had been left to their artificial intelligence.

The one being jerked around by Jasmine raised

both forearms and fired a barrage of bullets. Conthan ripped open the air in front of him. The bullets entered the darkness and exited through a portal next to the synthetic's skull. They pelted the machine, denting the metal exterior.

"Dammit," he said, "no laser weapons."

The head severed from the machine. Jasmine's muscles increased to cope with her mass as she grabbed the arm of another machine and tore it free. Metal rang out as she used the arm like a bat, clobbering the humanoid and knocking it to the ground. She slammed the heel of her foot down, crushing its skull.

"I see you have everything taken care of," he said.

Two of the synthetics grabbed on to her and wrestled her down to one knee. The third synthetic fired directly into her forehead. She grunted as the bullets pelted her skin. She once told him she could still feel, not as clearly as when her powers were off, but enough that she'd bruise later.

The base of his skull tingled, turning to a slight pain as he pulled from the internal well containing his powers. The portal resisted, and he pushed harder. He'd have a headache in seconds, and if he continued, he'd be bedridden with a migraine.

"Open," he yelled.

The top half of a synthetic was swallowed by a portal tearing through its midsection. A second portal opened next to him, dumping out the remains. Jasmine took the opportunity to throw one machine against a wall and climb on top of another.

Conthan kneeled down to see the small red light

in the synthetic's head still recording. Sparks shot out of the frayed wiring around its midsection. He leaned in closer to the synthetic's face. He pulled back his hoodie and smiled. "I don't know who you are or what you want with these people, but we're coming for you. The Children of Nostradamus are angry."

The crowd watched, their mouths agape, as Jasmine finished tearing apart the last synthetic. Conthan made note of one man, his face freshly shaven and his hair cleaner than any of the other vagabonds'. Looking at the shoes, he could see they had been freshly polished. Against the others, he stood out like a sore thumb.

"They'll be back," the man said. "You need to get out of here."

Jasmine stepped up next to Conthan and chucked one of the synthetics onto the ground. "We are not your gods. Now be gone before you get yourselves killed."

Conthan opened a portal and the two of them exited the church.

***

Half a city away, Vanessa seized the arm of a synthetic and snapped it in half. As the other arm attempted to take hold of her, she spun the machine around and tore at the head, severing it from its metallic spine. She chucked the body toward another synthetic, sending it to the ground.

"How come we can't just show up to a party and have a good time?"

51

Skits's hands turned blue as she spoke. Vanessa stepped back as the heat from the girl's hands started to swelter.

"I mean, don't get me wrong, calling me a goddess is sweet and everything…"

"Skits," Dwayne yelled. "More destroying, less talking!"

"Oh," she said, "I see you're in a mood."

Vanessa ducked behind a broken column. She watched as Skits burned through the closest synthetic, neatly cutting it in two. As another reached for her, a bolt of lightning struck its body, hurling it to the ground.

She didn't have to say it, she was glad to have the siblings with her. Her abilities were vast, but it was hard to compete with a girl who could superheat the air around her until it turned to plasma and her older brother who could hurl lightning from his body. No, her abilities were subtle in comparison to these two powerhouses.

The thoughts of two dozen parishioners occupied her mind. They were in awe of the three Children of Nostradamus. They watched the gods fight to save their human lives. Even though they were only trying to stop a massacre, the humans were going to see this as a divine act. It had taken her half her life to remove the image of the angel, and here she was being elevated even higher.

She tensed as the barrel of a gun pressed against her skull. Synthetics had no thoughts. They were artificial in every regard, making it impossible for her to detect them. Had it been a human, she would have had a dozen methods of removing herself from this situation. Now, she had to rely on her body and hope she had honed it as well as she did her mind.

The weapon hummed as it came to life. Vanessa gritted her teeth, but suddenly the machine was hurled against a wall, its skull completely blown away. Vanessa spun around to see a woman at the altar holding a rifle.

It seems like trouble follows you wherever you go.

Vanessa smirked. She hadn't encountered Twenty-Seven in almost a year and it was good to see the woman again. Twenty-Seven held up her rifle and shot again, striking another synthetic in the skull, obliterating its upper body. Her marksmanship was amazing; it was obvious she transitioned into the rogue lifestyle better than expected.

Dwayne stepped up next to Vanessa. "We're five by five."

"Really? You're going to try and sound all cool? Five by five? Jesus." Skits threw up her arms and tossed a melted skull onto the ground. "When we get back we're going to work on your dialogue."

Twenty-Seven stepped down off the altar and slung the rifle over her shoulder as she embraced Vanessa. "It seems things have changed a bit since I saw you last."

Vanessa forgot that not everybody had grown accustomed to her appearance. The people had collected near the altar of the church, huddled together, afraid of the gods they proclaimed to love. "The two of you go talk to the priest, see what information you can get about this gathering."

"Your god is here to save the day," Skits said, working her way to the crowd. The people pushed away from her until a young woman reached out and touched the girl's arm. Once they realized it was safe, they started making contact with her, basking in the glory of their savior.

"This is going straight to her head."

Vanessa nodded. "Alyssa will not be happy she missed out on the opportunity to see Skits start her own religion."

Dwayne followed his sister into the crowd. He held them back, keeping his admirers at arm's length as he walked up the altar. Vanessa turned to Twenty-Seven and eyed the woman. Something was significantly different about her.

"This," she said, holding up her arm. She pulled back the sleeve to reveal a cybernetic limb similar to the synthetics'. She pulled the fabric up to her shoulder. The metal seemed to go right into the socket, giving her a full robotic arm.

"It seems trouble finds you as well."

Vanessa could only wonder what mishap had caused this new development. She reached out with her mind to touch Twenty-Seven's. Vanessa gasped out loud when she found only silence. She had never found a human capable of hiding their thoughts. When entering the mind of Children, she heard distant chatter even if she couldn't make out individual words.

"How are you doing that?"

Twenty-Seven's smile faded. "It has been a difficult year, Vanessa. I've made some interesting allies since I came back to the States. The

Nighthawks aren't the only ones fighting back against this darkness."

Vanessa dwelled on the statement. She hadn't thought about the darkness in months. They all hoped the death of the Warden signaled victory over Eleanor's predictions. The mention of the darkness told Vanessa more than she needed to know.

"The darkness is still coming."

Twenty-Seven nodded her head. "Eleanor's predictions are far from over."

"What do you mean?"

A single voice entered her mind and eventually Vanessa heard Twenty-Seven's mind processing the information. Vanessa focused and listened to Twenty-Seven reading another letter from Eleanor. The image of the woman in her mind tucked the letter away and handed it back to a sturdy-looking man with dark brown hair.

"There was another letter?"

Twenty-Seven nodded. "The Warden was only the precursor to whatever is coming."

As fast as the thoughts projected from Twenty-Seven's mind, they vanished. Vanessa didn't hide her emotions, letting Twenty-Seven know how impressed she was of a woman entirely in control of her mind. If Vanessa hadn't known better, she'd mistake her friend for another telepath. The lines around Twenty-Seven's eyes had weathered and the scar across her cheek gave away that her life had been anything but easy in the last year.

"You can come back with us," Vanessa offered.

Twenty-Seven shook her head. "I have Troy. And it seems I'll be back in the thick of it soon."

Vanessa didn't know what to say. She had never found a human capable of avoiding her like this. She was very aware how much she relied on her abilities to bridge in the gaps between what a person said and what they meant. She didn't like having somebody dodge her proddings, but it did tell her that Twenty-Seven was expanding her role in the world again. She could only hope the skills she acquired would keep her safe.

"Understood. Do you know anything more?"

"We found a young man at this church not too long ago. I hoped to find more recruits here, but it seems the synthetics have become enough of a problem that the Children are hiding again"

"With the president overseeing the Eastern Seaboard, there is a good chance the government has returned to dissecting our people."

Twenty-Seven nodded. "We can only hope that it's something as benign as that. With this thing looming over us, who knows when we'll finally uncover what's happening."

Vanessa watched as a black portal appeared in the middle of the church. Jasmine and Conthan stepped out, inspecting the destruction that had just taken place. Conthan pointed to one of the synthetics on the floor. "I see you had a similar reception."

"Nothing they couldn't handle," Twenty-Seven said with a slight smile. "I have to go. But be aware, the president and the military aren't the only players anymore. There is something new, possibly even worse."

"Any clues?" asked Vanessa.

Twenty-Seven gave a slight nod. "Genesis Division. They're coming for us."

"They're with the military," Jasmine chimed in.

Twenty-Seven shook her head. "They had a military contract. They're the ones who made things like this possible." She flexed her arm, the metal bending to her will as she clenched her fist. "But they're much bigger than that. I don't know why, but they're very interested in all of you."

"Do you have any information on them?"

Twenty-Seven shook her head again. "Whoever is in charge, the Children of Nostradamus are their focus."

"Be safe, Twenty-Seven," Vanessa said.

"You too, Angel," she replied. "I'm glad to see you're finally owning who you are."

"Takes some of us longer than others."

"Are we going to hug now?" Skits asked as she joined the group.

Chapter 4

2033

"You were hired to do a job."

"But sir," the man on the screen sputtered, "there were unforeseeable circumstances."

"Are we not in the business of war?"

Wilson choked in reply.

"Do we not have a war outside our doors?"

Wilson straightened his tie and sat upright. He leaned into the camera. "Do not patronize me. You live off the wealth the board makes for you. You've spent our money like a spoiled child and you question my efforts?"

Jacob rolled his eyes. "Don't forget how you got these contracts. Without us, you'd be working at the local gas station selling Slurpees."

"Leave the business to the adults. You do whatever keeps you entertained and stop trying to act…"

Jacob didn't have to try very hard to hear Wilson's thoughts. It was easiest when they were angry. It turned up the volume and he could hear each word before it started. With a simple thought from Jacob, Wilson stopped speaking. Jacob focused on him, pushing with his mind, forcing him to lean back in his chair.

"That feeling is me forcing your body to do what I want. The next thing I do is have you reach for the gun in your desk and blow out your brains."

Jacob smiled as fear washed over Wilson. The board had stopped meeting with him in person, citing that his anger made them uneasy. It didn't surprise him. They ran a multi-billion dollar corporation. The board was put in place by a group of very discreet men in a secret organization, and now these pawns ran it, forgetting that without the Society's influence, they'd be nothing.

"Wilson, the only reason I'm not killing you is because I have no desire to train a new president of the board. You'll watch your tongue. You'll continue to fund my operation, and I won't feel the need to inform your wife about your particular brand of perversion."

Yes, sir.

"That's what I wanted to hear." Jacob pulled back, letting Wilson's thoughts quiet. He detested the man; every fiber of him dripped weakness. Jacob wished he had the luxury of being given such a posh position without working for it.

"Be sure the president gets what resources she needs…" He paused. "Within reason."

Before the executive replied Jacob waved his hand, forcing the video feed to vanish. If he desired, he could easily step in and take over the board. He might not be able to control each of them as easily as Wilson, but the power of suggestion had taken him far enough. At some point, when he got bored, he'd try his hand at running Genesis Division.

He loosened his tie, flipping open the top button of his shirt. His library held wall-to-wall books stacked neatly on shelves reaching nearly twelve feet to the ceiling. In the middle of the room sat two large high back chairs with a small table between them. On the table rested a chessboard, the figures laid out in a heated battle he had been attempting to solve for the better part of a decade. He walked to a giant globe resting next to one of the chairs. He spun the top until it revealed a bottle of scotch inside. He poured himself two fingers and took a light sip, savoring the amber liquid. Finishing off the last of the glass and sat at the edge of the chair.

He eyed the white chess pieces. Several sat adjacent to the board, his fallen soldiers. Once there had been a man he played against daily. His mentor had said that chess sharpened the mind and forced the players into a mental game. Each move weighed a thousand decisions and required knowledge of your opponent on an intimate level. His mentor abandoned this particular game, saying that all options had been eliminated and he won with only a few pieces moved. Jacob spent the last twenty years trying to understand the man's moves, guessing which would protect his king.

Like each time before, he started the mental game, moving pieces one, then two and three steps ahead of where they were. He found himself defeated, knowing the movements of his senior.

Then he began on the next group of movements and found the same result. Nearly twenty years and he believed there was still an answer he had yet to discover. With each new train of thought, he found himself questioning the moves like a thousand times before. Each time his opponent won. Jacob growled as he struck the board, knocking the pieces to the floor.

He leaned back in the chair, pouring himself another drink. He didn't attempt to savor the liquid as he polished off the glass. He closed his eyes. He didn't need the chessboard in front of him to see each distinct shape. The pieces would eternally haunt him.

"Ahem."

His eyes remained closed, but he sensed her leaning in the doorway. Her arms would be crossed, causing her breasts to appear even larger than they were. He cracked his eyes, and just like his imagination predicted, there she stood, bent in a way accentuating every curve in her body. The black dress touched the floor, but the slit up the side nearly made it to her waist, not hiding much of her long legs.

"What do you want, Lillian?"

"Are you done with your temper tantrum?"

He shot her a dirty look. Out of habit, his mind reached out, touching hers. Unlike in Wilson's, there were no stray thoughts for Jacob to grapple with and gain entry into her head. She stuck out her bottom lip, feigning a pout. "Can't get what you want?"

He growled. "What do you want?"

"Salvador and Dikeledi are waiting for you."

"Let them wait."

"Stop being a petulant child." He felt the invisible tug at his clothes, and a moment later found himself being pulled to his feet. She turned and walked out the door.

He couldn't hide annoyance at the way her abilities could affect him, when his were met with resistance every time. He followed her into the hallway. Just as he caught sight of her, the color in her dress bled away until it turned a pristine white. He touched the lapel of his shirt and his clothes followed suit. He had tried to convince the rest of the inner circle there was no reason in continuing with this wretched tradition, but they continued to fight him. They clung to a past he had abandoned long ago.

"Can't they function even for a moment without me?"

"You'd love to think we are helpless without your grand machinations."

They walked down a hallway leading to a large wooden door. The upper floor of their penthouse suite held their inner sanctum. Once upon a time it was where the Society of Paranormal Research, a group of humans studying and researching mentalists, gathered. Jacob wondered how many men and women had gathered to discuss the paranormal, none of them having abilities of their own.

Hanging on the wall were photographs of the Society's past presidents. The men appeared stodgy, holding a scholarly quality, but still inept in their inability to grasp what they were dealing with. Then came the first woman to sit as president of the Society. Unlike those before her, she was a mentalist, her abilities still discussed as some of the most powerful to date.

Jacob stopped to look at her photograph. Eleanor Valentine, a beautiful woman to behold. The records of her ascension in the Society were scattered at best. The history books the scribe kept became difficult to obtain and after a betrayal by several mentalists, the Society seemed to fall in disarray for years. Before whatever Eleanor did to darken their history, mentalists served as a slave class, lab for the people who researched them. After that tarnished moment, after Eleanor Valentine, it seemed things changed drastically and the mentalist rose to power. First Eleanor Valentine, and later her protégé, Jacob's mentor, Franklin.

Someday, Jacob would find his own protégé, train them, help them realize the gifts they possessed, and they would take over his position. Someday, far, far into the future this would happen. Then Jacob's photograph would adorn the walls of this sanctuary, and he would be immortalized as one of the keepers of the Society. But for now, he had a job to do with the others who partook in the honor of sitting at a table meant for the distinguished.

"What?" Jacob asked, annoyed he was being requested.

Salvador raised his eyebrow at the man. He knew Salvador didn't like him, tolerated would be a better word. The man had no qualms speaking his mind about Jacob as if he wasn't there. Jacob didn't like him either, and if Salvador had any ambition to take over the presidency of the group, he'd feel threatened. However, Salvador much preferred to spend his free time indulging in womanizing rather than overseeing a vast organization.

"Something has come to light that you will want to see."

A metal orb hung in the middle of the room, casting a blue light that created an almost three-dimensional image of a man's office. Salvador reached into the light and shifted the image, showing two figures standing on either side of a doorway. Jacob looked at familiar bomber jackets.

"So what? I often use the Barren like this."

The man rotated the image again. Jacob had first thought the image was one of the rooms in their penthouse suite. However, with the new angle, he could see a large man sitting behind a desk. He had never met the man face-to-face, but he knew of him well enough. The Warden's reputation preceded him. A burly man placed into power by the President of the United States of America.

Jacob's mentor had more than a hand in the election of Cecilia Jones as the President of the United States. When Jacob took over, he assumed the role of handler to the woman. Meanwhile, the president oversaw the Warden, a man who utilized resources by Genesis Division to perform research on the Children of Nostradamus.

"How does the Warden have two Barren standing at his door?"

Where Lillian had the beauty and sex appeal reflective of Hollywood nearly one hundred years ago, Dikeledi had an exotic beauty. Her ebony skin was so dark it almost held a purple hue to it. Her powers were most akin to his: where he could read minds, she could read emotions. Where he could influence thoughts, she could do the same with feelings. He controlled the brain, and she the heart.

She leaned into the image and closed her eyes. "They are still empty."

Lillian sat on the table, staring at Jacob. "We sent two Barren to execute the Warden. His control on the Facility was absolute. It was too much power for a single human."

"I assumed they were killed."

Salvador rubbed his two-day stubble. He made a slight gesture with his hand. The time stamp on the video feed sped forward. He let it continue playing.

"It's not going," Jacob said, watching the man behind the desk sitting rigidly. He looked back at the stamp and noticing time passing by. His eyes flicked up to the man again. Instantly he knew the man was physically sitting at his desk, but his mind was elsewhere.

"He's a telepath," Lillian said, eyeing Jacob. "I've seen you do the same thing when you're focusing."

"What the hell is he focusing on?" Had he been in the same room, Jacob might be able to get a sense of what was happening. Dikeledi was more likely able to pick up the emotional echoes of everybody in the room. Both of them at this distance, and with this much time passing, could only get faint hints of what might have happened.

"Wait for it," Salvador said.

A black circle appeared in the side of the room and a man stepped through. Jacob watched intently as a fight ensued between the young man and the Warden. His jaw dropped as the kid reached into the portal and pulled out what looked like a still-beating heart. As the Warden fell to the ground, Jacob was certain a Child of Nostradamus had murdered the Warden.

"A Child of Nostradamus killed him," Salvador said.

"That's not what I'm interested in," Jacob said. "There's another telepath in that room."

***

He stepped out of the void. The light of the street didn't reach into the alley; only a cloud-covered moon offered any peak into this dismal space. The space between the buildings was just wide enough to allow access for a garbage truck. To one side, scaffolding reached four stories high. It appeared as if there were renovations being done to the outside of the building. It surprised him that anybody cared enough anymore to make improvements. Lately people merely tried to survive. Perhaps it was the remnant of a more hopeful time yet to be destroyed by this new world.

A call had come in over the police scanner. There were so many to choose from it became an endless game. Each night he woke, exhausted, and as he shook away the nightmares, the look on the murdered man's face, he'd start his penance. Dav5d had given him a police radio accessing New York

City's emergency network. It had started with strikes against the synthetics, systematically removing them one at a time.

It was ironic, waking from the terror of killing a man and wanting to do justice by inflicting harm. It didn't slip by him. Destroying machines was all well and good, but there were times in which he wanted to feel his knuckles connect with something soft for a change. The mention of thugs in an alley told him he could teleport in and out as necessary. No synthetics. It wasn't his safety he was concerned with, it was the rush he got from ruining the lives of two men.

The call came in to dispatch. "They're terrorizing that poor girl in the street. I yelled and yelled, but it didn't stop them."

He stepped out of the portal. They had her on the ground next to a dozen trashcans behind a small restaurant. The call had been made less than a minute ago. In sixty seconds they had pinned her to the ground and one of them was pulling at the fly on his jeans.

Conthan scuffed his foot against the ground. He wasn't sure if they heard him over her whimpering. He prepared to do it again when the man on his knees spun around.

"What do we have here?"

The man stood from between the woman's legs. He reached into his pocket, pulled out a butterfly knife, and flipped it open. "I ain't into dudes, but maybe I'll make an exception this once."

The other guy laughed. They were like animals, terrorizing anybody they deemed weak. Conthan took another step closer, leaving only a few feet between them. He didn't move, instead waiting for one of them to attack.

"You some sort of freak?"

When he didn't answer, the man with the weapon started to signal to his buddy. "I think we have some sort of fucking idiot here."

The other guy laughed as he reached down to his boot and pulled out a long knife. Conthan wasn't impressed. With a single thought he could tear them apart and leave limbs of strewn across the alley. He could easily end this fight before it started, but that wouldn't give him what he sought.

The man shifted his weight to his rear leg. As he lunged forward, attempting a stabbing motion with the blade, Conthan responded. Moving both hands in a circular pattern, he caught the man's forearm and smacked the palm of his hand against the wrist holding the knife. The pressure caused the assailant to drop the blade.

"What the fuck?" said the second man.

Two knuckles extended, Conthan slammed his bony joints into the throat of the man. The guy fell backward, stumbling over the woman's legs, trying to scurry further away from Conthan.

The second man swung wildly, his right fist, then the left. Conthan leaned back, dodging the blows. Then he reached out and grabbed the man by the jacket. Conthan slammed his forehead into his nose. Pain seared through his forehead and reached down to his chest, staggering him. He shook his head, trying to remind himself his teacher had thicker skin than him.

"Grab him," the man said, spitting the blood out of his mouth.

There was no tingling as he accessed his abilities. The portal open and he reached through. His arms emerged behind the standing man's legs. Conthan grabbed his pants and pulled, sending the criminal to the ground. The thud from his boot didn't compare to the crunch as his foot connected with the man's jaw. He didn't need to see to know teeth had gone clanking to the ground.

"Had enough?" he asked calmly, trying to keep his breath under control.

The man with a bloody nose reached into the waistband of his pants and pulled out a gun. He readied the trigger and raised it to eye level. Conthan took a deep breath and let out a long sigh. He eyed the gun, then the man, and then the gun again, all while trying to keep the smirk off his face. He failed. "Are you showing it to me? Or are you going to pull the trigger?"

"What?" the man asked. "Don't think I won't do it, man."

"If you pull the trigger—" Conthan let out a slight laugh—"you're going to get hurt."

"Says the man with no gun."

Conthan knew the speed of the bullet at this close range only gave him so many options. He could fall through a portal and land behind the guy. He could open a portal in front of the weapon and redirect the bullet somewhere else. Hell, if he was feeling particularly whimsical, he could open a portal under his newfound friend and make the thug land on his buddy.

"So many options." The idea of having a bullet tear through his jacket and bore into his fleshy bits didn't make him smile. The thought of ruining this man's life, that, however, made it impossible to hold back laughter.

The hammer landed on the gun. His powers reacted before he knew what happened. Dav5d said the automated reaction was the part of the brain controlling the fight or flight response. Conthan's powers did the work to protect him if they could.

The portal opened in front of the gun, enveloping the bullet. Time slowed for a fraction of a second. Sound vanished and the world turned into a blur as he looked for a spot to open an exit portal. The knee. As the thug's kneecap blew apart and he fell to the ground, Conthan closed the portals.

"I didn't think I stuttered." The gun scraped along the ground as he kicked it away. The disabled thug's partner ran from the alley. As he cleared it, a metallic hand lunged from around the corner, grabbing him and hurling him against a wall. The bricks crumbled from the impact and the man slumped to the ground, at best, in a coma, at worst, dead.

"Shit," Conthan said.

"It's going to kill us," the woman cried.

"Ma'am, I didn't just go through all that to have a can opener kill you."

Conthan didn't break eye contact with her. He held out his hand toward the synthetic and opened his fingers. Pain seared through his head, drilling into the base of his skull. A hiss escaped his lips. The portal opened inside the metal of the robot, consuming the top half. A portal off in the distance expunged the head and torso, leaving two standing legs.

"What just happened?"

He dipped down to one knee, taking steadying breaths, and then toppled to the ground. The pain continued to shoot through his skull, but lessened to a dull roar. He had used his abilities enough for the night and they gave him the cue that he needed to rely on more human-like skills. The woman crawled toward him. Holding his head up, she checked his bruised forehead.

"Are you all right?"

"Yeah," he lied.

"You're one of them, aren't you?"

"A citizen with nothing better to do than save damsels?"

"A Child."

"Oh," he said. "Yeah, that too."

"Are you a hawk?"

He grabbed her hand, squeezing it gently. "What did you just say?"

"A hawk? You're one of them?"

He didn't realize his deeds were widespread enough that a random woman would know him. He assumed the president had the media in her pocket. Each time he wreaked havoc, the media found some new and interesting way to make it seem like a common occurrence. Nobody outside of the bar knew the name Nighthawks.

"There," she said pointing to a billboard on top of a building across the street.

Conthan slowly got to his feet as he saw the

symbol. The billboard had been tagged by a street artist. Nearly half was covered by a large circular tribal pattern with the head of a hawk at the start. His mind started to race through the list of people who would have been this daring. If he had been at the warehouse, he could ask Sculptee. He knew nearly every street artist in Manhattan.

"Gretchen," he mumbled. It couldn't be a coincidence. He thought he saw her earlier today and now some rogue artist took up the hawk moniker. It wouldn't surprise him if this was part of Eleanor's grand design; she could have sent a letter with the symbol to an artist to take up the cause. For a moment, he thought about returning to the warehouse to see who remained. But he couldn't deny the danger following him these days. A pair of metallic legs reminded him of who he dealt with. There wasn't any chance he could endanger the people in his former life.

"Can you get home?"

She nodded as he helped her stand. "I live right there," she said, pointing to a building at the end of the alley.

"Be careful," he said.

She motioned to the remains of the synthetic. "I should say the same to you."

He started deep breathing, trying to ignore the pain. The tingling was buried beneath a searing hot poker being prodded into the base of his skull. A portal opened and he stumbled into it, leaving the woman and the mystery of the hawk behind.

***

Dwayne let the electricity hum on the surface of his skin. The buzz of the current distracted him from the cold enveloping his body. If he discharged, his core temperature would rise for a few minutes, but then he'd feel the cold even more as he crashed. Instead, he focused on containing his abilities as he leaned against the cold stone of the church.

It had been almost two hours since Conthan woke him. He heard the kid yelling in his sleep through the wall separating their rooms. It was like clockwork, Conthan crying out in his sleep. With the frequency, he'd be concerned if it didn't happen now. Despite it becoming a nightly tradition, Conthan didn't confide in him, or anybody, as to what was happening. The kid's world changed in the blink of an eye, everything he knew torn out from under his feet. When it came to nightmares, there were plenty of things it could be.

The first few nights Dwayne had run to Conthan's room to check on him. He had thrown open the door ready to see a synthetic climbing in the window, but he found the space empty. The kid's jacket was missing. It took Dwayne a few days to realize he was teleporting away from the hotel and coming back a few hours later. He waited for him, concerned for the kid's safety. Conthan's face was bruised and he had a nasty gash across his forearm. Conthan blew off his worry. He wanted distance, and now instead of returning his quarters, he'd teleport to the church balcony.

Dwayne waited. The world was an eerie gray moments before the sun rose over the horizon. He admitted there was something impressive about watching it, trying to understand the world through Conthan's eyes. There was a part of him that longed for the innocence the kid clung to. Unfortunately he had packed away those feelings years ago and accepted that somebody had to do the job, no matter how dirty.

He didn't turn around as he heard the thud of a boot on the stone behind him. The kid stumbled as he fell against the rock wall surrounding the balcony. Dwayne wanted to greet him and make sure he was okay. Instead, he held fast, staring at the sun as it broke the horizon. He pulled his hoodie closer around his body. Conthan didn't mutter a word as they stood there.

The light began to change colors as the sun pushed through the fog. Dwayne turned and walked away, never looking at Conthan.

"You're not going to say anything?"

Dwayne didn't turn around. Things had been different ever since Conthan discovered what he had done to Jasmine when they first captured her. Even Jasmine had come to terms with what happened, saying she would have done the same if the tables had been turned. It was Conthan who had been most upset at the realization. Dwayne hadn't understood it at first, why the boy was so angry with him. It wasn't until Vanessa had a heart-to-heart with Dwayne that he realized the boy looked up to him. His anger stemmed from discovering his idol was less than perfect.

Other than Skits, it had been years since he felt affection for another person. He admired his team, even respected them and their hard work, but he had difficulty letting them in. For a short time, he thought Conthan might be a friend. The solitude made his heart ache and left him wallowing in memories of best friend and first love, Michael.

It pained Dwayne to know he disappointed the kid. His head hung low as he continued walking. "Whatever demons you're dealing with..." He paused and let out a sigh. "I wanted to make sure they didn't win."

Chapter 5

1993

"When are you coming home?"

He stared at the picture on his desk. Elizabeth Davis, the ideal of beauty with her brown hair falling around her shoulders. Her turtleneck sweater hid her long, slender neck. She had red sauce smeared across her face and her expression was a mix between shock and laughter.

Sitting across from Elizabeth, his nearly one year old son, Raymond Valentine Davis. His high chair was covered in a mixture of sauce and spaghetti pieces, as was his naked chest. He had a phase of throwing his food, which slightly overlapped with his phase of wearing food. The two of them were the happiest people in the world. He missed the sound of her laughter and more than that, he missed the sound of her reacting to his laughter.

"What was that?"

"You're being a bonehead." She gave a slight chuckle. "When are you coming back to us mundane folk?"

She was anything but mundane, but if he complimented her now, she'd giggle at him. "I'll be home in two days. It'll be nice to be somewhere without white walls and so much radiation."

"Are you following your diet?"

He looked down at his stomach. "Yup."

"Liar."

"Guilty."

"I'll make sure to go grocery shopping before you get home. Need to make sure you're eating right. I like my man with a little meat on his bone, but you're no good to us if you have a heart attack."

The pager on his belt buzzed. He looked down, eyeing the small screen with several numbers. He didn't want to cut the phone call short. The sound of her voice eased the tension between his shoulder blades and for a moment he felt rejuvenated. He wanted nothing more than to feel her nuzzled against his chest. He let out a long sigh.

"I know the sound of that," she said in a playful manner.

"I'm sorry," he said.

"Mark Davis," she scolded. "I am proud of you, we all are. There aren't many men who see injustice and stand up for what's right. You're making a world I want our son to grow up in."

"I love you, hon."

"Right back at you, champ. Now go save the world. I have a grocery store to conquer and an infant who thinks the cat is a squish toy."

They both hung up. He pulled on his t-shirt and grabbed his shoes by the door. He had the most lavish quarters in the center and it really only meant he had a living room, small kitchen, and a separate bedroom. The communal quarters shared living space. He appreciated having time to himself, not that he spent it doing anything but working. On a TV tray next to his recliner an open book rested face down, holding the same spot for the last three months. *Eventually*, he thought, *eventually I'll learn to take a moment to myself.*

The research center was built for long term occupancy. Within the building, the outer rooms closest to the exterior were open for the public, giving a slight glimpse into the more mundane projects they worked on. The windows had been removed to help shield them from radiation. In their place, massive televisions, showed a lush green vista that had once been around the building. As a person moved toward the interior of the complex the security measures increased exponentially.

In the middle, an elevator descended to the most important research being done at the center. Only two men had security clearance to the inner sanctum. As Mark rested his hand on the button, a biometric scanner checked for his thumbprint. The elevator shifted downward, journeying forty feet beneath the surface.

The doors hissed as hydraulics forced them open.

"Mark!"

She jumped into his arms before he registered she was in front of him. Flowing brown hair wrapped around his face, sticking to his stubble as she nuzzled his neck. Her arms locked behind his head, causing him to bend until her feet touched the ground.

"You need to stop growing," he said with a laugh.

As he pulled away, he admired just how green her eyes were. He couldn't tell if it was their real color or if her fondness of wearing dark green flannel over her jean overalls brought out the rich hue. Every day, the innocence of her youth was shed, replaced with the determination and rebelliousness of a tween. For the past year she had lived at the center, hidden away from the rest of the world.

"Ariel," came a gruff voice.

Mark recognized Ivan's tone. While the girl was a permanent resident against her will, Mark wanted her to have some sort of normalcy. On either side of this floor's lobby waited conference rooms, a small lab, and a fitness area tailored to Ariel. Across the lobby, double doors constructed of dense metal led to her personal quarters, similar to his and only accessible by Mark and her. They formed a private place for her to call her own, a small bit of normalcy in her life.

"I don't like him," she whispered.

"Ivan," Mark said sternly, "is there anything I can help you with?"

"Ariel and I were in the middle of running some preliminary tests to establish a baseline."

She squeezed Mark's hand tighter. The girl by definition was brave. She had often been poked with needles, her blood drawn weekly. He assumed that being a young girl she'd be frightened by the people who treated her like a science experiment.

Instead, Mark hoped his child viewed the world like her, as a challenge she had yet to overcome.

"I think that should be enough for today," Mark said.

"No," Ivan replied. "These need to be finished today."

Mark took several steps forward, nearing the scientist. He tried to whisper but found his voice louder as he flexed his authority. "She's a young girl. We don't treat her like a lab rat. Give her a break today." Mark began to turn back to the girl.

"Perhaps that is why your research has gone nowhere, Mr. Davis? We finish the tests today."

Mark squared off against Ivan, straightening his back to appear even larger than normal. Ivan was taller but Mark didn't find his size intimidating in the least. "You work for me."

"Technically..."

"For me," Mark said again, loud enough that it bordered on a shout.

"You may not like my methods, Mr. Davis, but I do not answer to you. I am here to get results and whether you like it or not, I will have them."

"Not like this."

Ivan's clenched fists and furrowed brow gave away his anger. Over the last month Mark found the man's methods to be questionable at best. The scientist had no problem treating the girl like an object and often forgot she was a kid. Mark had frequent conversations with him about intellectual endeavors and the more he learned, the more he found Ivan to be cold, almost completely removed of emotion. He might be a damned good scientist, but he was far from being a good man.

"I do not care what you think of me, Mr. Davis. My cold demeanor is what gets my job done."

"We're leaving now."

"No…"

Mark registered the slight twitch from the man ready to raise his balled fist. Before Ivan could lift his hand, he was tossed across the room by an unseen force. He slid along the floor until he came to a stop near the wall. He lifted himself up from his stomach, obviously confused at what happened.

Both men turned to Ariel, who was holding both hands in front of her, palms out. Mark knelt in front of the girl, using the corner of his sleeve to wipe the trickle of blood from her nose. "We had an agreement."

"You watch out for me, I watch out for you. You said that, Mark."

He gave her a slight hug. They walked to the elevator and as the doors closed he watched Ivan sit upright. The scientist needed to worry less about who was in charge and more about pissing off the girl. She stood close to him, almost close enough they could touch, but just far enough away they had separate space. Mark reached out and put his hand on her shoulder.

"He's not a good man."

"I find the smartest men are rarely good."

"Why don't you fire him?"

"I wish I could, trust me. But he's really smart and we need his help. I know you don't like him, but we need you to cooperate. The more you help him, hopefully the sooner we can figure out a way to convince the president to stop killing mentalists."

She continued to stare at him, her head tilted backward as she tried to gauge his expression. As the elevator stopped moving, he waited a moment before turning and making eye contact. "What?"

"Why do you care so much?"

"I don't want my kid to grow up in a world where people are hunted for being different."

Her shoulders slumped. She grabbed him by the hand. "Tell me the real reason."

"So you can read my mind now?"

"You're easy to figure out."

He often forgot her age. She had gone through so much in her short years that he begun assuming she was a young lady. He liked her. She had a way of seeing the world that reminded him of Elizabeth. He thought they would be close.

"You're not the first person I've met with abilities."

"Really?" she asked with a gasp. The doors opened and he walked down the long corridor leading to the lobby. He rested his head on the pad and for once got the scanner to work on the first try. As the door opened, they were covered in the soft light from the sun-filled lobby.

"When I was younger I met a very polite old lady. She had a gift too. She was the first mentalist I ever met. I'll never forget her."

Ariel tugged on his arm as they walked toward the fountain. Atlas knelt in the middle of the water, holding a disc above his head with the Earth resting atop. When Mark first arrived the Earth rotated as water spilled out from the disc into the pool below.

At some point, it stopped working. Mark stared at Atlas's vacant eyes and wonder if that was his destiny. Would there be a day the weight of the world became too much?

"Who was she?"

They sat on the edge of the pool. "Her name was Eleanor Valentine."

"That's a pretty name."

"She was a beautiful human. I met her at a time when the world was changing drastically for me. I was scared and unsure of what the future held. My mother was sick and my wife and I were newlyweds trying to have a baby. It only took a single conversation with Eleanor to change everything about me."

"Really? What could she do?"

"Eleanor could see the future."

"Wow," Ariel said. Mark looked forward to when his son grew up and he could tell the same story. He hoped his son grew up to be like Ariel and never lose his sense of wonder.

"Yeah. It was pretty amazing. She told me a little about my future."

"What did she see?"

"She knew my mom would get better. She also knew my baby would be born healthy. We were scared when Elizabeth's pregnancy had complications, but we held faith."

Ariel's didn't try to hide the wonderment on her face. Every other person who had heard this story stared at him in disbelief. Ariel's eyes held a sparkle of interest. She was the only person he had met who understood Eleanor. They may not be similar in any

83

way, but Ariel knew the woman was also different; it was the closest she'd have to a peer.

"Did she see me?"

"She never told me about you."

Her lip pushed out, pouting at the disappointing news. Mark smiled and put his arm around the girl. "But I've been thinking about it. She told me some things that started a series of events. Without her, I might not have taken this job, and if that hadn't happened I wouldn't have met you. So I think she did see you."

"She knew I needed you to rescue me!"

He pulled her in tight and gave her a squeeze. He had found her in the care of foster parents who were less than suitable as guardians, let alone the keepers of a girl with abilities. When they tried to capitalize on her gifts, he had them jailed and took Ariel away. What he didn't dare vocalize was, she had saved him every day in this temporary jail.

"I think she knew a lot of things but she didn't always tell people."

They sat on the edge of the pool, staring out of the windows that made up the front wall of the lobby. The sun was beginning to set and its heat bathed their faces. The light was almost too bright to continue looking at. Mark looked down, checking his badge to see if the radiation indicator had changed colors. When they had first moved into the center, engineers reinforced the windows, adding a layer of protection from the outside world. While he had been assured it was safe, he was convinced he felt the radiation along his skin.

"What happened to the fountain?"

"I think a rock got wedged between the globe and the pan with the water. They turned off the water when the top stopped moving. Eventually we'll get it fixed."

"I liked it. Was nice sitting here in the afternoon and putting my feet in the water."

She wiggled away from him and stood on the edge of the fountain. He reached up for her as her toes lifted off the rim. She steadily raised herself upward, hovering inches from the stone and then a few feet. Without effort she glided, nearing the Earth spanning almost twice her height. She pointed with her fingertips toward the water valve. It gave in to her will and turned slowly until the pipes moaned.

Water started to pour from underneath the Earth, but it didn't rotate in the disc, spinning in circles like it once had. He had seen her use her abilities hundreds of times. She acted as if they were no different than using her hand to pick up a pencil. He wondered if he would be as open about having powers. Would he train them? Would he even be brave enough to embrace this abnormal aspect of his person?

"Careful, Ariel," he warned.

"I can do it."

She raised both of her hands above her head as if she was lifting an invisible object. It took a moment, but the mammoth Earth shifted and started to rise into the air. He watched her arms shaking from the exertion. He had never seen her move so much weight. Only a few months ago she had barely been able to lift herself. Now, he had to remind her to use her legs instead of hovering just above the ground.

He stepped up onto the side of the pool, his arms ready to catch her if she should fall. She flicked her wrist and a trapped rock flew off the disk. She lowered her arms slowly, taking care to return the giant globe back to its resting spot. She waited a moment and the scaled Earth began to spin with the water falling cascading down onto Atlas below.

"Wow," Mark said in disbelief. "How do you feel?"

She spun around, her face revealing a giant smile. She floated down to his outstretched arms. He gave her a quick hug. "That was amazing."

Her body suddenly went stiff. "Mark."

Keeping her nestled against his body, he turned to see six security guards holding their weapons, each pointing directly at the two of them. In front of the guards, Goddard held a gun in his right hand while his left was held up in a fist.

"Put away your weapons," Mark said with a shout. "Put away your fucking weapons!"

"Not till I'm sure we're safe."

Mark slid Ariel behind him, making sure to keep himself between her and the guns. "Stay here," he said as he stepped down from the water fountain. He walked up to Goddard and met the man's steely gaze. Eventually Goddard tucked the gun into his holster, never looking away from him.

"She's a threat, Mark." Mark balled up his fist and lunged at the head of security.

Goddard blocked the blow with his forearm. Before Mark could react, the muscular guard drew back his fist and landed it square in his gut. Mark buckled over from the blow, the wind knocked from his lungs. He grabbed his torso and tried not to hurl on the man's shoes.

"Mark!" screamed Ariel.

He motioned with his hand for her not to move. He glanced up as the guards gasped. Mark watched the guns be pulled from their hands by an unseen force. Each weapon spun about, pointing at the guards. The gun on Goddard's hip lifted from it holster and moved closer until it touched his forehead.

The man's smile faded as the safeties flipped off on all the guns. Mark waved his hands at her. "Ariel, stop it."

"They were going to hurt you, Mark." Her feet hovered a few inches from the pool edge. He knew she was scared. Her body appeared as if it was moving in water, her hair floating about her face and the flannel starting to drift away from her body.

"It's over, Ariel. Mr. Goddard is an asshole. You're nothing like him. Be better than him, Ariel."

Her feet touched down on the pavement. With a flick of her wrist, the magazine in each gun released and she ejected the bullet from the chamber. The guns fell to the floor. Mark reached out and took her hand. He walked away with her in tow, never looking back at the security guards. Tonight, she would stay in his apartment and he'd sleep in his armchair watching the door.

Chapter 6

2033

Twenty-Seven admired the town's quaint charm, which made it difficult to believe New York City resided only an hour away. Where the city took on a life of its own, a thriving and living organism, Troy revealed a quieter atmosphere. The shops lining the downtown area had once been owned by real people and not large corporations. The barber shop and record store shared a sprawling red awning. Across the street was a small diner where she imagined locals gathered to drink plentiful cups of coffee while they gossiped about a new family moving into town.

It wasn't what she had grown up with, but it was something she was growing to love, even if the n primary occupants were the ghosts of its former residents.

Twenty-Seven started to laugh.

Once upon a time, she had wanted to vacation in a small town like this with her husband. The man never made time for her unless it was at the empty end of a bottle and he needed somebody to receive his insecurities in the form of a fist. A year ago, when Vanessa saved her from the perils of the Danger Zone, she had feared saying farewell to the ghost of herself. From the ashes of a broken housewife rose a woman whose courage knew no bounds. Not a soul in the town knew her name from before; now they only called her "Twenty-Seven," or "Twenty" for short.

A year ago she had been worried if she would survive the night. Now she served as the caretaker of a small town filled with Children of Nostradamus, people whose abilities were either too obvious for the casual world, or who wanted to hide away from the dangers of the modern society.

She stopped and stared inside the giant bay window of the barber shop. For some reason she always stopped to stare. She wondered who was getting their hair trimmed when the sirens foretelling the nuclear explosions were sounded. She assumed it was an ex-marine, getting the sides of his hair tightened as the barber and he swapped dirty jokes. Now it stood empty, t dust gathering on the black chair with duct-taped arms. They had talked about opening it up again, but the woman who currently served as their surgeon and barber much preferred to do her business at the former vet's office.

A breeze caught the back of her neck, sending a cold gust of wind down her shirt. She pulled the military jacket closed, tying the makeshift belt around it tighter. She pulled the rifle off over her head and slung it over her other arm. Gun metal clanked against her metal hand. Despite not having nerve endings in her bionic limb, her brain responded as if the weapon grazed her skin and for a moment she thought about the cold of the gun.

Twenty-Seven froze as a shadow caught the edge of her peripheral vision. Troy had a self-imposed curfew and only the watchmen roamed the streets at night. Their community housed forty-three individuals, all but four of them Children of Nostradamus. Three of the residents were loved ones and then there was her, somebody who owed her life to the Children. In the last year, she found being an Outlander and then a refugee with no home made her connect more with these hunted people than her own species.

A man at the next intersection stepped out from an alley, moving into the middle of the street. The flickering streetlight made the figure even more ominous. Every once in a while one of the townspeople would come out and join her on patrol, but this wasn't anybody she recognized. She started to close the distance between them, trying to figure out who it might be. The man wore a vintage bomber jacket and slacks, making him appear as if he stepped out of an old movie.

"Who are you?"

Her voice broke the silence of the night, but there was no reply. The man reached into his jacket and pulled out something shiny in the light. She expected a gun, but couldn't hide her amusement when she saw him holding a knife. She was holding a rifle with explosive rounds, something capable of winning a knife fight every time.

She stopped moving and lifted the rifle against her shoulder. The man took his first steps toward her. She eased down on the trigger. Before she fired, she found herself rolling along the ground from an impact from behind her.

She rolled along the ground and jumped back to her feet. A knee sped toward her face but she leaned out of the way of the blow. The second attacker, another bomber jacket owner, swung his knife, attempting to drag it across her throat. She grabbed his wrist and punched him across the face with her metallic hand. The blow cut into his cheek and spun his head to the side. She twisted his arm, threatening to pop it out of its socket.

"Who sent you?" He submitted as she used his bent arm to guide him to the ground. She had no problem throwing two goons around the street; it was the most action she'd seen in months.

The man looked up. His cheek had been pulled partway loose from his face, blood streaming down his neck. The wound didn't faze her—it was the twisted smile across his face that left her feeling uneasy. His shoulder cracked and popped out of socket as he stood. The pain would have made any other man scream, but the smile never left his face.

"What the fuck are you?"

His other hand latched on to her jacket, but he made no move to continue the assault. She grabbed him and spun him around as the other man slashed with an identical blade. She stared in horror, knowing the blade must have landed in the man's flesh, but his smile never flinched.

She drew back her arm. At her command, the hydraulics powering it would thrust into motion. With a single punch, the side of his skull collapsed and his brain was nothing more than mush. The man fell to the ground, and she was met with the original attacker. Like his dead friend's, the smile across his face stretched a bit too far and seemed to be stapled into place.

"Who are you?" she asked, backing up from the man.

Unlike his deceased comrade, he wielded the blade with superior skill. His swings were controlled, precise, and used to force her backward. She parried with her hand, sparks raining down every time the blade scraped across the metallic surface. She wasn't a close range fighter; it was something she had never taken to. She didn't like to get this close in a fray, but it didn't mean she wasn't without resources.

She grabbed his wrist. Before she could snap it, his knee came up, landing a solid blow to her rib cage. She staggered backward, swearing at the pain. There were more figures moving through the shadows, and she had to assume they were more of these ass-hats. She didn't care if they were some drugged-up gang, they were on her turf.

She was buckled over when he took another step toward her. She launched into an uppercut with her right hand, the knuckles landing squarely underneath his jaw. The man's body didn't lift off the ground as much as his head disconnected from the rest of it. Fluids covered her face and favorite jacket. Her stomach turned in disgust.

She grabbed the walkie-talkie on the back of her belt. She pressed the button and yelled into it. "We have intruders."

Clarice sat in the office, most likely dozing off from boredom. But her walkie was turned up loud enough it could wake the dead. Twenty-Seven ran over to her gun and grabbed it. As she stood up, an ear-piercing scream started to fill the streets. The scream grew until it pierced through the night and threatened to blow out her eardrums. Clarice, the equivalent of an emergency broadcast signal.

"We have men in bomber jackets. They're hyped up on drugs. No projectiles…"

She stopped speaking, recognizing the red dots hovering in the air. Somewhere in the darkness of the alley there were synthetics creeping closer. Twenty-Seven took aim with her gun and pulled the trigger. The round dipped low, just under the synthetic's head. The explosion tore through the metal and lit up the alleyway. There were a dozen killing machines. She pressed the button on the walkie-talkie again. "Synthetics. We have synthetics."

She took aim when one launched itself from a rooftop. As it hit the ground, she pulled the trigger, sending the heap of metal skidding across the pavement. Then she ran. She didn't have enough ammo to take out each of them, they'd swarm her. Their tactics were simple: overwhelm with force until the subject submitted.

There weren't many Children in Troy with active abilities—one of the reasons they came here to hide—but there were some.

The first scream in the distance was a warning. She reached into her pocket and fumbled around, looking for the plugs. The screeching started again as she tried to force the plugs in her ears. Her robotic hand wasn't the most adept at fine motor functions and she had to jam it in before the sound got worse. Even with squishy material clogging her ear canal, the screaming made her cover the sides of her head as she ran into a small bookstore.

"Thank God, Clarice," she said as she checked the magazine in her gun. She hadn't refilled from earlier in the day. She needed to make it to the armory and secure more rounds. She smashed the magazine back into place. The high-pitched screaming stopped abruptly and Twenty-Seven closed her eyes. "May you find peace."

***

Jasmine lay awake, staring at the ceiling. Another night when she didn't feel tired enough to sleep passed at a glacial pace. Barely midnight, and she could just as easily run a marathon as she could pass out. The ceiling was covered in a tacky popcorn plaster, giving it a rough texture. Every time she woke up, she found small bits of white on the floor, a testament that the building was falling apart.

It wasn't cool enough to need covers, but it wasn't warm enough to go without. She had the lower half of her body covered and her hands tucked behind her head as she stared at the ceiling.

She had given up on pillow; the military had trained her to be able to sleep anywhere at any time. It might not be as comfortable, but she preferred not having her hearing dampened. Only recently had she started sleeping on a mattress, originally opting for the floor next to the bed.

When she found sleep difficult, her mind wondered back to her life before the Nighthawks. She wondered where the Paladins were or what the General was doing. When civil war erupted on American soil, she found herself rooting for the team she knew. She trained with them for years before taking over as their commander. She had been part of an old initiative to put Children of Nostradamus in charge of military units. She ate, bathed, and slept with her unit. She cheered for them in the war, hoping the Paladins she trained kept their heads about them, at least enough to survive the onslaught.

Now she hoped they evaded death so she could be the one to squeeze the life from their bodies. The smile spread across her face. With all the do-gooding she participated in with the Nighthawks, anger still felt like an old friend. She'd drift off into sleep thinking of revenge.

***

"You can't be serious?"

Vanessa shook her head. "It is not something they promoted in the Church."

"I think it's important we change this immediately."

He stood up from the chair and held out his hand. The hotel lobby was one of the few spaces in the city they made sure to keep clean. While the rest of the buildings faded away, everything but the color of the rug remained vibrant and absent of dust. The desk where guests checked in stayed polished and the furniture kept clean. There were two high back chairs facing each other with a small table to one side. Despite the plush seating, Vanessa and Dav5d sat atop tall stools. While it was never said, everybody knew her wings presented practical issues. Dav5d refused to let her be the odd one out.

"You have to listen to him." Alyssa pointed at the man.

"What do you know of it, child?"

Vanessa listened to the girl's thoughts, the playful laughter echoing in her head. Alyssa stood, walked over to the grand piano, and pushed up the drawer covering the keys. Vanessa remembered the surgeon who had lived with them years ago. He claimed he needed the manual dexterity and kept his hands tuned by playing for hours each evening. With no television or even radio, it had been their entertainment for months. She thought about his mangled body, killed nearly two years prior.

Dav5d touched her chin, lifting her face. "Remember you are still alive."

His hand lingered for a moment. As he pulled away, he let the tips of his fingers graze her cheek. Her heart swelled and she smiled. He knew her so well, and there was no way he'd let her dwell on the dead when she had more living to do. She caught his eye and couldn't help but smile, her lips pulling back, showing both of her canine fangs.

Alyssa tapped away at piano keys. She pulled up the bench and sat at the mammoth instrument and continued. The sounds being produced made Vanessa wince. Alyssa persisted and within the minute she was playing chords, mastering the art. Vanessa turned her attention to Dav5d, who held out his hand again.

"Every beautiful woman should know how to dance," he said with a slight bow.

Vanessa extended her hand, taking his and standing in front of him. He guided her other hand to his shoulder and placed his against her waist. Vanessa couldn't help but be impressed with the melodies Alyssa conjured, the music so heartfelt and sincere.

"A waltz please, Alyssa."

"I don't know how to play that."

"Three four time, one chord per measure with the root chord on the first beat and up the scale for the second and third."

While Alyssa's abilities adapted, he took Vanessa by the waist and pulled her close. She was taller than him, his mid-five-foot frame to her six-plus-feet making the encounter comical. He stepped forward, forcing her right foot to take a step back. With his right foot he moved at a diagonal, then waited for her to repeat the step. With two more steps they completed the first rotation.

"We'll go slow."

Her feet were almost human, slightly longer and slightly more pointy at the heel, but for the most part human-like. She watched them, taking steps a second after Dav5d. His hand on her waist gently pushed her into place. She caught a glimpse of him staring at her, his eyes focused on her face. She could sense his admiration as she began to follow his footwork.

"Try not to look so scared," Alyssa encouraged.

"I'm sorry," she said, stopping mid-step. "I fear dancing will never be my thing."

He gripped her hand tighter, refusing to let her go. He pulled her back toward him, placing his hand on her hip again. "Put aside your insecurities and let me be in control."

She understood the statement. She had no doubt he kept track of the times in their relationship she lost control. The last time, she walked into a group of her peers and revealed her real form. Command over their abilities was an underlying requirement for a mentalist. She feared the day she ever completely let go.

The music continued and she watched as her feet moved just a moment slower than his. He lifted her head, forcing her to follow his eyes. As they continued he guided her from one step to the next until they were matching the speed of the music. She smiled at her mentor, appreciative of his persistence.

"Do you trust me?"

"Always," she replied.

His hand on her hip guided her as they twirled about the lobby. Her feet continued the same pattern, matching his, time and time again. They moved to and fro, spinning about the piano as if they had been practicing for hours. Between the measures of music, she nearly forgot she was a telepath, or that she was the so-called leader of a group of superpowered people. For a brief moment her world vanished and Dav5d was the only thing that mattered.

Her back went rigid, causing Dav5d to freeze in place. "There's something very wrong."

The music stopped. Dav5d and Alyssa stared at her, waiting for her next words. She shook her head, trying to sort through the voices at the edge of her mind. She was jealous of Dav5d for being able to sort through so much information in a logical manner. She had to rely on her gut and the fear of a wrong move clung to her as she searched the aether for something out of place.

"Twenty-Seven," she said. The name surprised even her.

"She's terrified." She paused. "No, she's angry. Something's happening." Vanessa tried to reach out and connect to the woman, but with Twenty-Seven's newfound ability to keep her out, Vanessa wasn't sure she could do it.

She stood in a small room. A bathroom, the mirror cracked and covered with layers of filth. Twenty-Seven glared into it, blood caking hair to the side of her face. Twenty-Seven's thoughts reached out to Vanessa. At some point they would have to discuss who had taught her these tricks.

Vanessa. We're under attack. We need help.

In the mirror, behind Twenty-Seven, a man in a stark white suit watched. Vanessa's mind recoiled, hurling back into her body. "Something horrible is happening. We need to go to Troy."

"Go wake the others," Dav5d said.

"Dav5d, think you can give me a hand?" Alyssa pointed to the computer screen wrapped around his wrist.

A dozen videos on high speed later, the remaining Nighthawks stood in the room with them. Conthan was the last to walk in the door. Vanessa didn't need to ask to sense the fatigue radiating through his bones. He had been experiencing the same bad dreams she had, and it seemed they were getting worse. Every night he vanished, his conscience taking him on a mission to undo the act of killing a man in cold blood. The pain in the back of his mind tugged at hers, a reminder they shared a taint of darkness.

"Can you get us there?" asked Vanessa.

She knew the answer before he shook his head. She tried not to pry, but the memories were fresh with a life of their own. She saw him saving an innocent woman. She pulled back, trying to leave him some amount of secrecy. "I can, if you do that thing you do."

I'm sorry.

Do what you must, Conthan. None of us can judge you. We have all been where you are now and had to make decisions about the lives we would live afterward.

"Do it."

It was familiar as she reached into his mind and triggered his powers. The portal opened and a moment later another one appeared in the middle of an intersection in downtown Troy. She ignored his blackened eyes, a reminder that she had pushed him further than she should. She would feel guilty later, but now, they had Children to save.

***

She pulled the trigger, aimed, and pulled again. The first machine exploded, its head nowhere to be found. The second she caught in the hips, removing both legs. The synthetic dug its digits into the earth and gained ground between them, determined to get at its target. Twenty-Seven, attempted to ignore the two teenagers huddling in the corner of the kitchen while she worked.

Twenty-Seven grabbed onto the machine's skull with her enhanced hand and squeezed. The metal resisted, but as she growled, the skull collapsed in. With the processor crushed, the synthetic slumped to the ground. "We're getting you out of here."

The boy nodded, holding the girl close to his chest. Twenty-Seven slung the rifle over her shoulder and reached out to the two. "We clear this building, get to the bunker. You know the drill." She could see he was trying not to shiver. The shock had worn off and the terror began to set in. *If they're going to get to safety, it has to happen now*, she thought.

The kitchen was modest, without the most state-of-the-art appliances, but it had managed to make a killer steak once upon a time. She grabbed a knife from the block on the counter. Not her weapon of choice, but if any more of the smiling people showed up, she was going to make sure they didn't have a chance to reach her wards.

She flipped the knife in her hand so that the blade pointed down, resting against her forearm. A year ago she thought she'd die from starvation in the Outlands. A year ago, she worried how she would manage without her husband. A year ago, she was another woman. In three hundred and sixty-five days she learned underneath a scared housewife, she harnessed the spirit of a fighter.

A shadow moved underneath the door leading into the dining room. She gestured for the children to step back. The heel of her foot slammed the swinging service door, which smacked into somebody, and she burst through, on them before they could react. It was another man in a bomber jacket, the sixth one she had come across at this point. His switchblade scraped across the metal of her forearm. She slashed across his chest, sending him backward, knocking into the empty pastry case.

She latched onto his wrist and with a simple spin of a gyro, it hung pulverized, his hand dangling useless. With the uninjured one he grabbed at her throat and she plunged the knife into his chest. The bomber jacket gave way and the blade sunk deep into the man's torso. She had no problem killing in defense, but she found the silent deaths of these men unsettling. She tore them limb from limb and there wasn't a single cry of pain. Whatever had been done to them, she wasn't going to leave them alive to tell.

The diner could seat fifty, but they rarely used it anymore. It was easier to cook food in one of the smaller houses behind the main street. The checkered tablecloths had a layer of dust and the cash register sat open, dollar bills still resting in the drawer. There was something mournful when she looked at the buildings thrown into disrepair or neglected. She hoped that in the next generation, there would be enough people that these abandoned dreams would thrive again. But as she caught her reflection in the pastry case, her face streaked with blood and her hair matted to her face, she knew this fantasy was far from a reality.

"Are you ready?"

She saw the reflection in the Ryan's eyes before he could reply. They were here. At least a dozen synthetics stalked the diner. He screamed.

She had studied each of the residents, learned who they were as people, their favorite ice-cream flavors. Tangled in the informal coffee conversations were their abilities, the things that made them Children of Nostradamus. Twenty-Seven felt her robotic arm go limp, refusing to cooperate or respond to her commands.

"Good job, Ryan."

"Sorry, Ma'am," he said, looking at her arm.

"I still have a good one."

His body generated low-level electromagnet pulses. The first time they shook hands, her enhancement had died, the power source drained. He had apologized profusely, but she could only laugh at this young man who literally de-armed her with a simple handshake. If he depowered her arm, then the nearby synthetics were nothing more than lifeless statues. It would take her body an hour to power the fuel cell that kept her arm functioning. Until then, she thanked God she was a leftie.

"We make a break for it. I'm heading to the armory, you head to the bunkers."

Just outside the town, scattered around in the parks and woods, were underground bunkers created by the townspeople for this exact purpose. He nodded again. It was the first time he had used his ability to fight the enemy. In a different time, he would have been a useful soldier. For now, it was her job to make sure he had the opportunity to grow into a fighter.

"If they come for you, use your abilities as much as you can."

"Yes, ma'am."

The girl in his arms was half his age. She clung to him, hiding her face away from the boogeymen. The girl's senses were heightened, nearly driving her mad. For the longest time she hid away in a safe in the bank in town, the only place with walls thick enough to block out the noise.

"Jenny." Twenty-Seven saw one eye peak out to look at her. "If you hear anything, you tell him. Help him."

The girl clenched her eyes. "They're dead."

Twenty-Seven didn't need to ask. The girl was listening to the inhabitants of the town being killed one at a time. The smell of blood must be reaching her by now. Twenty-Seven wanted to shelter her, save her from this madness, but right now, she needed soldiers. "Jenny, Ryan needs you to help him. Can you do that?"

Her eyes darted back to the boy she held tightly. She nodded.

"Now run." Twenty-Seven grabbed her gun and

bolted out the glass doors. The synthetics stood there, motionless. She wasn't sure if they had any way to charge their bodies again. If she had the ammunition, she'd dismantle them one at a time, but she had one round left and it was for an emergency.

They began their trot down the road. Ryan kept looking back and forth as he passed alleys. Twenty-Seven grabbed her gun and took aim at a synthetic on the roof of a building to his side. Before she could pull the trigger, the robot's shoulders slumped and she saw Jenny pointing. She took a deep breath and for the first time in the last hour, she thought somebody might make it out alive.

"Now for the rest of you."

There were no explosions, no bloodcurdling screams, just an unusual stillness in the town. She stepped into an alley that led her across the street from the armory. She ducked behind a trashcan as two synthetics walked past the entrance. She listened for their feet to stop moving. When there was no more scuffing, she knew they'd had seen her. "Fucking infrared cameras."

Before they could mount the lasers on their shoulders, she fired her last shot into the synthetic on the left. The explosion was enough to send chunks of metal in every direction and knock the other to the ground. She spun around and started running. The alley was clear, a straight path to the end and then a turn to the left. She skidded around the corner as pieces of brick exploded near her head. The thumping of feet behind her picked up speed. It was hard enough to run, but even harder with the dead weight of her arm rocking in the wind.

Across the street stood a hardware store. Inside, tucked underneath the counter was a loaded shotgun. All she had to do was make it in and she'd be armed. It was thirty feet across the street, another five to the door, and less than ten to the counter. In forty feet she'd be dangerous again.

The synthetic jumped from the roof, landing in front of the doorway. "Stupid machines," she hissed. She continued to build speed, running in a straight line. At the last moment, she dodged to the left, launching herself through the display window. She'd worry about the cuts later. Glass shattered as she flew through the case. She hit the ground and stumbled over the wheelbarrows, falling and skidding to a stop. She started getting to her knees as bullets flew overhead. Fertilizer and gardening chemicals rained down on her as the synthetic launched a volley of suppressing fire.

She crawled her way to the counter, hobbling from the useless limb. Hidden only a few feet away, a gun filled with enough shells to defend herself. It would give her a fighting chance to reach the back of the store where they used to repair broken screen doors and now stored their weapons and ammo. In the backroom there were enough guns to start a war. They had been a present from Jasmine after raiding a government warehouse. If she could get there, she'd remove every the threat in the town. Victory was only a few feet away.

She screamed as a synthetic jumped over and landed on the counter. It ripped away at the wood, and grabbed on to the weapon. The operator on the other end of the synthetic laughed. She could tell by the head tilt and slight shaking of the chest. He found her death amusing. She tried to flex her fingers on her right hand, but the limb remained dead.

The synthetic held out its arm and a compartment opened on the forearm. The laser started to charge and she found herself trapped by the counter. She spun about so the laser would hit her shoulder, the thickest part of her enhancement.

Her teeth clenched tightly in anticipation of the burn. Seconds passed and she opened her eyes to see the laser silently pulsing against an invisible shield between her and the robot. Twenty-Seven let out a sigh of relief. In the last year, there were many times she had been saved in a similar fashion, her guardian angel watching over her.

The synthetic's head cocked to the side. Neither the artificial intelligence nor the human operating the machine had any idea what was happening. As Twenty-Seven stood, she started to laugh. "You fucked with the wrong town."

A single screw loosened from its neck, hovering in midair. A moment later every moving part separated, suspended like a complex jigsaw puzzle. The machine parts fell to the ground in a pile of scrap. She turned around just in time to watch a synthetic from the alley be torn in half. An elderly woman stepped through the front door.

"About damned time," Twenty-Seven said.

"Let's be done with this."

"Deal."

***

Some of the Barren running through the streets were his own creations. The assassins were younger, more virile, and by far more destructive than their elder counterparts. Decades ago the Society forced its members to surrender their firstborn as an offering. Then, drugs mixed with the minor nudging of the resident telepath created empty vessels, the group's very own subservient army.

The ritual vanished for a time as Eleanor refused to partake in such brutal methods. His mentor restored the tradition and now Jacob continued. Instead of firstborns, he sought out the dredges of society, picking male prostitutes, criminals, and homeless off the street, subjecting them to the same brainwashing. Those who resisted he'd experiment on, testing the limits of his abilities. Those on which they worked became part of the Barren, a mindless group of people waiting for a mentalist to give them purpose.

Jacob's vision shifted, seeing through the eyes of one Barren and then on to the next. He experienced the world through each body he inhabited. Each time they brought down their signature razor blades, he could feel the resistance of their victim's skin. It allowed himself the pleasure of his bloodlust within the security of his own home.

Jacob sat quietly in his study, a glass of scotch in hand. His eyes remained closed as his body jumped again. He smiled as one of his men slaughtered a couple, murdering them without regard. The Barren were nothing more than mindless drones, but their tenacity for killing continued to prove useful.

As he hopped to another, he watched a woman with a robotic arm grapple his host. They struggled and she snapped his hand, crushing it with her enhancements and delivering a solid punch into his chest, collapsing his ribcage. Jacob left his dying husk and touched the mind of the woman. A wall surrounded her, preventing him from entering her thoughts. How did a human keep him at bay?

"A mentalist?"

He growled. If he were stronger, he might be capable of raping her mind. Compared to Lillian or Dikeledi, he was the weakest mentalist, capable of only minor tricks. His mentor had been exceptional, and showed Jacob a world where their kind took what they wanted. For now, he relied on those around him, needing to play a game of intrigue, using his cunning to further his goals.

A Barren waited for a synthetic to finish shooting a defenseless woman in her pajamas. The President of the United States controlled the synthetics his company created. His relationship with her was less than healthy. Knowing the Warden was a mentalist, he wondered if she put him there as part of a bigger conspiracy. She kept his company well-funded. In return the Genesis Division worked directly with her. For now, their relationship remained mutually parasitic.

Another Barren had his hands wrapped around the neck of a young man, his grip determined to squeeze the life out of the Child. Jacob smiled at the sensation beneath his fingertips, the pressure building as the man struggled to get free. He grasped at the assassin's fingers. A moment later his body went limp and the Barren grabbed its switchblade from the ground and folded it back into his jacket pocket. As his vessel started walking down the road, toward screams, Jacob forced the body to stand motionless, staring at a dark shadow standing in the middle of the street.

Abandoned storefronts stood dark. At one time they had housed a vibrant community, but now they remained vacated. The shadow should have been faint, diminished by a street lamp hanging above, but the thick darkness resisted the light.

Jacob started to speak but realized his host had wandered down the street in pursuit of new victims. Jacob projected his thoughts, touching the darkness, trying to wrap his head around what it might be.

"It's alive," he said aloud in his study.

Waves of anger washed off the figure. He poked and prodded with his telepathy, trying to sort through the overwhelming emotions radiating from the darkness. The Society had suspected there might be mentalists hiding among the Children. At one point he thought he might be the last telepath. In two days he discovered the Warden, and now this thing. Despite trying, he couldn't penetrate the figure's mind.

Who are you?

He thought about getting the others. Lily and Salvador wouldn't be of much use, but Dikeledi was adept with her abilities. She would be able to see through his eyes and read the figure's emotional state. Of the four of them, she was by far the most powerful, a banner she kept hidden away. Jacob gritted his teeth; he hated that he wasn't nearly as capable as his former mentor. His jaw began to ache, the anger tightening his chest.

Tell me. Who are you?

Between blinks, the shadow vanished. He spun about, trying to see the rest of the town. Without the eyes of the Barren the town became fuzzy, his anchor beginning to disappear. He let his mind drift until he found another Barren, this one knocking open the door of a small store. Jacob gave a simple suggestion and the Barren turned around, heading back to the spot he had been standing earlier.

"Fuck," he said in his study. The shadow had vanished and now all that remained were synthetics systematically going through the town looking for survivors.

Who are you?

Jacob jumped out of his chair, scanning his study for the voice. A fire burned in the archaic-looking fireplace, causing shadows to dance about the room. There were well over a thousand books, many he had read. Even under his mentor's tutelage, he found himself alone, and the only comfort was that of dead authors. He spent time reading through classics, absorbing their symbolism, and when he finished those, he began studying the history of the Society. He had learned there was power in knowledge, and if his measly gifts wouldn't give him the power he wanted, he would find another way.

"Who's there?"

He didn't see it at first, at least not with his eyes.

111

A wisp of anger touched his mind, telling him he wasn't alone. Jacob gathered his thoughts, leaving behind the massacre in Troy. He didn't need his senses to know he detected the same person from the street only seconds earlier. Distance meant nothing to a mentalist, and he assumed the figure tracked him from the slaughter.

Who are you?

"Jacob Griffin," he answered. It would only take the briefest thought and the others would be alerted to the intruder. While he might not be strong enough alone, between the four of them, this stranger couldn't persevere. It would only take a shout, and they'd come to his aid.

It infuriates you to rely on them.

Jacob knew his defenses were crumbling. The figure barely put in effort, hardly exerting itself, and already Jacob needed to play defense. If it had been an assailant, he could reach for the knife-shaped letter opener or the poker next to the fireplace. However, whatever this figure wanted, their confrontation would be played out in a mental battlefield.

What if I could give you everything you wanted?

Jacob had been given a similar offer by the president of the Society decades prior. The man said that under their guidance, he'd become a force to be reckoned with. He had offered him more money than he could imagine and a position in life beyond that of his parent's trailer park. Jacob had given up his entire life at the promise, and now that he had obtained his reward, he wondered what more could be given to him.

The shadows collected, merging until a solid figure appeared. Standing next to the books on economics and politics, the wisps seemed sentient, alive. The light from the fireplace didn't diminish the depths of darkness, instead giving them an almost eerie setting to call home. Whoever the shadow belonged to, Jacob couldn't deny the person's abilities. Underneath a tightly woven shield, there was a sense of power, more than he ever sensed from his mentor.

What do you want?

The figure moved closer, each step leaving wisps of smoke in its wake. Jacob couldn't help but tense up as it passed through the booze-hiding globe and the high back chair. Jacob knew he couldn't run, couldn't hide, and couldn't defeat the adversary. He should call for the others, cry out for help, but something in his chest prevented him.

The figure stopped, its head tilting slightly to one side as if confused by something in the room. Jacob found himself able to move, but had no desire to step away from the figure. An intoxicating sensation coursed through his veins from standing so close to such a powerful mentalist. Jacob thrust his hand into the figure and found there was nothing in the air. With a single thought, the mass vanished. Jacob inspected his hand, looking for any remains, but not even traces of the smoke remained.

The seconds seemed to freeze. Looking past his hand, he saw the flames on the fire move as if they were in slow motion. He was familiar with the sensation; his mind was adrift, removed from his body, and in this state it worked faster than the world around him.

A hissing sound started to one side. He spun about. The room remained empty. The hissing grew louder until he recognized it as a faint whisper, the thoughts of a person nearby. Another began, and then another. Seconds passed and he listened to the voices of hundreds of people. His mind scanned more thoughts than his abilities had ever been capable of. Every time he had attempted to read this many people, he'd find himself on the floor, straining to push them away once the floodgates opened.

Something clicked in his head. A sealed door, hiding away untapped power, was thrown open, causing his spine to bow. The voices shouted at him as more and more filled his head. He grabbed his temples, trying to focus as the thoughts echoed throughout his skull. He screamed out, wailing at the pain.

"Stop."

He was perfectly aware of a dozen people. A dozen people heard his telepathic command, freezing in place. A woman holding her child stopped moving, a man on a treadmill slowed to a stop, and a couple having sex ceased their carnal activities. Jacob panted, trying to catch his breath at the strain ripping through his mind. It was the first time he had ever controlled a person with his telepathy, let alone a dozen. His nails bit into his palms, but he couldn't ignore the thralls of ecstasy.

This is power.

Chapter 7

1993

Mark watched through the glass into Ariel's testing area. She sat in a chair, with little stickers attached to wires connecting to a machine used to read her brainwave activity. Ivan calibrated the machine while she read her junior detective novel. She devoured books, a trait Mark fostered. His chest swelled with pride.

Neither she nor Ivan seemed to pay any attention to the other. She didn't like him, but she continued to be a trooper while he ran his tests. Mark had his reservations about Ivan He wondered if Ivan had a soul or if it was only science that drove him. In the months since he had joined his research team, Mark hadn't heard the lanky man talk about his family, his home life, or even his past. He was incredibly guarded and rarely let personal factoids slip.

The scientist turned, staring directly at Mark through mirrored glass. Mark froze, unsure if Ivan was checking his reflection or if he knew he had an observer. There was something unnerving about Ivan. Mark had learned to control his feeling, but it taxed him at times, not letting his lead researcher know he found him to be incredibly creepy.

"Are you ready, Ariel?"

"Yes, sir," she said in a polite voice. She slid a bookmark into her novel and set it down on the table. She straightened herself in the chair. She had confessed to Mark that Ivan scared her. She couldn't quite put her finger on it, but something about him made her skin crawl. She had described their encounters to him each time they met, "He's looking at me, but not."

Mark was unsettled by her fear. With no effort, she had singlehandedly disarmed his entire security detail. She was the only person in the complex Goddard feared and somehow, the researcher gave her alarm. Mark had taken to watching the tests to make sure everything was being done above the board. Ivan hadn't held back his data, giving some early results, including that he had isolated the area of the brain responsible for her abilities. It was the first time the President of the United States had been pleased with him.

"I want you to lift this pencil for me, Ariel."

Her eyes didn't leave his, but the pencil jumped up in the air and hovered several inches above the table. Mark was well aware that her abilities allowed her to move far more than a pencil. With such a small object, she'd have nearly perfect mastery.

"Can you write your name in cursive on the paper?"

She didn't budge as the pencil lowered itself to the paper and scribbled out her name. She cleared her throat. "What are you looking for, sir?"

"I'm looking for how skilled you are with the fine motor control aspect of your abilities."

She huffed at his remark. The smile spread across Mark's face as the Rubik's cube on the table lifted into the air. The blocks twisted back and forth and within seconds she solved the cube. She lifted several bent metal puzzles and with quick shifts in direction each of them fell apart, solved without any effort on her behalf.

"We've done this before."

Ivan didn't hide his annoyance with the girl. Mark assumed the man didn't have children of his own. He was an excellent scientist, but dealing with a single child nearly crippled him. Mark had frequent conversations coaching him at how to coax the best out of her. Ivan rubbed his eyes, attempting to placate the girl.

"Want to try something a bit more difficult?"

"I guess."

Ivan set down the clipboard and stood behind Ariel. "I want you to close your eyes. In a room not far from here, I've placed similar items on a table. I want to test your abilities without relying on your other senses."

Mark hadn't seen him perform this test before, but he was indeed curious. If Ariel had the ability to affect physical objects from a distance, it would mean she held an entirely different level of danger for the outside world. Mark put aside the implications and quietly cheered her on. "You'll show him, Ariel."

"Close your eyes, Ariel. I want you to imagine yourself walking outside this door and turning right. Can you do that?"

"I'm at the elevator."

"Good girl." He rested his hands on her shoulders. "Step inside the elevator and go up three levels."

"It's moving."

Mark walked out to the door that would lead to Ariel's housing quarters. He was shocked to see the elevator doors close. It moved upward, just as Ivan had instructed. Mark was beginning to sense they were on the verge of discovering something terrifying enough it could end their work here.

"I want you to step off the elevator and walk down the hallway. Stop when you see a door with my name on it."

"I see it," she said softly.

Mark pressed his hands against the glass as he watched. He wasn't sure if it was his imagination or part of the experiment, but a pressure pushed against the exterior of his skull. It started as a mild buzzing but faster than he could explain, a headache started just behind his eyes.

"Go into my office. On a table in the middle of the room, you'll see a Rubik's Cube. I want you to solve it."

Ariel's hands lifted into the air, her fingers poking and gripping an unseen object. She spun the invisible cube in her hand. Mark had observed her use her abilities hundreds of times. It was only when she taxed herself that she started relying on physical gestures to complement her mind. She grimaced, her hands shaking as she continued spinning her fingers.

"Concentrate on the cube, Ariel." Ivan firmly gripped her shoulders while she moved her hands. Mark found it curious that Ivan physically interacted with the girl. The researcher rarely stepped inside her personal space. He would say something later. He gasped at the pain pulsing through his head, making it difficult to concentrate. He leaned against the glass, the cool surface distracting him from the thumping in his head.

"I can't solve it."

"Keep trying, Ariel, you can do it."

Mark touched the divot at the top of his lip. Blood smeared onto the back of his hand. He slid down the wall. He fought to keep his eyes open, but as the pain seared through his brain, he relaxed. He understood the edges of his vision going dark meant he'd be out cold in a moment.

Nothingness.

Seconds passed. Air rushed into his lungs as he inhaled, gasping for breath like he'd been drowning. He grabbed at the wall, looking for anything to help him sit upright. His movements seemed desperate, as if he was begging his body to respond to his commands. As he turned his head to examine the wall, he found he sat in an empty room. No, not empty—walls, floor, and ceiling were gray, seamless, and void of any exits.

"Hello," he said, his voice swallowed as if he whispered in a vicious storm.

The motion blur of his hand reminded him of

time-lapse photography. He tried not to think about how his skin appeared desaturated, as if the color was siphoned from it. Worry set in as he moved his legs. His limbs responded as if both had fallen asleep. He wasn't sure what was happening, but he had a feeling he wasn't in the observation room.

"Ariel," he whispered.

He got to his knees and then stood. Part of the wall faded, becoming translucent, allowing him to see through. The glass tinted and hid Ivan and the girl. A door faded into place on the wall. He reached for the handle to the door and found it was missing. He tried to steady his breathing, but his heart picked up its tempo as his fear grew.

"Ariel!"

He froze. The hair on his arms stood on end as an eerie sensation coursed through his body. Something in his gut told him there was another person in the room with him. He wasn't sure how anybody could get into the sealed room, but he knew somebody was close by. He tried not to hyperventilate as terror creeped into his mind.

"It's the girl," said a distant voice.

Mark spun, arms flailing, pushing his back to the wall. The far end of the room dissipated into the shadows. Somewhere inside there, another person hid from sight. He couldn't fight panic anymore; his heart raced. He heard the pounding in his head, a raging thumping, nearly deafening him.

Out of the shadows emerged Ivan. "The girl has more abilities than we thought possible."

The man's skin was as desaturated as his own, but on the scientist's stretched body, the lack of color almost appeared ghastly. Ivan's movements were slow, deliberate and calculated. He stepped up to the tinted glass and touched it, giving the material a firm push before admitting it wouldn't budge. He stepped closer to Mark and leaned in just close enough to inspect him.

"What's happening?"

"I have been working with her for months, but this is the first time I can say this has happened."

"What is this?"

Ivan gave a slight shrug. "I do not believe we're awake."

"How are we in each other's dreams?"

"How does a mentalist communicate without moving their lips?" Ivan asked, his sarcasm reminded Mark how they dealt with the unbelievable everyday. "Somehow the girl has thrust us together in this shared space. It appears as if it is some sort of limbo."

Mark's pulse slowed. Even with the awkward man in the room with him, at least he had a scientist handy. Hopefully he could bring some amount of reason to this conundrum. Ivan turned and studied the room, brushing his fingers where there should be seams, but avoiding the darkness at the far end.

"How do we get out of here?"

"I've worked with one telepath before. Her abilities only allowed her to hear faint whispers. She wasn't adept enough to send thoughts, let alone send two minds to a place like this."

"Do we wait it out?"

"I have a suspicion that hours could pass here while barely a fraction of a second has passed in the physical world. I wouldn't be surprised if my body has yet to hit the ground."

"What did you have her doing?"

"Guided meditation technique. Ariel strained to complete the task at hand. Then something changed in the air."

"The pressure? I felt it too. I was just about to pass out."

"Maybe because we're unconscious, this is possible?"

"How do we wake?" Mark reached for the handle again and found the fixture had returned. He pushed at the door open. Where it should have opened into the lobby of Ariel's quarters, it entered into the room she and Ivan had been in. As he stepped closer to the table, a putrid smell began to fill the room.

"Do you smell it?"

Mark couldn't locate Ivan. He took a step away, back toward the door. As he crossed the threshold, he felt as if he was thrust from the room. His eyes opened and he was lying on the floor with two of the security team kneeling next to him.

"He's awake."

"Get him to medical."

He was groggy, his mind trying to make sense of what happened. One of the men held a white capsule in his hand. *The smell*, he thought, *smelling salts*. The two men picked him up and carted him toward medical. In the elevator he finally got his bearings enough to stand on his own feet. The guards were curiously eyeing him. Both men had guns on their hips, replacing their standard issue

Tasers.

"What about Ivan?" Mark asked.

One of the men in the black turtlenecks eyed him curiously. "Dr. Volkov is with Ariel in medical."

Mark's blood pressure went up, the beeps on the monitor sounding closer together as he feared the worst. "What happened to her?"

"He had to sedate her," the man said. "You'll have to watch the video to believe it. Goddard thinks that man might be the only reason you're alive."

He wanted to see the tape, to see exactly what occurred in the seconds after he passed out. However, more than that, he wanted to make sure Ariel was being taken care of. He wasn't going to leave her alone with Goddard while she was unconscious. At least Ivan, no matter how unsettling he was, stood by her side. While he might not be Mark's first choice, he was the only other man in the center that wanted her alive, even if for less than righteous reasons. He needed answers and Ivan was the only one who might be able to answer them.

Chapter 8

2033

Jasmine believed the kid held back when it came to his abilities. Conthan grunted from the exertion. If it wasn't for Vanessa possessing him and using his powers for him, they'd still be standing in a street in Boston. She didn't like that the telepath could eavesdrop on their every thought, but certain uses of the woman's abilities were effective. Even now, she had no doubts that Vanessa heard everything passing through her mind.

"We split up," Vanessa said.

"Can't find them for us?" asked Alyssa.

Jasmine knew by the bothered look on the woman's green face it wasn't good news. Her eyes hovered just right of pain, but not quite anger. Shock gripped Vanessa, leaving her unable to continue. Jasmine said it for the telepath.

"They're all dead."

It had become their routine. Despite Jasmine's moments of cold ruthlessness, Vanessa remained the caregiver of the group. Each of them granted her a motherly type of respect. Jasmine didn't find the need for admiration or even acceptance; she often served as the bearer of bad news.

Vanessa nodded. "Unless they can hide from me like Twenty-Seven—" She let her eyes drop for a moment "—it does not bode well."

Jasmine watched the woman's serpentine eyes scan the street in hopes she may be wrong. Despite the horrific things Vanessa must know to be true, she tried to maintain optimism. It was unfortunate— the woman had the makings of a soldier, but underneath her thick skin, her emotions still got the best of her.

"As they did to you once not so long ago," Vanessa whispered to her.

Jasmine stormed away, her boots slamming down on the ground. The tingling started at her wrists, underneath the metal bands she wore on each arm. Responding to her anger, her powers sought out the closest material to mimic. Thanks to Dav5d, her bracers contained several alloys for her epidermis to interact with.

Pain flashed through her body, her muscles clenching tightly. At once, she increased in weight, her legs struggling to keep her upright. There were denser metals she could mimic, but the denser she got, the slower she became and the more the transformation hurt. Right now, she didn't want anybody to see her emote, much less show pain.

"Dwayne, take Conthan," commanded Vanessa. "Stay with Jasmine, cover east of here. We have the west."

While any of them would go to great lengths to protect one another, he was the only one willing to set aside his morals for the greater good. She admired a soldier willing to get the job done. Of all the people in this group, she probably respected Dwayne the most. It was Conthan who annoyed her. His aimless path in life and the liability he served as to this team, she didn't appreciate. The kid had more power than any of them, and he chose to remain naive.

She stopped to assess her surroundings. To her right a diner appeared abandoned, but in the alley behind something moved enough to catch her attention. She locked gazes with Dwayne, pointing to her eyes and then to the alley. He nodded in reply. Conthan ignored them, looking almost alien in his power-drunken state.

Her muscles adapted to the weight of her changed body, growing stronger with each step. It'd be another minute before she reached her normal speed, but she'd sacrifice speed for endurance. The alley separating the diner from a barber shop was wide enough to hold dumpsters. It would have been a tight fit for a car, but it was the perfect place to bottleneck a fight and catch prey off guard.

She stopped before entering the alley, listening for any sound. It was faint, but from somewhere, a scraping sound made the small hair on her neck stand on end. She clenched her fists and walked quickly through the alley. It was intersected by another lane. Through a pair of buildings she saw the source of the scraping, a synthetic dragging itself along the pavement.

She didn't wait. Her feet thumped against the ground, leaving small indentations where the ball of her foot pressed. The synthetic attempted to crawl away from her. One hand had been torn from the body and both of its legs were missing. There was no slowing as she grabbed the machine's skull. She braced her foot on its back and pulled with all her strength until sparks rained down and the head pulled away from its shoulders.

She inspected the street for any other synthetics, but found the town empty. Dwayne and Conthan caught up, trying to make sense of the battered synthetic.

"Do you think it was attacked by Twenty-Seven?" Dwayne asked.

Jasmine nodded. "Or one of her people."

"It was probably trying to escape."

Conthan shook his head. "It wasn't crawling away from us. They never crawl away from a fight. It was crawling toward something."

All three looked across the street to the edge of a park. Troy was small, but it was far enough north that nature butted against the town. The park had a line of trees with a playground located inside. Jasmine listened to Conthan's speculations. She would have to ask when he became so well versed in synthetic fighting tactics. Maybe he wasn't a lost cause?

She stepped onto the curb and followed a paved pathway into the park. She paused every few steps, listening for more attackers. The path opened up at the playground, an area filled with wood chips and equipment to keep kids entertained. The wooden structure came complete with a swinging bridge and plastic spiral slide. It was obviously an area heavily used by the residents. She couldn't recall if there were children in the town; the last time she had been there had been shortly after the liberation of the Facility prisoners. Jasmine helped bring supplies and gave the few residents training with firearms and how to maintain some semblance of security.

Dwayne and Conthan split up and approached different sides of the playground. They waited on her to make the next move. It had taken a while, but they learned to follow her lead in a fight. The respect they bestowed on her was appreciated.

Something underneath the bridge flickered. One moment a figure was there and the next it was gone. She held up her hand, signaling to the guys to stop moving forward. If there was somebody hiding, it was most likely a Child; she had never seen a synthetic be able to vanish from sight like that. More likely, a Child with the ability to camouflage.

Her heart skipped a beat. She held her breath as she thought about the last Child of Nostradamus she captured as a Paladin. The young girl had touched her red suit and her skin transformed into a matching red. Jasmine commanded her feet to move forward. With each step, her heart seemed to stop.

"No," she mumbled to herself.

She told the girl to run from home, to run before the military tracked her down. That action had sealed both of their fates. The girl no longer had a home and Jasmine was marked for death by her former employers. It was the first time she allowed her humanity to override orders from the

128

government. That act of defiance started a series of events liberating her both physically and mentally.

The outlines of the person shimmered, vanishing and reappearing in a sporadic pattern. Only distant street lamps illuminated the edges of the park. Here, the Child was hidden almost entirely in shadows. Jasmine hovered over the Child, afraid to kneel down and touch them.

"Heaven help me," she whispered.

The form flickered again and she noted the long hair and petite stature. She could only assume it was a female. She had seen several Children die while using their abilities, and each of their powers had done something similar, flickering until they realized the host had died. When she died, she wondered if her skin would turn to steel. With deep breath, and she looked down at the girl again. Jasmine had no doubt she was dead.

She stifled a gasp and dropped to her knees. She reached out, touching the girl, looking for her arm so she could roll the body onto its back. Jasmine's heart raced faster, fear gripping her chest. She pulled at the girl's shoulder, turning her over just as the powers faded away and a female face greeted her.

The nude girl had several holes in her body, penetrated by the bullets belonging to synthetics. Jasmine assumed she had ditched her clothes and attempted to hide. Her camouflage would work against the human eye, but for machines that could read her heat or listen for her heartbeat, her powers fell short. Jasmine moved up the girl's torso, lingering on the wounds to avoid her face.

"Rebecca," she mumbled.

In an instant, her skin returned to its normal density. As soon as her epidermis converted, Jasmine became aware of the girl's skin beneath her palms. She touched her cheek, running her thumb along the soft skin. There was no point in trying to stop the tears that fell from her eyes onto the body below.

She stroked the girl's face, trying to recall their conversation a year ago. Jasmine had defied orders and told her to flee. She assumed the girl was killed before she got out of the city. Jasmine never assumed the teen would have made it this far. She couldn't even begin to figure out how Rebecca had discovered a town filled with Children. Perhaps it had been by sheer luck, or perhaps Twenty-Seven and her people had gone looking for refugees.

She lifted the girl's body, enough that she rested on her lap. The blood around her wounds was still wet. Jasmine estimated she had died within the hour. Alone.

"I'm so sorry," she whispered.

Jasmine felt the weight press down on her body, the guilt of pushing Rebecca away from her home. Her fault or not, she had been the instrument that set the girl's fate into motion. Behind her decision, she thought about the man who made the commands. She had been acting under orders. Only one man gave those to the Paladins.

She sensed the two men closing in on her. "Stop!" she screamed.

The space got brighter as Dwayne used his electricity to generate light. Even with the faint glow, Rebecca's features showed more prominently. The girl was flushed, and her lips had already started to fade. The terrified girl from a year ago had grown up. She didn't look terrified now. Her features were a bit harder, and Jasmine believed that Rebecca had made something of herself in that short time. Perhaps she worked with Twenty-Seven protecting others, perhaps she cared for the wounded, perhaps she infiltrated locations saving Children. Jasmine took solace in the narrative she created.

She picked up the girl, cradling her in both arms. She let the metal of her cuffs help transform her skin again. The pain rushed through her body, forcing out a small scream. As her epidermis mutated and turned dense, the sensation of the girl's skin grew distant. She had felt enough for today.

Conthan had taken off his coat and hoodie, which he laid across the girl. Neither of the men said anything as Jasmine walked back into town. By the time she reached the cement pathway, the tears ceased. By the pavement of the road, rage replaced her sadness. By the alley, she plotted how good it would feel to push her thumbs into the eyes of the man responsible for this.

***

Vanessa's fingers latched onto the second story windowsill. Her muscles flexed, launching her upward to the third story and had her holding onto the edge of the flat roof. She pulled herself over the ledge and inspected Troy from her vantage point.

The town wasn't large, and from here, she could see the majority of the downtown area with only a few buildings standing taller.

The only whispers inside her head came from her own comrades. While the buildings remained more or less intact, the solitude reminded her of Boston. She hoped Twenty-Seven survived. It bothered her more than she cared to admit that somebody found a way to shield themselves from her telepathy. There was a certain security in being able to read a person; relying on faith and trust were not things she typically had to worry about.

Her chest heaved as she inspected the rooftop. Other than an access door and a few vents, it stood bare. Her feet picked up speed as she prepared to launch herself upward. As she passed the access door, she felt a sting on her arm before she caught a glimpse of a man holding a knife. The back of her wing launched outward, knocking him back.

Her toes dug into the roof, scraping until she skidded to a halt. The gash on her arm stung, blood already starting to drip from the wound. She eyed the man in the shadow. There were no thoughts. He shielded himself from her. She had to wonder if the government found a way to protect themselves from telepaths.

"Who are you?"

The figure picked himself off the ground and stepped forward. The light from the street barely reached the rooftop, but just enough did for her to make out the trademark smile. She recognized the man from the Warden's office. The smile pulled too far back on each cheek terrified her. Like before, there were no thoughts, just a vacant eyes staring off into the distance. She tried to listen to the man's inner dialogue, but there was nothing, more than nothing, it almost appeared as if there was a void.

"Oh shit," she said as she let her abilities cast out wide and found a dozen more of the blank spaces nearby. Before she could warn the others, a single image seared its way through her mind. The face of a young girl being held in Jasmine's arms. The woman's grief overwhelmed her, almost crippling her physically.

The man rushed at Vanessa. She flailed to keep him at bay while Jasmine's cries made it difficult to focus. The stinging from her forearm brought her back, anchoring her in the moment. She managed to push away Jasmine's grief. The assailant brought his knife hand out wide. She snatched him by the wrist, pivoting his arm, and punched with her other hand, breaking his elbow.

No screaming, mentally or physically. The man didn't react to the broken bone. His other hand aimed for her windpipe. She reached for his arm. He ducked low, sweeping her feet out from under her. She hit the roof with a loud thud, and he was on her, his knees attempting to pin her arms at her sides.

"What are you?"

The man reached for the razor several feet away. As he leaned to one side, she lifted him and rolled him onto the ground. She was on him in an instant, her legs pinning him. She reached down and clutched his neck, threatening to squeeze until it tore from his spine. There was nothing in him, no pain, no fear, an empty vessel with a single goal.

While he tried to wiggle free, she pushed at the man's mind. It was as if something pushed back. She had a moment to wonder if he might be a telepath. She pushed harder. Bit by bit, his defenses crumbled and she found herself slipping into his mind. It was unlike anything she had ever seen before. Hollow, with only a single thought bouncing around his head. Even the most basic thoughts about food, love, or even survival were absent. The man had been stripped of everything except a single command.

She burrowed deeper into his mind, looking for the source of the tampering. She found a barricade pushing back against her intrusions. With time, she was sure she could break through and sift through the damage done to the man. For now, a single entity consumed his thoughts, "the Society." She retreated from his mind. The man would never be a human again. She grabbed the sides of his head and spun his skull, snapping his neck.

"May God have mercy on your soul."

Be on the lookout for men. Capable of fighting close combat.

She ran to the edge of the roof and pushed off with every muscle. She launched into the air another ten feet and as she reached her peak, her wings spread out, catching a soft breeze. Once upon a time she had wished they were strong enough to and carry her like a bird. It took time to find pleasure in being able to drift among the birds even if she couldn't fly.

Below, Alyssa and Skits walked with Dav5d

between them. A man came out of the shadows, crashing into Alyssa. Most people required a mental push to block a blow, or at least a suggestion to knock away a knife, but not Alyssa. Her limbs reacted on their own, grappling the man's weapon hand and spinning him over her shoulder. As he soared above her, he pivoted his hips, landing on his feet. He brought up his knee but she had already stepped out of reach. She knocked his hand away again and brought up her boot, kicking him in the face hard enough to send him to the ground.

I can't detect them. They're invisible to me.

"*Well, shit,*" Skits said both aloud and in her mind.

Three of them emerged, stepping out of the doorway to a Mexican restaurant. Vanessa assumed they were on the hunt for any remaining survivors. A hint of pain struck her as Skits ignited the air about her arms. Two more appeared and another awaited on a roof nearby. Vanessa was starting to think the hollow men stood a chance simply by sheer numbers.

The man on the roof lifted a rifle and pointed it to the group below. Vanessa's wings pulled in close to her body, quickening her descent. He lowered his eye to the scope, and her three comrades below had yet to spot him. Warning them didn't guarantee they'd react fast enough.

Her wings went wide, catching the breeze and almost halting her body in midair. As the jolt pulled her back, she imagined her thoughts flying forward. She squinted, her yellow eyes focusing on the man on the roof. She felt resistance as her mind slammed

135

into his. Her thoughts were fueled by the need to save her friends. A quiet rage seeped into her thinking, battering the invisible wall guarding his mind. She almost heard the shattering as she penetrated his mental defenses. A moment later his eyes became hers and she stared down the scope, the crosshairs focused on Dav5d's forehead.

Kill them.

The echo of a command implanted in the man's head licked at her thoughts. She almost laughed. The telepath who had left the message was incredibly weak in comparison. The gun moved until the sight focused on one of the attacker's chests. The trigger eased back. She zeroed in on a target, a clear shot on his forehead. Another trigger pull. The need to climb onto the ledge pushed the man on top of the wall circling the roof. She let her mind drift back as the man took another step, sending him off the second story of the building.

Seconds passed while she manipulated the assailants. Skits removed the legs of one of the men while Alyssa grappled with the remaining hollow man. She tossed him to the ground in a flip over the shoulder. As he worked his way to a standing position, Vanessa slammed her feet into the man, sending her momentum into the blow, hurling him thirty feet down the road. With the last flap of her wings, she touched down.

"Who are they?" asked Alyssa.

"They're not real people. They're hollow, vessels for a telepath to control. There's a mentalist behind this."

"The Warden?"

Vanessa shook her head. "No, whoever this is, they're weak. They can only control people who are stripped of any humanity. They needed these men to be barren before they can be controlled."

Skits shook the bright blue fire from her arms as she joined the group. "Government?"

"No," Vanessa said. "At least, I don't think so. Why would the government be using these things when they have techniques far more lethal?"

Dav5d touched her hand. She gripped his fingers in hers. She let the information flow from her mind, the encounter on the roof with both men flashing quickly. She might be able to see inside the minds of others, but it was her better half who could interpret the information. His eyes glazed over as he stared off into nothingness. His mind was a deafening roar as he pulled from every piece of data he ever collected. He was attempting to draw connections where there might not be any.

She pulled her hand away. The moment they broke contact the roar diminished to something more like a distant waterfall. She had never heard him use his abilities on such a grand scale. She wondered how dangerous he could be if given the opportunity. He might not be psychic, but even Eleanor didn't have the luxury of making sense of her visions. Dav5d's ability to see the future might be limited, but his accuracy was uncanny.

"Oh no," whispered Alyssa. The three women held their breath as Jasmine walked down the street holding a body in her arms.

***

137

He couldn't see her face, and he was thankful he couldn't. Boots slammed against the pavement as she walked, each step angrier than the last. They had seen dozens of dead bodies by this point, and he couldn't fathom why this one was any different. The girl was young, perhaps she was her daughter or a relative of some sort?

The sound of her screaming still shivered along his spine, giving him goosebumps every time he thought of it. He assumed she was only capable of anger, and each morning she awoke with that default expression written across her face.

Anguish was not an emotion he'd assign to Jasmine. It terrified and unsettled him, but something about that moment made her far more human than he thought she was capable of. Her anger replaced more sullen emotions quickly. He stayed several feet behind her with Dwayne trailing him. He should have been looking into the dark corners of the streets as they walked, searching for signs of life. Conthan feared for anything willing to confront Jasmine right now.

Dwayne sped up his walking until they were shoulder to shoulder. The man's eyes were darting back and forth, scanning the rooftops and the alleys they passed. Dwayne remained vigilant, much better at playing hero than he would ever be.

"Should we say something?" Conthan whispered.

"No," Dwayne replied without a moment's hesitation.

"She's in pain."

The look from Dwayne conveyed more than

words could. The sharpness in his eyes and his relentless scowl prevented Conthan from talking to Jasmine. Her boots stomped as they turned onto a street leading toward the others. Each foot slammed onto the ground, the sound echoing even louder by the weight bearing down on the woman.

"Jasmine," Conthan said suddenly, "we're going to get them."

She stopped walking. He wasn't sure if it was for dramatic effect or for fear of them seeing her face covered in tears, but she spoke without facing them. "I assumed you wouldn't see this as a game after witnessing somebody you cared for slaughtered."

She continued. Dwayne passed by Conthan, shaking his head. Jasmine's words cut deep. She still believed he played a game, wrapped up in this idea of being a superhero. Conthan's pity for her was replaced with anger. She believed herself above him because of what she had endured as part of the military, and yet she made sure he knew his optimism was not welcomed.

"Fuck you," he whispered as they walked.

They approached the others, who hadn't budged. They were cautious with their eyes, avoiding the girl cradled in Jasmine's arms. Jasmine had no problem making sure they knew what happened. "They slaughtered everybody in the town. I'm calling in my favor, Vanessa."

"Jasmine, we…"

"I want to go after the government."

Vanessa didn't respond. Jasmine had been tolerant, letting time pass after the Facility attack. Their smaller operations against the government

139

paled in comparison to what she demanded. She
didn't want to attack a manufacturer of synthetics or
take out a holding facility, she wanted to strike at
the commander, the man in charge of the West
Coast military operation.

"It was the president," Dav5d said.

"You understand she's the most powerful
woman in the world, right?" asked Skits.

"I've heard you say that about yourself," Jasmine
spat back. "I've been patient. I've been cooperative.
I've been part of this team for a year. But we always
knew it was going to come to this."

Vanessa nodded. "We owe you."

Dav5d's gaze focused on Jasmine. "The
president is the only person who had ties to the
Warden, who had two of these men in his
possession. The president is the only person who
could have ordered the synthetics to attack. There is
a connection between these men, the Warden, and
president. I am missing something critical. I am
making an assumption, but I think there is another
player on the field."

"Did you just say assumption?" asked Dwayne.

The black man nodded. "I need to do some
research when we get back to Boston. I think I can
fill in the blanks and uncover the person."

Jasmine faced Vanessa, their eyes meeting.
Vanessa broke the silence first. "We discover who
did this and I promise you, we stop them."

Vanessa didn't add the underlying line, "We will
kill them," but Conthan understood the tone. He
knew they were going to extract revenge. Jasmine
might not have noticed it, but he was more than

okay with this. He was ready to infiltrate the people that caused Sarah's death and deliver justice, even if that meant his hands getting bloody.

"Did anybody see Twenty-Seven?"

Conthan shook his head. "There were almost no bodies. Just signs of fighting."

"We found a synthetic," added Dwayne.

"There is a conspiracy afoot," Dav5d added.

"And whoever is behind it has decided to start playing this game of chess without us," Vanessa said.

She gave a slight nod to Conthan and he knew it was the signal for them to return to Boston. He flexed his muscles and searched his mind for the well of energy used to open portals. It approached empty, but he thought he could still open one more before his powers refused to function. The pain started at the base of his brain and spread through his limbs. As it reached his hands, he flung his fingers open and a portal appeared in the middle of the group.

They each stepped out of the way as Jasmine walked through first. They followed and Conthan took a moment to look back at the town. He commended them for trying to lead a normal life away from danger. He wished this social experiment had been a success. Somewhere in his heart he imagined himself settling down and enjoying his life with other Children. But it wouldn't happen. Someone decided their community was a threat and destroyed it. He understood Jasmine in that moment. The more he thought about it, the more he agreed with her.

Somebody was going to pay for what happened here.

Chapter 9

2033

Jacob sat at the end of a long table inside a glass conference room. At each seat, a man in a suit attentively watched a display hovering above the table. They jotted notes as figures passed over the screen while one of the men talked about quarterly projections. Each of them held an important position within Genesis Division. Some worked directly with research and development with the president; others were number crunchers.

Jacob gave a passing glance to see that the numbers escalated quickly. He knew they would. While the General of the Free States and the President of the United States waged battle, those who dealt in war were profiting nicely. Only one man in the room belonged to the Society. At the far end of the table, nearly twenty feet away, his insignia remained visible: the white lapel pin sporting two wavy lines. The man had risen through the ranks of the company because of his dedication to the Society. Jacob gave a slight nod to his cohort who returned the gesture.

Jacob listened to the thoughts of every person in the room, picking apart the conversation and looking for interesting tidbits. A woman in a power suit told herself sleeping with her boss to get a promotion was worth every lust-filled moment. Another man nervously questioned if anybody else in the room could smell the Scotch on his breath. There was nothing worth listening to until a he heard a stray thought from a bald man in a checkered tie.

"Mr. Paulito, is it?"

The room froze. Jacob held the majority share of the company, but it was rare he got involved in the daily activities. The only time the board dared to call him was when something needed to be fixed. He had become known as the man with the golden touch, and every time he intercepted a problem, somehow, resolutions were made. Only one man at the table understood how Jacob obtained his resolutions.

"Yes, sir."

Jacob stood and walked toward the man. "I can read a person, and I think you have something that will help make this board a lot of money."

Paulito squirmed in his seat, then froze as Jacob's hand rested on his shoulder. Jacob's temper was legendary, and frequently he would fly off the handle. The edge of the table remained broken in the spot where he had brought down his fist hard enough to shatter it. It served as a reminder who they shared this pedestal with.

Jacob saw a wash of memories play out as if he was watching a film in a small, dark room. He saw the divorce of Mr. Paulito's parents, and the messy way his mom walked out on him, leaving him to fend for himself with an abusive father. He could almost feel the blows as the dad wailed on the kid, taking out his anger with his fists. The film sped up until Paulito held a rifle, walking through the desert with his unit on the way to overtake a crime lord in the Middle East. It jumped forward to the graduation where he spoke as the valedictorian of his class. Jacob tried to pull his hand away, but found the intrusion as addicting as any drug.

Let them wash over you, this man can hide nothing from you.

Jacob opened the floodgates and in a fraction of a second, he watched the entire life story play out. He pulled his hand back and saw the rest of the board waiting in anticipation for the man to speak.

Mr. Paulito cleared his throat, but Jacob whispered a single word. "Silence."

His ability to control others had limitations. He struggled to force even a single person's will into submission. These limitations were discussed openly by Salvador, who wanted to remind Jacob of his insignificance.

With a single word, something changed. He no longer cared about Mr. Paulito and his worthless life accomplishments.

"Sit," he said. The man sat down and nobody moved to open their mouths. He had no doubt these newfound abilities would let him wipe their memories of him ever being present. He walked toward the man with the white lapel, the only person whose eyes seemed to follow him.

"Call my car. I have Society business to attend to."

"Yes, sir," the man responded.

"Prepare for a council meeting. There are about to be some serious changes taking place."

The man's eyebrows rose, asking the question he didn't dare to. Jacob gave a slight laugh. He would normally yell, threaten, and even wail on the man for questioning his motives. Instead he gave him a slight smile. "I think we finally have the means to take what's ours."

The man nodded, tense as he waited for the aggression.

The walk through the building surprised him as nobody took notice of his presence. Typically they would scatter, or bend over backward to pay him compliments, terrified of his wrath. For the moment, not only did he go unnoticed, as he walked, it appeared as if people unknowingly stepped aside for him. When Jacob stood at the elevator, the doors opened but nobody made a move to enter alongside him, instead waiting for one of the other dozen lifts.

He took a moment to stare up the one hundred and twenty story building. It stood as one of the largest structures in all of New York City and it belonged to him. Housing classified secrets capable of toppling the government or sending foreign countries into war, he held an uncanny power in one location. Between the scientific discoveries inside and the sheer political power, he finally started to see what could be done.

For years he had been satiated, willing to reap the benefits of being a benefactor to one of the largest corporations in the world. He had the President of the United States in his pocket and her need for war only furthered his finances. However, he was beginning to feel that being wealthy might not be enough. There was something more, a new challenge beginning to emerge in the back of his head.

A valet opened the door to a town car and they drove away from the building. It was a light mental suggestion that started the driver in that direction. Jacob stared out the window and was amazed by people caught up in their everyday lives. They walked to jobs they hated and stood at food carts poisoning their bodies. He heard each and every one of them hiding behind lies, going through the motions, afraid to break out of the shackles forced on them by society.

They are nothing more than lambs for the slaughter.

The whisper in the back of his mind knew his thoughts; more than that, it knew his desires. He wondered how many of the people lining those streets fathomed the war being waged on American soil this very moment. He assumed they kept to their routine out of fear, worried that if they dwelled on the happenings only a few states away, dread would consume them.

The car stopped at his brownstone and he exited the vehicle, walking up nine steps leading to the main entry. A servant opened the doors for him and gave a slight bow as he passed by. There had been a time the grandeur of the foyer shocked him, along with the double winding staircase leading to the second story, but now it had become another symbol of his status. He had known poverty most of his young life, and with the Society, he had experienced riches beyond what a starving child could fathom.

The double staircase from the first floor led to a solitary staircase taking him to the third floor. He walked down the hallway toward his study, slowing as he heard the whispers of voices in his head. It was rare he heard the thoughts of other mentalist; something about their abilities making them immune to his intrusions. Now, as his confidence continued to build, he knew without a doubt that if he focused, they'd be an open book.

Meet me in the study.

The hallways on the third floor continued the grandeur of the lower two levels. The dark hardwood floors led to light gray walls where lantern-shaped sconces hung, preserving some of the qualities of the original brownstone. It wasn't particularly his style, but Lily had overseen the decoration of their acquisition, the largest collection of row houses turned into a single structure in the city. They had made the front page of the paper and to help mitigate the media's attention, she had done her best to preserve the charm of the original building. When they finished the construction, a banquet was held inviting the most prominent members of society to take in their home. It had been photographed for nearly every renovation

148

magazine on the Eastern Seaboard and finally, they had been able to finish the third floor, the private quarters, a place only Society members were permitted.

He veered right, pushing through a solid oak door. Inside he breathed deeply, the scent of books filling his nostrils. There had been a time in his youth where he hid inside the walls of the library, terrified to go home. The smell of first volumes and rare texts excited his mind in a way few things could. He poured himself two fingers of Scotch and sipped deeply, letting the amber liquid warm his insides.

Lily and Salvador entered his study; the looks on both of their faces presented mild annoyance. He knew they disliked being summoned, but he would need their support if he was going to move forward at the council meeting.

"What do you want, Jacob?"

Jacob paused before replying, hearing stray thoughts escaping the Salvador's head. He knew the man didn't like him; they had never gotten along. If the opportunity presented itself, Salvador would be the first to stab him in the back. His rival's telepathy was different than his own. Jacob's abilities catered to mindreading and manipulation. while Salvador had a knack for possessing humans.

"I think it's time the Society takes a more active role in this civil war."

The perfectly sculpted eyebrow above Lily's right eye rose in curiosity. It was Salvador's shaking head that showed him where his biggest opposition would lie. "The Society has survived this long by manipulating from the shadows. You want to make us public? A target? What more could we achieve? We already have the most powerful person in the world in our corner."

"The most powerful person in the world conspired with a mentalist in an attempt to remove us from the equation."

While the shock registered on their faces, he did his best to hide his amusement. He suspected something amiss with Cecilia, that she had her own agenda. He couldn't imagine she would ever do something to threaten her relationship with the Society. After manipulating Congress into amending the Constitution to let her stay in power, her every success was built on the work of their organization.

"How do you know that?"

"It doesn't matter," Jacob said. "Cecilia is growing unstable in this war. It's time we step in and make some decisions for her."

"Where are you getting this information from?" Salvador wasn't going to back down from the question. Jacob couldn't fault him. If they were going to participate in a war, there should be sound reasoning behind his decisions.

The push required little effort. A minor nudge at the barriers keeping their thoughts guarded. He slid around their defenses and he pulled from a memory, one he wasn't aware he had. The president stood across the desk from the Warden. The bulky man reclined in his seat, listening as she laid out exactly what his duties were.

"A change in your appearance hasn't changed

your mission. I want you to figure out what gives them their abilities. I want to know what makes them tick."

"You want to discover how they can be used as weapons."

"They are weapons. I want you to learn how to make them an army."

The man nodded.

Jacob came out of the memory and grinned at the shock written across their faces. He couldn't figure if they were surprised at the betrayal of their most valuable asset or his ability to inject his thoughts into their minds. He hoped Salvador felt violated, knowing that his thoughts weren't nearly as sacred as he believed.

"How did you…"

Lily cut him off. "It proves Cecilia acted in her own best interest. But how do you know she was preparing to turn on us?"

Dikeledi stepped from around the corner, skulking into the room. Her eyes went wide the moment she saw Jacob. She didn't seem shocked, or even unnerved by him. He disliked empaths, their abilities to see beyond simple thoughts and break into the underlying meaning of a person's actions. She was especially good at translating the energy she read from people. Much like his, her abilities didn't come built with an off switch. The woman endured a constant assault of emotions from those around her expending most of her talents to keep them at bay.

"Jacob, you carry more than just a few memories?"

He nodded, deciding against lying to the one woman with the ability to taste his intents. She gave a sly smile, showing her canine teeth. "You have seen the man, truly seen him. You carry his memories."

"Whose memories?" asked Salvador.

"The Warden," Lily whispered.

"How?" asked Salvador.

Jacob shrugged. "It was a moment of opportunity. I can't explain it, but I'm certain Cecilia is only our ally in name. The moment she's capable of fighting a war on two fronts, she will make sure we're removed from this equation."

"No," Salvador said sternly. "You put our biggest ally in jeopardy and Genesis Division will stand to lose billions in military contracts."

"Or Genesis Division will stand to be the sole military provider on the Eastern Seaboard. Without us, she'd lose this fight. No synthetics, mechs, or technology to her support her reign. She'd falter and fall in no time."

"You'd let the Free States take over the government?"

Jacob smiled. There was a moment when everybody in the room understood that his plan was less about subtlety and subterfuge and more about emerging as a world power unto himself. Salvador was the only person to shake their head in response.

"Fuck no," he said. "You threaten Genesis, you threaten the Society, and quite frankly, I'd like to not get shot due to your hubris."

Dikeledi's smile spread across her face as she became intoxicated by the surge of emotions. At first Jacob assumed she was receiving the anxiety or worry Salvador was radiating. She caught his eye and he smiled back. He understood she wasn't sensing anything more than the confidence permeating every cell of his being. He would have to ask her if strong emotions were euphoric or if she just got off on his cocky attitude.

"You have no say in the matter, Salvador," Jacob said.

"Like hell I don't," he spat back. He turned to the women, gesturing wildly toward them. "They get a vote in this matter. And it's three against one."

"Two against two," Dikeledi said, standing next to Jacob.

"Lily?" he asked.

He tried to read the expressions across her face. She had no problem being an upstart, but she would only take the bait if she knew it was a sure thing. Lily was many things, but foolish was not one of them. She had risen to power by exploiting her relationship with Jacob, and he had no problem reminding her when necessary.

"No," she said. "It's a risk I'm not sure we'd win."

"It's a tie," Salvador said quickly. "Defeated."

"I challenge the tie," Jacob said firmly.

"I'll kill you," Salvador said. "I have let you sit at the head of this table for long enough, Jacob. What you propose threatens a dynasty older than all of us combined."

"I challenge you," Jacob said again.

"You know I'm stronger. It can only end one way, Jacob. I offer you a chance to stand down."

Lily's eyes pleaded for Jacob to accept the offer. She had never been a fan of Salvador. Jacob hoped otherwise, but predicted she would side with his nemesis, leaving him a formal challenge. He hoped Salvador would accept. It would be his chance to show the man who was strongest. When the man submitted, he'd have a broken plaything to keep at his side.

They didn't move, their bodies remaining stationary in the study. Their minds were on a dark landscape. Somewhere off in the distance, lights twinkled, possibly stars or even the lights of a distant city. Each of them wore their white ceremonial garb. The ladies wore gowns seemingly taken from the 1920s, while he and Salvador wore tailored three piece suits. Once upon a time, when mentalists were plentiful, this served as a method for them to duel and strut their stuff, showing their abilities to one another. Now, it provided a ring for battles of the mind and to settle scores.

Salvador crossed his arms, waiting for Jacob to make the first move. The man's body seemed to vibrate to the point where there were no hard edges outlining him. Jacob had seen him fight, and it would only be a moment before a rush of those vibrating images stepped closer, hurling Salvador into Jacob's mind.

Jacob lunged forward, his hands in front. The fingers elongated until claws replaced his human limbs. The Latin man caught his wrists with ease and the two of them stood face to face. Jacob pushed, face blurring until it washed around Salvador. His telepathy pounded on the walls the man had erected to prevent Jacob from eavesdropping. Jacob's avatar turned to mist, surrounding Salvador, looking for any spot to seep through his armor.

"Good luck," Salvador said with a laugh.

He reached into the mist and ripped his arm back, and in the blink of an eye he held Jacob by the throat. He leaned in close, a faint image of him stepping outside of himself and into Jacob. The man possessed him like a mundane human. He tried to push back but there was little chance he'd be able to do anything other than prolong his demise.

The echo of the man settled onto Jacob, consuming his form. He could hear Salvador's laughter and for a moment he thought challenging him had been a mistake. Jacob pushed hard, shoving back with enough force that the image of Salvador was knocked to the ground.

"How the hell did you do that?"

He had never been able to push Salvador away. The man could take control of any of their bodies and frequently reminded them of this. Salvador might not access their minds like Jacob could, but he could make them a prison in their own flesh.

The darkness started to surge forward, wrapping itself around Jacob. He held out his arms, letting black wisps of smoke roll around his hand, until the white suit all but vanished. For a moment, it appeared as if a larger, more menacing figure stood about Jacob, hugging his back. Jacob let the tendrils touch his skin and the moment he made contact, he understood strength as it coursed through his veins. The devil he partnered with upheld his end of the deal and as he breathed in the smoke, he heard Salvador's thoughts.

"Why are you terrified?" Jacob asked. His voice had deepened and it sounded as if it came from everywhere at once.

"Who are you?"

Jacob smiled. The power touching every fiber of his being was so strong he found himself almost giddy at the possibilities. With the blink of an eye he stood in the study again. Salvador's expression in person held an even more amusing quality. He wanted to see the man's eyes with his own as he submitted.

"Do you yield?"

It appeared as if ghosts sprung from Salvador, transparent images of him moving in every direction. They swatted at Jacob, trying to push him backward. One of the faint images tried to jump into Jacob and with a simple thought, Jacob watched it tear itself to shreds. He had an accurate understanding of Salvador's abilities, but he hadn't given the man much credit when it came to fighting to the end.

"Yield, Salvador."

The man prepared to try another attack with his telepathy. Jacob eyed Lily and reached out with his hand, pointing at her. She responding by raising her own hands and without so much as a word, she hurled Salvador against a bookcase.

"It's your last chance to yield."

Lily tried to push Jacob out of her head, but she found his hold was absolute. She cast an angry glance at him while he smiled back. He turned his attention to Salvador, who braced himself against the bookcase, his feet inches from the ground. The man attempted to step outside his body, and each time Jacob swatted away the ghostly images.

"You're not this strong."

"But I am, dear friend."

"How'd you do it?"

"Do you submit?"

Salvador lashed out. His rage lanced forward, catching Jacob by surprise. Had it been a week prior, the attack would have left him comatose at best. Now, the raw energy coming off the man held no significance. He was insignificant.

With a flip of the wrist, Lily's telekinesis snapped the man's neck. Jacob pulled away from her thoughts and without his direction, her powers returned to her control. Salvador fell to the floor in a heap, his body looking like a broken doll.

"How did you do that?" Lily asked. Her concern for their dead comrade seemed to be lacking.

"Before we carry out this plan," Jacob said, "there are loose ends we need to see attended to."

Chapter 10

2033

The morning light cast funky shadows along the textured ceiling of his bedroom. Conthan's muscles ached like he anticipated. Using his abilities too much hurt on its own. When his abilities took over, it never left him feeling good, a brutal hangover from being drunk with power.

"Hangovers used to mean good vodka," he mumbled as he rubbed his eyes.

He had kicked the blankets off in the middle of the night. The room was oddly warm, and he couldn't muster the energy to crack open the windows before he face dived into bed. He tried to remember his dreams. For the first time in months, he hadn't been haunted by the Warden. He hoped it meant something about his life was going right. Perhaps the nightly wanderings were starting to win him some points with his conscience.

He knew at some point today he'd have to talk to Jasmine. She'd be a bitch and brush him off, but more so than anybody else's, her situation struck home. Somebody important had been ripped away. She was detached before it happened; now, he imagined there was a good chance her humanity was slipping away. He couldn't blame her. When she started tearing through people to get revenge, would he help her or would he try to deter her? At that moment, he couldn't tell. The black and white world he lived in for so long started to turn a murky gray.

Conthan wished there was somebody from his former life to talk to, somebody not tied up in this saving the world gig. There was nobody he could turn to for advice, or at least advice that didn't include the words power, destiny, psychic, mentalist or villain. He was beginning to think he lived in a comic book. At any moment the building was going to shake and they'd snap to action, fending off the newest in a long list of threats.

"I can teleport around the world and I'm whining about wanting to be normal." He laughed. Gretchen would mock him. She'd tell him to celebrate his differences and stop moping. She'd tell him to get out of his head and start living life. She'd tell him a long list of reasons why he was being dumb. He couldn't shake the feeling that she had been at the gathering. It wouldn't surprise him to see her lingering among cultists. No, if anything, Gretchen knew how to find trouble, and when she couldn't find it, she'd make it.

The room's temperature steadily increased as the sun beat against the side of the building. It wouldn't be long before he started sweating. He sat up in bed and pulled off his t-shirt and jeans as he moved toward the bathroom. He appreciated the luxurious bedrooms and the electricity they had in the evenings, but by the time morning came around, the water in the tanks tucked away in the damp basement grew lukewarm at best, and showers were more spine-tingling than refreshing.

The water beat against his back and he hissed out loud at the shock frigid temps. A year later and he still wasn't used to it. If he had time, he'd teleport to a working hotel and steal a quick shower tomorrow. He spun about and hissed even louder as the water hit his face and caused his testicles to shrink.

At some point today, he'd man up and talk to Dwayne. Things had become awkward between them and after watching Jasmine's anger last night, he didn't want to alienate his friends. He had fallen asleep thinking of the man and the conversation they had a year ago about doing what comes easy versus what's right. Dwayne had been the first one of the team he looked up to. He hadn't realized how high the pedestal stood until the truth of what Dwayne had done to Jasmine brought it crashing down. Now, even Jasmine had forgiven her torturer; only Conthan held a grudge. He wasn't sure it was even his grudge to hold.

Dwayne had gone out of his way to check on him every night he ventured into the city. It became something he expected. He wanted to be angry with Dwayne, wanted to hate him for being a prick, but there was an endearing quality about having the guy watching out for him. Every time he came home, he knew it wouldn't be long before Dwayne showed, making sure he returned from another crusade.

Something about the man tugged at Conthan. What started out as admiration had turned to anger and now, he almost felt dirty at the thoughts in his mind's periphery. As he dwelled on the man, there was a knock on his door.

"Coming," he yelled from the shower.

He turned off the freezing water and grabbed a towel sitting on the sink. He wrapped it around his waist, realizing the hotel towels were far too short for a chubby man to cover himself. He did his best to protect his modesty as he made his way to the door. He swung it open expecting to see Dwayne. He tried to hide his frown when Jasmine stared back at him.

"We need to talk."

He staggered over his own feet as she pushed her way into the room.

"I can see you're as pleasant as always."

She shut the door and eyed him. It was the first time she had deliberately been in a position leaving them alone together. It took him a moment to notice she was in the red tactical suit given to her by the Paladins. The leather hugged her body, emphasizing her curves. He knew there were bits of metal woven into the thread, making it nearly bulletproof. Where the leather parted, the fabric beneath almost appeared like chainmail, the small fibers linking together to create a modern day warrior costume. The sleeves ended part way down her forearms, leaving plenty of room for gauntlets to touch her skin. It fit too well not be custom, but he wondered

161

if there were other tricks to the suit that complimented her powers.

"I need you to get me to the General."

"Hi, Conthan," he mocked. "How's it going, teammate? I value your work on the…"

She shoved him backward. "It wasn't a question."

He dropped the towel as he pushed her back. Her jaw dropped as she caught herself. He gritted his jaw, waiting for her iron fist to club him across the face. He didn't want to fight her, but he wasn't going to let her walk all over him.

"You know I could beat you into the ground."

"I could tear open your innards with a black hole."

"Which one of us is more likely to follow through with our threat?"

The power in the base of his skull came to life and he waited to see if she would make a move. "If we're going to see whose is bigger, mine's already on the table."

She tried to keep her eyes focused on him, but he caught them flicking south for a moment. He laughed at her, not a fake laugh, but one starting from the pit of his stomach. He reached down and grabbed his towel, ignoring her and going back to putting on his clothes.

"What just happened?"

"You checked out my junk."

"I did not," she said, her face turning a shade darker.

"It's okay," he said. "It happens to the best of us."

"I should have assumed you wouldn't take this seriously."

"I'll do it."

He pulled on a pair of underwear and stood, dragging his jeans up one leg and then the other. He looked at her when she didn't reply. "That's what you wanted me to say, right? You want me to teleport us in so you can kill the General."

"Yeah," she mumbled. "I didn't think you'd agree."

"There's a catch."

She rolled her eyes.

"Don't test me, Jasmine. In this equation, you need me way more than I need you. So you're going to agree, and then we can both walk out of this getting what we wanted." He pulled a t-shirt over his head and met her face to face. "You're going to help me kill the President."

Conthan waited for her to speak, but found she was assessing him. She stepped back, nodding as she leaned against the wall. "For Sarah?"

"For the girl?" he countered.

Before she replied the building shook. The floor moved enough that Conthan had to sit down on his bed. He started to speak but another explosion rocked the building. A roaring sound came closer until Jasmine's eyes lit up. "They found us."

***

"What would you be doing?" asked Dwayne.

Vanessa sat on the bar stool, staring off into the distance. He watched as her forehead wrinkled,

163

giving his question consideration for the first time. It was a game the others played often, but he realized she had never given him an answer. Now, as her dark green eyebrows arched, he couldn't help but laugh.

"Of all the things you can be jealous of, Dwayne, my eyebrows?"

"Did you give yourself a compliment?"

They relaxed at the bar, each in their usual seat they had long ago claimed as their own. The large glass window let in the morning light, illuminating the entire bar, showing off the dust hovering in the air. Dwayne lifted a broken mug to his lips. He often found it funny, these mornings when they acted as if they were normal. He sipped his black coffee, ignoring the fact he could hurl lighting from his body. Something about the normalcy helped remind him why he endured the constant fighting and running.

She smiled. He assumed she was listening to his every thought. Her drawn-back lips formed a sincere expression. Not one of her coy smiles, something she had mastered as the Angel of the Outlands. No, this was entirely Vanessa, the gargoyle of the Nighthawks. He found her features fascinating, how it almost appeared she had animal properties mixed in with her human traits. He understood why she hid for so long, but he was glad his oldest friend was coming into her own.

"I wouldn't," she finally answered.

"You wouldn't?"

"This is my life. I wouldn't have it any other way. I have dear friends, people who rely on me. I

164

have a cause. It might not all be good, but I can't imagine a different life. Where would someone like me go? Can you imagine me a school teacher? Or a working in a bar?"

"And Dav5d?"

"I have Dav5d," she said with a bit of a smirk. Her eyes darted away, avoiding his. He knew she was being demure.

"And what is he to you?"

"How about we discuss your love life?" she said, poking him in the chest.

"What love life? You people are the only ones I see."

"And?"

The ground rumbled and the large bay window shattered, falling to the ground. They shielded their faces as the glass smashed along the bar floor. Dwayne hopped off his stool and grabbed Vanessa under the legs and behind her back, lifting her over the small shards. He set her down as they watched the street.

"What was that?"

"Gas?" she asked.

He shrugged. "You're not hearing anybody?" he asked, pointing to his head.

She shook her head in reply. They turned down the other street to see if there were any signs of movement. Just as Dwayne was about to speak, an explosion boomed only a few blocks away. The side of a building erupted, sending glass and steel into the street below.

"It's the machines," Vanessa said, panicked.

"Nothing?"

"I can't hear anything."

"It's like Troy. They're eradicating Children."

She nodded. He watched the muscles in her body as the anger washed over her. *There are machines coming. This isn't like before, there are no humans.*

Two large mechs rounded the corner and another airship hovered just above the city buildings. They were willing to wage a full-out war to eradicate his team. It had been more than an hour since he had discharged his electricity; the energy building up in his body was more than ready to release.

"What the fuck?" yelled Skits as she charged out of the hotel.

Dav5d pointed down the street. "It seems they've decided our time is up."

"Where's Alyssa?" asked Dwayne.

"She ran next door to the tower. I have no idea what she's doing."

Jasmine and Conthan trotted from the hotel to join them. He noticed she was in her old tactical gear and wondered if she had enough time to change or if something else had been going on when the explosions started. Nearly his entire team stood in awe. They could easily run from the chaos, or they could put up yet another fight and hope they walked away victorious.

"The decision is yours," Vanessa whispered.

He didn't want to put their lives in jeopardy or take any risks that meant one of them might not walk way. He was just about to tell Conthan to open a portal away from their home when an image of Jasmine holding the girl came to mind. Last night when they returned she had taken the girl to be

166

buried in a nearby park. They all stayed awake, waiting for their teammate to do her duty. She needed space, but they wanted her to know they stood by her side.

He turned to see Jasmine waiting for his command. "For Troy," he said.

The airships looked like giant U's with massive turbines hovering in their center. From forty feet above the ground several hatches opened and at least twenty small synthetics slid down steel cables. He knew they were entering a standoff. It wouldn't be long before the fight was literally on top of them.

"If you can bring down one of the airships, its forward momentum would put it between us and the synthetics. It would force them to come in waves."

Dwayne didn't need Dav5d to say it twice. The smartest man alive was standing at his side, something he would have to rely on.

Vanessa, go high, we'll need you as back up to one of the ships. Conthan, send Jasmine…

He stopped the thought as the window of a building seven stories up shattered and a chair went flying. He had no doubt what he was about to see. Alyssa soared through the air, her arms and legs stretched out wide, helping slow her descent.

"Conthan!"

She knew he wouldn't run from a fight. There was something comforting in knowing the mellowest member of their squad was willing to put her life on the line. There was something more satisfying about knowing Conthan would be there to save her from falling to her death. At least, he hoped that was what she was doing.

167

The black void opened in the air, intercepting her.

"Where to?"

"The cockpit. Fuck the President."

***

The chair hit the window and the glass gave way, a million razor-sharp pieces falling several stories below. Alyssa held the crowbar in her right hand and dug the ball of her foot into the industrial carpet. She shoved off, her body moving quickly, forcing her toward the broken window.

Wind.

She held her arms and legs out wide. The wind whipped at her clothes. She soared away from the building, her eyes focused on the ship below. If she landed correctly, she'd be able to roll to a stop before sliding into a turbine and getting herself chopped to death. Amidst the thoughts of being ground into bloody pieces, she had a moment of serenity. She always wondered what it must be like for Vanessa to fly, and as her body sailed downward, she understood the freedom.

A small black portal opened between her and the ship. It was nearly ten feet in the wrong direction. She had no idea what Conthan was attempting, but she trusted they had a plan. Tucking in her left arm and leg, she leaned to one side, coming closer to the portal. She knew if she hit the edges they would slice through her.

Moment of darkness and then she slid along the ground inside the ship. Her muscles reacted, applying a lifetime of training she watched on the computer yesterday before Troy. A single synthetic stood between her and what she assumed was the cockpit. The room was narrow, without much space on either side of her and the synthetic. She assumed they created the room as a hallway to easily kill invaders.

She charged. She didn't have space to jump around the machine, but she was trained in close-quarters combat. It reached out to grab her shoulder. She smacked her hand downward, denting metal as she swung the crowbar. She changed direction and brought the metal up, clubbing the machine in the head. It staggered.

Alyssa jumped up, slamming both of her feet against the machine. She landed on her back and with a kick of her legs, posed in a crouch as the machine fell. The synthetic reached out, its fingers gripping into the metal of the wall. Alyssa flipped the crowbar around and jammed the tip under the machine's chin.

The synthetic grabbed at her shoulder. She screamed as its fingers gripped tighter. For a moment she thought it'd crush her clavicle. Then its grip loosened. The machine didn't move anymore.

"That's how it's done."

She grabbed the crowbar and twisted, breaking several of the hydraulics in the machine's neck. She didn't dare risk the synthetic doing something when she wasn't paying attention. Between her and the cockpit stood a thick metal door. She smashed the keypad to the side until wires poured out of the wall. She held the crowbar between her legs as she started pulling at the wires.

"Dav5d, this is so much more your area."

The green wire. Tie it to the black and the blue to the yellow. The surge should unlock the door.

For a moment she saw through Vanessa's eyes as the telepath projected Dav5d's thoughts. The woman climbed up the side of a building. They stayed to protect their home. Alyssa began spinning wires together, a sense of pride washing over her. They weren't going down without a fight.

A hiss preceded the door popping open. She grabbed the crowbar, ready for more synthetics. The cockpit appeared vacant. Lights blinked and levers moved without hands guiding them. She had assumed there'd be a pilot she could beat, but whoever controlled this ship was hundreds of miles away. She didn't have time to learn how to fly, nor to figure out how to work the controls. Even Dav5d sending her commands wouldn't help them fast enough.

She shoved the crowbar into the command station and pried it up, exposing the wires below. She reached in and pulled, tearing them from their casings. Sparks erupted from the console. She repeated the process with every computerized piece of equipment she could find. Sparks scattered in the cockpit and before the sprinklers released their fire retardant foam, she crammed the crowbar into the ceiling.

Then something exploded. There was beeping and the ship jerked. She was worried they had a remote cockpit or some artificial intelligence had planned for her meddling. The ship leaned to the side as its nose pointed downward. She fell to the floor as it bumped into a second airship. She could only hope it managed to take out both of them.

"I need an evacuation, Conthan." *Please, I hope Vanessa is listening.*

A black portal opened in the floor. She scrambled to her feet and fell through into the darkness.

***

The ship tilted forward. Jasmine had no doubt it'd come down and by the looks of it, might very well land on the large mechs approaching them. She spun about, more concerned with the dozen synthetics racing toward them from the other direction. She hadn't seen this model before. They moved along the pavement like dogs, their bodies human, but almost appearing animalistic in their behavior.

Her skin morphed, the ripple starting at her bracers and flowing through her body. She screamed out loud as the transformation took place. She didn't have any reason to hide the pain. Her scream turned to a roar, a battle cry signaling her willingness to fight.

"For Troy," she yelled.

She ran. She lurched as her muscles adapted to the new weight. She winced as the pain moved through her limbs. The first synthetic approached. It jumped onto a car and lunged at her. The robot looked more like a feral cat than a synthetic. She slammed her fist into its face, spinning it around in midair. Another jumped on her. The moment it made contact, the body contorted until it looked similar to a standard synthetic.

She pulled at its arm, and the sound of bending metal told her they weren't much stronger than their predecessor. Her muscles strained for a moment longer. A wave of relief coursed through her body. Now, her muscles thickened. The arm ripped free and she grabbed onto the head, pulling back until it tore away from its body.

Another synthetic cat jumped at her. Before it could tackle her to the ground, a flare of blue light sliced through its torso, separating it into two pieces.

"Just as dumb as they were before."

Jasmine fell to the pavement as the first synthetic she encountered pounced on her back. She tried to stand but the machine clutched her wrists, putting her in a submission pose. Two feet landed in front of her and she heard the loud thunk of metal smashing into metal. The synthetic was off her and she scrambled to her feet. The portal in the air vanished and Alyssa rested the crowbar on her shoulder.

"You've been a busy girl," Jasmine remarked.

"You know, it's what I do."

A bolt of lightning flashed past them, searing into another synthetic. The machine tried to dodge, but the electricity followed the metal conduit. She couldn't help but be impressed with Dwayne; his abilities were astounding. At some point, when they weren't fighting for their lives, she'd have to ask him if he thought he'd ever control his abilities.

Keep your head in the game.

Jasmine turned to the rooftop where Vanessa grappled with a synthetic. She hurled the machine off the roof. Skits shoved her hand into its center, the blue fire melting its exterior. Jasmine felt the rumble as the airship hit the ground. Instead of scraping along the pavement, it drove nose-first, creating a crater.

"Holy shit."

The two large mechs vanished under the weight of the ship. The bar was destroyed as the ship's momentum sent up the ground in a ripple. Jasmine watched as Vanessa's expression turned to horror. She didn't need to be a telepath to know the exploding windows of Vanessa's home tore at her heart. The walls collapsed and the roof caved in, leaving the building in rubble. The ground under her feet shook and she had to steady herself to keep from falling.

"What now?" she yelled to Dwayne.

The synthetics were already climbing over the wreckage, passing through flames. Before Dwayne could answer the question, another airship appeared. She swore. Whoever initiated this attack wanted to make sure they didn't walk out alive. There were at least twenty synthetics coming from one direction and another twenty from the other.

"We can't win."

"I know," he said.

"Yes, we can," Conthan said.

His eyes were dark orbs, a liquid black that gave away the level of power he attempted to summon. He lost himself to his abilities, which meant he'd be far more lethal than normal. This was the Conthan she liked, the wild man, the dangerous one.

"Take 'em down," she whispered.

***

It wasn't only the spot at the base of his skull calling out to him; every cell in his body worked in overdrive. The euphoria left him feeling as if he was flying. The imaginary well in the pit of his stomach housing his powers overflowed and all he had to do was let it take control.

The expression on Jasmine's face gave away the state of his eyes, the blackness consuming them. He concentrated on opening a portal. In the middle of the turbine keeping the airship aloft, gear shafts worked in conjunction to create enough torque to hold up the vessel. The portal opened in the middle, swallowing huge pieces of metal, causing gears to grind.

Chunks of the craft fell into the void and his body reacted, determined to expel the materials. He opened another portal in the third airship, directly in the path of the massive spinning propeller. The edges of the black hole sliced through the blades, tearing the propeller to pieces. Material from one portal flew to the other and vice versa, destroying both airships.

"Holy shit," Dwayne muttered.

Conthan's heart skipped beats as the blades slammed into the portal. He never used his abilities to cut through a material, but he knew from practice with Dav5d that the edges were lethal. A person could slit themselves open on them if they weren't careful. He had scars on his arms to prove it.

"You're truly frightening," Dwayne said.

Conthan couldn't respond as the ships came crashing down. Explosions launched debris into the air, burning bright enough to be visible in daylight. Smoke plumed from the wreckage and synthetics attempted to force their way out of the crashing ships. He assumed the machines on the inside were still alive. There was no way to stop them if they got free.

A hissing sound came out of nowhere. Conthan turned just in time to see a missile flying at the three of them. The portal opened without a thought. The exit appeared next to the twelve-foot-tall mech working its way toward them. The explosion sent the machine to the ground, one of its legs completely removed from its body. Conthan shut the portals and turned to the others.

"I don't know how many more times I can teleport."

"What do you mean?" asked Jasmine.

"He's our exit strategy. We have to make a decision to stay and fight or to run," Dwayne said.

Conthan gasped as Vanessa swooped down and snatched one of the synthetics out of the air. She redirected its momentum straight down. With a flap of her wings, she stopped moving forward and fell onto of the synthetic. Her feet landed on its shoulders, sending it to the ground. She reached down, grabbed the skull, and tore it free.

"There are more coming," she yelled to them.

Dav5d stepped out of a doorway where he hid

while the active powers fought. He pointed across the street. "We can go underground. There are limited access points and they can't track us using satellites."

The subway entrance. Everybody hurry.

***

Vanessa stood point while Dwayne ushered the others into the stairwell leading into the subway. She accepted his plan, to retreat underground where the larger mechs couldn't follow and the airships would have difficulty detecting them. She wasn't fearful, this escape had been planned years ago for just this reason. They'd be gone and out of sight before the machines had any chance to stop them.

Her home was lost, the bar nothing more than a pile of rubble. There was a moment where she felt empty, unsure of what the next stage might bring. She was filled with emotion, possibly projections of her teammates. She wasn't an empath, but it was hard to push away so many emotions bombarding her thoughts.

She was about to turn and run toward the stairs when a lone woman caught her eye. Only a few feet away, a woman stood idly watching her. She knew whoever owned the image was nowhere nearby and that it must be some form of telepathy. Did this woman have anything to do with the attacks? Perhaps she was another telepath?

Who are you? the woman asked.

Vanessa didn't quite understand what unfolded in front of her. The woman spoke, but her words

176

were being cast mentally. She didn't discount an entirely new type of mentalist; it would only be fitting.

Vanessa blinked as a flash of a woman sitting in a small hotel room hit her. Sitting across from the woman was a burly man, both of them wearing clothes far too old to be a recent memory. Vanessa's eyes went wide, her jaw opening slightly from disbelief.

"Eleanor?" she asked aloud.

How do you know me?

Vanessa didn't know what she could and couldn't say. If she told her about the letters, would that mean she'd make them? By talking to a projection from the past, could she alter the future? She wished Dav5d saw this. He'd have already figured out the thousand ways every word they exchanged was altered the future.

"You do something that changes the world, Eleanor Valentine."

The woman seemed to balk at the mention of her name. Neither of them flinched as an explosion erupted from the fallen airship. The ghost tried to take in the scene, clearly uncertain of what she was seeing.

Did I do this?

"You prevented this from being so much worse."

I can do better.

"Vanessa!" Dav5d yelled from the stairs.

"Thank you for saving me, Eleanor."

The woman's ghostly eyes started to see through her. She knew it was only for a moment, but somehow, a woman from many decades ago was seeing their future. Vanessa assumed there was something about two mentalists crossing paths that made the encounter possible. She felt a sense of relief, finally able to thank the woman who rescued her from being killed as a child.

As she jogged down the stairs, she had to wonder—if the woman could do better, what would that change about now? Was this the better? Had the change already happened? Or was there another wave of interventions about to happen courtesy of Eleanor? When they had time, she would tell the others, and then it would be up to Dav5d to make sense of it.

For now, amidst the explosions and killing machines stalking her, she felt a moment of peace. She only hoped she survived long enough to enjoy it.

Chapter 11

1993

Mark looked up from his book, carefully wedging his bookmark into place before setting it on the stand next to his recliner. Of all the furniture he had in his small home away from home, the recliner was his prized possession. When he told Elizabeth how long he would be away, she had asked if he wanted anything to remind him of home. Other than some essential photos of his family and a series of books to occupy his downtime, the recliner had been the most important. It was the one comfort he needed to feel at ease in the evenings. Elizabeth had laughed as he dragged the chair into the moving van.

Without notice, the lights in his suite flashed, leaving him in the dark. It happened before. The first time, a hacker turned activist invaded their computer systems and rendered the electrical grid inoperable for days. The second time, a storm hit the center and fried their generators, plunging them into darkness. The emergency lights would kick on in a few seconds, bathing his living quarters in a dim red light.

He waited, counting out the seconds in his head. One one thousand. Two one thousand. It normally didn't take this long for the backup systems to kick in. Three one thousand. One of the research labs in the upper levels had wounded soldiers on life support. He hoped their power responded quicker than his. Four one thousand.

The red lights flickered to life, nearly blinding him. The bulb clicked to life, bathing his living quarters in a dark red light. It reminded him of the darkroom in his college photography class. It had been under the safety lights that he first caught a glimpse of Elizabeth. From then on he made sure to arrive early enough to watch her walk in the door and he'd stay until she left. As she fumbled with film in a pitch black room, he'd help her put it on the reel. Their first kiss happened in the darkroom. Long before that, he fell in love with a woman whose name he barely knew underneath those red lights.

"Such sweet memories."

Mark's muscles tensed at the whisper from over his shoulder. The voice had a slight hiss to it, as if the person dragged out the letters with their tongue. He wanted to turn around but his feet refused to cooperate. He tried to throw his hand backward, but found the same feeling as in his feet made his arms refuse to move. He turned his head slightly, but nowhere could he see a person in the room with him.

"There is only us, Mark," said the soft voice. The warm heat of someone's breath pushed along the skin behind his ear. The closeness made the pit of his stomach clench. The heat radiating from their mouth as they breathed on his neck violated his personal space. There was something oddly sexual about a person breaching his personal bubble.

"Who are you?"

"Who are we, Mark?"

"Answer the damned question."

"Fear, Mark," the voice said, accentuating the end of the phrase. "I can see you, Mark, what scares you most."

Before he could think of his biggest fear, the room shifted from his suite to a massive field. Unlike the dark room he had been immobilized in, here he breathed the clean air and felt the sun kissing his skin. The shift of location gave him a moment of clarity to figure out what was happening.

"I'm dreaming."

"Or is it a nightmare?" asked the voice.

It lost its scary edge, drowned out by the wind-rustled grass. He reached out and touched some of the tallest weeds, grazing them with his fingertips. There was a second when he wanted to stay in that moment, free of the fluorescent lights and lab coats. The carefree sensation running through his body had him elated to the point where he contemplated running through the field.

A gray object hidden amongst the overgrown weeds gave him pause, looking somewhat out of place in this beautiful scene. He wasn't sure why, but his pulse raced and he needed to be standing at the stone markers. He pushed his way through the grass, moving recklessly, tearing at the weeds as he moved. He bumped into the two large objects and began to tear away at the vines threatening to squeeze the stones into pebbles.

"No," he gasped.

He fell backward and pushed away from the monument. His hands sunk into the dirt, the cold soil wrapping itself around his fingers. He kept saying it over and over again, as if his denial changed the reality in front of him.

"Here lies Elizabeth Davis," whispered a distant voice.

"No!" he screamed.

"Yes," said the voice, its tone almost pleased with Mark's disbelief.

Mark stared at the carved letters spelling his wife's name. No date, nor cause of death, just her name chiseled out of granite. Horror gripped his heart as his head turned slightly to look at the smaller stone. Vines covered the name underneath, but he didn't need to claw at the vegetation to know whose it was.

His eyes watered as he tried to process the information. He didn't remember what happened, or what had taken his family away. He wailed uncontrollably and his nose ran as he filtered through his lifetime of memories. Just as he was about to start cursing God, a dark figure stepped up behind the tombstones. Through tear-filled eyes he tried to make out the person standing behind his wife's grave.

"Hello?"

Mark wiped his eyes as the person stepped through the stones. The figure loomed over his broken body, blocking out the sun. It dawned on him: nobody was really there. Its body consisted of smoke and looked as if a smoldering fire filled the air with black soot.

"I am very much here, Mark."

Between blinks the figure went from smoky apparition to his chief of security. "Goddard? Is that you?"

The man reached out and touched Mark's face, caressing his cheek far more intimately than their relationship allowed. Mark pulled away, never wanting the man to touch him, let alone make a sympathetic gesture. Whoever it was standing above him, it wasn't the chief of security he had grown to loathe over the past year No, this was somebody else entirely.

He blinked. Ariel stood above him. She gave a slight giggle. He recognized her voice, but there was something uncomfortably wrong about what was happening. *Hadn't she been somebody else just a moment again?* he thought. It seemed he couldn't remember what was happening in the dream.

"A dream," he whispered.

Ivan leaned in, grabbing both sides of Mark's face, black tendrils snaking their way along his skin. As Mark gasped, wisps of smoke threatened to coat his lungs. He pulled backward, kicking with his legs, trying to put as much distance as possible between him and the researcher. He flipped over and got his feet under him, trying to scurry away.

"You cannot run. I am everywhere."

Mark's eyes opened.

He found himself staring at the ceiling of his bedroom. The alarm clock next to his head read 2:47 am. They had released him earlier in the evening with strict orders to rest. Bed rest, he thought, a doctor's way of saying he had no idea what was wrong. They had the leading experts in cybernetics, parapsychology, and medicine at their disposal and a simple diagnosis reminded Mark they were far away from uncovering the source of mentalists' abilities.

The voice rang in his head. It was if an echo of the owner continued whispering just beyond his hearing. He shivered at the thought of the two solitary stones in the field. The many-faced man hadn't scared him, but the thought of his wife and child dying, that terrified him. As soon as it was a reasonable hour he'd call. He would be going home in two weeks and no emergency here would keep him away from his family.

He rubbed his eyes, pushing away the crusty bits. Other than his breathing, the room remained silent, one of the few good things about being surrounded by this much concrete. Even if the robotics lab had another explosion, he'd be able to sleep. The downside was waking up to dingy fluorescent lighting and never being sure the hour of the day. Eventually he'd paint a window on his wall so he could at least pretend he wasn't in a cement jail.

He tossed back the covers on the bed and sat upright. He pulled the gauze from his nostrils and inhaled deeply. As he pushed the light on his nightstand, the room shone a bright orange. He examined the pieces of rolled-up gauze and found only a small bit of blood on the ends. At least he didn't have to stay in medical overnight. The last thing he wanted was to sleep in a hospital bed.

Mark stretched his arms and stood, working his way to the bathroom. He flipped on the light and flinched at the brightness. He lifted up the toilet seat and relieved his bladder. He flushed and started to turn to the sink, but eyed the open seat. He flipped it down. Every time he went home, Elizabeth yelled at him through the closed door that she had nearly plunged into the freezing depths of toilet water. Living alone for so long brought out his bad bachelor habits.

He stared at his naked self in the mirror. He wasn't repulsed by what he saw, but Elizabeth was going to have a talk with him about his health. He had gained too much weight since he got the job and his stress eating was out of control. He gave a slight flex in the mirror. Maybe when he returned to the center, he'd spend the next three months at the gym and when she saw him next, he'd be ripped. He was sure one of the security guards would be more than willing to work out with him. She'd swoon over his giant biceps.

He chuckled. She'd throw the back of her hand to her forehead and fall back on the couch. She had no problem poking fun at him. He let out a sigh.

"I miss you, Lizzy-bee."

He grabbed his robe and covered up, tying the plush belt around his waist. He grabbed the remote to the TV and flipped it on. He reached for the cassette sitting on his side table and pushed it into the VCR. He plopped down on the recliner and leaned forward, resting his elbows on his knees. The tech who dropped it off had been kind enough to only record a few minutes near when he passed out. His TV was large enough that he could clearly see the two different scenes. On the left, the room with Ariel and Ivan, and in the other, him. The tech lined up the time stamps on both videos so he could see what happened as it unfolded.

It felt weird watching himself start to stagger. It was as if he was having an out of body experience after the fact. Ivan guided Ariel on her virtual walk down the halls of the center. Neither of them seemed to budge for the duration of the video. He watched until Ivan collapsed on the floor without any warning. Mark clicked the remote and rewound the video.

He leaned in closer to the television and took note of Ivan's shaking hands. It didn't seem like much, but they were shivering just enough to be noticeable. It was difficult due to the angle, but it appeared as if they weren't even touching Ariel. Mark sat back in the chair and pondered what it meant. They needed to stop testing and start developing theories of what might have happened.

The video played a minute beyond his collapse. Mark jumped at a loud sound from the television, the door busting inward. Goddard held up his gun, pointing it directly at Ariel's head. The security guard pressed the barrel against her temple, yelling at her to stop what she was doing.

They all waited. Ariel pivoted her body toward

the man. Mark thought he saw a smile flash on her face. Her voice was quiet, barely audible on the television set. "I did it."

She collapsed to the floor. Goddard put away his weapon and pulled out a small ceramic gun and pulled the trigger, sending a small dart into the girl. The tranquilizing effect caused her body to relax, shoulders slumping. Mark tried not to grit his teeth as he watched the man abuse the girl with his Taser.

He hit the pause button and stared at Goddard on the screen. His concern for the young girl competed with the anger he felt for the guard. The man was becoming something of a problem, constantly belittling the research they were doing, constantly trying to undermine his authority by crying to the president. Mark sneered as he thought of how he would show the man a lesson.

A knock at the door jolted him enough to see his hands were balled into tight fists. His jaw was clenched and his heart thumped against his ribcage. He was a difficult man to make angry, but it seemed Goddard was more than capable.

As he thought of the man's name, he had a flash of him standing on the other side of his door. He only hoped his imagination was right. Mark tried to put away his anger, but he was more than willing to give Goddard a piece of his mind. He didn't condone violence, but there was a time when it would be necessary.

He approached the door and paused for a moment, his hand nearly resting on the handle. If it was Goddard, what would he say? What would he do? The little voice of reason in the back of his head laughed; what could he possibly do to the brute of a man?

He pulled the door open and there stood the security guard. The man's bulky form stretched his uniform from spending too much time in the gym. His neck was nearly as thick as his head and the black turtleneck did little to hide the muscles in his biceps. Mark's blood started to boil with each observation, noting the more he admired the man's physique, the more he hated him.

"We need to talk about this…"

Mark's fist went straight for the man's chiseled jaw. *He'll block,* thought Mark.

Goddard stopped the fist, blocking with his forearm, but he couldn't stop the foot snapping outward, kicking him in the groin. Goddard fell backward, the air rushing out of his lungs so fast he spit.

Make sure he can't fight back.

Mark brought up his knee as the man buckled over, cracking him in the face. Blood erupted across Mark's thigh. As Goddard fell backward, Mark stepped closer, faster than anybody could have imagined a guy his size capable of. He snatched the gun from Goddard's holster and took a step back as Goddard spat blood onto the floor.

"The president is going to…"

"Shut the fuck up, Goddard." Mark flipped the safety on the gun and pointed it at the man's head. "The president is going to hear about this, because I'm going say that her militant lackey has been found insubordinate. Depending on the next words out of your mouth, she might also hear about you attempting to kill our asset and how it could be seen as an act of treason. Do you understand me?"

Goddard licked his lips and spat more blood. He ignored the blood rushing out of his nose. He stared at Mark, his eyes darting back and forth over him, attempting to assess the situation. Mark stiffened as he held out the gun. "All it takes is a pull of the trigger and every problem I have goes away."

Mark held onto the anger in the pit of his stomach. He recalled the numerous times the man used that condescending tone, trying to supersede him at the center. Mark had been unaware of the rage he locked away in the darkest corner of his mind. There was a bit of him that was elated, almost euphoric at the sensation radiating from his body.

"Do you understand me?" he repeated.

Goddard nodded. "Yes."

"That's what I wanted to hear."

Chapter 12

2033

"We should have stayed," Jasmine said. She hopped down off the platform onto the tracks below. Boston's Red Line, part of the busy network of subway tunnels that connected downtown, was at least thirty feet underground. It remained their contingency plan since meeting the rest of the group, but she had never taken the time to explore the miles of winding tunnels.

Frozen escalators brought them down to the first sub-level, and a small tunnel filled with broken tiles lead them to another escalator. Darkness hid the disgusting floors. The air smelled odd, and she assumed this was the first time a living person walked here in years. Cobwebs created false walls, looking more and more like something out of a horror movie.

Bronze sculptures of famous Bostonians lined the landing where patrons once waited for subway cars. They emerged from the shadows like penny-colored ghosts. Dwayne's body steadily produced light and Skits's hand cast an eerie blue light. Jasmine wondered how many people died here, trying to hide during the nuclear fallout. What had once been the easiest mode of transportation about the city had turned into a catacomb.

"They weren't going to stop," Dwayne said firmly. "I'd rather run than be dead."

She gritted her teeth, she wasn't done fighting. She wanted to tear each of the machines limb from limb and stare into their cameras to make sure their operators knew her face. The rage in her eyes would terrify them and when she threatened to come for them next, they'd be petrified. She wouldn't be satisfied until Genesis Division was destroyed from the inside out.

Jasmine held out her hand to Alyssa, helping the smaller woman down from the platform. She stumbled and Jasmine caught her from falling.

"Well, good to know I'm a klutz again."

The girl's abilities were limited; the more time passed, the more her muscles forgot. The more she forced them to learn, the shorter the time period she retained her borrowed skills. It wouldn't be long before she could recharge and be a fighting machine, but in this moment, she was nothing more than a girl.

"It's about a mile before the next stop. There's a pretty big station, we'll be able to find a way out without alerting the machines," Dwayne said.

"If they're not waiting for us," Alyssa said.

Dwayne stopped walking, letting the others continue further down the tracks. Jasmine watched as he planted his feet on the rails and braced himself. The light around his body dimmed for a moment and he shoved his hands up into the air. The flash was enough to hurt the eyes. She shielded hers with her hands at another flash from his palms. The crack of the lightning pulverized the roof until dirt started to rain down, filling the tunnel behind them. Several more cracks and the earth had nearly blocked off the tunnel.

"Might as well make sure they don't follow."

The man's glow dimmed considerably. For all the frightening power he wielded, the limitations were obvious. She noted each of them had similar limitations. Even her iron hide had to revert back. She didn't want to risk finding more synthetics with her powers incapable of working. She could maintain them for long periods of time, but even she, the veteran, had drawbacks. Fighting machines made Vanessa useless, and Dav5d had been quiet for most of the descent into the subway. Even Conthan kept his sarcasm to himself.

"You were right," she mumbled to Dwayne as he passed by.

"I know," he said. He was an ass, but at least he was an ass looking out for their best interests. If it had been left to her, they would have fought until depleted, and one by one they would have died. She sometimes questioned why she followed the man instead of being in charge. These moments reminded her why.

"Ass."

"I know."

NIGHT SHADOWS

***

The distant tingle at the base of his spine faded until it turned to a dull ache. His powers had taken over, used his body as a vessel all without his consent. Pumping through his body, a sense of pride at the destruction he caused. He had taken down two airships, something the others wouldn't have been able to accomplish. He walked a bit taller as he tried to think of the dollar amount attached to the damage he caused.

The downside in abusing his powers: they ignored his demands now, refusing to give them an escape route. In the meantime, he was nothing more than a liability. He took comfort knowing Alyssa shared a similar position, and even Vanessa couldn't rely on her telepathy. They were a deadly fighting force, for several minutes, and then when they ran out of juice, they were as human as the people hunting them down.

A year ago he sat in a warehouse with friends talking about art. YiYi was in the midst of a revolutionary breakthrough involving motor oil and chalk drawings. He and Gretchen must have given her less than stellar facial expressions and she went into a spiral of doubt. Her screaming about the project she loved was almost dramatic enough to be a performance piece on its own. Eventually Trish called for shots and they'd gathered around the bonfire and toasted to their failures. These artists, the people he chose to surround himself with, they were his family when he needed one.

Now, he couldn't remember the last time he

picked up a pencil and drew anything. His passion had been traded for training and his skills as a painter now fell by the wayside. They had been the family who held him up whenever he felt doubt starting to tear away at his self-esteem. Other than the brutish Rocks, the rest of them were exactly what you'd imagine for a group of artists. They wouldn't fit in with his current companions.

At first being a Child of Nostradamus had been thrilling, then grueling, but now, now he was concerned that running for his life barely stirred a response. His closest friends were a gargoyle and a human lightbulb. He had to stop and wonder if any of them considered themselves friends. Or were they compatriots by necessity? He knew Jasmine only stuck around out of a mutual need, which he respected, but it kept her from ever being anything more than a super-powered officemate.

He stole a glance of Dwayne and his perpetual stoic visage. The man wore jeans, but left his upper body exposed. He rarely wore a shirt, citing he didn't like the burning fabric scorching his skin. Conthan wondered if the human lightning bolt was able to produce electricity from any point on his body, or if it was easier from his hands. He had a lot of questions, but for months he barely spoken two words to the man not related to team responsibilities.

Perhaps it was coming down off a high from his powers, but the pit of his stomach housed a cage of butterflies laced with regret. He shared a dozen picturesque sunrises with the man, each one more serene than the last. However, as Dwayne tried to maintain a line of communication, Conthan had been a dick and shot him down. In the last year, wrapped up in his sanctimonious bullshit, he missed the one man trying to connect with him.

Conthan silently admitted to being an asshole.

He thought of Dwayne the night before, waiting for him on the balcony of the church. It had become a game for them to meet there. They'd exchange a few tense words and Dwayne would leave. The man didn't push himself onto Conthan; he just left the doors open for discussion if the kid needed it. Conthan hated to admit it, but he'd be lying if he said he didn't appreciate the watchful eye.

He held his breath as he reached out and touched Dwayne's hand. A short jolt snapped between them. Neither acknowledged the gesture until Dwayne gave Conthan's hand a slight squeeze. Conthan returned the gesture and pulled his hand back, a crack of lightning jumping between them. He didn't think the gesture quite summed up his emotions. Even the momentary contact calmed his worry. He only hoped it did the same for Dwayne.

***

"What are you thinking?" Vanessa asked.

Dav5d reached out in the darkness and rested his hand on her shoulder. His thoughts were a blur, moving too fast for her to comprehend. All of the others were in their heads, having a dialogue with themselves, and for the first time, she felt guilty listening to their thoughts.

"Who were you talking to?"

She didn't know if it was the time to share or if she should wait until they reached safety. She decided if there was a chance any of them might not make it out alive, they deserved to know. "I spoke to Eleanor."

"The dead psychic?" asked Skits.

Skits's hands cast an eerie blue light in the narrow tunnel. They hadn't been walking for long, but the sounds above them had already vanished. Dwayne would stop every now and then to check the rear of the group while his sister pushed forward. At the mention of Eleanor, both her hands flared brighter for a split second, almost as if the light responded to her excitement.

"Yes."

"She's been dead for forty years," she responded.

"I know."

"This is going to require a bit more explanation," Skits said as she continued walking down the tracks.

"I'm not sure," Vanessa said honestly. "How could I see a woman dead for four decades?—and even more so, I believe it was a much younger her."

She didn't need to see Dav5d to know his eyes were growing distant as he processed the information. "A younger version of Eleanor comes to the future. She witnesses Vanessa in the middle of a firefight. Vanessa may be able to see her because of her telepathy. There are too many uncertainties to know for sure."

"I get worried when Dav5d says he doesn't know something," Alyssa confessed.

"If we look at time as a non-linear system, it is

possible that her coming to the future will indeed change the past. However, if you apply the grandfather paradox, by her coming to the future, she would have that knowledge in the past and everything remains on its current course. But there is also a possibility that by affecting the future, she has created an alternate timeline from that fixed point in which the future diverged with new rules."

"What the hell?" Skits asked.

"There is no science to support one or the other. There is also no science to support a precog being able to see the future, let alone affect it through changing major events. To know this, I would need to know every future Eleanor witnessed and what she did to affect change. With that knowledge, I could indeed begin predicting the probabilities she witnessed with her powers."

Vanessa didn't attempt to understand the majority of his ramblings. Ultimately, she knew she saw a dead woman and somehow, the woman navigated her way decades into the future to make contact. She had wondered what questions she might ask the woman and her heart felt heavy with the long list of things she wanted to know. At the end of it all, she said her thanks, and even if Eleanor didn't know what it meant in that moment, she hoped someday it would make sense.

"We take it as a sign."

"A sign?" asked Dav5d.

"I can't see the future, and we don't know enough of Eleanor's past. So we take it as we can. We saw our founder in a time of need."

"We will persevere," Conthan said.

"We will," she echoed.

Skits's hands flared brighter as the tunnel widened. They reached the junction where four different subway lines intersected in one grand maze. Vanessa let her wings expand outward, stretching them for the first time since they entered the tunnels. She didn't like closed in spaces. Thankfully, she wasn't claustrophobic, but the idea of not being able to utilize her additional limbs made her antsy.

Inside the massive room, she located a giant metal box with wires exiting in every direction. She pushed a button and flipped a switch and a motor roared to life. Skits and Dwayne let their glows fade into nothingness, casting the room in pitch black. The roar seemed louder in the dark, consuming their senses for the moment.

Light. Lights illuminated the barren corridor. They were dim and far too few, but it was enough after being in the dark for so long. The generator forced lightbulbs several years old to come to life. Several exploded in a fury of tiny sparks and raining glass. The rest cast enough of a glow that the station almost seemed inhabitable.

The tunnel they were in led to a subway platform on both sides. Stairs led upward to the next level where three more lines met. To move any further in any direction they'd have to move toward the surface. Thanks to the confusion of the Boston subway system, they'd be able to lose the military without problem.

"If we take the Orange Line one stop north, we can take the Blue Line and regroup at the airport."

198

She agreed with Dav5d, they needed a place to rest, recharge and gather their resources. The airport had enough underground areas they'd be able to avoid any detection until they were ready. Hopefully by then, the pursuit would be called off and they'd be considered a lost cause.

She reached the ledge and jumped straight up. With a single flap of her wings, her foot cleared the lip of the platform. She reached down, took Alyssa with one hand and Skits with the other, and pulled them up. She pointed to the stairwell leading toward the streets. In a few minutes they cleared the stairs and were standing in a massive junction where several lines of the subway connected.

There were at least a dozen tunnels, each heading in slightly different directions. The platform were flush with the tracks and commuters were able to run back and forth across the station. She had a faint image in her head of the thousands of people rushing from one spot to the next in an effort to get to their jobs. Each abandoned subway car had carried thousands of passengers a day, sending them deeper into the city as they fought for survival. Reality set in as she realized nearly every face she saw in the echoes was dead, eradicated by a nuclear explosion.

She felt the concussive force before she heard it. An explosion strong enough it sent her flying backward into a turnstile, breaking the archaic machine. Dust filled the air and a new light source reached the dismal darkness they hid in. Metal beams collapsed into the subway station and rock fell from the ceiling. The scraping of metal on pavement filled the air. Her mouth went dry as she reached a new tier of panic.

"Machines," she screamed.

Chapter 13

2033

"You can stop lurking, Lily."

"Jacob, you c-can—" her voice stuttered "—sense me now?"

He turned from the computer screens hovering above the table to the woman in white standing in the doorway. Beneath tightly bound lace dress, he could spot her black bra and panties, enough sex woven into the fabric that he couldn't ignore it. There had been a time when she was forced to utilize her feminine charms to survive. He wished he could read her thoughts now; he wanted to know if she was attempting to survive with him.

"No," he said returning to his screens. "At least not yet."

Her heels made a clacking noise each time she stepped further into the room. Her steps were deliberate and careful. He had no doubt now, she was attempting uncover her position in Jacob's new order. The Society said there must always be four, and with one dead, did it mean they would replace Salvador or was the group dissolving? He wouldn't tell her just yet, but planned on getting rid of those who sided against him.

"Is your cleansing underway?"

"You think it's a poor use of Genesis Division's resources?"

Her laugh was condescending out of habit, as if she practiced it while looking down on her peers. He knew not to take it personally, but his slight growl sobered her. She shook her head promptly.

"These people killed the Warden," she said as if that explained it all. He didn't blink as she took a seat and crossed her legs, accentuating her sexuality. "If they are capable of killing a man who not only eluded us, but managed to take control of the most secure facility in America, I believe they deserve our attention."

The voice in the back of his head quieted, satiated by her explanation. It was what she didn't say that spoke volumes more. "You don't like the competition, do you?"

She waved him off with her hand. "Rivalry? Does it look like I have a rival? They're dangerous because they're unknown. If they want to meet me, I will gladly snap their necks myself." Dark blue eyes met his gaze, the jab at him stealing her abilities hanging in the air.

Explosions on his computer screen grabbed his attention. For now, it seemed Lily would continue surviving. As for the Children his company hunted, that was another story entirely.

Chapter 14

1993

"Goddard, you look absolutely a wreck."

Mark kept his composure at the president's assessment of the security guard. Goddard nodded, agreeing with her, keeping his eyes on the screen and avoiding Mark. "Things got a bit heated in the gym."

The television's pixelated screen projecting the image of the President of the United States of America did nothing to hide her suspicious glance. She didn't believe him and she let her slight eye roll give it away. She might be a thousand miles away, but the camera recording the meeting room was not hiding their tells. Mark wanted to punch the man again, just to make sure Goddard maintained a level of fear about him.

"Gentlemen, I have a country to run. Do you have anything new to tell me or am I just going to hear about you wasting taxpayer money?"

"The   cybernetics   division   has   begun

implementing the prosthetics you approved. The soldiers are not just able to function again, they'll be returning to active duty."

"Is that all you have for me?"

"We will be moving forward with the second phase of the cybernetics program. We have secured several volunteers who are willing to undergo installation of hardware directly into their brains. If it is successful, we will be able to speed up their cognitive functions, accessing their hearing and even visual abilities in due time."

"It sounds promising, Mr. Davis, but you know I'm only half-heartedly invested in your tinkering with soldiers' brains. What about the real reason for this call?"

"Ariel has been an outstanding subject, Madame President. She's been extremely cooperative with Dr. Volkov."

The president leaned in closer to her camera. She pointed at Mark with a scowl. "I do not care about her good behavior, Mr. Davis. She's not your friend, she's our test subject. What have you learned from her?"

Mark didn't appreciate the woman's dehumanization of Ariel. He understood he was too close to her, that he saw her as a daughter. Despite his fondness for the girl, he knew she was also a means to an end. However, he tried to always remind her she was a person and that her humanity remained essential to her survival.

Ivan cleared his throat. "Her abilities are immense, Madame President. She has shown amazing potential; these powers allow her to influence matter from a greater distance than we originally imagined. I understand with your..." He paused, eyes seeming to search for the right phrase "...particular connection with mentalists, you have no fondness for their kind. However, I think there is potential beyond simple study, research, and containment."

"At least one of you is working," she scolded Mark. "What are you hinting at, Dr. Volkov?"

"They have weaponizing potential."

Mark couldn't help but notice the shock on the woman's face. It couldn't have been much different from his own. Mark didn't care for Ivan's treatment of Ariel, or his pursuit of this pure science, but up to this point, it had only been for the sake of research. This was the first time he was hearing the man discuss the potential for weaponizing them.

"Explain."

Ivan cleared his throat again. "If Ariel was to be placed in a military unit, her ability to support them would be unparalleled. She would be able to trip bombs, defuse weapons, or even subdue enemies before the platoon arrived. If that isn't enough—I'm speaking hypothetically at the moment—what if we had the ability to put her abilities in your elite soldiers?"

The president paused at the thought, tapping her fingers against her desk. Her nails rapped loudly against the wood. She finally leaned forward, staring directly into the camera. "And how would this be different from that vile woman Eleanor attempting to put a bullet in my head?"

Mark ignored the dig at the woman. He was

amazed at how fast his concept for the center was being bastardized and turned into a military training ground. "I would advise against that, Madame President."

"Your objection is noted, Mr. Davis. Do you have an answer, Dr. Volkov?"

"From what little I know about Ms. Valentine, she was a guest in the White House. She was a friend of yours for many years. These aren't friends, these are tools. Putting a solitary mentalist into a unit of skilled soldiers would enhance their capabilities."

"And how would you advise we prevent a telepath from controlling their minds and forcing them into submission?"

"I'm not saying the science is quite there yet. However, I think with more studying of our asset and those like her, it is attainable."

She leaned back in her chair and pursed her lips. Mark noted she kept glancing over to where the couch was placed, the infamous spot where Eleanor bled to death. She grimaced when she caught him watching her.

"So be it."

Mark's eyebrows rose in surprise at the simple phrase. He had wanted to protect mentalists, save the kids from being slaughtered by overzealous police officers. He had never anticipated he would be overseeing a military training facility. He knew it would only be a matter of time before soldiers flocked to his doors, learning to work with people like Ariel. He wasn't sure if being a slave to the United States government was better than a fast death.

"Mr. Davis, I expect to see the first report on the transition within the week. Dr. Volkov, I appreciate your expertise on this. I'm looking forward to hearing more about this military 'body shop' you're creating to keep our soldiers safe."

She leaned in again. "And Mr. Goddard, you might want to be a bit more careful in the gym. Wouldn't want to send in somebody to replace the head of security." Her smile bordered on cruel. She knew how much power she had in this situation, and she had no problem flaunting it. With a wave of her hand, the video feed cut off and the three men stared at a black screen.

"Ivan, I can't believe you offered to weaponize mentalists." Mark felt the rage from last night returning. It fed through his chest and his hands clenched.

"She was about to terminate the program."

"How do you know?" asked Mark.

Ivan glanced at the dark screen again. "I don't, the tone in her voice perhaps? She was going to terminate the program and I have a sneaking suspicion she'd terminate every asset."

Goddard turned around to walk out the door. "We're assets," he said matter-of-factly as he left.

Ivan nodded. "That we are."

Mark let his hands open up, his nails leaving small half-moons in his palm. He didn't like the plan, but he had a feeling Ivan wasn't wrong. There was something particularly cruel about the president, and if they weren't doing something for her, it meant they were on the chopping block.

"You do whatever you must to survive."

"But at what cost, Ivan?"

Before the scientist could answer the rhetorical question, an alarm sounded through the building. A light on the wall flashed red as a blaring tone filled the room. Ivan ran over to the telephone and picked it up, punching the keypad. "What..."

The smile on the man's face, the near sick grin spreading from ear to ear, unnerved Mark. "Our new assets have arrived and one of them is going berserk." His bad news didn't overturn his delighted features. He listened to the receiver for a moment longer. "It's a pyro."

He dropped the phone as the men bolted for the door. Ivan turned to head toward the lobby. Mark turned in the opposite direction. "Do what you can, I'm getting backup."

Mark reached the elevator and put his hand on the scanner. The doors opened more slowly than he remembered. As he punched the button to head down, he was convinced he moved at lightning speed and the world around him crawled.

"Come on, come on, come on."

He jumped out of the small elevator as the doors opened. He didn't have time to hunt for her. "Ariel! I need you."

The tween's head popped around a glass door, the one leading to her play room, where she spent most of her time reading fantasy novels. She held one such book t her chest as she walked closer, the concern on her face growing. "Mark?"

"Come with me. We're going to need your help."

"What's wrong?" she asked as she creeped

forward.

He noticed her feet were lifting off the ground. "We have two new mentalists and their abilities are flaring. I don't want Goddard to kill them, I need your help."

Her feet touched down onto the cement and she set her book on a nearby table. She mustered a serious face and gave him a nod, determined to prove herself. She jumped forward into the elevator. She didn't speak; in fact, her jaw was tense, her teeth clamped shut.

He knelt in front of her. "I don't know what's going to happen. Whatever you do, do not put yourself in jeopardy. If you can help, go for it, but don't hurt yourself."

He wrapped his arms around her, squeezing her tightly. "Ariel, I don't want you in danger, but I need you to show everybody in that room how amazing you are."

He pulled back and stared into her brown eyes. The slight nod of her head was her only assurance. Barely fourteen and already capable of more amazing gifts than he would ever manage. He felt guilty using her like this, showing her off to make a spectacle, but he knew it was the best chance she had of surviving. She was an alpha dog; he needed everybody else to see it.

The doors opened and they sprinted down the hallway. They dodged through doorways and security guards did nothing to stop them. At this point there weren't many who dared to speak out against the young girl. As they reached the final door to the lobby, Mark pushed the button for the scanner to appear. He relaxed his eye, chin on the stand, trying not to blink. As the light flashed red, he growled and started over.

Grinding metal filled the air. One step, two steps, he moved back as he watched Ariel hovering off the ground, her arms pushing out wide. Her auburn hair floated upward as she exerted her abilities. Mark watched as the door threw itself open several feet. He was amazed at how strong her abilities had become since they first met.

As he stepped in front of her, entering the lobby, he thought he'd stumbled onto a movie scene. There were several security staff lying on the ground, barely moving. To one side of the giant water fountain, a man bellowed, engulfed in flames.

"Ariel, water," Mark said quickly.

Without further prompting, water from the fountain shot outward and knocked the man to the ground, stopping the flames. Mark continued to survey the room, looking for the source of the fire. He found a teenage boy on the far side of the lobby, nearly at the steps leading to the mezzanine. Mark pointed to the kid. "Ariel, can you knock him down?"

She looked at him, her eyes concerned.

"Don't hurt him, we just need to get his attention."

Before they could get any closer, Goddard stepped out of a side room with his gun drawn. "Stop or I'll be forced to kill you."

Mark wanted to yell, but he couldn't argue with the man. They had casualties, people whose families he would have to call later today. It didn't make it easier, but if he had to, he'd do what needed to be done to protect these people.

Goddard didn't wait for the teen to reply. As the teenager took another step up the stairwell, the trigger was pulled and three loud bangs filled the room. All three projectiles burst into flame, losing their momentum and falling to the ground. Before Goddard pulled the trigger again, the gun in his hand exploded, sending him screaming to the ground.

"Ariel," Mark said.

Water from the fountain hurled itself at the boy. As it closed in, the hiss of steam filled the room. Mark watched as Ariel approached the boy. Her feet weren't touching the ground, she was nervous, but she was putting on a brave face. Mark sprinted to the side of the fountain and ducked down behind the lip, near enough that he could see the two mentalists.

"Son, we need you to calm down," Mark yelled.

"He's terrified," Ariel responded. Her voice sounded distant, almost void of emotion, a sign she was starting to lose herself to the euphoria of her abilities. The boy's face didn't register their conversation. He was panic-stricken, looking more like an animal backed into a corner than a human.

She gently reached out with her hand. "It'll be okay. There is a nice man here trying to help us."

She must have passed an invisible barrier, a line the boy had drawn in the sand. Fire leapt from his chest, incinerating his t-shirt and trying to strike Ariel. Mark gasped as the fire brushed off to either side, deflected by an unseen force. He knew she was talented, but to see her in a dangerous situation accentuated just how vast her abilities had grown.

Mark searched for Ivan. He saw him lying on his back several feet away. Mark crawled along the floor, grabbing the man by the collar pulling him back to safety. Another fireball lit up the room, washing them all in heat. The few security guards remaining were backing away from the fight.

"Ivan, are you okay?"

The man didn't respond. Mark noted the tension in his chest. He suddenly felt an immediacy to the situation. *What if something happens to Ariel? What if the boy is shot? What if he dies? What if I die?* His thoughts started to race toward the worst possible scenarios.

He reached up to the fountain and dipped his hand in the water. The boy spewed flames at Ariel but none came close enough to even warrant concern. The boy had never dealt with somebody like her before; she wasn't moving to subdue him, instead just waiting out the situation.

"Want me to do something?" she called back.

"Keep doing what you're doing," Mark responded.

He splashed the water on Ivan's face. He tapped the man's cheek, aggressively enough to leave a handprint. He shook him. "Wake up, dammit."

Ivan's back arched as he shot up for a moment. He sucked in air and spun about, his eyes darting to and fro. They rested on Mark. The fear in them was palpable. Mark took the man by the shoulders. "What's wrong?"

"An empath."

212

He started to speak again but his body went limp. His eyes stared off into space like nobody was home. Mark reached into the man's lab coat and fished around. Without a doubt there would be a syringe with a sedative in it. Mark tried to recall everything he knew about empaths. *They can touch stuff and feel thing? No, that's psychosymmetry. Empath's read people's emotions and can project them outward.* Mark suddenly realized the racing of his heart. It was fear: there was somebody here capable of making him feel fear.

Mark felt the familiar plastic in the man's pocket and pulled out the syringes. He bit one of the caps and pulled it off. He stood up, scanning the room, looking for somebody who didn't belong. Ariel had pushed the boy against the wall and held him in place. Fire erupted around her and she swatted at it with her hand, knocking the flame away.

"Just a few more minutes, Ariel," Mark yelled.

He rounded the fountain, and was nearly to the front doors of the lobby when he discovered a small female hiding behind a potted tree. He paused the moment he saw the young girl huddled on the floor, trying to make herself look as tiny as possible. He wanted to take a step forward but something in his body told him to flee. He was sweating enough that his eyes stung.

"It's not you," Mark whispered to himself.

If he didn't get to the kid, they'd kill him. They'd kill the pyro and ultimately they'd scrub them all from existence. The rage in the pit of his stomach brewed. He wouldn't let this child scrap everything he was trying to build. *This fucking pathetic piece of garbage is going to kill us all.*

A moment of clarity washed through his body. He screamed as he charged toward the young female empath, syringe gripped tightly in his hand. With every step forward waves of doubt washed over him. He tripped and fell to the ground, skidding alongside the kid. *Fucking empath,* he screamed in his head. He jabbed the kid with the needle and pushed the plunger down.

She stopped shaking and slumped to the floor. Mark rolled onto his back and stared at the ceiling. Every muscle in his body relaxed, and he realized how drastically the empath's abilities had affected him. He couldn't help but wonder if that was also the cause of his rage-filled frenzy.

He turned his head while resting on the floor. Ariel cradled the pyro on the stairs, holding him tightly as the security staff rushed back into the room. She ignored them as they surrounded her. Mark tried to speak but found his body incapable of operating. He was thankful when he heard Ivan barking orders. "Leave them. Get the wounded. Goddard needs medical attention or he's going to lose both his hands."

Mark couldn't help it. He laughed. *Goddard, you sack of shit, you finally got what you deserved. I hope you lose both hands.* Lately he startled himself with the cruel thoughts dancing across his mind, but this was the first time he felt no remorse. The man deserved to die, but if that wasn't going to happen, he was best left to suffer.

Mark laughed out loud at the thought.

Chapter 15

2033

Dwayne stalked around the side of a subway car, trying to remain out of sight of the increasing number of synthetics. He needed to get close, enough to put his hands on the metal and near the battery that gave life to the annoying machines. It didn't require powers to be useful, but it certainly helped.

He scrambled along the ground, spotting one of the synthetics several cars down. If he could dodge the lasers, avoid the bullets, and not have his limbs ripped from his body, he had a chance. He didn't like the odds, but being the powerhouse in the group carried certain responsibilities. The obligation to save everybody fell on his shoulders, and the fight hadn't ended yet.

Shots rang out in the air, bullets ricocheting off metal subway cars. The machines were effective killing machines, and as more climbed down into the subway, it would become more difficult to hide.

Did they have thermal cameras? Were they trying to corral them? Did the assholes in charge of the assault want them alive? He didn't like not knowing the rules of the game. Until they figured out what was happening, it was a destroy-everything mission.

He crouched at the corner of a subway car, tucking himself under the transport, removing himself from the line of sight of a wandering machine. Metal scraped along the gravel, one step, two, three; it paused, examining the area. Somewhere a human watched through the camera, relaying information to the machine. Dwayne wanted to blow up the controller centers more than he did the robots—humans hunting his kind like it was a deranged kind of sport.

He barely moved his foot when the synthetic pivoted, head moving back and forth as it scanned the area. Dwayne raised his hands above his head, getting to his feet slowly. He hoped the operator was under orders to take them alive if possible, otherwise he'd feel the shredding potential of small projectiles piercing his flesh.

"No luck!"

Skits jumped down from a subway car, landing on the synthetic's back. Even with her weight it didn't fall to the ground like she hoped. She clung to its head, trying to bend it backward. The machine reached back, snapping at her face, trying to latch onto something it could pull.

The laser whistled as it powered up. He jumped at the machine, grabbing on to the metal bar resembling a collarbone. He siphoned in a breath, tasting the power held in the synthetic's chest. He

216

drained the battery, his emptied cells craving the power radiating off the machine. Light blasted through the metal chest plate and into his palm. He gripped the machine, holding on as Skits pulled at its hands.

The synthetic stopped moving, the hydraulics freezing in place. He let go, a weird sensation creeping along his skin. His body already wanted to expel the surplus of power; he had to focus his attention to keep it from escaping every pore of his body. "I can't hold it long.

"You won't need to." Skits climbed off the machine's back and pointed across the tracks toward a passenger platform. He followed her gaze to the dozen machines climbing down the fallen ceiling to the platform. Even if he was at his peak, he'd be hard pressed to hit that many man-sized objects with lightning. In the small space, he didn't have the luxury of them acting as conductors, or being able to blindly fire hoping to strike a large object.

"We're so fucked."

The world turned white. He feared he fainted, knocked unconscious by the sudden increase of electricity running rampant through his body. It took a moment before he realized Vanessa had stolen him away from his body into the white room.

"I need you," she said.

"I've got them." He nodded.

"No," she said, "that's not what I mean."

She reached out, touching his shoulder. He stood confused as her hand seemed to meld into his skin, leaving a green stain across his shoulder and chest.

He tried to pull back, unsure of what was happening, but found his legs refused to function.

"No, Vanessa." His voice didn't leave any question. He tried to swat at her but even his arms rejected him. The green stain spread quickly. He could feel it working its way to his neck and covering his face. A moment later, he could see through his eyes again, but like he viewed the world through a long tunnel.

He screamed for Vanessa, but his lungs didn't respond. The woman stole his body, trapping him within his own head. He raged, the sound filling the space, but never reaching his mouth. The telepath had taken over his body before, but always at his request or with his support. In those instances, they worked his body in tandem, a joining of abilities. Now, she caged him like an animal.

The surge of power discharged through his body. Instead of lightning tearing from his skin, she let the charge build until the strain threatened to rip apart his innards. At the last moment, she let it go, no light, no electricity, just a discharge of energy. She repeated the act until his body grew weak from the rapid expenditure of electricity.

From the corner of his eye, he recognized Conthan, his expression perplexed. Dwayne strained to see the synthetics on the platform, but found they were just beyond his perception. He had no idea what the woman was doing with his body, but he wanted her gone.

"EMPs?" asked Conthan.

Dav5d had theorized he could do it. If he let the energy reach critical mass, he could release it,

218

frying electronics like when his lightning struck near circuitry. As fatigue took hold, he was pissed at the woman. He had tried the tactic before but to no avail. She stole his body and mastered his abilities in seconds. He wanted her gone.

His hand touched Conthan's shoulder. The synthetics on the platform hadn't moved, but a new wave of machines was entering the subway. As he touched the skin on Conthan's neck, the long tunnel vanished and his vision returned to normal. He didn't need to see her; he knew she had jumped from one body to the next.

***

Survival instinct pushed aside the growing fatigue. Back pressed against a subway car, Conthan debated if a prayer was in order. At their best, they'd be outmatched; a dozen machines might require a little effort if they had their powers. But now, they were no more than walking bags of flesh waiting to be pulverized by lasers and torn apart by metal hands. He was caught between Jasmine and Alyssa, their faces both holding a fear he shared.

"Can we run?"

Jasmine shook her head. "There are enough subway cars here for us to hide. Once you run for the tunnel, they have a straight shot."

"What do we do?"

A machine rounded the corner of the subway car, gun raised, ready to start shooting. Bang. Bang. Bang. Jasmine absorbed the shots, her body buckling further as each bullet connected. While she grappled with the machine, tearing the gun away and reaching for its neck, Conthan turned his attention to the ground.

Alyssa slipped inside the subway car while he felt around for any object large enough to smash into the robot. Jasmine knocked him over as the synthetic shoved her against the car. A stone twice the size of his fist sat less than two feet away from his face.

With the rock in hand, he smashed it against the synthetic's skull. He hoped it'd disconnect the head, perhaps even destroy whatever artificial intelligence was housed inside. As the rock struck, it crumbled to powder. The machine clutched Jasmine with one hand and tried to grab him with the other. Conthan grabbed on to its wrist, trying to pull it away from his friend.

Jasmine raised her feet and slammed into the robot's chest. As it staggered backward her lungs inflated, sucking in air. The machine assessed the situation and decided Conthan, at least for the moment, was the bigger threat. He didn't have time to react as it latched onto his forearm and pulled him close, its free hand pointing the forearm gun at his chest.

The head of the machine jerked backward with a loud metal ringing. It jerked the other way with the same ring. Alyssa wielded a metal pipe like a club. She tossed it to Jasmine and the former Marine jammed the end of the pipe into the synthetic's neck and cranked it to one side.

Sparks erupted as it spasmed, trying to pull the pipe from its neck. Each of their faces mirrored

Conthan's panic. "We can't keep this up, we can barely take on one of them." Alyssa said.

"I see them." Jasmine pointed to the next set of tracks. Further down, Skits had her back pressed to a subway car, trying to hide from a synthetic rounding the corner.

The popping of guns stopped.

"No more gunfire?" asked Alyssa.

Conthan tapped Jasmine on her shoulder. "You two go get Skits, I'm going for Dwayne and Vanessa. Keep an eye open for Dav5d, he can't have gone far."

They didn't reply. They were already in a mad dash to reach Skits. None of them wanted to waste the sudden ceasefire. Whatever reason the machines paused, he had to assume it was nothing short of a miracle. They may have a chance to reach further into the tunnels and put distance between them and the synthetics. He didn't believe in a higher power, but he promised to thank God if they made it out alive.

"EMPs?" he asked as he approached.

He reached Vanessa and before he could ask why Dwayne appeared like a zombie, she touched his face. Her nails would have caused him to flinch, but his body didn't respond. The sensation of being pulled at wasn't unfamiliar. A year ago in the Facility, she asked to push aside his mind and control his body.

I hope you know what you're doing, Vanessa.

You can't save me. He recognized Dav5d's voice. The despair caused his heart to ache. For a moment, he worried the strain on his body was

221

giving him a heart attack. Vanessa's emotions boiled over, and the anger seared through his brain. He ground his teeth, preparing for a bloodcurdling scream.

"No!" It escaped his lips and Vanessa's at the same time. Vanessa's mind opened, and he knew the moment she tugged at his powers, they were leaving her love behind.

The portal opened. Jasmine grabbed Alyssa and Skits and dragged them through the black disc. His spine strained as his back bowed. Wherever his power resided, it threatened to snap his body in half to prevent him from opening another portal. Vanessa didn't stop, opening one last hole in the air as she closed the first.

"I'm so sorry," she said through both her and his mouth.

***

The subway lit up as gunfire erupted on either side of her. Vanessa tried to focus, gather her thoughts, but each time she touched the minds of her teammates, an explosion forced her back into her own head. It had been years since she exerted this much effort to reach out to friends.

Panic. The last time the emotion consumed her had been when the Nostradamus Effect started changing her body. She survived puberty, high school, and her undergraduate degree, and her body betrayed her. Already gifted with the ability to read minds, her body took years to be labeled as a gift. She panicked as Sister Muriel hugged her tightly, assuring her it was all part of God's plan. If only she believed in a God.

No. Panic scattered her thoughts, she needed to pull it together if she was going to save the day. Anger—underneath the panic she recognized the fire, the sheer disgust made her want to lash out at the synthetics. The human operators were well over a hundred miles away, making it impossible to fry their delicate brains.

The tunnel shook as large chunks of the ceiling collapsed. She hoped Dwayne or Conthan was the cause. Until she managed to shake off the distractions, she wouldn't be any good to the people who trusted in her to lead them. Fleeting thoughts from the others were just out of her reach but they radiated the same emotion; they shared her panic. They believed they were going to die.

"No."

Her resolve didn't have time to form as a synthetic leaned over the roof of the subway car. The sound of ripping steel assaulted her epiphany as the machine dug into the car, holding itself in place while it held up both arms. The guns pointed less than a foot from her face.

Her scream tore through the air as she reached up, grabbing the machine by the hands. Vanessa put her weight into the motion, yanking down hard, tearing the synthetic from the side of the car. She wouldn't win an arm wrestling match against Jasmine while the former veteran was powered, but at the cost of being green, the Nostradamus Effect had given her more strength than most.

She directed the forearms away from her as they

fired a series of bullets. Her hands vibrated from the recoil, and she almost let go. The synthetic matched her strength, but unlike the cursed machine, she'd tire in seconds, and then the next bullet would pierce her skull. She braced one foot against its chest, then the other, and pushed as hard as she could.

The strain hurt. Pain meant she wasn't dead. The aching muscles meant she could still fight. The machine's limbs snapped and with a flap of her wings, she landed gracefully on her feet. With one metallic forearm in hand and the entire arm in the other, she swung hard, clubbing the machine with its own limb. The lasers would fire next. She spun the machine about, grabbed underneath its chin, and pulled back, determined to sever its skull.

"Just. Fucking. Die." She found her anger as the wires popped and hissed. She threw the broken machine to the ground.

Vanessa.

Dav5d, where are you?

You can't save me, Vanessa. The ceiling collapsed on my legs. I'm pinned. If the blood loss doesn't kill me, the building toxins in my dying muscles will.

No.

I'm sorry, love.

She screamed. Anger; she understood this emotion. She wrapped the anger about her like a warm blanket. Her thoughts shot out wide, touching each of her teammates. She didn't need to see them to know where they were located. For a moment, she witnessed the world through each of their eyes.

Her feet dug into the gravel and muscles pumped, launching her across a set of tracks, between two cars, and farther down the tunnel.

"Dwayne," she yelled.

Her feet continued to close the distance between them. Her mind launched forward and she imagined grabbing on to his shoulders, ripping him from his body. The man's fatigue lowered his resistance. If he hadn't welcomed her into his mind on so many occasions, she feared being a Child would protect him from her intrusions. It might have, any other time perhaps, but not now.

She blinked. The white room.

"I need you," she said.

"I've got them." He nodded.

"No," she said, "that's not what I mean."

Her urgency pushed aside disgust. A year ago, a sadistic man showed her how powerful she could be if she put aside her morals. The Warden had stolen the soul of another man and turned him into a puppet. Vanessa had done it before with consent from the host, a symbiotic coupling that allowed them to work in tandem. Right now, she didn't have time to explain herself. She needed to save her beloved.

Dav5d had briefed her on their abilities, but more than that, he explained his complicated scientific theories of what each of them may be capable of. Vanessa didn't understand the science, but she listened to the man. She admired his intellect and ability to see each of his friends as more than they were. He didn't push them beyond their limits, instead encouraging them to expand and be more.

She loved him. She loved him more than she had ever loved anybody. She felt herself losing him.

The power in Dwayne's body built until she unleashed the energy in massive pulse. She repeated it once, twice, three times. Whatever invisible energy was discharged by his abilities left the synthetics empty husks. The machines froze in place, giving her the opportunity to reach Dav5d. If she and Jasmine worked together, they'd be able to save him. He could to coach them through any medical aid he'd need. She only had to reach him.

Before she could pull herself from his mind, bullets whizzed by their hiding spot. Another wave of machines had already started entering through the collapsed ceiling. Dwayne's abilities were emptied, and shouldn't be used again for hours. Just when she thought hope was lost, Conthan ran up to her.

"EMPs?"

She touched his face and her thoughts washed over him. Unlike Dwayne, Conthan welcomed the sensation. He had complete trust in her and relinquished control of his body without any hesitation. If they survived, she'd thank him for the trust he bestowed upon her.

No.

I can reach you now, Dav5d.

No, you can't. Not without killing Conthan, and perhaps yourself.

I can save you.

They need you, Vanessa. Without you, they'll be lost. Think of Eleanor.

Fuck Eleanor. Fuck them all.

I love you, Vanessa. For the longest time I didn't understand it. I couldn't make sense of the chemistry that elicited this word, love. I stopped caring, Vanessa. For the first time since my powers started, I didn't need to understand. I simply knew I loved you.

I can save you.

You can't save me.

The emotion gripped at her chest. She sensed his resolve. If Dav5d didn't believe there was a chance of being saved, she couldn't argue with the smartest man in the world. Despite believing it, her heart tensed and threatened to give out on her as his thoughts silenced.

"No," she screamed. The sound of her and Conthan belting out in unison caused the synthetics to turn in their direction. Conthan's powers were weak, barely recognizable as she tore at what made him more than human. As she screamed, she opened a portal near Jasmine, Skits, and Alyssa. She closed the portal after Jasmine dragged the two girls into the disc with her.

"I'm so sorry."

Vanessa ignored the pain emanating from Conthan. She opened another portal, and the screams inside his head sent her reeling from his mind. With a shove from her, Conthan's limp body knocked into Dwayne, barreling them both into the blackness of his portal. She ducked through the disc, saving herself and her teammates, but leaving the love of her life to die.

Chapter 16

2033

Dwayne rolled along the ground with Conthan under one arm and half falling on Vanessa. He didn't waste any time getting to his feet, crouching with one hand held up ready to fight. Vanessa staggered to floor with a thud. His emotions fueled him as he struck her jaw. He wanted his body to produce a charge, enough that when his skin connected with hers she felt the surge of energy pulse through her body.

She wasn't prepared as Dwayne's other fist connected with her torso. She tried to push him away, but he shoved her hands to the side. She batted her wings once, putting several feet between them. He charged again, his right fist drawn. She spun, dropping to one leg, and let her wing swing out wide in an attempt to knock him to the ground. He jumped, missing the sweeping motion. He brought up his knee, clipping her in the side of the head.

"How dare you rape my mind."

She screamed. She seemed larger as she stood, her muscles flexing as she drained her lungs of air. The sound dissipated into the large room. It was the first moment he realized they had teleported into a massive warehouse. They stood in the middle of the structure, a football field-sized room with them on the fifty yard line.

"I did what I had to." Her voice broke as she screamed the words. She closed the distance between them. With a flap of her wings she was off the ground and both feet slammed into Dwayne's chest. He flipped backward along the cement. He didn't have time to figure out if his ribs had been cracked. She was on him, lifting him off the ground with a grip on his neck.

"And look where it got you," he spat out.

She thrust him off of her, sending him onto his back again. Vanessa was a telepath. He had no doubt she read every thought as it crossed his mind. Every fist he threw, she knew it was coming. In a physical confrontation all he could do was survive long enough. He had only ever felt this hollow once before, when Michael died.

He could end the fight. He could turn his back and walk away, but he was mad. He rolled over and stood up again, clutching the pain in his chest, worried his sternum had been cracked. He balled his fist and prepared for another round with the beast.

"You would have done the same."

"No, Vanessa," he said. "You crossed a line."

"We're at war," she hissed. "There are no lines."

"And what? I'm a casualty of your war?" He

suspected she could utilize the same tactics the Warden used. He had wondered if she could do it to Children. He let her take over his body before, in a situation not so different than this. Before she asked, now, she took what she wanted. She violated him and even after that, Dav5d remained a casualty.

She screamed again. She couldn't stop. He hoped she listened to every thought and understood just how wrong she was. Nothing she could do would quench the rage pumping his heart, making it beat faster. He wanted his pound of flesh before this fight was over.

He took two steps and lunged at her. He didn't try to punch or use tactics he learned with Alyssa. He grabbed her shoulders and rode her to the ground. He sat up on her chest and brought his hands together, swinging them like a club. He connected with her jaw once, then again, and again a third time. His cells fired to life and the charge sped through his body.

He put his hands on either side of her head and let the electricity escape. Her body convulsed as she screamed. He pushed, emptying out the last drop of power. It might be enough to stop the fight, but for now, he wanted her in pain. He wanted her to experience her entire body revolting against her if only for a moment.

He spat out the air in his lungs as her fist connected his chest again. He flew backward along the ground. The rafters faded in and out of focus as he tried to roll over. His muscles fought, refusing to cooperate with his brain. He tried sitting up, but pain radiated through his body. He blinked several times as his vision blurred. Between blinks a person stood over him. The last thing he saw was the tattoos covering half of the woman's face, then his vision gave out on him.

"You look like shit, mate."

***

Jasmine hurt. Her chest heaved as she tried sucking in air. The machine lay across her body, its hand firmly pushing down on her sternum. It leaned forward, almost straddling her as it used its weight to push harder. One of its arms was missing, severed, leaving sparks raining down on her body.

There was a sense of peace knowing she didn't have much longer to live. It hurt like hell, but she had gone out swinging and did more damage than she ever thought possible. Her only regret, other than being killed, was not being able to see the face of the General as she crushed his skull between her bare palms. No, death didn't bother her. An incomplete mission, that would stir her ghost in the afterlife.

The metal of the claw-like hand touched the side of her breast. If it had been an hour earlier, her power would reach out, seeking the material to mimic. Had it been an hour earlier, she'd be nearly impervious and she'd have the strength to match. She'd throw the machine off her and with no effort, she'd beat it to death. Instead, she waited.

A loud clank sounded behind the synthetic as its head was knocked clear to the side. She waited for the killing blow, but something smacked against the machine again. It moved just enough; behind it, Alyssa held a fire extinguisher. Jasmine's chest might be about to collapse, but the gymnast looked as if she had been hit by a bus. Her bruises and cuts were impossible to count.

"Get off her!" She swung the canister again. It connected with the machine's head. The red metal broke open and white powder flew into the air, creating a smoke screen. Jasmine caught her breath as the machine turned and lunged at its attacker.

She couldn't move. She listened as metal clanked against metal. Somebody grunted. There was another voice. Skits. The two of them were fighting now. She hoped they succeeded. Her teammates fought for all of their survival. They fought for her survival.

Tears welled up in her eyes despite her resistance. She had been a killing machine for so long, the leader, the one who barked orders to subordinates. That had been torn away and now she was given a set of people who called themselves a team. She lay there, hoping her teammates succeeded. They, the ones who had her back, two people who were threatening their own safety to protect her.

She forced the muscles in her arm to cooperate. Her limbs were like jelly, barely able to follow her commands. She reached down and touched the piece of metal protruding from the side of her body. The moment she touched it, the pain returned and she screamed into the white cloud. The powder touched her lips and she tasted it, similar to milk gone bad.

Her powers attempted to reach the metal, draw it into herself. She had never transformed before with a wound this bad. She had no idea what would happen, but she couldn't let them fight for her. She couldn't let them die for her.

The skin touching metal tried to mimic its density, but her powers vanished. She turned her head quickly as a piece of metal landed next to her. She looked back to see the head of the machine, its blank metal face staring at her.

Skits stepped forward. Behind her, she dragged the body of the machine. Alyssa followed. Skits dropped the non-functioning body onto the ground and fell to her knees. She toppled, lying on top of the synthetic, staring Jasmine almost in the eye.

"You owe me."

Jasmine nodded, her voice escaping her.

"I mean big, you owe me so big."

Alyssa lay down next to her companion. "So big," she repeated.

Jasmine nodded again, tears building momentum down her cheeks.

***

He couldn't feel his legs. He knew they were crushed. There was zero percent chance he'd ever walk again. He'd be lucky if the toxins in his muscles weren't building to a dangerous crescendo. Once the beam was off his legs, he'd be lucky if he survived.

He was okay not being able to walk. His body had always been the fragile vessel for his mind. It

233

simply held what he was most proud of. If he was bound to a wheelchair he'd learn to survive. For a moment, he thought of Vanessa and what her reaction would be if he couldn't walk again. What a pair they'd make, the soaring gargoyle and the hyperintelligent paraplegic.

He tried not to smile. His brain shut off the pain receptors. Shock was setting in, and once it took hold, he'd be incapable of functioning. He tried to focus himself. The sound of small explosions and falling debris reminded him he was in the subway, dangerously close to the enemy. He breathed in deeply, letting his thoughts clear.

Did they escape?

He glanced to his side. A subway car lay half demolished by the support beams in the tunnel. Machines were littered about. A giant mech stood frozen with a missing leg and of the thirteen synthetics, none moved. Their damage wasn't sufficient for them to shut down; he assumed somehow Dwayne's powers had evolved. He had thrust an electromagnetic pulse outward, draining every energy source around them.

"Smart man," Dav5d whispered.

The letters. His eyes glassed over as he started to examine the conundrum of Eleanor Valentine. He exhausted every bit of data he could uncover about the woman. He had hacked every government network with the hopes of finding files. What few he found had been redacted, scrubbed of any useful information. Utilizing common phrases, patterns of writing, and contextual clues, he rebuilt every piece of data available.

Her past wasn't the answer. If there was a cause for her altering the timeline, it was emotional, something he'd never be able to uncover from third party files. The woman saved Vanessa, he knew that, but his partner never elaborated. He assumed that as Eleanor worked as an aide in the White House, she somehow used her influence to save Vanessa from being exterminated. It was a subject Vanessa had kept secret, even from him. He didn't push.

The psychic spoke about a dark coming. She had seen the future her entire life and there came a point where she couldn't see further. He wondered if there were limitations of how far she could see beyond her own death. He wished he had a precog to study, then he might know what real limitations they encountered.

"The Warden," he whispered. The man had been the binding element for their group. This one singular evil had initiated this hurried comradery. Vanessa's letter led them to Skits, who in turn became the reason Dwayne stayed with Vanessa. Conthan had come to them because of Dwayne's letter and his singular purpose was to rescue Sarah. All signs turned back to the Facility and the man who controlled it. There was no doubt that he was the reason the team formed. But now that he was dead, killed by Conthan and Vanessa, what purpose did they have together?

He froze.

"He's alive."

Chapter 17

2033

"You overstep your boundaries, Jacob."

The blue screens hung in the air over the table. There were a dozen, all but one showing a state of chaos unleashed within Boston's city limits. But it was the woman in the largest screen making all the noise. He was amazed at her ability to threaten. The lines on her face were deep, giving away her age, but underneath a weathered body, her mind remained sharp.

"Madame President," he said with a bite, "I think you know little of my boundaries."

He didn't like her. She served a necessary evil created by the Society. A young woman with every advantage, giving her the most potential to take the White House during an election year. It was a challenge even for the Society, raising a woman to a position of power like this. Every resource had been used. What they couldn't manipulate with money, they relied on their extraordinary abilities. The

Society's mentalists had exhausted themselves manipulating the minds of politicians, pushing back their worries and creating a carefully crafted backstory of support. The Society used these people for the very reason they were feared.

"Mr. Griffin, I think you underestimate my position. You and the Society only remain intact because I have decided you're more useful to me than not. The moment you cross that line…"

"You seem to forget who manufactures the synthetics that protect your position. You forget that with almost no effort, they could turn on you, take you down, and the General could unify his America again."

He laughed, making sure to evoke as much condescension as possible. He wanted her to know that her and her position meant little to him. She was anything but stupid, and he knew just how much she needed the Society to support her during this civil war. No, she knew who was in control.

"Are you finished, Mr. Griffin?"

"Cecilia, the only reason you remain president is my lack of desire to see another assume the mantle. Make sure you know your place or I'll be at your door to tear you down myself."

Do it. Take all that power for yourself.

Jacob ignored the voice creeping into his thoughts. It was only a matter of time before he turned his attention on her. But in the meantime, he needed to do away with other loose ends.

"There is another mentalist. There is an entire team of Children who have no love for you."

"The ones from the Facility?"

237

"Yes," he said. "And I think they have a grudge against anybody involved in the Facility."

"The Warden is dead."

"You think he didn't give you away? I'm sure he told them who placed him into the position. I would be surprised if they were aware of the Society. The man was a wretched human being."

She rubbed her forehead, the loose skin moving back and forth. She was annoyed. Seconds passed as she considered what this could mean for her. If there was one thing he could rely on, it was her desire for self-preservation. She would go out of her way to survive. At seventy-five years of age, she had every intention of making it well past one hundred.

"Do you know any of the people on their roster?"

"One. It seems all facial recognition has been wiped. For all intents and purposes, they never existed. Somebody they're in league with is extremely savvy with computers. The only person we know by reputation is Jasmine Gentile, the former Paladin."

"Gentile," she said with disgust. "I've met her before. She's the lapdog for the General. He'd parade her about whenever he wanted to show his absolute control."

"Well, she's rogue now. She's the only way they would know how to disable the computers at the Facility, stop the alarms, and prevent a call for help. I can assume the only person higher on her hit list is the General himself."

"So what did today achieve?"

"We had a lead that Troy was a community of

Children. When we sent in the synthetics, they wiped the town clean. Death toll 42. We suspect only a few managed to evade our efforts."

"Why them?"

He smiled. "Who do you think has been locating these Children and sheltering them? Our teleporter and rogue Paladin. They've been rescuing Children and we wanted to make sure the backbone of their army was annihilated."

She didn't argue with his logic. He wondered if she was even aware he repositioned the synthetics to take the town. With her keeping a war off her front doorstep, he doubted she missed a few dozen synthetics. As she furrowed her brow, the wrinkles turned to dark lines, making her look even older.

"And what of the multi-billion-dollar, very public, very loud attack on Boston?"

It was his turn to frown. He didn't like to admit it. He had taken nearly four billion dollars of machinery into the Danger Zone. Only minutes into making a visual, the group of Children destroyed half the fleet. The synthetics had been decimated within minutes. He underestimated the abilities of each Child and what they were capable of when working in tandem. Now he understood why they remained a group.

Her laugh was haughty, filled with arrogance. "They escaped? Even after you threw everything you had."

His teeth ground at the sound of her cackle while his ribcage seemed to tighten against his heart. He wondered if his newfound abilities could work from this distance. He could reach out and with a stray

239

thought, her hands would grip her own head and spin her neck. A long sigh escaped his mouth as the tension in his body vanished. Vindictiveness decided for him; he'd rather savor the look on her face when he tore her down as the president and stood atop her crumbled empire.

"No, we didn't walk away emptyhanded."

On cue, Lily entered the conference room. Her white gown matched his suit. She wiggled her fingers and the screens on the table rearranged themselves. With a couple swipes, the president was shown the back of an armored car. A medical team raced to save their patient. An uncanny amount of blood pooled where his legs should have been. His eyes were fixed on the ceiling, blinking in regular intervals, oblivious to the severed limbs.

"Who is this?"

"It's one of the Children from Boston."

"His powers?"

"We won't know until we get him to Genesis Division."

The emptiness in the woman's emotions surprised even him. When she resolved to think deeply about an issue, not a whisper transmitted from her mind. He wondered if she had a way to dodge mentalists, or if some technology prevented him from hearing her. His mentor had been clear there were ways for humans to avoid his abilities, but they were few and far between.

"We will also be increasing our production of synthetics. Both the New York plant and the Jersey plant will be maxing their output. We will have more than enough units to replace everything I borrowed."

The raised eyebrow gave away her surprise. When it returned, her eyes shrunk to slits. It was only a moment before her faculties returned and she realized there were no favors between them.

"My position is better secured with you in power than the General. For now, you still serve a purpose."

"For now," she echoed.

Lily waved her arm and all of the screens vanished. She lifted herself onto the table, folding one leg over the other. She eyed Jacob, studying him, her eyes going up and down his body.

"Yes?"

"Something has changed. Your arrogance has..." She paused as she pondered her options. "Become confidence."

"Arrogance?"

"You're anything but a fool, Jacob. You know exactly what I mean. Before, you were a petulant child, constantly fighting for approval. Whatever has happened to you, there is no longer a man looking for validation. Your doubts have been removed."

Jacob waited for the little voice in the back of his head to whisper something, but he could only discern a content sensation from the darkness in his mind. She was right; before, he wouldn't have had the confidence in his abilities to make such a bold move in the face of the most powerful woman in the world. Now, he wondered if he'd be capable of fear again. Underneath his skin, in the depths of his mind, he could only describe the feeling as limitless.

"I have a purpose now."

"The White House?"

He smiled. "Why stop there?"

The edge of her lip curled. She was the voice of reason, but underneath her logic was a sinister lust for power. Her origin story started with a young poor wretch begging on the streets; now, she would never stop wanting more. And if he was to aim higher, she'd be the first to support him, pushing him to the brink. She might be the voice of reason, but there was a propensity for chaos at the root of her being waiting to spin out of control like an addict with an endless supply.

"Get Dikeledi. We're going to Genesis Division," he said. "I want to interrogate the prisoner myself."

"Do you think you can break the mind of a Child?"

It wouldn't be the first, the voice in the back of his head whispered. The silky smooth seduction of power wrapped about his being. Once upon a time, Jacob might not have been able to tear away the protection awarded to a Child's minds, but now, he felt excitement at testing his abilities against a more formidable foe.

"It's not the first time I've done it," he echoed.

***

The doors to the elevator hissed as they parted. The bright white of the lobby nearly blinded him as he stepped out. It had been just over a month since he last set foot in the building, preferring to let the board run their company. With the change in plans, he had a feeling the path to the White House began here.

A woman in a white lab coat with her hair pulled back in a tight bun gave a slight nod. "Mr. Griffin, we weren't expecting you so quickly. The lab directors—"

"I'm here to see the Child of Nostradamus brought in earlier today."

She nodded again. Her disappointment was easy enough to read on her face, but her thoughts gave away its severity. She had been sent to greet him, but more, a group of researchers hoped she'd have the ability to bring him into their lab. He commended them on attempting to divert his attention.

"You may speak while we walk."

"You're so gracious," Lily said in a sly tone.

The scientist's eyes lit up. She flipped through her papers and he listened as she tried to prioritize the work being done in research and development. They moved through the lobby and into a long corridor with glass rooms on either side. The bright white lights gave it a sanitary appearance, removing their shadows from the floor.

"We've started to push forward with an upgrade in the Body Shop. We've found there has been a problem with underground bodyhackers stealing our technology and reverse engineering it. To keep the elite coming back for more, we've started to infuse nanites into the technology, allowed for overall endurance upgrades as well as speed. There have been extreme developments in the area of male virility enhancements."

"You prioritize telling me your achievements in making a man's cock work?"

Her face turned red and she tore the sheet off her clipboard. She shoved it into her pocket. Ignoring her, he faced the other side of the hallway. Inside were several synthetics, their bodies slumped, a familiar sign they had yet to be activated. They weren't much different to the naked eye, their frames slightly slimmer, and where they had blank faces before, now they had eyes.

"Tell me about them."

"You and your machines," Dikeledi said.

He eyed her. She had never been fond of the Genesis Division. Where she typically was a mystery to him, he could sense the unease radiating off her. He stepped closer, lording over her slender frame. She didn't flinch at him invading her space; instead she reached out, her fingertips touching the side of his face.

For a moment he was aware of the feelings of all two-hundred-and-thirty-two people on the floor working. His heart jumped, racing as if he had finished running a marathon. The sensation overwhelmed him. He knew her powers were like his, always active and reading the room, but he was constantly amazed by just her strength. While Lily exploited her abilities for her own gains, Dikeledi's motives were rarely understood. For a moment, he grasped the amount of control the woman had, warding off the emotional intrusions of so many humans.

She leaned forward, grabbing the back of his neck to bring his ear close to her mouth. She whispered as softly as possible. "I can hear you in there."

"We know," Jacob whispered back.

As she rocked back on her heels, the smile spreading across her lips wasn't missed. She appeared just as delighted as him with his newfound abilities. He could smell the respect wafting off her. For the first time, she saw him as an equal. It was the first time he realized she'd seen him as weak. For the years they had known each other, she never let on.

"Tell me about the synthetics," he said, turning away from Dikeledi.

"These are the newest models. They're completely integrated artificial intelligence. We're hoping sometime in the next year, we'll be able to remove the human operators. We're finding the symbiotic nature of pilot and synthetic has become cost prohibitive and our technology has started to reach a place where it can move faster than human reaction."

"Interesting," he said. He knew very well the machines would be the gateway to his ascension. The same machines that protected the president against the West Coast invasion would be her downfall. He was thrilled they were making progress. "Why next year?"

"It's much more complex than standard artificial intelligence. On a plane, the craft knows if it flies into a mountain, everybody will die. These have to make millions of threat assessments, some of them beyond even our understanding."

"Children."

She nodded. "If we send them out, we need to make sure they have the ability to adapt to unique abilities we haven't encountered yet. We wouldn't want to send them out and have them killing humans."

She paused. He could hear her thoughts come to a standstill. She feared she had just insulted him and his friends. She was the executive director of research and development, and member of the Society, sworn in to perpetuate the exploration of science and a brilliant scientist. Like everybody inducted into their secret organization, they knew about the four mentalists and their involvement in the organization. The sense of duty was strong in the scientist, and the undertones of fear were almost as obvious.

He did nothing to alleviate her fears.

"Take us to see the Child," Lily said. She pushed past Jacob, giving the woman a slight nudge. Her fiery temper excited him, constantly allowing his lust to override his commonsense. For a moment he thought he could hear her thoughts, but as he pried further, he found himself butting up against her natural abilities to resist. The fact he lusted after something he couldn't have was not lost on him either.

"Soon," Dikeledi said as she followed.

The empath's words excited him even more. He wondered how long it would be before he could force Lily into succumbing to his abilities. She already volunteered her body, but he looked forward to the moment he could take her mind and pull away the layers like one of her evening gowns.

They walked through several glass doors in research and development. The more scientists he saw working at lab tables and punching on computer screens, the more confident he became. Once they reached the metal blast doors, he was certain they could take the country by force if they must.

A card swipe, an eye scan, and a drop of blood opened the doors and the woman escorted them into a room with a single glass window overlooking an operating theater. Unlike the area by the elevator, there was little glass in the decor, replaced by thick steel. The strengthened structure warned him: this was where they worked with things far too dangerous for the rest of the world.

"He lost both of his legs," she said.

"Did you sedate him?" asked Lily.

"No," she said. "He's been awake throughout his entire operation. We've been monitoring his brain activity and it seems he has the ability to shut off his pain receptors."

Jacob wasn't impressed. When one can hurl lightning and another can teleport through space, the ability to not feel pain seemed less than thrilling. "Is that all he can do?"

"The MRI of his brain throughout the surgery is showing more activity than we've ever seen in a human before."

"You mean he uses his whole brain?"

She shook her head. "The idea that the humans only use ten percent of their processing power has been known as a myth for years. In fact, over the course of the day, you use nearly one hundred percent of your brain."

"You learn something new every day," Lily said as a woman in the operating room set the scalpel down in a metal tray.

"What is more captivating, we believe he has more neurons than any human on record. Typically the brain only holds about ten percent neurons while the rest of the mass are glial cells supporting its function. He, however, has more." She stopped to see the glassed-over effect on Lily's face.

"We are each computers. We are capable of incredible amounts of data processing, but if we had to write it out, it'd take forever. His brain can process, synthesize, and respond to that data in seconds. For all intents and purposes he's a living computer."

Jacob felt the sting of her dumbing down the science. She used words beyond his understanding as she thought about the situation. She flipped through papers on her clipboard and eyed the data, a smile appeared as she processed the information. Her jubilation was overwhelming and he almost sent her away to avoid the taste of her perky thoughts.

"Share, child," Dikeledi said. Her hand snaked along the scientist's shoulder. Jacob had no doubt the almost giddy expression on his companion's face was a byproduct of the woman in the lab coat. He pitied the empath for having to constantly ride an emotional rollercoaster when in close proximity to people.

"I need to consult my team. This Child of Nostradamus might be the answer to our problems."

Jacob didn't care to listen to her babble. A doctor stepped from the operating room into the decontamination room. Jacob let his thoughts touch the surgeon removing her gloves. She was satisfied with the job and she was creeped out that the man was capable of enduring the pain without so much as a wince. Despite that, she was certain he'd survive the ordeal if he ever came out of his trance.

The surgeon came in and before she could speak, Jacob interrupted. "I need to talk with the patient."

"He'll be in recovery for the next few days. After that—"

"I meant now." His voice echoed. She stepped out of the way of the door and held it open for him. He went past her and through the prep room into the operating theater. He was amazed with how much blood laced the white floor. He wondered if there would ever be a chance the Child could walk again or if he'd even be capable of a simple conversation.

"He's there," Dikeledi said. "I can sense his confidence. He knows we're here. He has no fear. He hardly has any emotions. He's either repressed or in control, I cannot tell."

"I can," Jacob said as he placed his hand on the man's bloody thigh. He ignored the thick, wet sensation of the fluid and focused on his eyes staring at the ceiling. The Child and Jacob blinked in unison. Their eyes opened to an empty white room. Jacob's formal suit transformed into a dark red, standing out against the nearly blinding emptiness of the infinite space around them.

"Who are you?"

"You don't seem surprised to have your legs. Or that we're standing on empty air."

"Should I be?"

Of all the psyches he had delved into, this was the first where the owner didn't seem shocked by the switch from one plane to another. The man wasn't nearly as dark skinned as Dikeledi, but in the bright white room, he practically stood like a shadow. Even his scrubs maintained the blood stains, looking out of place on the pristine white.

The man grabbed onto the bloodied shirt and tore it away from his body. As the fabric vanished into thin air, he stood wearing a nearly identical suit as Jacob. The white room blinked out of existence. They were standing in the middle of decrepit street, the pavement cracked, grass forcing its way to the surface. Behind them a pyramid of steps led to the front door of a grand cathedral, its wooden doors seeming to stretch three stories high.

"I am not your first telepath."

"You won't be my last," the man said.

"My name is Jacob Griffin."

"You're a mentalist, and I assume the company you keep are also mentalists. I'm assuming you work for the Society."

Jacob couldn't hide the expression on his face.

The man smiled. "You didn't think anybody outside your organization was aware? Or is it just that it took somebody with the ability to see the big picture to put the pieces together?"

"And that somebody is you?"

He shrugged.

"Dav5d," Jacob muttered.

"Eventually you'll wear me down and be able to read my thoughts. That's if..." the man's chest puffed out "...you can keep up."

"I want to know about your friends."

Dav5d shook his head. "You'll have to pry that out of me."

"I wouldn't have it any other way."

With the first step forward, Jacob's body exploded, leaving behind a smoky figure twice the size of his previous form. It wasn't a voice in the back of his head, it wasn't that darkness touching his mind, it was him now. The power coursed through his veins and he understood just how strong he had become. With each step forward the anger fueling his transformation grew. Reaching for the man, he was determined to tear down the Child's defenses.

A single punch threw Jacob backward, knocking his body from the smoky armor.

"How the fuck—"

"I've been sleeping with a telepath for as long as you've been able to read thoughts."

In the operating room, Jacob let his abilities wrap about Dikeledi and Lily, granting them entrance into the man's mind. They appeared on the steps of the church before the telepath understood what happened. He had once acted as the bridge between two people, but strained to maintain the connection. Now, his abilities called to them like it was second nature.

Jacob's body levitated upward until he was standing on his feet again. It was the first time he found an opponent to test out these newfound abilities. He wondered what limitations the man had, or if there were any at all.

Kill him.

Jacob's body vanished and reappeared behind Dav5d. He clutched the side of the black man's skull, letting tendrils of smoke pour out of his hands and wrap about his neck. Dav5d spun about, ducked out of the hold, and with a single palm forward slammed into Jacob's sternum. Unlike before, Jacob hardly budged.

"Fool me once," he said, waving his pointer finger.

Dav5'd body was thrown, hurled against the steps. Jacob watched as Lily motioned subtly with her fingers. She raised her hands, lifting Dav5d into the air until they were face to face. She inspected him, curious about what made him so special. "You don't seem so dangerous."

"That's the funny thing about mentalists. Your powers are limited by your mind." He dropped down to a crouch. With a swift fluid motion, his fist landed on the underside of her jaw. "My mind doesn't have any limitations."

"Like a mentalist," Dikeledi said. "So complex. Your mentor taught you well."

Jacob didn't try to hide the anger. The man was stating he was better than them. He claimed he was capable of outmatching three mentalists. Jacob didn't attempt to strike the man's avatar with his own. The mentalist was familiar with this battlefield, but he wondered how often the man's lover had tried to maneuver his thoughts. He didn't need the visuals of this scene to infiltrate the man's psyche.

Dav5d's avatar froze.

The smoke poured off Jacob until a shadowy form stood next to him. The figure stomped toward Dav5d and latched its arms onto him. In a rush of sound, Jacob heard the million thoughts being processed by Dav5d at once. He attempted to understand what was happening, calculating the powers being exerted on him.

Jacob watched as the shadow grappled with the Child. For a moment fear entered his mind. He understood there was no difference between him and the shadow consuming his thoughts. At first he believed the relationship between them was symbiotic, but as he witnessed memories of the green woman fighting a person, him, his sense of self vanished into the darkness.

"Warden," Dav5d whispered.

Jacob had suspected it before. But as he listened to a memory of the Child's lover describing a dream where a shadowy figure tried to consume her essence, he became certain it was the Warden. As the man struggled, Jacob smiled, the power of the dead mentalist wrapping around him.

"Yes," Jacob hissed. He drew back his hand and plunged it into Dav5d's chest. The man's thoughts slowed as the shadows strangled him. Jacob clenched his jaw, forcing his will onto the man, determined to break him.

Dav5d's eyes were glassy again. Jacob sensed him trying to lock down parts of his mind, to hide somewhere inside his psyche. With every barrier

Jacob's powers encountered, he blew apart the doors, invading every ounce of the man's mind. Jacob screamed out at the awesomeness of his abilities. His former self would never have been able to keep up with the Child, now it hardly seemed fair.

"Vanessa," Dav5d whispered as his eyes filled with black smoke.

Jacob staggered back from the man. He knew the sensation of consuming a person; the Barren were similar, dolls ready for his command. He didn't think he'd be able to do it to a person without the numerous synthetic cocktails they fed the Barren volunteers. The victory was only made sweeter knowing he had broken a Child of Nostradamus, one of last bastions against his abilities.

"Jacob?" asked Lily.

He turned to see the two women on the steps leading to the church. He sensed their fear as they watched the smoky outline about his body appear more akin to a monster than his normal self.

"Is that you?" she asked.

"And so much more."

Chapter 18

2033

A stillness in the warehouse made it even creepier than it appeared. He felt the cold cement against his cheek as he stared off into the distance. It took him a moment to realize he was in his warehouse. As Conthan grasped at memories, he fought to keep exhaustion from consuming him.

It had been a year since he sat on the scavenged car backseat while drinking around a fire. He remembered the rest of his collective cheering on his opening show. It had been the night before his world changed and he went from up and coming artist to Child of Nostradamus. As the pounding in his head moved in time with his pulse, he wondered if there was any vodka left.

"Dwayne," he whispered, his voice hoarse from yelling in the subway. The man lay on the ground, his body unmoving. Conthan let his muscles scream at him as he pushed himself up to his knees. The world spun and his stomach threatened to hurl its contents.

He crawled the several feet to Dwayne. He moved his ear close to the man's nose, listening to the faintest of breaths. He touched Dwayne's neck like they did in the movies and the pulse was almost nonexistent. Conthan touched his cheek, giving it a light tap, seeing if he could wake him.

"I don't know what to do," he whispered.

"We can't do anything," Vanessa said, her green form sprawled out on the ground.

"What do you mean?"

"He's in there, I can still hear him. But his body—"

Vanessa stood, her feet staggering underneath her. She almost appeared drunk, unable to hold herself straight. She rubbed her eyes and blinked several times. Conthan couldn't figure out what she was looking for as she spun about, eyeing the shadows.

"What are you doing?"

Vanessa lunged, grabbing at the air. She growled as her hands passed harmlessly through the empty space. She spun about and tried again, missing her invisible enemy. Conthan thought she lost her mind. With her third lunge, his eyes widened as it seemed a woman appeared and vanished quicker than he could make out.

"Who's there?" he asked.

"There's another Child in here, Conthan. I can sense them, but they're skilled at hiding their thoughts."

"Conthan?"

She stepped out of nothingness. The signature

shaved side of her head and long neon pink locks resting on her shoulder gave away her identity. He thought back to the church and was certain he had seen her. The tattoos snaking their way up her neck and onto the side of her head were one of a kind. Before he could speak, Vanessa tackled her to the ground.

"Who are you?"

He tried to stand but his legs gave out under him. "Vanessa, no!"

The gargoyle paused, turning back to her friend. She held the woman to the ground with one hand firmly planted on her chest. "Who is she?"

"Gretchen," he said, his voice giving away his disbelief.

"Long time no see. Now get off me, you beast," she said shoving Vanessa backward.

"It was you I saw at the church."

"Yeah," she said. "Sorry about that, couldn't let the synthetics catch me."

"Why were you there?"

Gretchen vanished from sight. It felt like an eternity as Vanessa reared backward, uncertain with what was happening. A few seconds later Gretchen appeared again, dusting off her ripped jeans.

"Funny fucking story." She smiled. "The people there kind of worship me."

"Why?"

"Cause I'm a Child."

***

Jasmine shielded Skits and Alyssa with her body

257

as her back skid along the ground. Her shoulder blades dug into the flooring, threatening to break through the surface as she came to a stop. She let go of her passengers and they were fast to their feet.

Alyssa stayed low to the ground, inspecting her surroundings to see if they were followed. Jasmine had no doubt the girl's powers had faded. Her stance was awkward, and it appeared as if she mimicked movies more than showing the skill of a martial arts master. Skits was in a similar situation, her hands barely able to glow. Jasmine wondered if the plasma burned the same temperature or if it grew cooler as the girl tired.

"Where are we?" She groaned as she worked her way to her feet.

"I've been here before," Alyssa said.

Jasmine's skin loosened and her muscles relaxed as her powers slipped away. She felt as if she had been holding her breath and as she let go of her tough exterior, she breathed easier. She hoped they were alone and that she wouldn't need her abilities.

The room wasn't huge, perhaps a hundred people could fill the space. It was empty, the floor littered with napkins and plates. Smashed glass seemed to be scattered here and there. The walls were painted a solid white and evenly spaced frames hung along the wall. It dawned on her she was standing amongst walls of art.

"A gallery?"

The layer of dust on the floor and the mess left by patrons told her it hadn't been used in quite some time. She watched as Alyssa's body eased to a standing position. The young girl inspected the burn mark along the wall. Her attention was captured by one of the poster-sized frames.

Skits joined her and finally Jasmine walked over to see what drew them. She gasped out loud as she saw the figure in the painting. A young girl sat for the artist, wearing a man's button down shirt, her shoulder exposed for the viewer. Where the supple skin of her breast should have been, a rock-like formation broke through the skin, obscuring her femininity.

"It's Sarah," Jasmine whispered.

The woman's face was covered in similar bone growths. The girl appeared bashful, almost ready to blush at the artist, but she held her cheeks in check. However, from the majority of her skin, bones emerged, consuming her flesh, making her look more like a golem than a pretty young girl.

"We're at the gallery where Conthan discovered his abilities," Alyssa said.

"That's a creepy coincidence," Skits said.

"I'm not sure I believe in coincidences anymore," Jasmine said as she moved to the next painting.

"Vanessa sent Dwayne and me to keep any eye on him. The party was great, people were admiring his work. I mean, they said he had real talent, and then she got up and gave a speech about him. That's when his life changed."

"He's never talked about the specifics," Skits commented.

"I don't know, he went out the back door and we provided cover for him. The Corps showed up. They swamped the place and we stopped them."

"He is quite talented," Jasmine said as she inspected a charcoal drawing. She had never been big into the arts. She hardly listened to music, and she couldn't recall the last movie she watched, but she saw the beauty in his work. Underneath the transformation of his friend, there was a beautiful young woman and she understood the world stopped seeing that as the bones pushed to the surface. Whatever she was before, now she served as a freak show for the public.

To everybody but Conthan, she thought.

Jasmine admired how every push of the black lines seemed to take a gentle approach in showing her calcified exterior. She had to wonder if he felt this way before her transformation or if he idealized the beauty he thought existed in all people. He captured a memory of somebody lost to him.

She thought of the young girl from Troy.

Tears streamed down the side of her face. She could handle machines sent to exterminate her or even fighting to a point where she might die. She had no problem with the physical. But as the emotions rolled over her, she reminded herself that beneath the tough exterior, she was human. She wiped the tears off her face and caught the girls staring at her.

"Why here?" Skits asked, avoiding an awkward bonding conversation.

"Maybe it was what he was thinking about when he made a portal?" said Alyssa.

"I'm sure there's a reason we're here," Jasmine said. "I don't buy that it's a coincidence."

"What about the others?"

Jasmine couldn't ignore the worry on Skits face. "Let's get ourselves in shape to travel, then we'll figure out what's going on."

"I could sleep for days," Skits said as she slid down the wall.

"You have two hours, soldier," Jasmine said. "Then we find the others."

"Then what?" asked Alyssa.

"We're going to find who is hunting us down and kill them."

"Sold," Alyssa said, sliding down the wall next to Skits.

Jasmine gritted her teeth. She was ready to begin killing anybody who got in her way. It wasn't enough to think about revenge. Somebody wanted to eradicate their existence, and the only way she knew to fight back was to kill everybody involved.

***

Conthan checked on Dwayne, covering his half-naked body with a flannel blanket. His prone form hadn't moved since the attack earlier. He breathed deeply, little snores slipping in here and there. His body barely fit on the backseat torn from an old car. Conthan rested his hand on the man's chest, taking comfort in the warmth of Dwayne's skin while it rose and fell in time with his breathing. Conthan wished he could make him more comfortable, but for the moment, this was the best they had to offer.

Vanessa, on the other hand, sat on the roof of the warehouse. He thought about joining her, but she needed to work out her demons in solitude. He didn't have to ask; he knew she was torn up over what happened with Dwayne and losing Dav5d.

He wondered if he could find the man. In a few seconds he could teleport in, vanish, and be back before anybody knew he was gone. He wished he had the ability to locate people. Perhaps Vanessa could do it and guide him. For now, he'd have to wait until she made peace with what she had done.

"He looks weird without eyebrows."

"Says the girl with enough piercings to set off a metal detector."

Gretchen had procured a black shawl, wrapping it tightly around herself. The cold of the water started to set in. He stood up and inspected Dwayne's face again. "Not weird," he said, "more like unique."

"Did you just say that out loud?"

"You and Skits are going to get along too well."

"The gymnast?"

"The plasma maker."

"Hi," she said, "you open black holes. He shoots lightning. The gargoyle on the roof can fly and read minds. And you have a girl who makes fire? My name is Gretchen, I go invisible." She took a moment to let the reality soak in—that she harbored jealousy for powers a little flashier than her own.

"They treat you good?"

He smiled as Dwayne snorted in his sleep. He hadn't thought of it in a long time. There had been a time it had been weird; they had been strangers, and he was a struggling artist. Now, he wasn't sure he could go back to his old life. He'd miss the morning coffee in the bar. He'd miss the people, present company included.

"They're family."

"I thought I had family issues."

She put her hands on his shoulders and leaned against his body. He wrapped his arm around her. He wasn't sure what to say. She had been such an important person in his life. But that life didn't exist anymore. He wasn't sure if she'd like the person he had become.

"Who is he to you?"

He smiled again. "Great, another telepath."

"Ew, I wouldn't want to hear what goes on in that head."

"He's somebody…"

"Special?"

"Yeah."

She nodded in silence. He appreciated her knowing when to avoid asking more questions. He wasn't sure he'd have answers for her at this point. Seeing the man unconscious on the couch caused a tightness in his chest. Whatever demons Vanessa dealt with, Dwayne had them as well. Conthan realized he had his own to deal with at this point.

"I need to go."

"I'm going with you."

"You can't," he said. "I don't want you to get hurt."

"I'm not staying with a human lightning bolt and a woman who could eat me alive."

She yelped as he thrust his hip into her. Her voice ceased as the blackness of a portal swallowed her. He took a step to the side and fell after her. The cold caused the hair on his arm to stand on end. His body violently shook in an attempt to push away the chill.

"What the fuck?"

He held a finger up to his lips. She stood up and shoved him. "I am not going to be quiet. What the hell did you do? Are we in hell? Why is it so cold? How did you do that?"

He grabbed her. Spinning her around, he placed a hand on her mouth. He ducked behind a half crumbled stone wall and leaned in close to her ear. "You wanted to see my world."

"Illegal trespassing."

The mechanical voice had become common to him. He didn't have the police scanners Dav5d built to locate damsels in distress. He teleported to the one place he knew would still be crawling with synthetics. The church looked even more eerie without parishioners lining the walls. Despite the clouds, the moon cast a faint light through the windows. He wasn't certain if there was a God, but if there had been, he had turned his back on this place years ago. Now, its charm came from its determination to survive without its savior. He found the archaic building to be empowering.

"Stay quiet."

"What about—"

"I said quiet," he snapped.

The sound of metal tapping on tile filled the chamber. He found it difficult to believe that after all the machines they destroyed, it wasn't even a small fraction of what littered the streets on patrol. The tapping grew louder as it reached the doors leading into the main room of the church.

"Trespassing is punishable by death."

Just hours ago he had opened the most portals he ever had in such a short time. He knew he only had so much juice for the fight, but there was aggression he needed to take out on the enemy.

The red dot flared. The light filled the end of the weapon and was ready to punch through the center of his skull. With a flick of Conthan's wrist, a portal opened and the laser redirected itself, punching through the head of the synthetic. Its body hit the floor, clattering like bones against the tile.

"What the hell—"

"Shhh," he hissed.

Another synthetic appeared, this one standing almost perfectly in the way of the rose window, the light casting an eerie shadow. He had suspected there would be plenty of machines watching the church. He imagined they waited for people to come back so they could exterminate the cults worshipping superpowered gods.

He waited for the machine to move. If it jumped, he'd send it into the bay. If it fired, he'd redirect the shot again into its head. He wished he had the ability to fight fist to fist with them like Jasmine. He could only imagine how many innocent people had been killed by the tin bucket. Or tortured. If they weren't killing the cults, they were forcing them to confess about their gods.

The heat in the pit of his stomach washed over his body. He was mad. It wasn't about survival anymore, it was about revenge. Just as he decided to open a portal in the machine's torso, metal shots clanged against the robot. Bright lights appeared as guns fired, the ammo ricocheting off the synthetic's hide

The synthetic turned to and fro, looking for the people firing. Before it could move to stop the attackers, a hiss filled the room and a small explosion tore the machine into pieces. The grandeur of the rose window came crashing down as the machine was hurled backward by the explosion. Glass fell to the floor in a wave, covering the far end of the room.

A minute passed while he froze in place. The crunch of glass on the floor made him turn to Gretchen. He expected to see her running, but she remained huddled in the corner where he had left her. He held his breath for a moment and was certain he heard at least two sets of feet moving.

"Shit," he said.

The room lit up as a man rapidly pulled a trigger. Conthan dove across the floor, sliding behind another column. He had been prepared to destroy machines. He wanted nothing more than to take the fight to the president herself, and stop her marshal law. He hadn't been expecting humans.

His back pressed against the column. He turned to yell for Gretchen but she had vanished. He wasn't sure if she was standing right there or if she had run for cover. Another bullet fired, chipping away at the cement near his head, causing him to scoot further out of the line of sight.

"Who are you?" he shouted.

"We're the ones with guns."

He could teleport out of there and be gone without much more than a thought, but not without

Gretchen. He wasn't sure if she was safe or even capable of surviving on her own. He had a suspicion the girl learned to keep herself alive, but he refused to leave another friend.

The image of Dav5d being pinned down by falling rock as Vanessa stole his body came to mind. He couldn't save the man. They relied on him, and in the most dire situation he let them down. He didn't like that Vanessa raped his mind, but he understood why. The feeling of grief raced along his spine, so overwhelming he thought his heart would explode. He'd have done the same thing.

"Vagrant or Child?"

"Your mom."

"Dead either way," said another voice.

Conthan laughed. They were only alive because he was holding back. He understood it now. He understood why Dwayne did what he did. Somebody had to be willing to cross the line.

The fire in his stomach sent waves of warmth through his body.

"What's so funny, boy?"

He let the anger touch his skin, all his hair standing on end. He closed his eyes and let the sensation at the base of his brain wash through him. When he opened them again, the world seemed almost monotone, as if the color had been sapped away. This was his reality now.

"Doesn't matter," he shouted. "You're dead either way."

***

All three stared at the hole in the wall. In a fit of anger, maddened by the events unfolding around her, Jasmine slammed her fist into the surface, dislodging several bricks. As she pulled her bruised knuckles back, bricks fell to the right of Conthan's drawings, leaving a gaping hole in the structure. Jasmine continued to huff and puff, but none of them spoke up as another brick clacked down onto the floor.

She shook her fist, willing the pain to fade away. Being a Child of Nostradamus awarded her more strength than the average human, but her knuckles would hurt for days. She turned to Alyssa and raised an eyebrow. The young girl shrugged her shoulders in response to her quizzical look.

"What are the chances this is random?"

Jasmine hated the idea. Whenever something unusual happened, it always pointed back to one person. She wondered if this was the same. Was the hole a freak coincidence, or did a tampered fate strike again?

"You know we're going in," Skits said.

She did.

She pulled at the bricks, tearing away at the drywall as she went along. Alyssa started peeling back the plaster and Skits kicked at the failing brick wall. Once the hole was big enough Jasmine stepped through, the fine powder of plaster coating her uniform. The faint light from the gallery gave away the hallway leading to a much larger room.

"The air is stale. Nobody has been in here in decades."

Skits crawled through after her. The teen held up

her hand and a wave of blue light appeared. Jasmine ran her hand along the tiled walls. The dank hall continued until it opened into a much larger room. Every step echoed about the space, bouncing off the ceramic.

Jasmine discovered a light switch. With a flip, the overhead fluorescent lights surged to life. Several of the bulbs refused to ignite and another buzzed loudly. She let out her breath, feeling the reveal was anticlimactic.

"A locker room?" asked Skits.

In the middle of the room, a bank of two dozen lockers stretched from floor to ceiling. Surrounding them on all sides were benches anchored into the floor. Toilets with no stall doors lined one wall while the other housed a communal shower.

"Not what I was expecting," Alyssa confessed.

"So the art gallery has a locker room? Maybe the owner just covered it up and ignored it instead of converting it to another room?"

Jasmine shook her head. "The gallery is where Conthan found out he was a Child. The same gallery where you first saw him. The same gallery where he discovered his first letter. I'm not buying it."

"Conspiracy much?"

Jasmine ignored Skits. If it had been a year ago, she would have agreed. But now, she didn't believe in coincidences. There was something about this place tugging at the pit of her stomach. It didn't have the same aggressive sensation of her former boss, but Jasmine felt as if she was being pushed in a direction against her will.

Several lights shorted, plunging them into darkness. Their surroundings vanished into shadowy depths. She couldn't imagine what the place had been at one time. Maybe it was a dorm or perhaps a gym. She had no idea how old it might be; the tile along the floor and walls reminded her of something out of a movie from the last century.

"Subhanallah."

Jasmine followed Alyssa's line of sight. The lone flickering light illuminated the group of lockers. The tape stuck at eye height had all but fallen off, clinging to the closest locker within an inch of its life. Scribbled along the tape, a single name.

"Eleanor," Jasmine whispered.

"That woman is everywhere," Skits said.

Jasmine pointed to the lock. Skits grabbed it in the palm of her hand and metal melted away until it hardened again on the ground. Jasmine admitted the girl's abilities were impressive.

"What are the chances?"

Jasmine looked over her shoulder to Alyssa. The woman's eyes were still wide in disbelief while she muttered a prayer to herself.

"With Eleanor? One hundred percent."

Jasmine pulled the door open. On the inside several pictures were tucked into the metal lip. One showed a young woman with a man in a firefighter uniform. Another black and white photo showed two young kids, a girl and a brother. She imagined the woman had looked like a spinster since the day she was born. What she saw in a half dozen photos was a young woman full of life.

"She's beautiful," Skits said.

270

Alyssa pushed between them to see the photos. Jasmine rummaged through the articles of clothing hanging from hooks. She tossed the shirts and pants to the floor. She reached down for the last shirt and found underneath it was a thick book.

"Holy shit."

Jasmine agreed with Skits. In just a handful of letters, Eleanor had manipulated the world. She altered the future to such a degree it was difficult to think what she could do if the woman wasn't dead. Now, in a book at the bottom of a locker in the middle of an art gallery, it was almost as if she was alive.

"What do we do?"

Alyssa grabbed the book and tucked it against her chest. "Allah save us, but we're taking it."

"We can read it while we find the others." Jasmine started to follow Skits and Alyssa out of the locker room. She paused and snatched the photograph of Eleanor and the fireman. She tucked it away in her breast pocket as they left.

"Where do you think they are?" asked Alyssa.

"If he sent us to some place familiar, maybe he did the same for the others?" Jasmine replied.

"His house?"

Skits shook her head. "He'd go to the other artists. There's a warehouse near the bay."

Jasmine wondered what brought Eleanor to this place. The oldest image of her was in her early twenties, and at that time the gym would be a place where you'd never find a woman. Was the man her father? As with every encounter with the Eleanor, she was left with more questions than answers.

271

Somehow, locked away in this room, she had a feeling this had been the start of something for the young woman. Did she work out here? Or was she just there as a byproduct of her father being in the gym?

The questions running through her mind calmed the need for revenge. She wondered if the woman knew what would happen. If she couldn't predict their future beyond the letters she sent, did she even know they would find the book?

Jasmine froze at the thought. *Are we on our own now?*

Chapter 19

1993

Mark's opponent jabbed and went wide with his right glove. Mark ducked down and took several hits to the man's exposed torso. The other fighter took a step back out of reach and held his hands up in a defensive position.

For the last three months a couple of the security guards had invited him to work out in the gym. Two of them had been knocked to the ground during the first encounter with Arturo, their resident pyro. The third guard, the one currently putting him through the motions, had received the worst of the attack that day; part of his neck and the side of his face were covered in burned scar tissue. Even with all their technology, it was the most they could do for him. Other than Goddard, Mark's sparring partner received the worst of it.

A jab to the face brought him back to reality. He continued dodging and punching, taking safe punches where he could. As he huffed and puffed, his endurance finally started to wear out on him. He took a step back and waved the man off. "You're going to kill me, Sanchez."

"Somebody has to keep you in shape."

Mark bent over, gloves resting on his knees. He took a couple of deep breaths, trying not to sound as out of shape as he felt. For three months he built his endurance, toned his muscles, and even gave himself a reasonable physique he was proud to show off, but he wasn't nearly as in shape as the guards. They trained to keep their jobs; he did it so he wouldn't have a heart attack by the time he was thirty.

There was a clanking sound from behind him. He didn't need to turn around to know that it was Goddard clapping. Mark fought down the bile in his throat. The man had become even more insufferable since he had his hands removed and replaced with electronic prosthetics. Instead of having them coated in a skin-like material, he preferred to show off his cyborg body parts.

"The Tinman decided to come play with the rest of us," Mark said.

None of the security staff would speak out against him, but Mark was well aware they thought their boss was a monstrosity. Many of the guards were even coming to understand Mark's need to work with the mentalist, but for every step they took forward, Goddard was determined to push them back. A single man made progress nearly impossible. Ivan demanded Goddard have his security clearance to the mentalists revoked, and under duress of his quitting the project, the president reluctantly agreed.

"Someday, we'll have to see how well you fare against somebody a bit closer to your weight class."

Mark smiled at the offer. He faced the man. "Are you making an idle threat or asking to get in the ring?"

Sanchez stepped out next to his coworkers. They watched, unsure of what was about to happen. Mark studied Goddard's face; by his expression, the guard was taken aback by the brazen offer. Mark had discovered the bully backed down before his enhancements. Now that he was part robot, he felt the need to prove his manhood more often than not.

"Let me get some gloves," Goddard said with a sneer.

"Not necessary," Mark said. The warmth in the pit of his stomach would turn to anger at any moment. He started working out to control the anger more than improve his body. Something about the dark side of his personality frightened him. It got to a point where he wondered if the empath projected her feelings beyond her medically induced coma.

Goddard fumbled with the buttons on his shirt. While the limbs were highly advanced cybernetics, their fine motor control left something to be desired. He ultimately ripped off the button down shirt, leaving him in his off-duty pants and a wife beater. When they first met, Mark had been terrified of the man, but now, there was something satisfying about standing up to the bully.

Mark stepped into the center of the ring and held out his gloves to bump with his opponent. Goddard tapped them and held up his fists. Mark started, a jab, a jab, a hook, a jab to the man's gut. Each punch was blocked by the superior fighter as Goddard returned the gesture, punching the gloves defending Mark's face. The impact caused his own gloves to hit him in the face. Mark was surprised with how strong the guard was.

A moment of distraction prevented the Mark from seeing the steely fist coming in low, jabbing him hard in the gut. He doubled over, the wind knocked from his lungs. Mark stepped backward to gain his composure. Goddard looked ready to celebrate his victory. Mark pushed forward, a jab, a jab, and a left hook connecting hard enough it knocked the spit out of the guard's mouth.

Mark jumped back and smiled. "You're nothing more than an annoyance, Goddard. Don't think you matter to me any more than dealing with a crying child."

Goddard didn't wait for him to finish. He punched Mark in the gut twice and with his metal forearm, slammed him on the shoulder, sending him to the ground. "Work out a few times a week and think you're something I should be worried about?"

Mark looked across the gym equipment to see Ivan watching the fight unfold. Since the incident in the lobby, Ivan had become Mark's biggest supporter. They agreed their intentions weren't in aligned, but they both had goals requiring cooperation. After a night of furious vodka shots, they made a truce. Now, standing behind the free weights, Ivan gave a slight nod. He was the only man who hated Goddard more than Mark.

Adrenaline coursed through his veins, and he became aware of his vision narrowing, almost to the point where he thought he might pass out. He turned and focused on Goddard, who started to hop back and forth in the ring, acting like a champ.

"Try me," Mark whispered.

The man's fist thrust forward. Mark ducked underneath the chunk of metal and jabbed him hard in the ribcage. Before Goddard could defend himself, Mark jumped backward, dodging a fist to the face.

"Glad to see you're not a complete pussy."

"Says the cyborg," Mark said with a sly smirk.

Mark could tell by the stance, Goddard would come in with his fist wide, hoping Mark blocked, leaving his ribcage exposed. As he stepped forward Mark watched his movements seem to slow. He ducked under the hook and punched the guard solidly in the lower torso. He had the groin shot, but he didn't want this to end. He wanted to make an example.

"You're predictable, Goddard. Stupid men always are."

The charade of boxing vanished. Goddard moved in tight, wrapping his hands around the Mark's head. He rolled, landing on his back with Mark in tow. He wedged his foot against Mark's stomach and kicked hard, sending the novice fighter down in the ring. Goddard jumped upright to see Mark was already waiting for him.

Mark's knee crunched against the man's lower jaw, threatening to shatter his teeth. Goddard rolled backward, getting back to his feet. His eyes narrowed, studying his prey, trying to figure out how Mark had gone from a soft, whiny man to a fighter.

"Are we done? Or do you need me to school you some more?"

"You're itching for a bruising, aren't you?"

"You have to hit me first," Mark spat back.

Goddard was going to step inside his reach. He was going to try and pull Mark's face down onto his knee. While he cradled his broken nose, Goddard was going to slam him down on the mat, leaving him immobile. Mark knew exactly what the man thought in that moment.

As Goddard rushed him, Mark dropped down low to the ground. He reached through Goddard's legs and lifted hard, sending the man onto his back. Mark jumped onto him, slamming his gloved fist into his face over and over again. He finally got his moment, his chance to pulverize the annoying, useless security guard.

"Mark," cried the men on the side of the ring.

As he brought his fist back, he examined the bloody face. Goddard's nose had broken and both of his eyes were swelling shut. Mark wanted to continue, go until the man's body stopped moving. He wanted to feel the muscles slump underneath him. He wanted to hear the final breath escape Goddard's lips.

"Oh my God," Mark whispered.

Blood coated his gloves and the front of his shirt. He was covered in Goddard's blood. He wanted the man dead. He wanted nothing more than to watch the man die. He pulled at the gloves until they

278

finally slid off. He sat back, staring at his rival, watching the man's head tilt from side to side as he tried to make sense of the world.

Mark stood, his legs trembling from the lack of adrenaline in his system. He turned to the three security guards. "Take him to the medics. Make sure they patch him up."

"What if they ask what happened?"

Mark raised his eyebrow at the questioner, appreciative of their loyalty. "If they ask, tell them he rubbed me the wrong way." What was he saying?

The guards didn't try to hide their surprise. The man standing in the ring, he wasn't the same man they had grown to know. Goddard's presence irritated Mark until the worst of him came out. He wished he could say he didn't like it, but there was something seductive about the power as he hovered over the man. He had to pull himself back before he did something he'd regret for the rest of his life.

Ivan gave a slight nod. Mark assumed he was there to discuss the empath again and what they should do to bring him out of the coma. Mark wasn't entirely sure what they were doing to the kid was ethical, but it sedation or the entire center trying to kill one another again. For now, he'd keep to arguing with Ivan about best practices.

Mark stepped off the ring and walked to the door leading to the locker room. He turned to watch the three men climb into the ring to pick up their supervisor. Pulping Goddard wasn't the smartest idea, but eventually gossip would start and people would realize he wasn't somebody to take lightly.

He wasn't stupid, however; there was only so much pushing he could do with Goddard before it escalated to something dangerous. Right now, he remained too satisfied to care about the risks.

With only a dozen lockers, two benches, and three showers, the room was modest. The sleeping quarters had more space for the security detail stationed with the center for the long term. He pulled off his bloody t-shirt and tossed it into the trash can. He slid his shorts down and grabbed his towel hanging on the door to his locker. He stopped for a moment when he caught a glimpse of himself naked in the mirror.

Despite the blood strewn across his face, he admired what the mirror showed him. He still had a gut, but he had more muscle than he had in years. He almost had definition on his chest. He flexed his pecs for a moment to make them more pronounced. His legs had always been thin, the legs of a runner, but now they were starting to show some bulk. He was impressed with his physique.

"I'd fuck me." He laughed.

He hoped he could keep up this progress and eventually he'd be ripped. There was something satisfying about his work shirts starting to feel tight some place other than his gut. He would catch himself flexing, showing off his muscles, making the secretaries stare at him. He wasn't perfect, but he was well on his way. Even Elizabeth had been shocked to see him last time he visited.

He snatched his towel and headed to the shower. He turned the handle, giving it a spin until it reached the perfect temperature, scalding hot. He stepped into the stream and let the water pulse against his face. The blood washed down his body, disappearing into the drain. As the fight began to slip from his mind, he started thinking about the last time he had seen Elizabeth. She had been thrilled when he mentioned he started going to the gym. She had even commented on how bulky he had become as he lifted her off the ground with one arm.

"Looks like the prison life is treating you well, Mr. Davis," she said jokingly.

"Have to make sure I don't turn into somebody's prison bitch," he returned.

She paused at his candid language. "Since when did you start using words like 'prison bitch? I'm not even sure you knew what that meant a year ago."

He laughed a little at the memory. She was right, something about this place was rubbing off on him. It wasn't enough he tried to look like an Adonis, but now he started to play by their rules. He wasn't sure if he liked what it was doing to him, but he couldn't refute the progress he made.

He leaned his face into the spray, letting the water wash over his head and down his back. Between power plays with a scared, childish security guard, they made progress, real progress. The cybernetics division was being merged with a private company and housed at the center. The Genesis Division had been doing similar research, and with their breakthroughs in human-robotic integration, they were on the verge of a revolution.

Then there were the mentalists, three individuals he had hoped would pave the way to save an entire subset of their species. They were years away from making any serious developments warranting attention, but for now, small victories happened daily. They developed, with the aid of the Genesis Division, a method to help inhibit Penelope's empathy. Even Arturo learned to control his abilities with the help of Ariel. Project Nostradamus made strides, even if not as quickly as he hoped.

The thought trailed off into nothingness. The image of Elizabeth, his sexy wife, naked on their bed, filled his head. The expression on her face was priceless as he pulled the shirt over his head and dropped his PJ pants. She stared at him in fascination, blushing when she realized she had been caught. He climbed on top of her, brushing his lips along her torso, working his way slowly up her body. He paused at her breasts, kissing the spot where they touched her sternum.

He stared into her eyes, waiting for her to make one of her goofy comments about how he worshipped her body. She pushed him to the side and climbed up onto him, straddling his torso. She kissed along his neck and bit his ear, her signal that she was ready for something a little more energetic than usual. He watched as she adored him, and he couldn't help but think he was the luckiest guy in the world.

The next two hours they traded positions, playing a game of one-upping in the bedroom and working harder to satisfy the other. He ultimately found himself on top of her, holding her hands above her head as he thrust. She cried out and at some point he heard the sound of her cries turn from ecstasy to pain. He continued, determined to make them both climax.

"Mark," she said, "you big lug, you're a bit stronger than you used to be."

He refused to relent as he pinned her wrists. There was something satisfying about watching her writhe each time he penetrated her. Tears streamed from her eyes as she tried to pull her hands free from his grip. With two more thrusts he felt the wave of pleasure start in his groin and radiate throughout his body. She arched her back, crying out as they both came. He fell to her side, basking in the radiance of his orgasm.

"You asshole," she said, sitting up. "I guess the bigger the muscle, the stupider the man," she said as she stormed off to the bathroom. It took a moment for him to realize what happened. They had both been rough in the sack before, but nothing like that. She hadn't been thrilled. He thought about getting up and knocking on the bathroom door to apologize. Instead he closed his eyes and drifted off to sleep.

The memory excited him. He stared down to see he was erect. He thought about taking care of business but decided it'd give him motivation to speed through the day. He shut off the shower and stepped outside to towel off. As he wiped the last of the water off his body, he could see a single red spot on the white towel, a speck of blood that must have sprayed onto him earlier.

"It's one thing to be cocky, it's another to be a cock," Elizabeth said the next day. The rest of his week with her had been magical, but they had avoided discussing that night again. As he stared down at the drop of blood, her words continued to loop through his head.

"Being a cock is going to keep me alive," he said, throwing the towel into the trashcan.

Chapter 20

2033

The flash grenade sent him wheeling backward. Pain radiated through his back as he hit the ground, bruising the base of his spine. He blinked several times, trying to remove the bright orbs dancing about in his vision. Sound seemed to come and go, waves of silence followed by the rushing of water and then silence again. He tried to stand but he couldn't get his bearings.

A man stepped through the smoke. He wore body armor similar to Jasmine's Paladin uniform. Conthan held out his hand and tried to find the spot in his mind that gave him access to his powers. With a simple thought he'd remove the man's head. All he found was the likelihood of hurling all over the ground.

The orbs began to vanish. He could make the man out more clearly now. He wasn't much older than Conthan, maybe a year or two. The Corps recruited them young and raised them within their ranks. He had no doubt the man was laced with artificial muscle enhancers or synthetic eyes. He tried to focus, but there were no superhuman abilities for him to grasp at.

The man pointed his rifle at Conthan. With only a few feet between them his brains would certainly smear across the floor. Conthan's mouth moved, but there was no voice. The soldier laughed and raised the gun sight to his eye. Conthan pushed backward, trying to put distance between them.

The man jerked his gun to the side, firing off into nothingness. Conthan flipped over to get to his knees. He swallowed down the bile rising in his throat. He turned just in time to see the man's head jerk to the side like he was hit with a sledgehammer. The man swung his arm out and Gretchen flickered into sight. She landed on her back with an "Oomph."

"There's two of them," came another soldier's voice.

"She didn't show up on the infrared."

Conthan could barely make out the voices shouting at one another. The moment Gretchen's eyes opened, she vanished again. It was hard to believe she was a Child of Nostradamus. Unlike him, she hadn't spent the last year training. She didn't have Dwayne chucking lightning at her, or Dav5d telling her how to optimize her abilities.

"Where the hell did she go?"

Conthan didn't think as he hurled himself at the soldier in front of him. He grabbed the gun, pushing it to the side. Gripping the man's tactical vest, Conthan lifted his legs, pulling the man to the floor.

Instead of hitting the weathered wooden planks, biting cold encompassed their bodies. The darkness of his portal wrapped around them. As quickly as it vanished, they emerged twenty feet in the air.

The soldier's face tightened as he threw a fist, connecting with the teleporter's jaw. Conthan grabbed on tight to the man's vest and braced for impact. They slammed into the ground, the floor boards splitting and cracking from the crash. The man's head battered a piece of stone fallen from one of the columns. Conthan rolled off him, his entire body radiating pain.

"What the fuck?" yelled the other soldier.

He raised his gun but before he could pull the trigger, Conthan watched the color in the room shift. It took him a moment to realize he was seeing the world desaturated, almost as if they were in a black and white painting.

"He can't see us."

Conthan looked down to see Gretchen clutching his ankle with both hands. He had seen her use her abilities, but she might be more capable than he gave credit for. The punker had more tricks up her sleeve than he thought. He touched his ear and then pointed to the soldier.

"No sound. He doesn't have anything that can find us."

"Damn," Conthan whispered, impressed with her abilities.

"Can you teleport us out of here?"

He nodded.

"Sir," the soldier barked. "Both are gone. I can't see them on thermal or motion sensors. It's like they were never here." He waited for a reply. "No, he's dead. Fucker just got accepted to be a Paladin."

Conthan's ears perked up at the mention of Jasmine's former team. He didn't know much about them, but he couldn't resist getting more intel on the situation. He held up a finger to Gretchen, telling her to wait.

"Yes, it was her," he said. "The synthetics were waiting. Seems the president wants her too."

Conthan couldn't imagine what they would want with the owner of an art gallery. Even with her abilities, she wasn't very high on the list of dangerous Children. It seemed there was more to the story than Gretchen let on.

"Let's get out of here."

He reached down and took her by the hand. They stood and he watched as the soldier checked the magazine on his rifle and started surveying the damage. Conthan didn't feel remorse. He didn't feel anything in the pit of his stomach as he flicked his wrist. The portal was small, but it was enough to sever the soldier's spine. Conthan closed it as fast as he opened the rip in space. The man's body froze and collapsed to the ground in a thud.

"What did you do?"

He didn't answer. He opened a portal next to them. Gretchen stepped through. He eyed the dead man's face one more time before he entered the cold. They were at war. It dragged him down, forcing him to become one of them. He wasn't sure if it was worth fighting or if it was time to make peace with what he had to do to survive.

***

"Better hope you're right about this," Alyssa said.

"Do you have a better idea?" Jasmine wasn't thrilled to be barreling through the streets in the old beat-up car they found near the gallery. She couldn't hijack a modern car, the tracking system would alert the police within a matter of seconds. Instead, she found one that had been on the road since before she was born. The odometer was nearly at 200,000 miles and by the sound of it, the vehicle might drop dead before it got there.

Skits sat in the passenger seat with the book open wide, her fingers grazing the old pages. She had snapped the visor off the ceiling and used the vanity mirror light to read the psychic's scribblings. She flipped through quickly, looking for anything that would explain how the book got in the art gallery.

"Eleanor P. Valentine's maiden name is Bouvier."

"I don't care," Jasmine said, trying to hide her annoyance. She spun the wheel, sending them into a slight spin as she banked left toward the location of the warehouse. Both Skits and Alyssa pressed against the door, holding on so they wouldn't fall out of the speeding vehicle.

"It's like a diary. Some of it is dated, some of it doesn't make sense. Maybe she was crazy?"

"Maybe?" asked Alyssa.

"Hey," Skits barked. "I know crazy when I see it."

She flipped through the book again, starting from the back pages. She skimmed and continued flipping. "Got it," she said. "She hid the book outside of the sanctuary so Malcolm couldn't find it."

"Who's Malcolm?" asked Jasmine.

"It seems he was her protégé."

"This damned woman is a royal pain in my ass," Jasmine said as she spun around another corner. The car thumped twice as it jumped over railroad tracks. They left the part of New York City that outsiders knew so well. Now they were heading into the industrial complexes and the shipping areas that most New Yorkers ignored. It was a treasure trove of jobs, but it wasn't where the residents of Chelsea would find themselves at this hour.

"We don't have much time," Alyssa said.

Jasmine looked to the clock. They only had a half hour before the curfew began. Anybody on the streets would be deemed a criminal and eradicated by synthetics. She assumed they were crawling about the streets of downtown, but how many synthetics found themselves near the harbor? It had been a while since they had seen any machines. She hoped they wouldn't come this far away from the residents.

"He was a telepath," Skits added. "Apparently she found him impressive. Though she said she didn't think he'd be fitting for the head of the Society."

"The Society?" asked Alyssa.

"I don't know."

"Read faster," Jasmine barked.

"Stop driving like you're angry at the road," replied Skits.

"We need Dav5d," Alyssa said.

"Look." Jasmine pointed to the warehouses. Skits closed the book and pushed the mirror out of her lap. Jasmine waited for Skits to start giving directions. She held her breath, hoping they would be able to find the others.

A crack of lightning flashed in the sky.

"Found them," Skits said. "That way, I guess," she said with a smile.

"Thanks." Jasmine pressed down the gas and started speeding down the access road toward the origin of the lightning. She hoped they got there in time to join in the fight.

***

"To what do I owe this pleasure, Mr. Griffin?"

He fought to keep the smile from his face. He forced each muscle to withhold its excitement. He held his breath, letting it pass slowly between his lips. Adjusting his cufflink, he fidgeted for a moment to help burn off the energy. She grew impatient. Her crossed arms got tighter and she proceeded to tap her finger on her arm.

"You seem impatient," Lily said, her voice obnoxiously innocent. Both women were more than ready for this to take place. Dikeledi wanted nothing more than for him cause havoc, stirring emotions so strong she'd be intoxicated. Lily on the other hand, she kept chiming in, playing devil's advocate, making sure Jacob wasn't going to destroy her meal ticket.

"I have things I need to attend to," she said, adding, "It happens when you're the President of the United States." She dropped her title as if it mattered to him. He was aware of how much she disregarded him, nothing more than a nuisance in her schedule. She violated his trust, the very principals that sustained the Society, and yet she required their aid to maintain a war she couldn't win. He found it ironic to say the least.

"We need to meet."

She stopped tapping her fingers. Their relationship had been one-sided for too long. She requested troops to support her war and keep her in power, they provided. It had been years since they had done anything more than sustain the symbiotic relationship that kept the Society in power. The mere mention of calling in a favor put her on her heels.

"Concerning?"

"Best to discuss it in a more secure manner."

"The situation is a bit tense at the moment. I cannot leave the White House."

"We expected as much."

He noted the moment her shoulders relaxed and she let out a deep breath. He wondered exactly what she had hoped to accomplish by recruiting the Warden. Had it simply been to create an army of powered people? Whatever reasoning she had, she had felt it threatening enough to keep it secret from him. He didn't like the idea of her gaining independence from the Society.

"We will arrive at the White House shortly."

Her back straightened again. He enjoyed watching the physical reactions he elicited from the elderly woman. He wondered how she would react the moment he mentioned he planned to remove her from power and replace her as the most dangerous person in the world.

"I will make sure synthetics are available to greet you."

A thinly veiled threat, he thought.

"I shall be bringing Lily and Dikeledi."

"Whatever happened to Salvador?" she asked.

"He crossed me."

She had practice, years of training her body to not react. The news of their visit startled her; the news of him killing a comrade, that didn't faze her in the least. He took solace in knowing she was very aware of what he would do if pushed. The president remained comfortable and a bit too relaxed in her position, but she was not stupid.

"I see. Well, I look forward to talking to you in person," he said. Before she could reply, Lily pressed a button on the table and all the images vanished. He wanted her worried. He wanted her terrified. Whatever she planned, he was more than willing to meet it head on.

"She suspects," Dikeledi said. "She can't know what, but she doesn't trust any of us."

"I'm not an empath and I could have told you that," Lily said. "The woman is a snake. She'd have been dead for decades without the Society."

Jacob waved his hand over the table and one large screen appeared. He scrolled through several Genesis Division security camera feeds until he

293

found the one. He leaned in on the table, excited by their handiwork. The captured Child of Nostradamus had been a saving grace. The moment they left the Facility, teams of scientists began to pour into the room. They pressed diodes against his body and pumped him full of drugs. Within two hours they fused a hardline into the base of his brain. Jacob believed their technology integrating the human brain to the machine was worth its investment, but he hadn't suspected it would be so perfect.

"Do you think it will work?" Lily asked, unfolding her legs and standing next to him.

"They used the same drugs necessary for the Barren."

"He's not human," she replied.

He shot her a dirty look, annoyed at her statement of the obvious. "I know. Once he was drugged his psyche turned much more malleable. When I was done, there was no difference between him and our foot soldiers."

"And if it doesn't work?"

He smiled. The man was strapped down to the table. The surgical equipment had been removed and now the room was filled with computers and servers. The team of surgeons was down to one keeping vigilant watch on their investment. The others in the room were the smartest computer technicians housed at Genesis Division. He had faith they had jumped every hurdle necessary in the last few hours. Simulations had been promising and now there was nothing to do except flip the on switch.

"It will work." He didn't hide the smile on his face. "It must."

***

"How dare you?" he yelled.

The pain radiating off the man hit her, strong enough it left a bitter taste in her mouth. Dwayne woke only a few minutes ago, and already, the memory of what happened in the subway consumed him. Vanessa heard every thought cross his mind, the betrayal, the disgrace, the humility, all of them and at the source, the moment she stole his body.

"I did what I had to," she yelled back. Her voice was shrill, loud enough it sounded off the metal walls of the warehouse.

His thoughts were less coherent, primal, a growl unable to stop. She found it difficult to keep them at bay and not let his anger drown her. Several metal sculptures separated them. She stepped backward, wanting more distance between them. She shook as one of the towering metal dragons toppled to the floor. She caught a glimpse of his face, the huffing and puffing as his anger continued to rise.

"Dwayne," she yelled, "I would have done the same for you!"

Another metal sculpture toppled, this one a massive horse with a human torso. The crashing metal filled the room with a screeching sound. He moved closer, closing the distance between them. Vanessa swatted at the air in a futile attempt to bat away his thoughts.

"I can't keep you out."

"Ironic, isn't it, Vanessa?"

She understood his bitterness, even his rage. She had been torn, had violated his trust, but she knew if she was given the option, she'd do it again. "Dwayne, don't do this," she yelled.

Dwayne creeped behind the next statue, its wide bent metal standing nearly twice his height. He didn't attempt to push it out of the way with his hands. A surge of lightning leapt from his chest, lighting up the warehouse, throwing the metal to the side. The statute slid along the floor, the smell of burnt rust wafting from it. Only one remained between them and then she'd be forced to meet him face to face.

She ducked low to the ground as the last statue flew overhead. The heat lines were visible from his chest. His eyes glowed a surreal gold, lost to his powers, a victim of his abilities. She thrust her thoughts against the wall of rage and tried to calm his anger. He resisted, pushing her aside as if she was a novice.

"Stop this, Dwayne."

The warehouse melted away and the two of them stood in a blinding white room. She grated her teeth, tensing her muscles as she dragged him into her mind. For a moment, he stopped moving and then the room faded. She stared at him again in the warehouse. It was the first time anybody had been able to resist her like this. She wondered if the Warden would be capable of stopping him.

The moment she thought it, she stopped moving. The anger pouring from finally made sense. She focused on her own anger, the wish to be like the

Warden tugging at her. She knew he was a deadly man and prided herself on being nothing like him. For a moment, his ways made sense, and that terrified her. She crossed a line with her friend, and with a single action, the shadows haunting her at night had been able to take hold of her mind.

Vanessa held her ground. Had she been capable of crying, rivers would have flowed down her cheeks, giving away her remorse. She dropped to her knees, resting her wings along the ground. Her chest heaved as she tried to drag air into the depths of her lungs.

"I'm sorry."

Dwayne stopped his approach. She wasn't sure if her submissive pose or the painful thoughts she broadcasted did it, but she caused him to hesitate. She heard him thinking about Dav5d. He stopped seeing her as a rapist and focused on her passion for the man who saw her as more than a gargoyle. He thought about what he would do if he was in her shoes and somebody threatened the man he loved.

He screamed. It started in his belly and worked its way through his throat until it threatened to give out on him. Lightning poured out of his shoulders and surging upward from his face. It punched through the roof of the warehouse and lit the sky. She watched as the man drained his internal battery, and as his body ached, the anger subsided.

"This does not make us right."

She shook her head. "I'm so sorry."

Conthan appeared out of nowhere and tackled Dwayne, taking him to the ground. Conthan held him, his arms locked around the man. He had no ability to stop Dwayne from electrocuting him, just blind faith he wouldn't hurt a teammate.

Gretchen materialized out of thin air. The moment she appeared, the whisper of her thoughts returned. Vanessa heard insecurities, her worry about revealing herself to them. She feared Vanessa and Dwayne, but most of all she feared her former friend. The young punk held her composure, but the worry racing through her mind betrayed her.

"I'm not really sure what's normal for you. You okay?"

Gretchen helped lift Vanessa to her feet. "I'll be fine, Child."

The girl had tattoos down the right side of her face and numerous chains locked around her neck. Vanessa understood she had a high threshold for weird, but even this was pushing her limits. Vanessa couldn't ignore the image of Conthan murdering a man in the forefront of Gretchen's mind. The girl was concerned the friend she knew had been replaced with a ruthless killer.

"It seems we are all doomed to confront our darkest selves," she said to Gretchen.

"I'm starting to see that. Would you all mind toning down the psychotic behavior? I'm losing my fucking mind."

They froze as the door to the warehouse flew open. Gretchen's body tensed and Vanessa gasped as the color in the room faded. There was something impressive with how fast Gretchen utilized her abilities. Jasmine walked through the doorway with Skits and Alyssa behind her. Vanessa let go of Gretchen; the moment their skin lost contact, the color came rushing in. All three women gasped as Vanessa moved toward them.

"So, we miss the party?" asked Skits.

Vanessa turned to see Conthan helping Dwayne to his feet. The older man looked over his shoulder, making eye contact, the disgruntled expression still present despite the lack of eyebrows. She turned back to the three women, glad to see they made it safely. She had no idea where the portals led as she possessed Conthan, instead relying on his memories to provide a destination.

"Where were you?" asked Vanessa. Her voice was shaky, but she coughed, clearing her throat, brushing away the heavy feeling still clinging to her chest.

"He put us in an art gallery."

Alyssa stepped around Jasmine. "It was the gallery where he did his final art show. Dwayne and I were there when everything started." She was about to say something more when Gretchen appeared out of nowhere. "It was her art gallery, to be precise."

"How'd you find us?" asked Vanessa.

"We followed him for days. This was the only other place he came to regularly. It was either this or we wandered around lost."

Jasmine nodded. "Then we saw a bolt of lightning and figured we were on the right track."

"Hey lady," Alyssa said, "did you know you had a secret room in your art gallery?"

"A what?"

Alyssa held up the book. "It seems Gallery Girl is part of Eleanor's plan."

Chapter 21

1993

The only things housed in the great empty space were a single table and four chairs. Mark walked through the space, frequently amazed by its sheer size. As he made it into the room, the door behind him shut and several pressure valves hissed, sealing them inside. Above them, contained in the ceiling were sprinklers and fire suppressant foam, all part of the adaptions for their newest assets.

Ivan sat on one side of the table and Ariel and Arturo sat on the other side. Mark was happy the two mentalists had started to get along. At first, it had been a tedious friendship. Ariel was excited to talk to somebody like her, but Arturo wanted little to do with her, claiming she was just another person trying to kill mentalists. It had taken them months to finally come to terms with one another. Mark assumed it was her constant pestering that broke Arturo down; the girl certainly had a way to make people agree with her.

Mark slowed his step as the lights darkened. The room was nearly pitch black except for the occasional blip from one of the security cameras. Ivan had been working with both of them for hours each day. From mapping their brain waves to testing their hormone levels after using their abilities, he was the world's expert in mentalists. The media named him the face of mentalist research and with the President of the United States' blessing he had even given television interviews. Mark was happy to let the man have the limelight, especially since his confidence in the science demystified their work for the public.

Small balls of flame appeared throughout the room. Just to his side, a small bit of fire hovered in the air, producing enough light to see the majority of the expansive room. He was impressed with how quickly Arturo developed his abilities. The young man was the opposite of Ariel; where he had to push his abilities, she found herself trying to restrain her telekinesis. *No*, he thought, *Arturo's abilities prove even mentalists start at different calibers.*

There was something beautiful about the two or three dozen balls of flame hovering in the air. It started as a slight tugging of his shirt, as if somebody grabbed ahold of his clothing and pulled him forward. His shoes started to drag a little on the floor and he realized it was Ariel's abilities pulling at him. His limbs were immobile as she lifted him off the ground and pulled him toward the table they gathered at. The sensation wasn't like flying, it was more like being wrapped tightly in a blanket and dangled over the ground.

As his feet touched down, Ivan gave him a nod. "Glad to see you could join us."

"Thanks," he said, staring at Ariel. "It was becoming tiresome using my own two feet."

"Told you he wouldn't find it funny," Ivan interjected.

Mark ignored the man's attempt at humor. In the last couple of months Ivan lost some of his awkward tendencies and started acting normal. He even reached a place where Ariel didn't want to hurl him across the room. Arturo wasn't as fast to warm up to the Russian's scientific pursuits, but thankfully he followed Ariel's lead. Where Mark had once been Ariel's only confidant, now she had people around her she might dare call friends. Mark assumed the envy he felt was the same every parent experienced as they were replaced by friends.

"I believe they might also be ready," Ivan said. "Arturo has demonstrated near mastery of his abilities. While his prolonged usage needs more conditioning, he has been more than capable of handling himself with environmental stressors."

"You do realize that environmental stressors are a bit different than having a group of men firing weapons in an attempt to kill you."

"Same diff," Ariel said.

"No, it isn't," he said, no longer trying to hide his annoyance.

She leaned across the table, resting her hands on his. "If we don't do this, we're dead. So how about we go with the least horrible option."

He had been at the center for so long, and it still

came down to them risking their lives. He started to wonder if it would just be better to break free and hide them away. If he could get them out of the country, there was a good chance they could go into hiding. He might be able to save Ariel, but there was no way the government would stand to lose Arturo, and at the moment Penelope was little more than warm body.

"Fine," he said through gritted teeth.

"Go get suited up," Ivan said.

"Suited up?"

Ivan turned to Mark. "I made suits that will record Ariel and Arturo's biometrics. Otherwise, everything they're about to do would just be for the sake of the military."

As the two trotted toward the entrance, the small balls of flame vanished from sight. After a moment in the pitch black, the lights came back on, the harsh fluorescent bulbs humming as they snapped into action.

Ivan stared at the man, studying him. He had his nose tipped down so that he was staring over his glasses. "I don't need to be a telepath; what do you want to ask?"

"We've been working together for nearly two years, and I've never asked you why."

"Excuse me?"

"Why are you here? Why this, them, why all of it?"

Ivan leaned back in his chair, pushing his glasses even further up his nose. He rested his hands on the desk, fingers neatly folded together. His affect didn't change as he cleared his throat.

"I grew up with 'them', Mark. I know so much about a mentalist's abilities because I spent my entire life next to one."

Mark tried to think back to the personnel file he received on Ivan. Nearly every line had been redacted. He hadn't been surprised, it came with the job. Each of them had exposure to extremely sensitive information; he had assumed Ivan had too.

"No guesses?"

"Ivan." His tone made it clear to stop playing games.

"Her name was Natalia."

Ivan stood up and continued toward the door without another word. Mark mulled over the four words. He wondered if she was his girlfriend, or a mother, or perhaps his sister. He wanted to ask, but he knew better than pushing the man. Ivan was egotistical, even pompous on his worst days, but Mark couldn't think of a single moment he had been reserved and reluctant to provide information.

He decided that it was a sister. He wasn't sure why he needed that piece of information, but something about it gave Ivan another dimension, something more than a man in a lab coat. If he was right, Mark was surprised by how tame the man seemed and how dedicated he was to his work. Mark couldn't explain it, but if it had been him, he imagined he'd be a psychopath killing people for revenge.

Mark followed the man, working his way through the corridors to the more military-oriented projects in the building. They had been given an ultimatum, either push through with military applications or have the mentalists washed from the program and refocus on the cybernetics. The term "washed" was used loosely, and he had no doubt that it meant the majority of the center's personnel would not survive the corporate restructuring.

He pushed his hand against the sensor and stepped through as the door whooshed open. Inside, he stood next to Ivan. There were was a comfortable silence between them. Mark didn't dare ask any more questions; instead he thought it best to focus on work. "I'm worried this is not going to end well."

"You need to stop viewing them as kids."

"You need to stop viewing them as weapons."

"When you realize they've been burdened with abilities that have forced them to grow up, especially in a world that would see them dead, you'll understand they never had the option to be kids."

Mark wanted to argue the point, but Ivan was right. Neither of these kids had the chance to watch cartoons and go on dates. They were born into a time when their parents had to make tough choices about survival. Ariel's mother abandoned her, and if a mother not wanting you wasn't a way to grow up quickly, he couldn't think of a harsher catalyst. Arturo had no family to speak of, and even now, his story basically started with him wandering the streets. No, nobody had it easy in that room.

Mark and Ivan stood at the observation window looking down into another training facility. Ariel and Arturo entered on the far end. There were large objects placed throughout the room to give a bit more of a realistic setting. Mark knew there were a dozen security guards entering from the other side. He pressed the intercom on the wall. "Remember, they're using rubber bullets and stun guns. It won't kill you, but it will hurt. A lot."

Ariel gave a thumbs-up. Goddard watched from another observation deck across the football field-sized room. A monitor came to life; the security guard looked annoyed. Goddard held the microphone close to his mouth. "Rubber bullets. Are you sure your brats aren't going to hurt my men?"

Ivan pushed the button back. "The room is filled with fire suppressant. If Arturo gets out of control, we can shut him down quickly."

Goddard shook his head. "I'm talking about the girl."

Mark ignored the man. He switched the microphone to the room. "Begin the exercise."

Ivan sat down at a computer, watching the meters and charts move back and forth. Mark didn't understand exactly what Ivan was reading. Mark was a visual man; his assessment would be based on how well the two held their own against the security guards.

Mark noted Ariel's feet were firmly planted on the ground. Either she overcame her nervous tick, or she really was as confident as she let on. As the first security guard rounded the corner of a giant metal cylinder sticking out of the ground, she raised her hand. The man stopped moving, his gun yanked away from his hands and the thrown across the room. The second guard managed to pull his trigger once. She didn't flinch as the rubber bullet was slapped away by her abilities. The man was knocked backward, dropping his gun.

"She's remaining calm," Ivan said. "Her heart rate isn't fluctuating and her norepinephrine levels aren't moving. She's completely under control."

Two sets of guards flanked Ariel, their weapons raised. They didn't hesitate as they fired at her. Arturo's fists clenched and flashes of lights burst from the end of two of the guard's weapons. The end of the guns were warped, useless to their owners, who opted for their backup sidearms.

Ariel's attention must have been focused on the flash, because a stray bullet struck her in the shoulder. She yelled as she hit the floor. Mark pressed his hand against the glass. He reached for the microphone, prepared to call off the exercise. Ivan held up his hand and Mark froze at the gesture. The scientist shook his head. "It's only a bruise."

Mark watched as a stream of flame appeared on the ground in front of two guards, causing them to take several steps backward. Ariel latched onto one man with her abilities and hurled him into another, sending both men to the ground. She didn't make any move to find cover, opting instead to stay in the open and draw them out.

Out of the corner of his eye, Goddard barked orders into his headset, providing his guards with information. Mark wanted to reach through the monitor and punch the man, but he kept his emotions in check. There would be time for a confrontation at the debriefing.

Arturo sent a line of fire from one of his hands at

two oncoming guards. Both men dropped to the ground. One rolled onto his back and fired his gun to the ceiling. After several attempts, the sprinklers spat out white foam. The flames vanished and Arturo and Ariel were covered in the fire retardant. Mark didn't want to see them lose, but he had to admit there was something genius about taking Arturo out of the fight so quickly.

Ariel stepped between the boy and the guards. The guards held down the triggers on their guns, sending waves of bullets at her. She flung out her hand and the projectiles froze in the air. With a snap of her wrist they cascaded onto the floor. She no longer stood on the ground. She hovered, and her hair moved as if it had a life of its own.

"Her heart rate is elevated. Her respiratory rate is increasing."

Mark wanted to yell to her. He wanted to tell her that two guards clad in all black had managed to circle around behind her. They approached a position that they'd be able to strike. He watched helplessly as they raised their weapons to their cheeks and took aim.

He couldn't count how many times they pulled the triggers, but each time, Ariel's body jerked. She fell forward onto all fours and even through the bulletproof glass, he heard her screaming. He grabbed for the microphone. He jolted backward as the two security guards were hurled against the glass. Both men slumped to the ground, unable to move anymore.

"Her hormones are rising quickly. Her abilities are flaring."

The foam coating the ground dispersed toward the walls. Mark was impressed with how strongly she forced her surroundings away. Two guards smacked against the far wall. One held up his gun and fired it at the girl. After the projectile froze several feet from her face, it exploded into a fury of bright colors.

Ariel shielded her eyes from the bright light. The guards capable of moving positioned themselves quickly, scattering about the room. One ran forward and skidded to his knees, holding out a small gun. He pulled the trigger and two wires sunk into the girl's shoulder. Arturo attempted to grab the wires, but jolts of electricity shot through them, sending her to the ground.

Mark pushed the button on the microphone. "Stand down. The exercise is complete."

He ignored Goddard's laughing in the monitor. He watched as the battered guards helped one another to their feet. Mark flipped the switch to speak with his nemesis. "Twelve men to take down a single teenage girl. Looks like they're softer than you."

He gave a middle finger to the monitor and flipped off the switch.

Ivan shook his head. "Someday I'm going to snap his neck."

Mark nodded as Arturo rolled Ariel onto her back. The boy checked her pulse, making sure she was breathing. Mark didn't want to admit it, but what little innocence endured in the girl was about to be wiped away. There would be no more use of the word "restraint" or "safety." No, Mark was going to tell her if it came down to them or her, she should always make sure she walked away the winner.

"You won't get the chance," Mark said in a quiet voice. "I'm going to kill him first."

Chapter 22

2033

Conthan led Dwayne through a door to a dock overlooking the river. He held the man's arm, guiding him along as Dwayne continued to curse under his breath. The moment they cleared the metal door, the smell of rotting fish filled his nostrils. He gave a slight shove to the older man.

"What the hell were you doing?"

Conthan leaned back as Dwayne threw a punch. He ducked under swinging arm and stepped behind him, locking his hands around Dwayne's head. For a moment, he thought Jasmine would be proud of the maneuver. He tightened his hold on the man's neck, forcing him to stop struggling.

"Dwayne, I'm not your enemy."

He let him go. Dwayne slammed his hand against the metal of the warehouse wall. As his knuckles connected, electricity shot out, snapping against the steel. Dwayne leaned against the wall, banging his head just hard enough to have hurt.

311

"She got inside my head," he said. "Conthan, she fucking mind-raped me."

Vanessa had done the same to him, but he had invited her to take over his body. He knew the woman could push his abilities further and it was the only way they'd survive. He understood the sensation of being a prisoner in his own body. He didn't know what it was like to have the choice ripped out from under him.

"It's over, man," Conthan said.

"It's getting to me, Conthan. This whole thing, it's finally getting to me."

Conthan raised his eyebrow, confused by the confession. He wasn't sure what Dwayne was speaking about. Despite the last twenty-four hours, things had been going fairly well for the group. "What do you mean?"

Dwayne turned around and leaned against the wall, banging the back of his head. Conthan could read the pain on his face. He processed his mentor's emotions, each of them neatly displayed on his face as the lines creased his forehead. Conthan didn't know if he should reach out and console the man, or let him deal with his demons.

"I would have done the same," he whispered.

"What?" Conthan asked, confused at the statement.

"I would have fucking-mind raped you to get out of there. I'd have done the same thing."

Conthan nodded his head in response. Considering Dwayne had tortured one of their teammates before she joined, he wasn't shocked he would do the same. Twenty-four hours ago, the

312

thought would have turned his stomach, but having just killed a man, he didn't have the moral high ground.

"This isn't me," Dwayne said. "There was a time when I was a mellow pacifist. I didn't blow things up, threaten to kill people—"

"I killed a man in cold blood tonight."

The statement took Dwayne by surprise, stopping his self-loathing pity party. Conthan felt for the man. He wanted a life outside of the hero gig, he wanted something more than trying to survive. He understood the feeling.

"So we're in the same boat," Dwayne said. "We're slipping down into that dark hole."

Conthan shook his head. "You want to go back to something you had before this. Skits tells me you had a pretty good life once upon a time. I get that you want it back."

"I hear a but coming."

"Gretchen and I went to the church today. We were attacked. I stopped the man who attacked us. Then, I snapped his neck."

"I'm sorry."

Conthan shook his head again. "I'm not. A year ago, you said to be worried if it came naturally."

"I remember."

"It's not natural. It's not easy. But I will kill anybody who threatens me or mine."

While Dwayne hoped to find redemption, Conthan found himself willing to abandon the hope of being saved. Every night he put himself in harm's way, he told himself it was to save the victims of the government, but he understood it was the allure of being powerful. The government took something from him; he wanted to make them suffer.

"I spent so much time mad at you for what you did to Jasmine and it didn't have anything to do with you. I was mad at myself. I didn't think I could do what I would have to get the job done. I was mad I couldn't do what you did. But I can, Dwayne, and I will."

Dwayne lowered his eyes. Conthan understood that he wanted to find peace and go back to who he used to be. For the first time since becoming a Child of Nostradamus, Conthan discovered some truth to himself. He found comfort in this revelation, even if it wasn't as clean cut as he once thought it should be.

Conthan placed his hands on each side of Dwayne's head and forced the man to see him eye to eye. It had been a trying day for Dwayne, but he hoped it was a momentary setback. Conthan wanted to slap him and tell him stop whining and own it. They weren't normal, and they weren't going to encounter normal situations; they'd have to check their moral compass more frequently than most.

"You can do this," Conthan whispered. He was close enough that even the quiet words sounded loud between the two of them.

"But—"

Conthan closed the distance between them. He leaned in and pushed against the lips of the older man. He was surprised by the smoothness of Dwayne's skin, most likely a side effect of pumping electricity out of his body all day. The kiss lasted a few seconds, and his heart sank as the man didn't return the gesture. He prepared to apologize as Dwayne pushed him away.

Dwayne grabbed him by the shoulders and spun the two of the around, throwing Conthan against the wall. Conthan gasped, about to beg for forgiveness, but the bigger man pinned him to the corrugated steel and his lips pressed against his. Conthan ignored the spark between them as Dwayne bit his lip.

Conthan grabbed the man's head again, forcing their lips together tightly. Dwayne grabbed his arms by the wrists and pinned them to the wall. Conthan stopped fighting and gave into the man's assertiveness. He had thought about it for months, and for the last couple of weeks he found himself imagining this very scenario. When they fled the subway, he realized what it would do to him if Dwayne didn't survive.

He bit down on the man's lips and heard him gasp in response. All the nights he teleported to the church after scouring the streets for a fight, Dwayne waited to see his safe return. They had spent dozens of mornings watching the sun rise in silence. Conthan thought the man was atoning for his past, but it hadn't dawned on him there might be something more admirable behind the check-ins.

Dwayne pulled at the leather jacket, dragging it down enough to ensnare Conthan's arms. His hands pushed Conthan's shirt over his head, exposing his chest. Conthan took a moment, unsure of where the exchange was heading, but excited at the prospect. He let the jacket fall off and pulled the shirt the rest of the way, leaving him in a similar state as Dwayne.

"You sure?" Dwayne asked.

Conthan reached for the button on Dwayne's pants. He let his hands hover for a moment, staring at the older man's torso. Everybody had hinted at the potential of this exchange, but giving Conthan space to dwell on his own truths. He wanted it.

"Oh yeah," he said as he unsnapped Dwayne's pants.

***

Vanessa flipped the pages of the book, her fingers grazing the indentations from the sharp point pen used to scribe. She held so many questions for so long, and she often thought if she could only talk to Eleanor, it would all make sense. By either a freak encounter or the product of stress-induced hallucination, she met the woman and not a single question was asked, let alone answered. Now, she held the woman's life in her hands and none of it seemed to matter.

Her feet dug into the roof of the warehouse, the perch placing her high above the rest of the bay. Other than a massive crane near the water, she could see clear across the warehouse district. The smell of low tide mixed with whatever diseases floated along the tainted bay filled her nostrils. She had spent the last hour as close to the sky as she could muster. She hid from Dwayne, from her teammates, from the questions they asked and the answers she had yet to uncover. Emotions ran amuck. Anger. Sadness. Loss. She missed her other half and had no idea how to find him. Instead, she held Eleanor's book, something to distract her from the gruesome reality that was her life.

She turned the page, squinting at the handwritten text, forcing her eyes to adjust to the low light on the roof. With only the moon hanging in the sky, she could barely make out the woman's ramblings. Her perfectly etched script reminded Vanessa of the thoughtful and elegant loops she had painstakingly written on each of her teammate's letters. Despite her cryptic and less than pleasant messages, she took care with every letter she wrote. Her journal was no different, and it appeared she spent as much time scribing her thoughts as she did thinking them.

"There is no way you left this for us to find with nothing inside."

Vanessa growled as she flipped another page. *The woman detailed the most benign aspects of her life,* she thought to herself. *I wonder if this is the plight of a psychic, wondering if every moment of your life may have some outward ripple?*

She flipped another page.

Then another.

She moved to the end of the book and started to flip forward. It didn't take long before she found a spot worth reading. She made note that in the journal of Eleanor's life, it seemed her entries toward the end became fewer and further between.

I am not enthused by my position amongst the Society. I have discovered the unpleasantries of this group of unsavory individuals stretch far deeper than I had been led to believe. I am hoping that my position will award me the opportunity to change our purpose in life. I believe there is potential and I am determined to reshape this foundation into something far greater than itself.

Vanessa reread the word, "Society," several times before it soaked in. The woman was part of an organization, the leader of a group of people that knew about the existence of mentalists. She suspected the woman had lived a full life, but she wasn't prepared for just how intriguing it was.

It wasn't the first time she had heard of the group, but much like the Illuminati or the Masons, she assumed they were figments of the paranoid imagination. Just how powerful could a group filled with mentalists be if they turned their energies to the world around them? What change could they bring about, all while the people being manipulated wouldn't be aware of what took place?

It has been forced upon me. I refused, but the board has decided I must follow in the footsteps of those who came before me. I have decided to concede and I will be taking a student to begin teaching our ways. I hope I can find somebody with a positive outlook on life, with an iron will capable of withstanding the constant sinister nature of this organization. I secretly hope I may find somebody who can replace me, thus giving me the ability to fade into the ether, away from this dreadful responsibility.

"A protégé?" Vanessa thought about the possibilities. What if there was another mentalist out there with the ability to see the future? What if they had the heft of this organization behind them? Vanessa shivered at the thought. A psychic with unlimited resources would be capable of reshaping the future as they saw fit.

"Is this why you brought us together?"

Perhaps it is, came a distant whisper.

The muscles in her body didn't flinch at the deep voice. Vanessa remained sitting on the roof, holding the book, but her mind slipped away to the white room that never seemed to end. She left her body and stepped into the blinding light, a room only telepaths could reach. She had no doubt the whispering voice knew she would be there.

"Jacob," Vanessa whispered, the name slipping into her mind. Another telepath was nearby, maybe not physically, but they were probing her mind, testing her abilities.

She knows my name.

Vanessa quieted her mind. A moment of peace flowed through her body and she heard the thoughts of another person. Her wings flared out as she thrust her hand into the open air. Her nails dug into soft flesh as she dragged a man into existence. She

319

wasn't surprised to see him wearing a perfectly tailored suit.

"Why are the obnoxious always well dressed?"

The man didn't respond to the power behind her grip. His eyes were nearly as dispassionate as his demeanor. She was surprised he had no fight in him. She pushed him backward. He caught himself from falling. The perfectly groomed man brushed off his jacket, making sure his cufflinks were correctly in place.

"I've noticed you," said the man.

"I appreciate your concern with me. You should be more worried about yourself, young man."

"Young man." He laughed. "It's been a long time since anybody has referred to me as young."

Vanessa took a step back, her wings folding behind her. Something about the man felt off, wrong, like he attempted to deceive her. It took a moment, but she had spent the better part of her life masking her identity; she knew a telepath's mirage better than most.

The man wasn't big by any stretch of the imagination. He was what might be described as petite, small enough that she found it hard to be intimidated. With a thought, the slightest push of her mind, she watched as he dimmed. As his body sunk into the blinding white of the room, a shadow remained, a smoky figure.

"Warden," she hissed.

"I missed our interactions, Vanessa."

It had been a year since she encountered him. She wanted to lash out at the former caretaker of the Facility and rake her nails across his face, but a year

320

brought with it maturity. She imagined the light of the room siphoning into her body, creating a barrier along her exterior, securing her inside its brilliance. The room grew dark as the light coated her like a second skin. Despite her muscles tensing, wanting to lash out, she knew she'd need every defense she could muster.

"I appreciate your melodrama."

"What do you want, beast?"

He laughed. The body he had stolen was younger than the Warden, but she knew there something had changed. She wanted to reach out, let her mind graze his, but she worried he'd break through her mental barriers and drag her into a fight, or worse yet, steal her body.

"He's a mentalist," she said in awe. The body the Warden occupied was a mentalist himself. She understood now, his need to subdue her until she submitted. The man had been determined to compound his gifts with hers, but being a Child of Nostradamus saved her from his intrusions.

"This could have been you." He gestured toward his chest. "Think of how few limitations you and I would have. Jacob is a quaint vessel, but he lacks your maturity."

"He also lacks the ability to keep you at bay."

She understood Dwayne's concerns. Seeing the man in front of her, a pawn of the Warden, she realized it would be easy to reach out and steal the bodies of those around her. The man was evil, but he had shown her the lines she refused to cross. He existed as a dark reflection. Vanessa imagined the line between her morality and his continued to blur.

"You are still filled with fear," he said, his head cocked to the side. "So powerful, and at the root of it, I can taste your terror."

"What's your name, Warden?"

As she asked, she let her defenses break, a slight crack in the light as she reached out with her mind. The heat of his mind washed over her as she caught a brief glimpse into it. It happened faster than a blink of the eye, but she saw Dav5d. The love of her life was missing his legs and he remained suspended in liquid. He floated inside the tube, dozens of wires hooked to his body. She didn't need press further to know the Warden had something to do with the state of her love.

She spun. Her wings smacked into the shadow, sending it backward. He didn't fall as he skidded along the white floors. She launched herself forward, her wings taking her off the ground, and at the last moment, she slammed her feet into his chest. This time he fell backward and rolled along the ground of the white room.

Vanessa jumped into the air and with a flap of her wings she soared higher. She pulled her wings in tight and fell toward the shadow's chest. Her knees drove into his torso. She thrust her hand into the Warden's chest and pushed through the surface until she could feel the empty cavity where his heart should be.

"You've become more assertive, Angel."

He reached up and without so much as a grunt, he pushed her away. The smoke swirled and reformed until he stood in front of her kneeling body. There was a laugh at the disbelief on her face.

"I applaud your confidence, Angel, but you're not the only one who has grown in the last year."

"I didn't have to steal my powers."

He laughed louder. "I can smell it on you. I'm not the only one who has been taking hostages." He reached down, letting the wisps of smoke snake along her cheek. "The only difference is my vessel invited me. Can yours say the same?"

She didn't know what to say to the man. She couldn't tell what he had gathered from Dav5d or what he was reading off her in that moment. She couldn't wrap her head around what it might do if she possessed another telepath. She imagined their abilities working in tandem, allowing her access to more power than she could ever muster on her own.

"What is it you want?"

"I hoped in your despair I could overcome you. You would make a delectable trophy, a highlight in my career."

"You can't," she said with a smirk.

"You're mistaken, Angel," he corrected. "I no longer need you. Jacob's Society has offered me every reward I could imagine."

He misstepped.

"Eleanor's Society," she said as she rose to her feet. She didn't need to see his face; the temperature of the room changed subtly, giving away his concern. The cold rolled off him, both of them, at the mention of the dead psychic. Both of them feared her.

"You are the darkness on the horizon," Vanessa said.

"Eleanor Valentine—"

Vanessa let her defenses roll along her skin, the light gathering about her fist. Her hand burned almost as bright as the rest of the room. It wasn't fear she sensed from the Warden, but at least it was concern.

"We're coming for you, Warden." She shoved her fist into the torso of the shadow. The light vanished for a moment, swallowed by the Warden's avatar. A moment later cracks emerged throughout the man's body. She could feel him being hurled from the white room.

"Eleanor's Nighthawks are coming for you."

The figure burst, smoke dissipating into nothingness. The moment the man vanished she opened her eyes, still sitting on the roof. The book in her lap suddenly felt heavy. She looked down at the diary scribed by the dead psychic. She knew the woman still worked through them and one way or another, she was going to stop the Warden.

***

In one corner of the warehouse, the former occupants created small rooms with corrugated steel as walls, looking like something out of an apocalyptic office building. Jasmine contemplated crawling into one for sleep, curling up next to Skits in an attempt for at least a few hours of shut eye. Even with the thought of a firm mattress welcoming her, there was something peaceful sitting this close to a fire. The warmth of the flame and the flickering light dancing across her eyelids were hard to give up, even if it meant feathers and springs.

The team is crumbling, she thought.

Dwayne and Conthan had walked out, the younger trying to keep the older from losing his shit and attacking again. Vanessa sat on the roof, removing herself from everybody, wanting to stay deep in her own thoughts. Jasmine didn't blame her, whatever had gone down wasn't pretty. The veteran imagined a thousand scenarios, but none of them involved Vanessa and Dwayne tossing aside their mutual respect to slug it out as they had.

The fire popped and cracked, the same thing her spine was going to do from lying down on the backseat of an old car. On the opposite side of the fire, Alyssa was nestled in a chair with a blanket wrapped around her body. Gretchen sat next to the girl, her chair pulled close enough to the fire pit she didn't need a blanket.

"How long have you known? I mean, about your powers?"

"The Nostradamus Effect happened when I was three," confessed Alyssa.

"That early?"

Jasmine opened her eyes into slits. She had known the girl for nearly a year and in all that time she hadn't asked her much about Alyssa's past. She wondered if that made her a bad person, keeping the girl at arm's length. She didn't want them asking about her past, so for the past year she kept her distance.

"Yeah," she said. "I don't even remember it, to be honest. Both of my parents are conservative Muslim but even though the Quran doesn't permit dancing, Mom wanted me to be involved with other kids. They attempted to assimilate to American culture. I was a bumbling ballerina. There's a tape of me at a dance recital a couple years later where I was almost majestic. I was six and already at the top of my class."

"What do you do?" asked Gretchen.

"Muscle memory. If I see it, I can do it. I used to watch the big girls dance. Mom would sit there and tell me if I worked hard, maybe that could be me. I didn't work very hard and it was me."

"She must have been thrilled."

"They wanted to blend in, not stand out. It was bad enough their ballerina wore different clothes." She pointed to the hijab wrapped about her head. "Then their six year old stole the show. They pulled me out of dance."

"Can you still do it?"

There was a pause. Jasmine could see the expression on Alyssa's face. She stared into the fire, remembering a long-forgotten memory. The girl's ability made her a keen fighter, one of the most efficient killing machines Jasmine had ever witnessed. It had never crossed her mind that the gift might be used for something else. *Goes to show where my head is.*

"No," Alyssa admitted. Her statement held a firm period at the end of it. Jasmine knew the girl's abilities faded if she didn't relearn them. The quantity she could absorb directly impacted the duration of her muscle memory. Even with that knowledge, she felt there was something else beneath the statement, something less related to the Nostradamus Effect and more to do with her past.

"You?" Alyssa asked.

"I was in sixth grade, so maybe eleven or twelve?"

"How did you get around detection?"

"My dad has money, I was tutored at home and my parents never questioned it. It was a dirty secret in our family."

"I'm sorry."

"Don't be. I threatened my parents with it all the time. I was quite the bitch. That's how I convinced them to let me go to art school. When you can become invisible, it's not like they can keep you in the house."

"So that's what you do?"

"I can't explain it really. Science was never my thing. I can bend waves, like light and sound. When I go invisible I'm there, but there's no way to see me. I tried figuring it out. But every time I started reading a physics book I figured it was just better to do it rather than study it."

"We have a friend whose job is to figure out the science stuff."

"Here's hoping he can help me."

Jasmine closed her eyes and basked in the heat of the fire. She wanted to roll over so her other side could warm up, but she didn't want to ruin the bonding moment between the two. She found it fascinating how easy it was to relate to them now that they were speaking openly.

"Did you know about Conthan?"

The rattle of chains told Jasmine the girl shook her head. "I wish I did. It'd have been awesome to know somebody else with abilities. But he was a late bloomer, I guess."

There was a long pause between them. "How is he?"

"Good, I think," Alyssa said. "I don't want to lie, we're not the kind of family that talks about this stuff. When the woman watching over your group is a telepath, you don't really need to share much. And Dwayne is a bit repressed. And Jasmine, she's military, so she's not exactly a talker."

She felt the eyes on her. They were studying her, trying to make heads or tails of her involvement. She had to admit, Alyssa was right, she didn't open up much. It had always been better to be quiet and observe.

"He seems more confident."

"He thinks we don't know about him sneaking out at night. I'm not sure what he's doing, but he always comes back banged up. He's got demons he's trying to exorcise."

"More demons than I remember."

"This life isn't easy," Alyssa said, letting her voice trail off.

"I was twenty when it happened." Jasmine's voice surprised even her.

"The Nostradamus Effect?"

She turned her head and eyed Gretchen through the fire. "The effect happened when I was sixteen. I was twenty the first time my powers did their thing."

"What is your thing?" asked Gretchen.

"My skin touches metal and can change its density."

"Ouch."

328

"Yeah, a lot of ouch. They took me to the doctor. The needle broke on my arm. It took days before my skin turned back. I had no idea what was going on. I went for years without it happening again. Eventually it did. This time I figured it out. But back then nobody bothered to test us or track us down."

Alyssa asked, "How'd you join the Corps?"

"The fucking Corps?" Gretchen yelled.

"They found out about me. They recruited me. It was more like they'd kill my family if I didn't go with them."

"Why didn't you leave?"

She had asked herself that question for years. Gretchen's candidness was a breath of fresh air. She appreciated that the woman didn't hold back. "I don't know."

"You could have run, or hell, could have kicked their asses."

"I didn't want to."

Gretchen didn't push further. Jasmine rolled her head back on the couch, staring at the ceiling almost three stories above them. She loathed the General, and she counted down the minutes until she could crush his windpipe and tear him limb from limb. Yet despite her disdain for the portly man, there had been something comforting about the armed forces.

"They were like a family," she admitted. "They knew I was a freak, some of them even liked the fact that I was made to be on the battlefield. I belonged."

"How did you join the Corps?" asked Alyssa.

"I was part of an old project. They used to have

mentalists as part of the military, and even after the Culling, the experiments continued. The project ended when a mentalist escaped. They resurrected it after I moved up the ranks. This time, though, they took more precautions. They stuck a damned explosive in my head and made sure I knew just how willing they were to kill me. They let me select my unit and eventually I became the commanding officer."

"Didn't you capture Children?" asked Gretchen. "I mean—"

"You're right. The last girl I was supposed to capture, I let go. Eleanor's letter told me to think about what I was doing. I told her to run."

"The girl in Troy," Alyssa said in a hushed voice.

"What girl?"

Jasmine's chest thumped quickly as she imagined the still corpse on the ground. Eleanor had told her to let the girl go, and despite the psychic's prophecy, the girl died. She wondered if Eleanor had foreseen the girl's death; perhaps the anger pulsing alongside her heartbeat was part of the mad woman's plans. Maybe she was supposed to go off the edge and kill the person responsible.

"We'll stop them," Alyssa said. Jasmine appreciated the girl lending herself to the cause. A small part of her wanted to spare her the atrocities she'd witness when Jasmine got a hold of the General.

There was a long pause, an awkward empty lull in the questioning. Jasmine sat up at the sight of Gretchen's face. She had seen that expression

330

before, the one where a person recalls every decision made in their life. Jasmine leaned in, ready to ask what she was thinking.

"Eleanor," she whispered.

Gretchen evaporated from sight. Jasmine noted the impression in the chair growing faint as she left the seat. There were no footfalls or the sounds of breathing, just a crackling fire playing with the shadows of the room. Jasmine turned about, looking for where the punk may have run to.

The lights at the end of the warehouse came to life. The fixtures were suspended from the rafters and projected onto the far wall of the warehouse. They were perfectly spaced apart, providing light to the entirety of the wall. Jasmine didn't understand art, but she could tell somebody had spent a significant amount of time painting the wall. Along the corrugated steel, there were paintings of synthetics tearing apart people and several figures lying on the ground reaching outward, their faces in agony as they tried to stop the act.

"Gruesome."

Behind the scene of brutality, a large black shape stretched from top to bottom of the wall. At first, she thought it was a giant circle emphasizing the center of the scene, but the more her eyes scanned the artwork, the more it appeared as if the circle was a swirl with a bird-like head.

"A hawk," she whispered.

"A Nighthawk," Gretchen corrected.

Jasmine turned to see Alyssa's pale face. The young girl stood from the chair and pulled the blanket tight around her shoulders as she took

331

several steps closer. Jasmine turned back to the wall and inspected the shape again. It was obvious, a stylized image of a bird.

"I got a letter from Eleanor Valentine. I couldn't figure out why a domestic terrorist paid me any attention. I figured she must have seen the future and felt the need to send a message to me."

Jasmine's stomach turned uneasy as she felt the psychic pulling their strings again. "What did it say?"

"Not much," Gretchen admitted. "'Await the Nighthawks'."

Gretchen stepped out in front of them and turned. The fire made the light on her face dance; the shadows deepened the lines, making her look older than she was.

Jasmine tried to hide her annoyance at the psychic. "We're the Nighthawks."

Gretchen shook her head and tried to process the words. "I knew it. I knew it had something to do with Conthan."

"How?" asked Alyssa.

"Have you ever asked him about Edward Hopper? He won't shut up about the man."

"What does it mean?"

Jasmine put her hand on Alyssa's shoulder. "We need to get the others."

"What the fuck is going on?" asked Gretchen.

Her face gave away her insecurity. The woman was covered in piercings and tattoos, and if you met her on the street, you'd probably shy away from her. Despite her tough exterior, Jasmine felt a tinge of remorse for stumbling into the woman's life.

"We're going to war."
    "Oh, fuck…"

Chapter 23

1993

The atmosphere was quiet, other than the beeps of the monitor attached to the young girl. Her hospital room lacked any bells and whistles, only monitoring equipment, her bed, and a chair by her side. Mark had been sitting next to her for nearly an hour, watching her chest rise and fall in time with the pulsing light on the machines. There was something calm and relaxing about watching over her, almost as if her abilities exuded her sedated state.

A deep breath filled his nostrils with the smell of bleach, reminding him they lived in a sterile setting. The vile scents made him want to cough.

His nightmares had been worsening, getting more terrifying each night. When he woke, images of creatures clawing at his clothing lingered. He stopped sleeping for pleasure and only did it out of necessity. Even now, he approached the twenty-four hour mark of no sleep. He reached a point of exhaustion, but his body needed to push forward. Sitting here in the dimly lit room was the closest thing he required to sleep. He hovered in a state between being awake and nodding off. At least in this state, the dark, violent images couldn't reach him.

Penelope had been in a coma for months, medically induced by Ivan and his staff. They weren't sure how to control an empath's abilities. Even Ivan, with all of his knowledge on mentalists, wasn't sure how he could protect them against somebody capable of pushing emotions onto others.

Mark wanted to speak with her. He wanted to ask her questions about his own state of mind. There was something weighing on his soul, and he feared the dreams were less the cause and more a symptom of his own deep-seated issues. Beneath the surface, he feared the dark rage emerging whenever his fortitude faltered.

He leaned forward and touched her hand, careful not to disturb the IV penetrating the skin inside her elbow. Her skin was soft, to the point where it almost felt fake. The muscles in her hand didn't respond as he clenched her fingers. He was sure it was in his head, but even the slightest contact seemed to give him a moment to breathe. His mind quieted.

He looked to the bag hanging near her head, the fluid dripping consistently into the tube below. He reached for the chart at the foot of her bed, the red stamp, "Project Nostradamus" pressed onto the cover. He started flipping through the pages. He could barely make out the notes by Ivan, but he finally found information on treatment from when Penelope was first admitted.

Mark looked at the device controlling the fluids being released into her body. He pushed several buttons until the Propofol slowed and then stopped. A buzzer in the machine sounded. He flipped the switch, silencing it. The room quieted. Now the fluid dripping into her body was nothing more than saline. He sat back in the chair and waited, his hand still clenched around her fingers.

He leaned forward in his chair, startling himself awake. His eyes darted around the room as he wiped the sleep from them. As he tried to read the clock above the head of the bed, he became aware of two soft brown eyes staring back at him. She looked incredibly young with her eyes resting shut, but with them open, she didn't appear to be any more than a child. He glanced at the door to see if any of the staff were present. Even drowsy, her lips curled in a faint smile.

"Hi, Penelope." His voice was soft but it felt as if he was shouting in the room.

"Hi, mister," she said, her voice quiet and coarse from months of not speaking. She gave a slight cough. He grabbed a paper cup and filled it with water from the small sink in the corner of the room. He held it up to her lips and let her take several tiny sips. She rested her head back on the pillow and let the water wet her mouth. "Where are my mamá and papá?"

"Penelope, what's the last thing you remember?"

She closed her eyes for a moment, and they darted back and forth behind her lids. "Men were

336

grabbing me. They were saying bad things. A boy said he'd make sure I was safe."

Her eyes opened and asked the question before her mouth could. "His name is Arturo, he's safe and doing very well. He's been asking about you, Penelope. He wanted to make sure you knew he did his best to keep you safe."

Her eyes closed again, appearing almost too heavy to keep open. She gave a slight nod with her head. "I remember, sir."

"We had to keep you asleep because of what you're able to do, Penelope."

Her face was delicate. Her tan skin and dark hair mixed with her accent suggested she might be Latin American. Nothing in the report mentioned her family. As with Ivan, large portions of the document preceding her was scratched out, thick black lines removing any details worth knowing. The moment he saw the black marker he knew something horrible happened to her. He assumed her family was dead, most likely at the hands of American soldiers.

"Why are you sad, mister?"

Mark realized every emotion dancing across his mind was out in the open for her. Ivan explained to him empaths were similar to telepaths in the fact that they could read another person. However, where telepaths could read thoughts, empaths focused almost entirely on emotional states. They also learned the day she arrived that not only could they receive emotion, they could project it outward. Her being awake was potentially influencing everybody in the center.

"I'm not sad," he said. "I'm just thinking really hard."

"You can't lie to me, mister," she said. "I can tell." The words weren't a threat, or even accusatory, just a simple fact.

He didn't mind being a human amongst these titans, however, their ability to invade the one space he didn't want them, that made him worry. She was only picking up on his worry at the moment, but if a panicked guard walked in, or a shocked doctor, how would that change her state of mind? If she became panicked, it could wreak havoc with the entire building.

"Do you know what you can do, Penelope?"

She nodded.

"Do you know how dangerous it can be?"

"Mamá would tell me that. She was always concerned the men would find us. She said if they knew what I could do, they would kill me."

Her tone was flat. For a child, she was extremely adept at keeping her emotions in check. Mark wondered if her parents had trained her to be numb to the world or if she had come by that on her own. The distant look in her eyes told him she was processing what happened, but if she had any feelings about it, he couldn't read it on her face. Despite her childish features, she was the most skilled poker player he ever encountered.

"Can you read my thoughts?"

Her head gave a slight shake. She opened her eyes; the brown in her iris was so dark it almost appeared black. "I feel a lot. I can tell what you're feeling. I can tell if you're happy or sad. If I try

338

really hard I can make you feel happy."

"How did you learn to do that?"

She stared blankly at him, as if she didn't understand the question. He pulled his chair closer, resting his arms on her bed. "When did you know you could do that?"

"You're eager," she said softly. "But, you're worried about something. Something has been bothering you lately and it makes you..." she paused as she glanced him up and down "angry."

"Penelope, I need to ask you a personal question."

She instinctively held her hand out for him, her palm facing upward, waiting for his hand. It hovered just above hers; he felt hesitant about what she might be able to see in him. He didn't question her abilities, he questioned whether he could handle hearing his doubts confirmed by the young girl. She lifted her fingers, locking them around his much larger ones.

He couldn't tell if the tingling along his skin was her doing or his paranoia being overactive. She closed her eyes, shutting them tight as she let out a slight grunt. Her face distorted, as if she was smelling something rather unpleasant. He waited for her to say something, but her face continued to contort.

You're scared she'll confirm your fears.

Mark ignored the voice in the back of his head. It had gotten louder the last few months and now he felt crazy as he held conversations with the throaty man just out of hearing range. Mark focused on the girl, hoping she would tell him something, anything at this point. All he wanted was confirmation he wasn't going crazy.

She knows I'm here.

The voice most often mocked him, poking at his insecurities. It was only when he felt the rage building in his chest that the voice became confidant, determined to give him an outlet for the violence brimming just below the surface. He kept it in check, but only as long as he stayed awake. When he slept he saw the shadow in his dreams, pushing at him, taunting him, determined to break down his armor.

"Anger. Rage. Underneath the worry, there is a bubbling rage, sir."

Mark resisted the urge to draw back. He didn't want to hear what might come next. Before he pulled his hand away, her fingers dug deeply into his hand, nails biting into his skin.

"There is something wrong. Your dreams are haunted. There is something growing inside you. Something dark."

Her grip refused to relent. "It's going to kill you, sir. It's going to consume you. It's evil. It wants you."

Her back arched as she sat bolt upright in the bed. Her nails cut deeper, drawing thin lines of blood from his palm. Her eyes glazed over, staring off into nowhere. She hissed through her teeth, as if she attempted to scare away a cat.

"I see you."

She paused as if somebody spoke back. "You are an evil, evil man. Go away, bad man."

Mark reached for a needle resting on the table

next to Penelope. If she grew angry, it would flood the center and with trigger-happy security guards. He wasn't sure how long it would take before they came storming the room and shot them both. She continued looking at the corner of the room, talking to some invisible person.

"Leave him alone."

Mark paused at the statement. "Leave who alone?"

"Don't touch me."

She attempted to recoil, letting go of his hand. Mark didn't dare risk her losing control. He poked the needle into her arm and thrust the plunger down, flooding her body with a sedative. She gave him a sad glance before her eyes shut and she drifted off.

"I'm sorry," she whispered as sleep consumed her.

Chapter 24

2033

Jasmine heard the glass shatter before she saw the fractured shards falling. High in the rafters, a window broke as a large object was hurled through the panes. Vanessa followed, jumping through with her wings tucked behind her. As she neared the ground they shot open, sending her speeding parallel to and only a few feet above the cement.

They're here. The call sounded through her head as if yelled by Vanessa. It dawned on her the fallen object was a synthetic. If there was one on the roof, there'd be another somewhere on the ground. She couldn't imagine they'd be trolling through the warehouse district without backup.

"There's probably another one," she said to Alyssa and Gretchen.

"Gretchen, do you have a computer here?"

The girl produced a piece of clear plastic and held it out to Alyssa. "Will my phone do?"

"Can you keep both of you invisible?"

Gretchen nodded. The punker grabbed onto Alyssa's hand and both blinked out sight. Jasmine hoped the girl could find quick inspiration for her powers. She didn't need to worry about people who couldn't take care of themselves.

Vanessa landed a few feet away. "I only saw one, but they know we're here. They're going to come in force again."

"We won't be staying very long," Jasmine said.

A scream sounded from the room Skits had claimed as her bedroom. A flash of blue light burst through the cracks in the corrugated metal wall. A second later she stepped out, a head in her hand. She dropped the metal skull onto the floor and eyed the two women. "I think we have a problem."

The fallen synthetic started heading toward the group at a light jog. Jasmine focused on the skin underneath her bracer and on the softest metal. With a simple thought her skin tightened and her epidermis changed density. She ignored the pain searing through her muscles. With the less dense materials, she could shift without collapsing onto the ground. For a single synthetic, she wouldn't need skin impenetrable enough to withstand tank munitions.

Her muscles followed suit, strengthening in response to the added weight of her body. She started charging toward the machine as the tension in her limbs tightened. She imagined it wouldn't be long; they'd wipe the floor with these two. Then they'd be on their way, hopefully to take this fight to the doorstep of their attackers.

The machine dropped to all fours, running more

animal like than human. She launched herself into the air, ready to tackle the synthetic to the floor. It dropped, sliding harmlessly along the pavement underneath her. It continued running, directing itself toward Vanessa.

"What the hell?" Jasmine whispered as she tried to get her footing and change direction.

She chased after the robot. It was going to charge into Vanessa, and while the woman was strong, she wasn't quite a fighter. Jasmine watched as Gretchen appeared out of thin air along with Alyssa. She let go of the younger woman and grabbed onto Vanessa's arm. As quickly as the tattooed woman appeared, she vanished.

The machine halted its pursuit. Jasmine knew in that moment, whoever was coming after them wasn't after the rest of the team, they wanted Vanessa. Somebody out there wanted the mentalist. At least this observation narrowed the list of attackers.

"Come here," Alyssa yelled.

The machine stood upright and stalked toward the girl. She slid the glass phone into her pocket and ducked its first swipe. She went to sweep the robot's legs out from under it, a well-rehearsed maneuver. The machine jumped, avoiding her attack. As it landed the synthetic launched a kick toward her head. She managed to block it, but not before it sent her rolling backward.

"Something's wrong," she yelled.

Jasmine caught up to them and grabbed the arm of the robot. It spun around and jabbed her in the throat. Even in her armored form, the impact caused her to choke. It followed the shot by reaching down and grabbing her at the knees. It lifted her up, then dropped her, sending her flat onto her back. She caught the machine's foot as it attempted to stomp on her.

Vanessa blinked into sight and slammed both her fists down on the machine's back. Jasmine kicked the thing off her and scrambled to her feet. Gretchen appeared and grabbed both of their shoulders. The moment her skin touched their bodies, color vanished.

"We're good," she said.

"It's smart," Jasmine said. "It knows us."

"I know," Vanessa said. "It's Dav5d."

Jasmine didn't need to see the woman to know the pain she must be feeling. She had a thousand questions, but she couldn't ignore that the machine was faster than its predecessors. Its forearms shifted and small guns rolled out.

"We're invisible, not impervious."

Gretchen was right, at any moment a stray bullet could kill them. If there were more, this would get out of hand quickly. Jasmine broke free from the girl's grip and the machine snapped to attention. The guns fired and she felt the biting sting of each bullet. Bullets dented her flesh, and if she let the synthetic focus its fire on one place too long, it'd tear through her metal hide.

Alyssa brought down a piece of rebar on the machine's neck. It spun around, catching the metal pole, and threw it to the side. She grabbed its arm and sidestepped, bringing it behind its back. She lifted hard, the gyros fighting to keep the limb from snapping.

"The not-strong girl needs help," Alyssa yelled.

Small panels flipped open on the machines shoulders. Jasmine knew those compartments housed the synthetic's lasers. It seemed they always resorted to lasers. They hurt, a lot.

Skits.

"Duck," Jasmine yelled. Alyssa leaned forward, tucking herself into a ball. The flash of blue light shoved through the machine's shoulder and the laser melted, half encased in its own metal. The synthetic tried to pull away, but Skits grabbed onto its arm with her other hand. The light flared again and the arm fell to the ground in a puddle of molten goo.

Jasmine stood in amazement of the girl's abilities. Skits's shirt had caught on fire, the fabric evaporating from her arms as the air around her burned brighter. Alyssa scurried away from the droplets of metal. Even Gretchen and Vanessa appeared again.

Skits pulled her hand out of the synthetic's shoulder and grabbed the machine by the pelvis. She screamed, blue fire turning white as she dragged her hand up the torso. She pulled both hands back and kicked the machine to the ground.

"Skits saves the day, bitches," she yelled. The girl did a quick cheer. Modesty was not her super power.

Jasmine stood over the machine as it tried to get up. It attempted to continue fighting. She wondered how long it would try before it finally admitted defeat. Vanessa reached down to the machine and rested her hand on its cheek.

"Are you in there?" she whispered.

Jasmine understood, she hoped to reach out to Dav5d through the machine. There were examples of powers mingling with unusual effects, but she had no idea how a telepath could read the mind of a machine. She wondered if Dav5d's conscious was somehow wrapped up in the circuitry. It was starting to get a bit too science fiction even for her.

As she was about to say something, Dwayne and Conthan worked their way through a bay door. Dwayne held an arm, certainly another synthetic they had dealt with. She turned about, looking at the darkest corners of the warehouse, waiting for another one of the machines to attack her.

He's in there.

"He's in there," Vanessa said, echoing Jasmine's thoughts.

The expressions on her face went from hopeful to dismal. She caressed the machine's cheek and stared at empty space. Dwayne caught Jasmine's eye, glancing down at Vanessa, trying to get a clue what was going on.

"It's Dav5d," she said.

The warehouse vanished and they stood in a blinding white room. She knew they were in that weird space telepaths went to communicate with one another. Even here, Vanessa kneeled on the floor, cradling the machine, whispering softly to it.

Off in the distance, a stasis tube could be seen, fainter than them, as if the atmosphere between them attempted to obscure the machinery. There was a man inside, and she knew without asking it contained Dav5d. A man in a finely tailored suit rested his hand on the glass of the tube and the moment he made contact, black tendrils of smoke appeared.

His mind is gone. The Warden did this.

They eyed one another, nervous glances, unsure of how to process the new bit of information. Conthan touched Vanessa, his hand resting on her shoulder, a firm grip offering solace. "The dreams were real."

As she looked to him, her eyes were bare, cold, and filled with hatred. Jasmine knew the look all too well, similar to the one that stared at her in the mirror. She knew the running was about to come to an end.

"The Warden?" asked Dwayne.

"He's latched onto the head of a secret society, another mentalist."

"Shit," Skits said.

"It seems they have a connection to the President of the United States," said Vanessa.

Jasmine's ears perked up at that. She started to wonder how it all fit. The president was connected to Eleanor from when they worked together. The Warden was put into place by the president. She couldn't figure out how this secret society played a role.

The white room vanished and they were standing in a circle in the abandoned warehouse. The sudden transition back to reality made her stomach queasy.

"Jasmine is right," Vanessa said, ignoring the fact nobody else had been able to read her mind. "Eleanor and the president are connected. The

348

president and the Warden are connected."

"But what about the secret society?" Jasmine asked, taking a deep breath.

"Eleanor was their leader for a while," said Alyssa.

"The book." Jasmine started seeing the last year of their lives coming full circle.

There was a collective gasp, except from Gretchen, who didn't quite connect the dots. "Somebody mind clueing me in here?"

Conthan was up to bat. "For the last year, everything we've done has been the manipulation of a dead psychic. Eleanor brought us together to stop something. We thought we had." He eyed Vanessa. "But it seems it's only getting worse."

"How does this involve Dav5d and the synthetics?" asked Dwayne.

"Genesis Division," whispered Jasmine. "They're the society?"

Vanessa nodded. "I fear so."

Jasmine clenched her fists. Genesis Division was the backer of the military, the people who helped supply the Corps with weapons. They were the ones who created the device still embedded in her neck. They were the ones who supplied the synthetics. Rage started to build in her chest. *It's time to end this*, she thought.

It is, Vanessa whispered back to her, her voice echoing the anger.

"We're going to the White House," said Jasmine.

"Gretchen, you need to stay back," said Conthan.

She shook her head. "This is a race war. I was a Nighthawk before you made it cool." Her smirk gave away the devilish side of her nature. Jasmine liked the spunk in the girl. In one fight, she had already proven herself useful.

"We're glad you're with us," she said.

"So what do we do?" asked Dwayne.

"This is going to be a fight like we've never encountered before," Vanessa started.

Before she continued talking, she reached down to the machine still scraping along the floor. She whispered words quietly enough they couldn't be made out. With a growl she pulled at the synthetic's head, tearing it from the metal. She pressed her hands together, crushing the skull until the machine stopped moving.

"Conthan, we need to make a stop along the way."

"Where to?" he asked.

"The art gallery."

"Why there?" asked Jasmine.

"It's where this all started."

***

"You're baiting them," Dikeledi said in the chair across from him.

They had boarded the company jet, bound to D.C. to meet with Cecilia. The jet was state of the art, and the trio sat comfortably in plush leather chairs opposite one another. Lily had started pacing the moment she could, her dislike for flying quite obvious. Dikeledi took a moment to calm her, soothing Lily's worries and relaxing the woman's body.

"Of course I am," he said.

"Always the risk taker. Both of you," she added.

He smiled. Lily accepted his additional abilities, the compounding of his telepathy along with the mysterious man haunting his dreams. She didn't question the favors he promised to receive such awesome power. Dikeledi on the other hand, she understood the occupation of his body, the two people who were slowly merging into one.

"We have a vacant seat on the board now. It'd be delightful if the Child of Nostradamus mentalist joined us. Between the four of us, there would be little we could not conquer."

"There will be unrest," Lily said, the constant voice of reason.

"The United States is at war, they will bow to anybody willing to provide them safety. Once we've taken the White House, we will set our sights to the General. Once we have squashed the military, then we consider our options."

"You won't stop until you've conquered the world," she said.

"Why should we?"

"If you get me killed," she said, "I'll be less than pleased."

"Lily, you're always less than pleased." Lily gave a slight roll of her eyes. He listened to her thoughts slipping out, and he knew without a doubt she was as excited as him. She would never let them know, but more than him or Dikeledi, she liked to fight. She itched for a confrontation. He knew deep down, she was getting exactly what she wanted.

The jet was a luxury of their wealth. Normally

several attendants rushed back and forth to make their trip as comfortable as possible. Now, a single woman stood at the end of the cabin near the bar, mixing a drink. With a thought, she turned around and walked toward him, holding out his drink along with a cocktail napkin.

"Excellent," he said with a sip. "Now be gone."

The woman turned around and walked to the back of the cabin and through a door to the staff area. He smiled, his lips stretching from ear to ear. He liked having the ability to force people into submission. Now, his charm paled in comparison to his telepathy; nobody would be able to resist his beck and call.

The pilot came over the speaker. "We are preparing our descent into D.C. Please remain seated until further notice."

"I can smell your excitement," Dikeledi said. "From both of you. This will be absolutely delectable."

Jacob admired the woman. Her ebony skin and high cheekbones were highlighted by her shaved head. Large golden earrings dangled, drawing attention to her face at all times. Now with the compounded abilities, he sensed just how wild of a person she was. He wondered how much of their excitement emanated from the aura she radiated, or how much of it was her reacting to their emotional state.

He looked out the window to the lights of the city below. It would be his, one way or another; he had earned it. There only remained one person between him and victory. *Thankfully, you underestimate yourself, and because of that, the world is mine, Madame President.*

***

Vanessa crossed her legs as she sat on the cold tiles. It wasn't the most comfortable position for her wings, but it gave her the most contact with the floor without lying down. The lockers towered above her while the smell of mildew made her scrunch up her nose. There was something electric about knowing she was in a location occupied by Eleanor forty years prior.

"What's she doing?" Gretchen whispered.

She didn't need to see Conthan to know he raised a finger to his lips. They were accustomed to her unexplainable witchcraft. Their abilities followed a sense of logic, science, and obeyed the laws of the universe. Even Conthan, who could tear open gaps in reality, could read about his abilities in a textbook. She was not like them. She was like this before the stars aligned and a cosmic event caused the Nostradamus Effect. She didn't have to obey the laws of the universe.

Her childhood had been a curse, bombarded by the constant thoughts of others. It only worsened as the Nostradamus Effect washed over her, altering her body until she was nothing more than a reflection of a devil. The irony of being raised by nuns was not lost on her. Now, as she looked back to her childhood, she could only see herself with green skin and leathery wings. She wondered if the priest who had beaten her had seen the same thing.

353

None of it mattered now. She had been an infant when Eleanor saved her life. She never knew what happened to her parents, just that a woman had stepped in and kept the government from taking her away from Sister Muriel. She had been raised ignorant of her savior, the same woman who died by security guards in the White House.

The memories of her youth washed over her. The pains and hardships of knowing every thought of those around her. For Vanessa's entire life she knew pain. The emotions brought a sniffle, and she understood it was pain that allowed her to embrace every moment of joy in her life. She held those memories close to her chest, embracing every building block of her existence. She knew she wouldn't change her past for the world.

She ran her hand over the book resting in her lap. The worn leather cover brought her back to the locker room. Around her stood six people, five of them her family and another willing to fight for a cause she hardly understood. They fought because of her, Eleanor. This battle wasn't like the Facility, it wasn't against a single man. This time, they were going against power they didn't understand wielded by institutions hundreds of years old.

She imagined her telepathy rolling out of her skin like smoke. It crawled along the ground, touching each surface in the locker room until she could chart every nook and cranny. With a gentle shove, she heard the thoughts of every person behind her. She pushed harder, looking for thoughts not belonging to her companions. She gripped the book, focusing on Eleanor, the woman with the pen, writing down her life for them to find.

I cannot believe I finally did it.

Vanessa heard the whisper. It sounded distant, as if breathed across a forest. She wasn't sure if it was real or her hoping to find something. She gritted her teeth, reaching out, searching for the voice. Her powers pulsed, filling the room, causing the people behind her to stagger. She rested one of her hands on the floor and shoved the entirety of her thoughts through it, into her palm, and along the tile floor.

"Holy shit," gasped Skits.

"A-ozu billahi mena shaitaan Arrajeem."

Vanessa felt the room breathe as if alive, the energy touching upon memories decades old. A woman stood naked at the locker in front of her. She toweled off, drying her skin after a shower. Despite the naked flesh only feet from her, Vanessa could only see the woman's face.

What do you mean, you did it?

A man's voice came from somewhere in the room. Vanessa couldn't see him, but she could sense he was a strong man, a role model, somebody Eleanor cared for. She wondered if the man was her father, or perhaps a sibling?

I changed the future.

Vanessa understood why this occasion spoke loudest. There could be many times Eleanor walked through this room, but this was a moment charged so powerfully its ghosts spoke to her. She hoped she could speak to the woman like earlier, perhaps glean some insight for the battle to come. She hoped her soldiers would see the exchange and be inspired. But this, this was something altogether more eye opening.

I can't explain it, Frank. I saw something happen, and I changed it. It wasn't like before, I was able to change the future. Do you know what this means?

The man grumbled.

If I can see the future, I can change it. I can make it better. I can save people.

Vanessa strained, the pounding in her skull interrupt the image. She tried to push harder but realized there was no way she could continue resurrecting memories from a half century ago. With one last push, she knew they was only seconds from disappearing.

What do you mean? Maybe God gave me the ability to see the future to change it. If I don't do it, who will?

Vanessa let out a breath she didn't realize she was holding. She clutched her chest, her heart thumping loud enough she feared the others could hear. She dragged herself up onto a bench near the lockers and stared at her companions. They stood in a line, their faces pale from witnessing long dead ghosts.

"If we don't do this, who will?" asked Conthan. She eyed the young man. There were moments such as these when she understood Eleanor's plan. He was the embodiment of everything good they stood for, even if he didn't know it. Each of them played a role, and with his single statement, she asked herself again, was this Eleanor's plan all along?

"Nighthawks?" Gretchen said.

"Nighthawks," Vanessa managed through

clenched teeth.

Chapter 25

1993

Mark leaned against the wall outside Penelope's room, reading through the chart taken from her door. The medical wing of the research center was extensive. They had areas for wounded soldiers, rehabilitation, and even testing new technologies. This area fell behind thick doors requiring high security clearance. Penelope's room had been selected for privacy.

Since the day he awakened her, they started to adjust her meds to let her remain conscious for short periods of time. Most often Ariel or Arturo sat with her. Ivan noted by observing recordings of their interactions, it appeared Penelope was incapable of using her abilities on the others. Ivan had assumed there was some sort of natural resistance. Now, the two teens sat with her and told her stories. It was almost as if they were finding some normalcy in their lives.

Mark took a deep breath as he rubbed his eyes.

He tried to ignore the pulling pain at the base of his brain, an early sign of an oncoming migraine. He hadn't slept a full night in almost three months and even now, he only took quick naps when his schedule allowed. He started living on coffee and Tylenol. Today was the first day in a week he didn't have a list of meetings scheduled. It seemed the headache knew when to rear its ugly head.

He jolted upright as a loud crash sounded across the hall. He slid the chart back into place and peered through the small window in the door leading to one of the labs. There was a quiet hush as he pressed his ear against the cold steel. He pulled at the door and poked his head inside the room.

"Hello?"

A privacy curtain obstructed his view. It was where they did their research into the cybernetics being applied to soldiers. A table in the middle of the room held microscopes and vials with liquids being pushed through them. Mark knew that it wasn't all the pursuit of academic research; a bone saw sitting on the table told him there were also experiments being conducted. Only a few rooms away, soldiers volunteered for the next wave of cybernetic enhancements. With the support of the Genesis Division they already progressed leaps and bounds. Now they were talking about covering the cybernetics with synthetic skin, something he honestly didn't believe would ever be possible.

Mark could see movement on through a curtain hanging near the door. He pulled it back to Goddard holding Ivan against the wall, pinned by the neck. Ivan grappled with the man's arm, trying to pull it away from his windpipe.

"Goddard, put him down."

The cyborg didn't turn his head to see who entered the room. Goddard leaned into his stance, holding Ivan several inches off the ground. Ivan's face transformed into a deep purple.

"Put him the fuck down."

"The doctor is refusing to upgrade my hands."

"That's no reason to kill him, Goddard."

"He says that my limbs wouldn't work well with the new interface. He thinks he's funny by leaving me with second rate gear. I seem to think it's funny that he's going to choke."

Ivan reached out, trying to grasp at the security guard's face. Goddard batted away his hand like it was nothing. "I can't even feel him. I can see him suffering, but I can't even feel him struggling through this metal limb."

Mark hadn't been sure how it was going to happen, but he knew it would eventually come to this. Goddard had been an ass to begin with, but it only magnified after the incident with his hands. He stayed clear of Mark after the fight in the ring, but now he was determined to harass Ivan until the scientist quit. Mark knew this was the line in the sand and Goddard stepped far over it.

He didn't remember picking up the bone saw from the table. Mark didn't remember the cold sensation of the metal running through his palm. He didn't remember his vise-like grip holding it like a weapon.

"Put down Ivan or I'll kill you."

"You can try," Goddard said.

Mark swung the blade at the man. The swing was messy. He fought to keep his eyes open, fearful he'd miss if he let them shut. The metal sounded loudly, ringing as it struck Goddard's hand. He swung again, the blade scraping along the back of the man's jacket, just enough that it grazed skin.

"And you," Goddard said, thrusting his hand out and grabbing onto Mark's tie. Mark used his free hand to punch the man in the kidney, causing him to take a step back from Ivan.

The scientist fell to the ground. Mark expected him to suck in air, like in the movies, but the man didn't move as his body slumped to the ground. Mark assumed Goddard killed him, all because he wanted an upgrade.

Mark slashed through his tie with the blade and kicked hard at the security guard's knee. Goddard knocked his foot away. Mark hissed at the impact of the club-like fist. He took a couple steps backward, jumping outside of the guard's reach.

"You think because you beat me once I'll be your whipping boy?"

Mark ducked under Goddard's fist, realizing too late the man's knee already lifted to meet his face. The impact launched Mark backward, threatening to send him to the floor as his nose exploded. Before he registered the pain, he tasted the copper on his tongue. He had been so confident in the ring, determined he could take the man down. Now, it seemed as if they reverted to their original relationship, Goddard the bully and Mark the weakling. Even the blade in his hand didn't provide him any comfort.

Mark lunged, swinging wildly with the saw, determined to catch whatever blocking limb he could. Goddard's metal hand clasped at the blade, gripping it, crushing the tip, and ripping it from Mark's hand. Goddard laughed as he tossed the weapon to the side.

"If I kill you...H" he panted, his lips turning upward, as if he pictured his 'happy place.' He took a step in closer, sending Mark jumping back, trying to stay out of his reach. "If I kill you, nobody will miss you."

Mark had a moment to realize the man's assumption was horribly wrong. In fact, Mark understood that he was the last man standing between all the Goddards in the world, the people who would kill them, and Ariel, Arturo, and even Penelope. There was a fraction of a second in which Mark realized if he fell today, everything he built would crumble. The stupidity of a single power-drunk man could destroy all his hard work.

"Over my dead body," Mark said.

Mark wanted to move forward, for his foot to kick as swiftly as possible in the hopes he might catch the man in the groin. His muscles tensed but stopped as a headache bit at the back of his head. The pressure threatened to make him hurl. He fell to the side, grabbing onto a table to try and keep himself standing. He clutched at the piece of furniture, wrapping his fingers around a microscope. As Goddard stepped closer, he swung the piece of equipment, catching the man in the neck, causing him to stagger backward.

As quickly as it began, the headache vanished.

He needed to be done with Goddard so he could check on Ivan. Mark spun around just in time to duck under Goddard's attempt at a bear hug. Mark studied the man.

Right foot forward. Then he'll swing. He'll hope I duck. He'll try for the knee again. He wants to drive down my spine and I'll be helpless.

Mark saw Goddard's hand come out, a slow left hook. He caught it and spun around, using the man's momentum to hurl him over his shoulder. As Goddard landed on the ground, Mark grabbed onto the metal forearm and twisted hard, causing a loud pop as the arm came loose from its socket.

Goddard howled.

Mark smiled.

The edges of his vision was starting to cloud, as if a blackness was moving in around the edge of his sight. He went to stomp down on the man's face, but got knocked backward by the other cybernetic limb. Mark gasped. For a moment, it was as if Goddard was slowing down until he stopped.

Goddard is going to lunge at me and try to take me down to the floor. The room sped up, and Goddard prepared to jump at him again. Mark stepped to the side just in time to watch the man fall down onto all fours. *He's going to reach into his boot for the knife.*

His vision darkened. It was beginning to look as if he was seeing the world down a long hallway. His foot stomped on Goddard's hand, pinning it to the ground. He reached down and grabbed the man's head, wrapping his arm around his neck. He held him in a sleeper hold, giving him just enough room that he wouldn't collapse.

Mark's limbs moved, but he wasn't aware of what they were doing. There was a distant sensation of the man's neck pressed against his forearm, but it was like a memory that happened years ago. He shook his head, trying to get a grasp of what was going on.

"I'm going to kill you," hissed Goddard.

The tunnel grew longer and longer until Mark could barely make out Goddard. He watched as his hand slid to Goddard's jaw. His other hand rested on the back of the security guard's head, and with a fast spin, the body fell to the floor. Mark watched as his eyes stared off toward the wall of the lab. Then Mark's vision closed, turning entirely black. Before the darkness swallowed him whole, he made out Ivan, standing unharmed to one side of the lab smiling.

I had hoped we would have more time to benefit from one another, but my hand was forced. But out of necessity, what amazing things we discover about ourselves.

Mark tried to respond, to yell at the scientist, but he couldn't find his voice. His limbs refused to respond, and it became obvious he was trapped inside the dark room. His heart started to race as he panicked. He wanted to claw at the walls, but his immobilized body did nothing.

Mark knew he wasn't standing in the lab anymore. He glanced down and could see his hands, bright white flesh shining against the darkness. Everywhere he turned, the room was perfectly black, swallowing any light that might enter. He screamed and this time, his voice came out as a guttural cry.

"You can scream all you like here," said a vaguely familiar voice.

Mark turned around to see Ivan several feet away, his lab coat perfectly white, almost blinding against the endless void of a room. Mark tried to understand what was transpiring. They weren't in the lab anymore.

"No, we're not," said Ivan.

"How did you know..."

Ivan's body seemed to absorb the darkness of the room until wisps of smoke wrapped itself around his limbs. His body faded from sight until all that was left was a spindly shadowy man. Mark recognized the form from his dreams. It struck Mark all of a sudden, everything falling into place.

"A telepath."

A cackle filled the space, seeming to echo off surfaces he couldn't see. There had been so many questions building over the last two years and now, with a single statement, it made sense. *There had been something dark coming,* he thought. *Is this what Eleanor had foreseen?*

"You'll never know. But with you working side-by-side with me, I'll achieve great things in this prison for mentalists."

"I'll never help you."

"You won't have a choice." The smile appeared to spread across the smoky figure. "Warden."

"I said to leave him alone."

Mark spun about, looking for the source of the second, soft voice. It was just above a whisper, sounding as if it was coming from across the room.

"I told you he was mine," said Ivan. Mark cocked his head to the side as the telepath spoke. He followed the man's downward facing eyes. Whoever he spoke to was short, hovering just over five feet.

The response was distant, impossible to understand. Mark was aware of his heartbeat speeding up and his muscles tensing. He couldn't see it, but he knew the hair on his arms stood on end. His body reacted as if he was having a panic attack.

"It doesn't seem your abilities work on a telepath."

Mark's eyes went wide in disbelief.

Penelope. Oh, God, no.

Chapter 26

2033

Jacob walked through the White House with Lily and Dikeledi two steps behind him, their feet falling in time on the plush rugs. He wore his white suit while Lily wore a white gown showing off ample cleavage and Dikeledi wore white slacks and a white blouse tied behind her neck. Behind them, three Barren followed, their bomber jackets and frightful smiles making them stand out. They were being led down the hallway by two Secret Service agents while another two took up the rear.

He made note of the number of synthetics stationed about the White House. He wondered how many extra were there to deal with the constant barrage of attempts on Cecilia's life, or was this a special occasion for the Society? She wasn't a fool. She knew the Secret Service agents were nothing more than cannon fodder and they'd be weapons with a simple thought from Jacob.

They passed by executive offices passed as they

continued down the hallway to the Oval Office. At the door, massive security guards stood at each side. They all had a look about them: stiff backs, clear plastic earpieces, and folded hands ready to reach into their jackets and pull out weapons. He stifled a laugh; they had no idea how close they were to dying right now. A thought is all it would take.

They waited a moment as one of the guards reached up to his earpiece and waited for commands. If it wasn't him that killed them, it'd be Lily tearing them limb from limb or Dikeledi dragging out their suffering for days.

Yes, he thought, *this is going to be fun.*

"With so many studs around, I can see why she doesn't want to give up office." Lily tried not to pout as the guards refused to partake in her verbal sparring.

The man at the front of their troupe opened the door and stepped inside and to the right. Jacob walked in to see the President of the United States standing in front of her desk, arms crossed, trying not to look displeased. Synthetics waited, stationed about the room in a manner to intimidate visitors. The room held the same iconic pieces of furniture as it had a century before. He pondered if the carpet was the same. Despite its historic appearance, he noted the security cameras located along the molding at the top of the room. Behind her, a giant blue virtual display revealed she had been watching them walk through the hallways.

"We appreciate your attire," he admitted.

She glanced down, dismissing the compliment. A formal gathering for Society businesses required they wear white. Her pure white pantsuit made her skin appear dark in comparison. The four of them contrasted with the security guards and their pitch black uniforms.

"What is it you want, Jacob?"

"It's a bit crowded in here, don't you think?"

She smirked. "They are loyal, you can speak openly in front of them."

He didn't doubt her. She could be paying them copious amounts of money, or perhaps she blackmailed their families. What she lacked in abilities, she had in resources to get her way. Her guards were ex-military, some were even mercenaries, but they were human none the less.

"Be gone."

The guards turned toward the door and walked out in unison. He smiled as they obeyed his command. They waited in the hallway, staring at the wall. Lily flipped her wrist and the door shut. With a simple gesture from the President, six synthetics came to life. They took a step closer, closing the distance between the president and her potential threat.

"Showing off to somebody who already knows your abilities seems like a wasted effort," she said.

"I like to remind you who sits in charge."

"They will kill you if you try."

"You'll be dead before they take another step, Madame President."

"Their orders are to kill you if anything should befall me." The smug grin wiped away the wrinkles at the edge of the president's lips. She laughed, a condescending laughter that felt like daggers in his chest. He closed his fist and let the nails bite into his skin. He could tear her mind to pieces, but watching her lose her humanity wasn't enough for him. He wanted to make sure she was aware he pulled all the strings before he killed her.

"I know you put the Warden in charge of the Facility."

"I'm sure you do." She didn't move more muscles than absolutely necessary to answer. "You've come a long ways to share information about the obvious."

"I know he was amassing an army of Children of Nostradamus. I have my suspicions you knew exactly what was going on. More than that, you were using Genesis Division resources to allow it."

She placed her hands on the edge of the desk and leaned back on the oversized piece of furniture. Her right pointer finger tapped against the surface. Through her legs he could make out the sigil for the United States of America. He reached out with his mind and brushed against hers. He wanted to hear her panic, but all he got in return was silence. The one woman he wanted to violate with his newfound talents had an immunity to his psychic abilities.

I must uncover how you do that, Cecilia.

He sat in one of the chairs facing toward her desk. The women sat on each side of him on the stately love seats. The Barren stood behind them, their bodies appearing almost as robotic as the machines in the room. Cecilia made no move to join. Instead she continued tapping away at the desk.

"What are you hinting at?"

Before he could respond, Dikeledi blurted out, "The Warden is a mentalist."

He stared at Dikeledi, who motioned a "sorry" with a shoulder shrug. He had no doubt she received his impending giddiness. The woman appeared on the verge of giggling, unable to suppress her abilities.

The president didn't respond. Her lack of a response made it clear what she knew about the man. Jacob might not be able to read her mind, but her body language helped make her understandable.

"Why do you suddenly have such an interest in a dead man?"

Jacob ran his hands along the leather of the chair, admiring the craftsmanship. "It's not him I'm interested in. What has caught my attention is you, my subordinate, raising an army without informing me. You wasted Genesis funds and decided to hide it from us. I'm hurt, Cecilia."

"It could have—"

"I'm not done," he stated, motioning for her to stop. "But the crime I can't forgive you for, the one that really makes me question our business relationship, is knowing your Warden is a mentalist."

"How would I have known that?"

"She's good at hiding her emotions," Dikeledi said, drawing a disgusted look from Cecilia.

"You carry more secrets than not," Jacob continued. "I have no doubt you were fully aware of what you were preparing to unleash on the world. And even if you didn't know his intentions, you made it possible."

"Your grandstanding has gone on long enough. What is it you want, Jacob?"

"I want your job."

She gave a slight nod, barely a twitch. Her security guards poured through the door, their guns drawn and pointed them toward him. He didn't flinch. He assumed humans to be beneath him, and this was another example of their feebleness. Each stood up straight and turned their guns toward their temples. He smiled as the guns fired, dropping all of her guards.

"Really, Cecilia, did you think that was going to end any other way?"

"I think my reliance on the Society ends here."

Two synthetics near the door took steps forward. The lasers on their shoulders hummed as power pulsed through the machinery. She made no attempt to hide the smirk on her face. "Lily may survive these two, but there are over one hundred synthetics close enough that you will not walk out of here alive."

"Isn't this the very spot where you were nearly assassinated before?"

She tried to hold her smile, but the edges of her lips couldn't maintain the farce. He stood up and adjusted his tie. He eyed a spot on the carpet. "Is this where she died? I was always curious."

"You think she's the only one who's made an attempt on my life? Mr. Griffin, men have come with armies to remove me. You have two lackeys and three mindless sacks of flesh."

Dikeledi started to laugh. Her laughter gave away who had the upper hand. Cecilia couldn't fathom the forces at work, but she believed Dikeledi borderline crazy. The president almost cracked a smile, a light chuckle escaping her lips. She motioned with her hand, and both synthetics aimed their weapons at the empath.

"Make an example out of her."

Everybody froze, everybody except Dikeledi. The laughter faded and she raised her eyebrows. "She's confused. Her fear has a hint of anger." She verbalized the president's emotional state, unnerving the powerful woman.

"It should."

Jacob motioned with his hand for the synthetics to stand down. As Cecilia's eyebrows rose and her jaw dropped, he smiled. "I've been waiting for years, Madame President."

"Finally, a crack in that armor of yours," Jacob said. Her thoughts were muddled, as if they were being swallowed by ambient noise. He adjusted the tie around his neck. As his hand slid down the fabric, Jacob shoved power into the president.

There was a moment of silence as Cecilia tried to comprehend what happened. Where Jacob had been standing, another man stood in his place, somebody she hadn't seen for decades. She leaned backward, half sitting on her desk, grabbing the edge to steady herself.

"It has been years," he said, his voice taking on an entirely different timbre. "I've missed the games you used to play, child. A powerful woman, scared by her own genetic limitations."

"But how…"

"What amazes me is you didn't have the

foresight to predict the product of your own machinations."

Lily rested her hand on his shoulder, taking delight in the befuddled expression on the face of the most powerful woman in the world. "The irony, Cecilia killed the only woman who could have foreseen this."

The president stuttered, unable to complete a single word. The curtains of the Oval Office shut with a quick flick of the telekinetic's wrist. It was the first time he shared in the memories of the other man, the sensations of his past washing along his skin. He had difficulty separating himself from the man he portrayed.

He dragged one foot in front of the other, creeping toward the terrified woman. With each step the image in front of her faded. One man transformed into another until a familiar man from her past stood in front of her. He watched as the reflection in her eyes aged into a thick powerhouse. It took a moment, but the terror flooding her eyes let him know she finally connected the dots.

"Davis? No, Volkov..."

***

Conthan stepped through the portal with Gretchen in tow. He clenched her hand tightly, their fingers interwoven to be sure they didn't lose contact. He only had a moment to pull her to the side of the portal and duck. The air on his neck stood on end as the first burst of searing white light shot through the room.

Dwayne held out his fists, electricity pouring out of him as he exited the black disc hanging in the air. The synthetics were hurled across the room, the metal covering their torsos ripped apart by the ferocity of his abilities. Not long before, Conthan had watched the man break down and question his role; now, he served as their heavy artillery with frightening efficiency.

Electricity tore at metal, frying wires and melting circuit boards. Seven people occupied the Oval Office, but he only recognized the president. The most powerful woman in the world and three people in white dress clothes dropped to the floor. The men in bomber jackets with their creepy smiles didn't budge at the destruction.

The two synthetics hurdled into the wall, breaking century old plaster. Dwayne looked for his next target. The smell of charred carpet, burning fabric, and gunpowder hung thick in the air. Dwayne directed his fist to the two women clad in pristine white garments on the ground closest to him. After the display he put on, Conthan didn't think anybody would dare to put up a fight.

"Lily," the man said.

Nobody moved a muscle. Dwayne emptied his lungs as something thrust into his gut throwing him from his feet into one of the charred curtains and out the window. Sunlight poured into the room, illuminating the damage the human lightning rod inflicted on the Oval Office. Conthan expected the president, but he didn't know the extra two women were. For a moment he thought he saw the Warden standing near Cecilia. He had the look of a villain, a certain arrogance only cultivated by a man trying to destroy the world.

Conthan started to step forward, but Gretchen tugged at his hand. She grasped his fingers tighter, reminding him this wasn't their battle. The others could yell at him later; he focused on the man in the middle of the room and opened a portal. When nothing happened, he raised his free hand for dramatic effect and tried again. The man's innards hadn't been torn from his body. For a moment, he stared directly at Conthan.

The teleporter didn't hesitate as he flicked his wrist and another portal opened. Skits dropped out of the black void. She kicked hard, her foot catching the white woman in the face and sending her onto her back, unmoving. Skits's hands flared blue as she pivoted to slam her fist into the black woman's chest. With her hands drawn back, she stopped attacking.

"You do not want to fight," said the black woman as she got to her knees. Skits froze instantly, the light around her hands dimming to the point the liquid fire vanished. Her shoulders slumped, her body appearing as if it might crumple to the ground.

"But she does," Skits said with a smile.

Alyssa fell through the portal, landing on the ground. As she touched down, Conthan clenched his fist, closing the black void. Alyssa, already in motion, punched her. The black woman threw her up hands to defend herself, obviously unaware of Alyssa's level of anger. She changed the direction of her punch, knocking blood from the woman's mouth. Her victim fell backward as Alyssa landed an uppercut.

"Get them, girl," Skits said with a lackluster tone.

She was fast. Conthan's stomach tightened as the three men in bomber jackets approached her. She spun about, the heel of her boot connecting with the closest bomber jacket. As spit flew from his mouth, Conthan realized where he had seen the creepy face before. He turned back to Gretchen. "They belong to the Warden."

"There's a plan," she said. He realized her hand shook. She gripped him tighter. There would be no improvising, no changing plans for her. She put on a brave front, but she had no idea what she got herself into when she agreed. Right now she had one job, and despite the shaking grip, she was determined to do it. He squeezed her hand back.

"You're doing fine."

Alyssa snapped the man's neck and punched another in the throat, sending him to the ground. She was about to block a punch from the third bomber jacket man when her body rose up off the ground and slammed into a blackened wall. When she hit the plaster, she crumpled. She slid up the wall, thumping harshly against the ceiling before she fell to the ground.

Conthan saw movement as the white woman pushed herself up from the rug, her hand balled in a fist. He didn't need to ask questions to know she must be a mentalist. He had never seen a telekinetic before, but he was amazed at how easily she took out two of the most skilled fighters he knew. He wondered if an idle Skits would be the next tossed about like dog's chew toy.

"What the fuck, Jacob?" asked Lily.

The man, his name was Jacob. Conthan remembered a time when the Warden was possessed by another man. He recognized the smug man, the body might be different, but the Warden resided inside the pompous looking man. The remaining man in the bomber jacket reached into his pocket and pulled out a razor. Could the Warden be stopping him from opening a portal in the man's chest? Would that even harm the source of the problem, or just this temporary vessel?

"No," Gretchen said.

She snapped him back to reality. He wanted to kill the man, but he didn't know if it would actually kill the Warden. He wondered if this would happen to Vanessa if she died. Would her mind run rampant, possessing other people?

"Something is not right," Jacob said.

The man surveyed the room while straightening his jacket. Vanessa had assured them as long as Gretchen's powers extended to them both, they'd be invisible to the telepath. He squeezed her hand again. "Keep focusing. You can do this." He didn't know if it was because Gretchen was terrified, or if Jacob was that powerful; either way, he didn't want to falter.

A snap filled the air before the flash of light burst through the windows. He pulled Gretchen close and wrapped his hands around her. He held her tight as the room exploded around them. "Don't stop, Gretchen," he said in her ear. He lifted her and worked toward the back of the room, hovering over her, shielding her from debris.

"Fucking Children," Lily screamed.

***

Jasmine hit the ground and somersaulted forward. Her muscles pumped with adrenaline; she was ready to kill. She wanted to feel the woman's skull in her hands, squeezing until the bone snapped and drove into her brain. She'd wait just long enough for her screams before finishing the job. Every muscle in her body moved with a purpose, to destroy the woman while savoring her pain.

She froze, scanning the scene around her. The shrubs shook in the breeze while the dozen beds of roses left the air smelling fragrant, almost sweet. The landscape stood in juxtaposition to her current mood. The portal dropping her into the rose garden blinked out of existence. She knew people were being put in position around the White House, preparing for an assault against the president.

The sound of pumping hydraulics broke the silence. She turned just in time to see the machine's fist closing the distance between them. Her jaw spun, snapping to the side, and she was impressed with the accuracy of the punch. She wondered if it was the machine or Dav5d making the newest model of synthetics so dangerous.

She grabbed at the arm, grappling it just above the elbow. The metal tore as she pulled. She planted her foot on the machine's chest and continued pulling. The weapon on the forearm sprung to life and she dug her fingers into the barrel of the gun before it fired. The laser on the shoulder popped up, but instead of firing, the synthetic drove the knuckles of its other hand into her temple once and then again.

"Jesus," she grumbled.

She stabbed her fingers into the machine's throat and latching onto the metal conduit connecting the wires to its head and torso. She ripped the pipe keeping its head afloat, sending the machine falling onto the ground. As it landed in a bed of roses she kicked, the toe of her boot tearing the head off its body.

Picking up the machine, she tossed it behind the shrubs in an attempt to hide the deed. She stayed low as she worked her way through the rose garden, taking care to avoid the delicate flowers. She admired the bushes' determination to stay bright and vibrant even while the world fell apart around them. It wouldn't be long before the White House itself joined the rubble of the rest of the country, another building in disrepair, victim of a war nobody understood.

She had a moment of clarity. *What if the world knew their problems were due to a conspiracy?* she thought. On one side, Children of Nostradamus, and on the other, a secret organization filled with mentalists. Humans were in the middle, unaware they were the fodder of this war.

Even in the daylight, a bright light flashed from the circular room to her left. The exterior of the building cracked, barely able to contain whatever unfolded inside. Whatever Dwayne was doing, the noise would bring wave after wave of synthetics running to defend their president. She wasn't sure she'd be enough to stop them. She watched the doors and windows, waiting for the onslaught, hoping she could slow them down enough for Dwayne and the others to do what they needed.

"Holy shit," she said as a window exploded.

Smoke billowed out of the broken window as something landed in the flowers. She watched as the burning fabric rolled about in the dirt until Dwayne threw back a layer of cloth. He tried to get to his knees but toppled, unable to get his feet to cooperate. She ran to his side and grabbed his arm, helping him up.

"They're in there."

"Thanks, genius."

"The others are in place," he said, slumping and relying on her to keep him on his feet. He held up his fist and sparks shot out, barely leaving the surface of his skin. "I need more juice."

The doors leading into the garden burst open as two synthetics rushed toward them. She let go of Dwayne, sending him to the perfectly manicured grass. The first machine rushed at her, hands extended, as if it would grab for her throat. She grappled with its hands as it knocked her to the grass, trying to use its weight against her. She slugged its head as it tried to grapple with her fists. The second synthetic pinned her free hand, its claws biting into her metal hide. She tried fight back, but they moved quicker than she recalled.

"I liked you better when you just shot me," she hissed.

The laser popped out on both shoulders. Red

lights lit up in the barrel, preparing to fire. She turned her head and closed her eyes, expecting the stinging in her cheek. The high pitched hiss of the lasers made her freeze, but the lack of pain made her partially open one eye. She was surprised to see Dwayne on the synthetic's back, each of his hands covering a laser. She imagined the powerful weapons would slice his hands from his body.

The man's eyes glowed red. She had seen him overcharge himself several times when they sparred. She knew his body was in pain, and he'd start screaming at any moment in an attempt to burn through all the power stored up in his cells. Still, she wasn't used to seeing his eyes leaking energy, and red was a new color on him.

"Oh shit," she said.

The electricity poured out of his skull, pushing through his eyes and out of his mouth. If he screamed, it couldn't be heard over the hissing metal and popping hydraulics. He turned his head and red lightning slammed into the standing synthetic. The machine held up its hands to block the blast, but all that remained were metal stubs when its skull went limp.

"There," Jasmine yelled, pointing toward the wall he came out of.

Now he roared. The bloodcurdling scream grew louder as the lightning tore out of his chest, leaving his skin blistered. She shielded her eyes from the light as it intensified. Like his sister, he was typically immune to his own abilities, nature's gift for giving him so much destructive force, but now, a rash spread across his bare torso and burns started to show.

The side of the Oval Office exploded and debris flew in every direction. The windows shattered, sending glass into the room. Plaster and wood tore apart as Dwayne bombarded the structure with energy. She squinted through her fingers; he gritted his teeth as he pushed out every last ounce of energy. He had spoken about giving in to the euphoria, and there was no doubt, as his eyes relaxed and his lips turned upward, he was experienced a moment of bliss.

She shoved the synthetic on top of her off to the side. She pulled at its stubby arm and used it to smack him along the base of his neck. He staggered, but the blast didn't stop. She drew back her fist and punched him squarely in the jaw, sending blood into the air, which evaporated as it hit the lightning. He'd be mad, but at least he'd be alive.

"Jesus," she said, "the only victory we have is downing my own team member."

Chapter 27

2033

The chill worked its through her skin and deep into her muscles as she slid through the portal. Her feet touched down in the small control room. Men barked orders at one another while hovering over monitors showing the White House's interior.

"Sleep."

The dozen men were out cold, draped across the computer equipment. With the security center out of commission, the others had a chance to do what they needed. Even as she kneeled onto the floor, her vision blurred, the world washed away until only the bright white room remained.

From the corners of her vision, black gobs of liquid oozed, coating the walls. It only took a moment, but her white room had turned dark, corrupted by an unseen presence. She rested her physical hands on her legs and took deep breaths, steadying her mind.

"It's not like last time, Vanessa. Not even by a

little."

"Who said it was?"

She wanted to ask who was in control. She saw the young man in a white suit appear, but something about the way he stood reminded her of the Warden. Despite having killed him once, the man's arrogance remained the only thing more powerful than his telepathy.

Vanessa stepped backward, her wings fading into the darkness, and slowly the black ink washed over her body, removing her from sight. She watched the man smile at her parlor trick. He took pleasure in her newfound confidence, admiring her willingness to play his game. She couldn't understand his satisfaction in the situation. *Is he so sure he'll win?*

With a thought, she appeared behind him. She lunged, her hands stretched out, claws ready to tears through his flesh. He moved quickly, faster than anybody should be capable of. With a simple swipe of his hand, he effortlessly knocked both of hers to the side. He thrust his other palm forward, catching her in the chest and sending her reeling into the shadows.

He's baiting me.

"I'm glad to see you've matured since our last encounter. I hoped you would take my words to heart and let the shackles of morality fall away. It seems unfortunate you can't shake being human."

She knew her friends waged a war in the physical world, attempting to thwart the man who had brought them so much misery. She only had to distract him. Her goal was to remove his abilities from the playing field, and she knew his hubris would make it possible. The man in the white suit might be a new vessel, but underneath, the arrogant bastard remained.

The white room, limbo, this place, contained no walls, no beginning, no end, and no up or down. He might be stronger than her, but she still remained far superior at guile. Sinking into the shadow, she positioned herself under him, then grabbed onto his legs. She pulled hard, sending him flying. Before he reacted, she vanished again, knowing her advantage was striking and running. If she was forced to confront the Warden face to face, she wouldn't be capable of winning.

"This game of cat and mouse is the best you have?"

"I had to warm up somehow." Her voice echoed through the space.

His arrogance was abundant, a scent rolling off him she couldn't ignore. With the slightest suggestion she followed the smell through his memories. The jumble of images pulsed like a heartbeat, washing over her. The memories flashed in front of her so quickly she had difficulty sorting through which belonged to who. One scene appeared over and over, and she knew she found the origins of the man.

The blackness around them shattered and behind it was a scene she barely recognized. When they first assaulted the Facility, she recalled Dav5d showing her footage of the building before it became a prison. Glass windows let in the light, bathing a large man made of granite. He knelt in the fountain, and on his shoulders he held a replica of the Earth. She knew it was Atlas, and had she the time, she'd reflect on how they weren't so different with the burdens they carried.

"More daring than I anticipated," he said.

She stepped out of nothingness, bleeding into existence. The Warden's avatar didn't flinch at her dramatic appearance; even his muscles remained like steel. With the brightly lit windows to her back, she stretched her wings, casting a shadow upon the man. "I've seen you before you possessed Jacob Griffin, before you destroyed the life of Mark Davis. I've seen the original you."

He stepped upon the edge of the water fountain. Even with the extra height, it was difficult to look at the pasty white man as anything more than fragile. Vanessa knew the body; his delicate bones housed underneath paper thin skin were only feeble compared to the mine it protected.

"You have?"

"Ivan Volkov." The words were hardly a whisper, just loud enough to be heard over the water trickling from the globe into the pool below. "The president did indeed assign you to the Facility. It's starting to make sense," she said, stepping closer to the man.

Vanessa flapped her wings, lifting herself off the ground. She half expected the Warden to stop her from flying closer. The wind from her wings hit the man and parts of his body crumbled. With a strong whoosh, the image of the man turned to ash, carried into the air, until only broken legs remained.

Hands wrapped around her neck, locking in at the elbows, placing her in a sleeper hold. She welcomed the touch of his skin, the cool fleshy part of his arm touching her face. She focused on the spots of her body making connections with the man. The chink in his armor looked more like a chasm once he touched her. He had no idea just how much she had grown in the last year.

"You want maturity?"

He yelled out loud, a bloodcurdling scream swallowed by the infinite space. She reached into his brain, forcing the organ to fire every synapse at once, drowning him in pain. The moment he let go, she spun about and grabbed both sides of his head. She brought her face close, her eyes staring into his. She smiled, her fangs showing as she leaned in and let their foreheads touch.

"I am not without my tricks." Her breath was sweet and wet. He tried to focus on her, bring himself back to the moment, but his face remained contorted in pain. She appreciated his subtle attempts to circumvent the power she unleashed in his brain.

"Test me," he said between panting.

She fell forward, stepping through his body as if he was an open door. On the other side she stood in a room where a man yelled angrily in Russian. She remembered when he pulled the same trick, forcing her to endure a past torture. She gladly returned his abuses. She wanted to make sure she left scars on the man before her teammates killed him.

She emerged in a dark room with torn wallpaper and holes broken through the plaster in the walls. The bed sitting in the middle maintained the only clean spot in the room and the sconce on the wall fought against the darkness, slowly losing the battle. A man stood at the end of the bed, looming over a woman, his fist drawn back as both of her hands were held up, trying to ward off the impending blow. He decided to change his tactic and pulled the belt from his pants.

He swung the belt wildly, striking a woman across the face. When she screamed out, he used the back of his other hand to stop her. Vanessa flinched at the sound of the man's fist hitting her, knocking the spit from her bruised lips. She hesitated, unsure if she had the fortitude to bring a man into his darkest memories.

She had to.

She grabbed Jacob by the back of the neck, forcing him closer to the carnage being wreaked by the man. The woman heaved as she cried and the man brought back his fist, the belt wrapped around his knuckles. There was nothing human left about the look on his face; the sounds coming from his mouth were primal, as if he forgot he was still a man.

The blow left the woman limp on the ground. The swelling on her face made it impossible to know what she looked like before, her cheeks cut, her eye swollen shut, and her lips three times their original size. A final gurgling breath and her body went limp. She was dead.

"No," he said.

"Seems we have belts in common," she said.

"But that's all we have in common." He pointed to a kid in the hallway. The kid must have been there the entire time, witnessing the brutality of his father. For a moment, she felt sorry, then it turned to horror.

The gangly child held a small knife in his hand, clutching it tightly enough his knuckles turned white. There were no tears on his face, just a detached anger, a low growl escaping his lips. He huffed and puffed as if he had run a marathon. He looked down to where the floorboards from the hallway ended and the carpet started. He lifted his foot, creeping it across the threshold.

His toes touched down on the carpet. He burst into a fury of movement. He lunged at the man, swinging the knife wildly, striking him across the arm. The man hissed and brought the belt down across the kid's face. The kid lurched backward, falling on his butt. The moment his aggression subsided, the man reached down, holding him by the neck, refusing to let air into his lungs.

The man muttered in Russian, a threat for his ungrateful wretch of a child. Vanessa prepared for the strike that would kill the kid. She eyed the man more closely and wondered if he was Ivan. They had a similar brow line and the same sinister pointy chin. Had she gotten the entire scene wrong? Was this his personal victory?

The kid jabbed the knife forward, striking the man in the throat. He turned his wrist and pulled out the knife. The man reared back, holding his neck, failing to keep the blood from spilling over his hands and down his shirt. The kid sat up, stabbing the man in the cheek and with his free hand, putting his thumb into the man's eye, imploding the eyeball.

Jacob laughed. Mark laughed. Ivan laughed. The echoes of the three men filled the tiny room. "You were struck and you cowered. I was struck and I struck back."

Jacob reached back and grabbed her wrist. She fought him, but as he turned, he forced her to submit, bending down to her knees. She looked past Jacob to see the kid smiling, declaring victory over his fallen father. This wasn't his greatest fear, he had navigated them to the moment the man in front of her had been born. She wasn't fighting a man, he was nothing more than a monster.

"Monster," he said, "I can agree with that."

"I'm not done here," she said as she pushed back, trying to knock him off her. She found his grip on her hand was absolute. In the battle of the minds, he wasn't simply winning, he was dragging out his prize fight to savor it.

He leaned in close to her ear. "You missed the best part, Angel."

He bent her wrist, an action that in the physical world would have left her with a broken hand. The move forced her closer to the ground. She could only see his legs and the child covered in his father's blood. She almost felt pity for him. It was bad enough his father beat his mother, but a devil was born as he exacted his revenge.

Jacob laughed. The image of the man in white faded until it was Ivan towering over her prone form. "Revenge? Angel, I question your senses now. I'm a mentalist, controlling people it is in our nature."

She froze in horror as the kid stood up and sat on

the bed next to his dead mother. The kid lifted the knife and drove it down into her breast, piercing where her heart would have been. He repeated the action several more times before taking the knife and sliding it into his pocket.

"My father didn't kill her." He laughed.

***

"Get me to her."

Conthan clutched Gretchen's hand for all it was worth. The lackluster monochrome world around him continued burning, fires breaking out among the remaining people in the room. Gretchen managed to keep them invisible while Dwayne destroyed one of the world's most recognized monuments. He and Gretchen stepped over a piece of burning carpet as he inched his way along the circular room toward the desk and the woman lying unconscious at its base.

Skits and Alyssa were within arm's reach of one another while the president was a few feet away. The elderly woman didn't move, her body partially covered by a massive piece of plaster. He hoped she was alive; she would only be useful in getting Dav5d back if they had a living woman to barter.

He moved around a bloodied bomber jacket man and kneeled down next to the president, reaching out to take her pulse. Gretchen pulled at his arm, yanking him away from her.

"Skin on skin," she said. "They'll see her vanish or we'll show up."

Alyssa slowly climbed to her knees, inspecting

her fallen comrade. He waited for Vanessa to shout through his head, to offer some sort of guidance. He missed those moments when she chimed in without asking. He wished she was ready to take over his powers again.

"We're getting out of this room," he said.

"How?"

He let go of her hand and the color washed back into the world. The moment reality returned to normal, he felt pressure at his head. He recalled the sensation, the Warden trying to force himself into his mind. He turned and saw Jacob eyeing him from the ground, a distant look on his face.

"Be lucky I need you," Conthan said.

Alyssa and Skits blinked out of existence. He was the only person preventing the death of the president. Jasmine would kill him for changing their plans of murdering everybody who stood in their way. It was left to him to make the call; it all revolved around the president.

The plaster broke apart as he pulled at it, freeing the president from the fallen wall. Conthan looked over his shoulder at the Warden, who seemed vulnerable in that moment, most likely occupied by Vanessa. He thought about the satisfaction he'd feel as the man's heart was sliced in two. Unfortunately, the Warden had proved that killing the vessel wouldn't end his tyranny.

Conthan hugged the president close to his chest. The telekinetic stirred. If the Warden was dangerous in regards to the mind, the woman had nearly killed two people barely moving her hand. He didn't want to be in her line of sight when she woke. Retreat.

The pain raced along his spine, jabbing at the base of his brain, telling him to stop. The darkness responded to his demands and a portal opened along the ground. He didn't need to see it; something about his powers told him Gretchen and the others had passed through. He clutched the president to his chest and fell backward. The portal opened wide enough that they both fell through, escaping the close quarters of the Oval Office.

Cold coated his skin, eliciting a shiver. He welcomed the sensation, preferring the cold over the numbing feeling of the Warden's persistent intrusions. He landed on his back, grass and invisible bodies cradling his fall. He pushed the president off him, jumping to his feet as quickly as he could.

"What the hell," Jasmine said. "Since when is rescuing her part of the plan?"

"Trust me," he said.

He pointed to the destroyed part of the White House. Gretchen blinked into sight along with Skits and Alyssa. Jacob and his telekinetic moved into sight in the ripped-open section of the Oval Office. It wouldn't take much for the woman to snap his neck—he'd ponder her mercy later—or perhaps she only acted when the Warden allowed her. He wondered if she was nothing more than a pawn for the man.

"I know you want her dead, Jacob. Give us Dav5d and you can have the president."

"What the hell?" Alyssa said.

"Otherwise, she goes with us and stays under our protection," Conthan yelled, "and the United States keeps its president."

"Lily—"

"She bats an eye and I open a portal in her chest."

The Warden's vessel didn't finish his sentence. He froze for a moment, taking stock of the scene. Conthan hoped he was weighing his options, because there was only enough juice in him for one more portal. He could feel the power trying to make a decision, possess his body or sleep. If it went in either direction, they'd have more problems than a psychopathic power-hungry telepath.

Jasmine propped up the president, holding the woman by the back of her neck. Conthan knew more than the rest that she wanted to slowly squeeze the soft flesh, forcing the life from her. He wanted something similar, but it seemed he wouldn't get his wish today.

Thud.

He threw up his hands to shield his eyes. Liquid splashed across his face, working its way between his fingers. He opened his eyes and his brain refused to register the red on his hands. He caught the shock on Jasmine's blood-covered face. He followed her gaze to, her hands still holding the president's neck. Where the neck curved outward to the skull, there was an empty space, covered in red goo.

Gretchen grabbed his shoulder and despite the color fading into shades of gray, he couldn't help but still see the red. She screamed in his ear, yelling at him to run. Their bargaining chip was gone. From the carnage of the Oval Office, Lily and Jacob floated toward them.

It was over.

He let the darkness wash over him. He imagined the black racing outward, wrapping itself around his body and consuming him. He knew his eyes turned a dark ebony, void of any light. The well of power in his mind was low, but it remained furious. He fought back, wrangling it in, keeping it from lashing out towards the first thing it wanted, the death of the Warden and his lackey. Emotion flooded his brain, trying to subdue his rational mind.

The portal opened inches in front of his face, blocking his line of sight to Jacob and his woman. Conthan pushed Gretchen through while Dwayne grabbed Skits by the arm, dragging her into the void. He followed the Alyssa and Jasmine, and the moment he cleared the disc, it vanished. He didn't know what to say at that moment. They failed, losing more than they gained. The president was dead, Dav5d was gone, and he hoped Vanessa found a way to escape from the White House roof before they found her.

His knees gave out on him, his body forced to the ground by the weight of the situation. He thought Eleanor had given him a note a year ago to stop the Warden, that she had mastered a plan to prevent the man from ruining the young artist's future. He hadn't thought the note was going to put him on a path to fight for the world itself.

"Eleanor, I'm sorry."

Epilogue

2033

The grass between her toes reminded her of playing as a child, barefoot, ignorant to the world around her. She scuffed her feet along the ground, letting the grass slide under her foot, tickling, almost eliciting a smile. Despite the metal gauntlets, and her ability to make her skin as dense as steel, it was the simple sensations that brought her moments of joy.

The cemetery was in the middle of a war zone, in a state caught between the east and west. Strip malls had been destroyed and citizens who remained lived in constant fear of becoming the victims of a senseless civil war. Somehow, even under the assault of man and machine, the cemetery remained largely untouched. The stone arches at the front had fallen, and the metal fence fell into disrepair, but otherwise, the land inside the gates appeared undisturbed.

The grass hadn't been cut in months, in places

reaching her waist. She pushed it to the side as she looked at the tops of gravestones. She wandered the cemetery for the better part of the morning, hoping to find one stone in particular. She trailed along until she came across a part of the cemetery removed from the rest.

She stepped over a decrepit wrought iron fence and pushed aside the grass. The stone was modest, a perfect rectangle three feet high sitting on a marble base. She removed the moss collecting on the front of the stone and realized it had been years, perhaps decades since anybody cared for the site. The stone held two names, a husband and wife. She pulled away and saw a military sigil etched into the rock.

Her fingers caressed the stone, running along the grooves made by the symbol. There had been a time when she expected her headstone would bear a similar sigil. There had been a point when she would have given her life for this country, and as the rage washed through her body, she knew she had given more than just her life to the military.

To the right of the stone, two smaller but otherwise identical markers were placed within arm's reach. She pushed aside the grass and made note of the names. Benjamin. In quotes, the nickname, "Benjie" adorned the middle of the marble. She smiled at the discovery, the name bestowed upon on a little brother. It was unfortunate somewhere in a box beneath the surface of grass, there was a box filled with somebody's sibling. She imagined him to be a handful, something of a wild spirit, and she thought for a moment she could hear somebody shouting his name.

She knew the occupant of the next gravestone. She dropped to her knees in front of it and pulled at the grass, breaking down the wall of roughage between her and the tombstone. She stopped as she cleared enough to see the name.

"Eleanor P. Valentine."

The marble had been chipped and scratches were etched in the form of numerous swears. The spray paint that once tagged the grave was all but washed away by time. Jasmine imagined how upset people must have been when they asked to bury the assassin. She wondered if the family had once been buried somewhere else in the cemetery. The isolation of the markers made her think they had been moved for the sanctity of the entire graveyard. She was happy to see Eleanor with her brother and both parents. It warmed her heart.

She secretly hoped there would be an envelope waiting on the stone, the next in Eleanor's mystical guiding steps. No letter waited on the base, no name etched in beautiful calligraphy, the hallmark of the psychic. With no letter, she was left with her own thoughts, herself and the psychic alone together for the first time since their paths crossed a year ago.

"I hate you," she admitted. "I hated you the moment I told the girl to run. I listened to what you said. I did the one thing you asked of me. I saved her."

Jasmine let her chest heave, an attempt to stop the tears from welling up in her eyes. "You gave me hope. You gave us all hope. Look where it's gotten us." Once they fled the White House, they knew it was only a matter of time before they were marked as public enemy number one. The videos given to news outlets showed her holding the President of the United States, and moments later squeezing her head until it exploded. The Children of Nostradamus had gone underground because of them. Had Eleanor never gotten involved, she would still be part of the military, removing deadly threats from the streets.

Emotion overtook her and she didn't have any outlet except to cry. She hated this feeling, the uncertainty of what unfolded around her. In the Corps, she had to be in control, and now she was victim to the ravings of a madwoman. "You didn't tell us how bad this got."

She didn't know what else to say to the ghost of a dead woman. She was angry. She wanted to scream at Eleanor, but found she was even more upset that she had fallen short. She had been part of something bigger, and even as a collective, they failed. She didn't understand how Eleanor could have brought them together and given them no hope for success.

"You tried to change the future." She thought back to the image in the locker room. "You said you could change it. Does that mean we can too? I need answers." The anger subsided, drowned out by the weight of responsibility pressing down on her from all sides.

She reached out and touched the stone. Her abilities were heightened from her emotions and they looked to synthesize the marble and change the density of her skin. She looked at the base of the stone to where a dandelion rested. It took a moment to realize the weed's white fuzzy tips hovered in the air. A pebble hovered off the ground along with several blades of grass, suspended like they had always been there.

She stood and took a step backward. She bumped into somebody and spun about, fist drawn back, ready to swing. The woman wore a green body suit, similar to something you might see on an old school mechanic. The wrinkles in her face gave away her age, but even with the obvious years written along every line, her eyes made her appear even older.

"Who are you?"

"That doesn't matter," she said. Her voice was warm, exactly how you would imagine your grandmother. Behind the words was a confidence allowing her to stand without flinching at Jasmine's drawn fist. Jasmine lowered her hand and wondered who could have found her here of all places.

"Eleanor sent me."

Acknowledgements

I must acknowledge some awesome people who helped bring about this book. The Metrowest Writers, my Wednesday night crew, for helping guilt me into writing instead of watching reruns. Thank you to Cristina Alden for keeping me energetic while writing, Jennifer Allis Provost for wasting time on Facebook with me, and E.J. Stevens for talking about writing until 3 A.M. in the hot tub. Thank you to Erin & Marc Fitch for reading early copies and helping shape the story into what it eventually became. And thank you to the New England Horror Writers and the many fellow writers who have given suggestions and support during this project.

About the Author

I'm high school graphic design and marketing teacher, at a large suburban high school in Massachusetts. Working as a high school educator and observing the outlandish world of adolescence was the inspiration for my first young adult novel, "Suburban Zombie High."

My inspiration for writing stems from being a youth who struggled with reading in school. While I found school assigned novels incredibly difficult to digest, I devoured comics and later fantasy novels. Their influences can be seen in the tall tales I spin.

I took the long route to becoming a writer. For a brief time, I majored in Creative Writing but exchanged one passion for another as I switched to Art and Design. My passion for reading about superheroes, fantastical worlds, and panic-stricken situations would become the foundation of my writing career.

I participated in my first NaNoWriMo in 2006 and continue to write an entire novel every November. Now I am the NaNoWriMo Municipal Liaison to the Massachusetts Metrowest Region. I also belong to a weekly writing group, the Metrowest Writers.

Facebook:
https://www.facebook.com/writeremyflagg

Twitter:
http://twitter.com/writeremyflagg

Website:
http://www.remyflagg.com/

Reviews help authors. If you enjoyed this story or Nighthawks, please leave a review on Amazon or Goodreads.

For more about Jeremy Flagg, visit
www.remyflagg.com

40408183R00244

Made in the USA
Middletown, DE
11 February 2017